I0637576

Almost Anonymous

by

Christine Bush

Dedication

To all the strong and wonderful women in my life, who get back up when they're knocked down, start over when the path has to change, find the joy in the day despite the clouds, and keep on loving, no matter what. You know who you are!

ALMOST ANONYMOUS

Chapter 1

The scene was so beautiful, it seemed almost disrespectful to be thinking about death.

The sun was going down. It cast a colorful glow in the sky, a variety of oranges and purples, making shadows on the menacing rocky cliff beneath her and reflecting off the frothy, rapid river below.

Cassandra's eyes took notice of the colorful display, but the beauty didn't reach her soul. Her soul felt dead. It was all over. She had given up.

She rested her head for a minute on the smooth steering wheel of the almost new BMW, its soft leather upholstery matching the metallic bronze of the car. It reeked of class, success. That was a joke.

Cassandra felt emotions well up, threatening to choke her. Her brain screamed "Failure! Disgust!" And then the quiet, overpowering and ugly thought flashed through her mind. "I can't do this anymore. I want to die."

The cool feel of the steering wheel felt good against her hot cheek. She rubbed her eyes with her fists, paying no heed to her makeup, knowing that it was probably already smeared and running down the tear tracks that marred her usually perfect face. Perfect. That was a laugh.

Her shoulder ached when she moved her arms. It was a broken collarbone, she was certain, even though she hadn't remained long enough for the final diagnosis. She had known before she had even entered the emergency room at the hospital. Why had she even bothered going? Why had she even tried? Just what exactly had she expected, after all this time?

She closed her eyes tightly, as if to block out the vision of Frederick's face as he had approached her in his latest rage. But even with her eyes tightly closed, she couldn't stop the vision, couldn't stop the memory.

"Ungrateful bitch!" he had rumbled in that horrible, low pitched voice that he reserved for only her and the boys. "You WILL listen to me. You WILL do as I say."

He grabbed her by the shoulders then, his long hard fingers, strong from hours of tennis and golf digging into her flesh, into her bones, shaking her until her teeth felt jarred. She felt the horrible pressure as her collar bone popped, as the searing pain flashed through her.

She collapsed onto the plush sofa in the family room as he abruptly let her go. Her legs wouldn't hold her. A strange weakness had come over her, along with the pain.

"See what you make me do?" he rumbled. "See what your foolhardy behavior has brought about? WHEN are you going to learn? WHEN are you going to understand?"

"I'm sorry, Frederick," she had heard her tired voice automatically utter. "It was just a haircut. I just wanted a new hairstyle."

She heard the tired, apologetic whine in her voice, and the very sound disgusted her. The pain in her shoulder filled her like an enormous toothache, her head started to pound along with the throb. <u>Why, why had she made the appointment?</u>

"You will wear your hair the way that I request, my lovely wife."

The word lovely seemed to drip from his tongue. "Your hair pleases me just as it is. You have no right to go against me like this. You have been very, very, bad."

<u>Why had she left her phone number with the hairstylist? And why did Frederick have to come home early on this particular day</u> and intercept the message that the stylist was running late?

"Now, this incident is over." His voice was firm, back in control. "Don't think for a minute that you are going to tell me that you are hurt too badly to cook a decent dinner. Get into the kitchen. I have a class to teach tonight, and I have no time for any more of this nonsense."

She shuffled silently to the kitchen, and did the chores she knew so well. The meal was served in an amazingly short time. Her shoulder ached horribly, but dinner had been served.

<u>What would he have done if she had actually come home with a new, short haircut?</u> The thought made her feel queasy.

Her hands worked automatically, her mind raced with incoherent thoughts. It was like a pattern. At first, anger would well up in her, and she would envision herself doing something crazy like charging from the kitchen swinging a carving knife, it's sharpened edge honed right for Frederick and putting an end to his cruel ways. After another incident, she had dreamed that she had killed him as he had slept in their big, expensive bed. She had woken up with a pillow wet with tears. But, of course, she never really took any of those vengeful actions.

Because the fear and guilt would silently creep into her subconscious, and she would begin chastising herself for her violent and misguided thoughts, eventually turning her feelings around so that she was more angry at herself than she had been at Frederick for his horrible actions. And she would end up apologizing. And apologizing. It wore her down.

The boys, Duncan, 15, and Peter, 12, came to the table and ate silently, as usual. They returned to their rooms, their faces blank, hiding the pain she knew lurked there.

"Delicious dinner, Cassandra," Frederick said in a cheerful voice a short time later. It was as if the whole thing had never occurred. "Boys, be sure to finish your homework. I'll see you all after class."

And then he was gone, smelling of expensive aftershave and looking like a model husband/father/professor, and sounding totally, perfectly normal.

The pain in her shoulder had grown by the minute, and when she could bear it no longer, she told the boys she was going to run an errand. She backed the BMW out of the garage. She pulled into the emergency ward, desperate for something to kill the pain that was enveloping her.

The starched nurse had been efficient, cool. She took the insurance numbers and asked questions about the injury. Cassandra had been though this routine before.

"When did the injury occur?"

"About an hour ago."

"How did it happen?"

The answers here varied. "I fell down the stairs". "I slipped on the ice." "I walked into a door."

But tonight, something in her had snapped right along with her collarbone. Frederick's menacing voice, the boys' blank stares, the pain, the pain..

"My husband grabbed me and shook me."

The nurse's eyes flickered for a minute, and then were professional, cool again.

"I see." She stopped writing, paused for a moment, and then went on. "And was this done in anger?"

"Rage. It was done in rage." Her own voice was flat, dead.

"I see." She paused. "Just a moment, Mrs. Ellington. I will be right back."

Cassandra closed her eyes, trying to fight the fear rolling over her. She felt bad, she felt disloyal. Images of Frederick's face swam before her.

Then the nurse was back, with a young, tanned doctor behind her. He took her into a small office to the right of the nurse's station.

"Hello, Mrs. Ellington. I'm Doctor Watson. Nurse Bates tells me that your shoulder is injured. How did this happen?"

His voice was kindly, concerned. Cassandra felt a ray of hope. Would someone help her?

She found her voice. "My husband, doctor. My husband grabbed me and shook me. I felt a sharp pain here. It really hurts." She raised her good arm and pointed to the spot that hurt the most.

"I see." The doctor wrote down a few notes. "And is this the first time that this has happened?"

"No, no. He hurts me alot." The story came surging out, like water suddenly released from a dam. "He broke my arm once. He broke my finger. Once he threw me down the stairs." She was crying now, and the tears were flowing rapidly, her voice punctuated by sobs. "I don't know what to do."

"Now, now, Mrs. Ellington. Everything will be all right."

He called the nurse and gave her instructions for medication.

"I am going to give you a shot that will dull the pain a bit."

She didn't even feel the needle when she got the shot.

"Later, we'll get an x-ray, and set you up with a sling for that collarbone." The doctor patted her good shoulder and sat down before her.

"Now, let's talk."

Cassandra looked up at him hopefully, expectantly. He was tall, strong, and looked capable, intelligent. She felt the glimmer of hope grow.

"Please."

But his words floored her.

"Cassandra, I know all about the problem you have been having with your drinking. I want you to know that Frederick wants to help you in any way that he can."

Her mouth opened dumbly. She stared back at him. "You know Frederick? Concerned about my DRINKING?" she squeaked out. She squeezed her eyes shut, then opened them again. She wasn't dreaming.

"Certainly, Cassandra. Frederick and I have shared an occasional round of golf at the country club. He has been, well, open about his worry for you. In fact, he even feared that you might do just as you are doing now, coming to the hospital and trying to cover an unfortunate accident with a tale like this."

"He told you that?" The dark cloud was descending on her now. Her head felt fuzzy.

"Certainly we discussed it. He's had a notation made in your file, right here." He tapped the manila folder her carried. "It's for your own good. Frederick is an important man, Cassandra. He's a well known professor, successful author and speaker. Don't you realize the damage you could do him by trying to solve your problems this way? And think about your boys."

His voice was still kind, still compassionate, but his words made no sense. A fact registered in her brain. He truly believed Frederick. Like others before him, he had been taken in by the sparkling, interested blue eyes, the dazzling smile...

The doctor was still talking, and she tried to concentrate on what he was saying, but the effects of the shot he had given her were starting to work. Her mind felt wobbly.

"Evidently, for your own good, Frederick and your family doctor have been anxious for you to get some help for your problems, Cassandra. But the best scenario would be that you take that first step yourself. Which you have by coming here. I commend you for that. The place that he is sending you is just about the best in the country, and they will help you more than you could ever believe."

"You are sending me someplace?"

Her voice was groggy, her mind was more and more confused by the minute. The pain medication had taken effect.

"It's called Hillmeadow House," he went on. " It's a private psychiatric and addictions hospital. Very exclusive. They have a very effective program. They will help you to conquer the underlying neurosis that is driving you to drink." He made a notation on the file. "We'll call Frederick right away. He'll be more than delighted that you've finally come for help. Since the basic arrangements have been made, there need be no delay. An ambulance can take you directly there. Tonight."

She shook her head. It must be a dream...a nightmare. "But that's ridiculous. I don't even drink. What on earth are you talking about?"

"Nonsense, Cassandra. Don't panic. It's time to face up to it, my dear. Alcoholism is no crime. It's a disease. And you can be helped. Look at Betty Ford..."

"YOU look at Betty Ford," she snapped. "I DO NOT drink. And I am not going anywhere. I have my boys to take care of, my house to take care of. You can't make me go."

The doctor shook his head sadly. "I understand your fears. But your boys and your house will be better off, later. You'll see. I'm afraid at this point, once the ball is rolling, you wouldn't have a lot to say about it. Frederick has been in the process of taking the legal steps necessary to...well, to insist that you get some psychiatric help...To keep yourself safe...to keep the boys safe…"

"Frederick doesn't even know that I'm here!" she yelled.

"But he knew that sooner or later you would come, Cassandra, and so he had the foresight to do the necessary footwork to take care of things. He is, after all, a very caring husband. You should be grateful."

His beeper went off. He stared at her for a moment, slumped in her chair, her eyes starting to droop. He turned toward the nurse standing nearby.

"Watch her, Nurse Bates, and please be very kind. She is a very troubled woman, and this must be very hard. The medication is taking effect. I'm sure Frederick will be here soon. He'll be able to help her to accept things. I have to answer this call." He was gone.

"Would you like some coffee, Mrs. Ellington?" said Nurse Bates gently. "Maybe that will help."

"No thanks. Coffee isn't going to help this mess," she mumbled, trying desperately to clear her head.

"I'm sorry, Mrs. Ellington. Things have a way of working out."

"I think I'll just rest, if you don't mind."

She closed her eyes, her head leaning against the back of the chair, her mind trying to fight off the effect of the painkiller. She had to think.

This was crazy, positively unbelievable. In all the things she had seen in her 36 years, this was absolutely the craziest. One thing was for sure...either she was losing her mind, or the entire world around her was. How had her life come to this?

Above her head, a speaker squawked. "All personnel, report to ambulance entry at the ER. Multiple ambulances arriving with injuries from a bus accident. Repeat. All available personnel report to the ambulance entry."

The medical world around her spun to life. Nurses and orderlies, pushing gurneys and carrying oxygen zoomed past her to the glass doors at the emergency room entry way. Nurse Bates, clipboard in hand, rushed out the door to greet the first of the ambulances as it pulled up, sirens wailing, lights flashing. It was pandemonium.

Quietly, purposefully, surveying the confusion around her, Cassandra Ellington rose from her seat, picking up her leather designer handbag that had fallen to the floor beside her. Calmly buttoning up her suede coat, she put her bag strap over her good shoulder and quietly, elegantly stepped briskly out the side door of the emergency room. The door swished softly behind her as she stepped quickly to the bronze BMW that was still parked right where she had frantically left it when she arrived. She slipped inside, jamming the seat belt closed when it offered resistance. Then she drove smoothly away, her outside calm demeanor absolutely no indication of the overwhelming pain and hopelessness that filled her heart.

Chapter 2

Duncan clicked the off button on telephone with frustration. He lifted his headphones from where they had lay around his neck while he answered the phone and plugged them back into his ears. The hard beat of the music enveloped him immediately, and he lay back slowly on his bed and let the sound fill his brain.

Man, his father drove him crazy. His mom, too, for that matter. But mostly his father. At fifteen, he was in the middle of a growth spurt that had left his arms and legs so long he looked like he needed a body transplant. And with a face that sprouted pimples as reliably as the tide ebbed and flowed, he wasn't so hot on himself, either.

The song changed, and the rhythmic words rang through him. He really loved his music. But not on an iPod like some of his friends. He liked live radio, especially the station he was usually tuned into. He listened to an upbeat commercial claiming that a certain kind of toothpaste would solve just about all of life's worries. If only that was the truth!

No matter how hard he tried to concentrate, his mind wandered back to his phone conversation with his father. It was about his mother. His father's voice had sounded strained and worried, for once. Somehow, Duncan took a kind of enjoyment in that. His father usually either sounded gratingly cheerful and upbeat, mostly when he was with his friends or students, or he sounded low and growling and mean, like he had when he took after mom before dinner. He always sounded like he was the boss. In control. Which he was.

Didn't his father think that he saw the things he did? Didn't his father know how he looked, how he sounded? Probably not. Probably he didn't care what Duncan thought.

Duncan turned the music up, trying to drown out his thoughts. It didn't work, so he turned it down again. No sense going deaf over his old man and his crazy temper.

But the phone call had been weird. His dad had said that his mom was REALLY upset and that she had disappeared. Disappeared? He knew his mom had gone out, he had seen the BMW pull away when she had said she needed to do an errand. But she hadn't seemed overly upset. I mean, he had seen her upset plenty of times before. He always wondered, actually, if she'd ever get upset enough that she'd just get in the car and never come back. God knows he'd wanted to do that.

But she never did. No matter what his father did to her, no matter what he did to all of them, the sun went down and the next day it came up and life just went on.

Only this time it felt different. It was almost like his father wasn't afraid of her NOT coming back, but like he was afraid that she WOULD come back. To do what?

Duncan shook his head. He was having crazy thoughts.

But his dad had said explicitly that he wasn't to talk to her, he wasn't to listen to her, he wasn't to do anything but to hang up and call 911 if she called. He said "We have to protect her from herself.." Whatever that was supposed to mean. Just what was his old man up to? The question gave him a stomach ache.

But so far, she hadn't come back, she hadn't called, and his old man hadn't bothered him again. He kept listening to the music. The DJ came on and said the normal things about the time, the weather, and traffic conditions. He loved listening to "Your Pal Cal", the night time DJ that crossed the airwaves of his favorite station. He was a funny guy, and really calm, like he could find humor in just about anything and didn't let things get him down. But it wasn't just the jokes and the wild stuff he did that made Duncan want to listen to him every night. Cal had this way of listening to people, like when he had his call-in show. It was like he understood the problems that kids were having, the problems with school, parent stuff, the urge to take drugs, or to drink your brains out, and the pain you felt when the coolest girl in the class made fun of your complexion. Cal was ok. Even though he was an adult, he was ok.

Duncan lay on the bed and listened. A kid had just had called in about running away. Her parents had grounded her, made fun of her friends, and all the usual routine. She was crying, and ready to take off. Within minutes the girl was laughing with him, and making fun of her parents and their funny ideas instead of packing her bag. Cal told her a story about when he was her age, and how things worked out in the end. Hell, it may not even have been true, but the way Cal said it, it was like it COULD have been true, and that was enough. She got his point. He helped her come up with a plan to get her parents off her back, and not "cut off her nose to spite her face", as he put it.

God knows Duncan had thought of running away often enough. Probably not as much as his little brother Peter though. Peter actually had a little knapsack packed and stored under his bed, just in case.

But all they did was think about it, actually. His dad was all about control. He wouldn't even let them have a cell phone. Not even mom. He wanted to know where they were every moment of the day.

No matter how ugly things got around the house, the very thought of incurring Dad's wrath for something like running away was just too awesomely gruesome to imagine. Dad was, after all, Dad. He seemed to find out about everything, about everyone. He didn't honestly think that either one of them would get too far without getting caught by Dad. That's for sure. And that would be even worse.

And then there was Mom. He really loved his mom. Not that he would admit it to his friends. They all said they hated their parents. But he didn't hate his mom. He was just disappointed in her a lot. He wished she didn't take so much crap from his mean old man, no matter how rich and important he was. But he didn't really blame her, either. She was as scared of him as they were. And he was scared for her. So that was really the main reason that he'd stay put, never run away. He had to stay and make sure that nothing really awful happened to his mom.

So what was happening tonight? Why did he have this funny feeling in the pit of his stomach? Why did his father sound so darn weird?

Another rap song came on the radio, and he turned it up again, adjusting his head phones. This time, he lost himself in the beat, and he didn't even notice that the house phone had begun to ring...

Chapter 3

Peter was in his room doing his homework. He had a headache. It was always a mystery to him why teachers felt the urge to give so much homework, especially if you already understood what they did in class. But he liked good grades, so he did it.

Line after line of problems practicing the fine art of multiplying fractions filled the page. Repetitive, boring. But he did it. He always made the Honor Roll.

Sometimes it was hard being so smart. Especially when you were 12. He was anxious for the time to go by so that he could be older, maybe 17. Then, maybe, adults would listen to his ideas, would realize that he had something to say. Sometimes they all treated him like he was just a little kid and they didn't realize just how much he understood, or just how smart he really was.

Especially Duncan. And his parents. His chubby freckled face pulled into a frown at the thought of his parents. Mom had really been upset tonight. She thought they didn't notice it when she made the dinner and all, but he could see. Maybe the others couldn't see. She was really upset.

He wished Dad could control his darn temper and stop hurting everyone. What was the big darn deal, anyhow, if Mom wanted to get her hair cut? She'd be beautiful no matter what. That's for sure. But dad just had to have the last word. Always the boss. It made Peter sick to think about it. Not that he was going to argue with him.

When dad had called, and talked to Duncan, he had lifted the receiver and listened. That was starting to be a habit. It gave him a certain sense of power to listen in on people's phone conversations, especially since they all seemed to forget to tell him stuff, anyway. So he heard what Dad told Duncan, about calling 911 and all. That was really stupid. But Dad had sounded weird.

And it was pretty dangerous to cross dad, no matter what crazy thing he said. But he was afraid for his mom, for some strange reason, not just a little afraid, as he was every time his dad started up on something, but deep down afraid, like something really horrible was going to happen. He wished he could warn her.

The phone rang. Duncan usually picked it up on the first ring, but for some reason he didn't. On the second ring, Peter reached out his hand and picked up the phone.

"Hello?"

It was his mom. "Peter, honey, this is Mom."

"Hi, mom." It seemed like a strange, regular thing to say when he felt so upset, but he didn't know what else to say. He wished he didn't pick up the phone. In school, he always had all the answers, he could always figure out every puzzle and solve every problem that came up...but with this family stuff, this just baffled him, and he wasn't too proud to admit it.

"Peter, is your father there?"

"No, but he called."

"Did you talk to him?"

"Duncan did." He hesitated, then went on. "But I listened."

"He told Duncan to call 911 if you called, and have them find you."

Cassandra swallowed. "Are you going to do that?"

"Of course not, mom. Dad doesn't even know that I heard that conversation, " he said with child like logic. "If I called 911, he'd know I listened."

She smiled, despite her pain. She really loved her boys.

"Where's Duncan?"

"I think he's listening to the radio. That guy he likes."

"OK. Peter. I am in a lot of trouble, and I don't know what to do. Your father is very, very upset, I think."

"I think you're right."

"I just wanted to let you and your brother know that I love you very, very much, no matter what happens."

Panic started to well up in him, his face was turning red and his eyes began to water.

"Mom, mom, don't come home. I'm afraid."

Pain pulled at her heart. She could almost see his bright, sensitive face. But she could also picture herself being forcibly put into an ambulance, on her way against her will, committed to some strange private hospital, and she knew deep in her bones, that she would never come out.

"Me too. I'm sorry, Peter, and I know you are right. I know I can't come home right now. I'm just too afraid, too. I have to figure some things out. I'll call you back." She wished she could think better, her mind was so groggy from the pain medication.

"Be careful, Mom. Be careful." He banged down the phone.

Right then, he heard the sound of his Dad's car in the drive.

Should he call 911? Would his father figure out that she had called, that he had listened in, that he had not called 911?

Would they be able to trace her call? Would her father look to see what calls had come in? Quickly, he hit the settings button on the phone, and reset the system. The lights blinked, and the information was gone. There were some benefits to being a techie, despite having to listen to Duncan call him a nerd and a brainiac. He swallowed hard.

His mom was so afraid, she wouldn't come home. He wasn't going to let his dad find her, no matter what.

Just as the door opened, Peter lifted the receiver and with all the speed in his plump fingers, he dialed his friend Tommy's house.

Tommy answered.

"Hi, Tom," he said, trying to keep his voice from shaking. His dad had come in the front door, and he was wearing his "angry face".

"I just wondered if you finished all those stinking math problems? Yeah, me too. See you tomorrow."

He hung up the phone carefully, saying a little prayer his mom had once taught him before he turned to face the wrath of his father. But no matter what had happened, he had had eliminated the chance that his father would be able to trace his mother's call with return call.

He took a deep breath, and turned to face the man who was his father.

****

Frederick slammed the front door behind him. Cassandra's car was not in the driveway. He was really agitated.

His mind was racing. Where would she have gone? How much had that stupid doctor said to her? He could almost hear his own heart beating, his breath was short. So close, so close to victory. So many years, so many plans. Where was Cassandra? She could ruin it all.

Peter, his youngest son, stood before him as he entered the kitchen. His chubby freckled face looked pale as he talked on the phone. Cassandra?

"Hi, Tom," Peter had said, and has mumbled something about math problems. A quick hang up, a nervous expression. Had Peter been talking to his mother? He looked at the boy in anger, critically aware of his chubby face, his uncomfortable look. He was soft, he was certainly not tough. But he was smart. Very smart.

"Peter," has your mother called? He kept his voice modulated, tried to sound casual.

"No, Dad, I was on the phone," said the boy softly. He paused for a moment. "That was Tom Johnson on the phone. Math homework." The words were smooth but Frederick didn't like the look in the boy's eye. He was lying. He was covering up. Maybe not everyone would pick up on it, but he was a master. His very understanding and perception of the human personality had gotten him far.

"I see, son," he said, casually walking to the phone. He picked the receiver up quickly and hit the button to check for prior calls. Only one number was there.

He hung up the phone, and glared at his son.

"Get Duncan," he growled in his angry voice, and Peter tore down the hall to his brother's room and found him lying on the bed, earphones in place.

"Dad wants you Dunc," he gasped, out of breath and scared. "And he's mad."

Duncan sighed, turned off the radio, and followed his brother to the living room.

"Did your mother call?" his father asked gruffly. "Did she contact you?"

"No, dad, I haven't heard from her. The phone didn't even ring since you called." Duncan looked, concerned, sincere. Frederick sighed, and tried to calm himself down. Duncan was obviously telling the truth.

****

Peter looked down at the floor and said a silent prayer for his mother, wherever she was. Then he said a silent prayer of thanks that she wasn't there. Wherever his mother was, he had a very strong feeling that it was better if the angry man who was his father didn't know.

Chapter 4

After her brief and painful conversation with Peter, Cassandra found herself driving mindlessly up the windy road that paralleled the river. She pulled off at the top of a hill and looked down over the forceful river, swelled with spring rains and the last of the melting snow from the mountains in the north.

She watched the sun drop gently below the horizon. Her watch said 8:00 pm. At the hospital, they would have realized she was gone by now. Would there be an uproar? Or would the fact be simply noted, not important, like every other factor in her life.

And Frederick? The class he taught at the University began at 7:30. They had evidently reached him before his class began, if he had called the house as Peter said. He'd be mad, livid, she knew, to be disturbed before beginning a class...He was so tense and tightly wound before he began a presentation. She'd have to apologize...

A fresh sob broke from her throat at the thought. The pain killer had made her shoulder feel better, but her thoughts were unfocused, her feelings were in a jumble and she felt confused.

What was the matter with her? Where was her self respect, her pride? Frederick had actually insinuated to the doctor that she was an alcoholic, as well as neurotic, to cover up his latest episode of abuse. He had gone so far as to convince a local judge, probably another golf partner, to begin the proceedings that would allow him to commit his wife to a hospital, rather than to allow her to take a stand about what he had done to her. What he would continue to do. There was no stopping him. Fear gripped her. It nauseated her, despite her pain, the she automatically worried about calming him, soothing him.

She felt trapped, hopeless, like an animal in a cage. There was absolutely no where to turn. She covered her face with her hands. It was not as though she hadn't occasionally gotten the gumption to try. It just hadn't worked. Nothing worked. Frederick had it all sewn up. Things always seemed to go his way.

First, she tried to talk to the minister in her local church. Here, she naively thought, she would be able to get help. It was almost funny. The minister looked at her in a rather bizarre way, and promised to pray for her. He asked her to go home and take her "medicine" and get some sleep. He simply had not believed a word she said. He had been told that she was "emotional" and "depressed" by her dear husband. His words hit her hard, piercing like nails driven into her coffin.

Later, she learned that Frederick had dropped off an $8,000 check as a donation for the new organ that the congregation needed. The church bulletin was generous with praise for their supportive parishioner, Frederick Ellington III, the following week.

Cassandra's stomach had been tied into a tight knot as she had read it, sitting demurely beside her handsome husband's side as he graciously accepted their thanks and applause during the next Sunday service. Of course, the bruises didn't show with her long sleeved woolen dress.

Up until that day, Cassandra had often prayed, perhaps a bit haphazardly, to God, begging him to solve the dilemma that she lived with, her anger prone husband, who ruled with unbendable rules and an iron fist. As she had listened to the hymns flowing from the brand new organ, however, she had quietly let that aspect of her life fade away. She hadn't prayed again.

There was the time that she had gone to the family doctor, concerned about the pain in her back that resulted from being pushed down wide stairway in her house. A back sprain, it had been diagnosed. But the issue that set Frederick off at that time concerned the boys, and he had scared her to death.

"They are getting just like you, with your crazy ideas, Cassandra, and I simply will not have it!" He roared with anger and the sound had filled the house."I will have to teach you all a lesson about who is in charge here!"

Truly afraid for her sons, she had gotten the courage to talk to the doctor, who had known the family for years.

"Cassandra," the doctor said gently, "You are getting very paranoid. I have known you and Frederick and the boys for a long time, and I know that Frederick is absolutely devoted to you all. This is nonsense." He had picked up the phone. "Shall I call Frederick to come here and we can all sit down and have a little talk about this?"

The very thought of facing his angry face, the thought of what he would do, to her, or even worse, to the boys made her feel sick, her hands clammy. "No, doctor," she heard herself saying, feeling as though a new nail was being added to her own coffin.

"I'm sorry."

"There, there, dear," he consoled, writing out a prescription of Valium to go with the pain pills for her back. "The back will heal, and these pills will keep you calmed down. Go home, now, and take care of that family of yours."

There had been a momentary, fleeting thought of taking those pills, all of them, to end the misery she felt in her soul at that time. But she had thought of her two young boys, and she had not. She had flushed the whole bottle down the toilet as soon as she went home, and life had gone on. She wished she had the pills now.

The sun was gone now, but she still sat in her car staring out into the darkness before her, memories flowing over her like water over the rocks below.

It wasn't just the physical abuse. That was actually the definable part. It was the verbal abuse, the psychological games that had eaten away at her soul for so many years. The years of being told what to think, what to say, what to do had taken their toll. She was 36 years old, a college graduate, and had once, she angrily told herself, possessed a brain.

But she had been told so often, and by such force, that the things she thought were stupid, the things she did were useless, and the things she said were ridiculous. Sooner or later, somewhere along the line, she had taken to believing it. From that point, taking the direction from Frederick had been easy, since everything about her was evidently so unacceptable.

And the boys...her heart clenched as visions of their faces came before her. Two loveable, intelligent, interesting, lively boys. Duncan, so deep and thoughtful, athletic, and amazingly clever with words and music. And Peter, so cuddly, so warm and loving, and so absolutely bright the school deemed to call him "gifted". She loved them with all her heart.

Frederick loved them, too, she knew, in his own way, but the vicious kink in his personality kept the positive feelings trapped. "Duncan, you should have made that last basket, what good are you? " "Peter, how can you eat all that, you're already a disgusting blimp?" "Duncan, why are you listening to that ridiculous music? Only a fool would enjoy that!" "Peter, so you think you're smart? I'll show you smart!"

They had grown so quiet, both so withdrawn in the past year, and the thought made her feel panic. It was her fault, probably, bringing out the anger and pain in Frederick and they would receive the brunt of it. Lately, it seemed as if Frederick was getting worse and worse. Duncan was constantly listening to his radio, every minute he could, and Peter would lose himself in his math puzzles by the hour. Neither seemed to have friends. It was really sad.

Her mind began to replay the words that Peter had spoken on the phone. She had heard, felt, his fear and anguish.

"Don't come home, mom," he had cried in his childish way. "Don't come home."

The words rang like a mantra in her brain. It was true, the feeling suddenly settled over her, that their lives would probably be better without her. Without her, Frederick would have nothing to be angry about. Without her, they might be able to have peace.

The doctor's words in the emergency room came back, "Your family and your home will be fine without you, you'll see."

Maybe it was true.

Chapter 5

"Your Pal Cal" took off his earphones and took a big, deep gulp from the can of soda he had gotten from the machine in the cafeteria of the radio station. His mouth felt dry, and he was really, really tired. But he had a job to do. More often than not, he absolutely loved his job, and was thankful for it every day.

The song on the turntable ended, and he flipped a few switches to play some ads, keeping a careful eye on the clock before him.

"When it's time," cheerful voices sang to a rhythmic tune, "To make the team...

Get your sports shoes, From Queen Maureen."

The commercial blared on, advertising "Queen Maureen", the local sports supplier who gave discounts to all the high school athletes. The commercial ended just as expected, perfect timing. Cal flipped a new switch, which made the red light go on over his head in the broadcasting booth. He was on the air.

"Yep, that was the latest message from "Queen Maureen" down on State Street, and if you hurry up over there this month, make sure you tell her that Your Pal Cal sent you, 'cause it's good for another 5% off the price of your sneakers!

"The time, my friends, is 8:00PM, and if you didn't get the chance to catch the most beautiful spring sunset yet this year, you're turning into a couch potato. Plan on seeing it tomorrow! Now, after the next mind boggling rap song you hear, these little old phone lines will be open for your calls. Want to talk? Make sure you call, 'cause I just might go off my rocker with boredom sitting here in this little booth with only old Paul here keeping me company!"

He smiled at his young assistant, who silently made a face.

Buttons flipped, and the turntable started spinning, the sounds of rap coming over loud and clear. The red light went off over his head, showing that his mike was dead.

"You're a good sport, Paul," he grinned at the young man who sat on the stool next to him, filling out the broadcasting log and putting the next songs in order for him to play. They ran a classic, old fashioned radio station, most of the music on vinyl records. The very newest songs were played digitally. Progress happens, whether you want it or not. But they'd play the vinyl as long as they could get away with it.

"No problem, Cal, you know I'll get you back." Paul laughed. "Just lay off the hair jokes, ok?"

They had a running commentary about Paul's long dark hair, which hung halfway down his back, tonight braided and anchored with a hair band running across his forehead.

"You know you look like a Comanche today," said Cal with a wide grin.

"You know you're just jealous, man, with that sparse crop you have on top." The two men laughed, several years and different lifestyles apart, but still close friends.

"That does it, Little Big Man, you've had it," Cal shot back.

The record was ending, and Paul pulled two telephones over within reach and Cal switched the mike switch on again. The red light cast a glow in the booth.

"That, my listeners, was some long song. But if you really want to see long...you should see Paul's hair here. This guy is making a statement, he says. Today he looks like he's trying out for a role in a western movie. Playing the role of Tonto."

He was outrageous, he was funny. The polls showed how his young listeners loved his kindly jabs, his quick humor. They also loved Paul.

"Yeah, well man," Paul drawled out in his low, slow voice that he reserved for his minutes on the air. "The next scene in the movie was where we scalped the white guy, but looking over here at you, I see somebody already beat me to it...."

"A low blow, Paul. My ego, please."

"Say you like my hair, man," Paul drawled. "Say it or you'll end up playing very golden oldies all night..."

"OK, OK," Cal cried in dramatic defeat. "The hairy one wins. However, the phone lines are open now, if you have a good insult for Paul, listeners."

"Or for Cal Your Pal," added Paul.

"Dial 555-talk, and if you get a busy signal, just keep trying." Cal's voice got quieter. "And if you really need to talk about something in your life, I'm here, you guys. Pick up the phone and you're not alone."

The lights on the phone started to blink like crazy.

The station loved Cal Your Pal, and his unexpectedly successful assistant, Paul. Cal had spent five years at the station, gradually focusing on the 7pm to 12am show. Most DJ's fought tooth and nail to get a spot on morning drive time (6am to 10am) or evening drive time (3pm to 7pm) because of the wide listening audience and the chance to gain fame on the airwaves, but Cal had already been there and back, and he was doing just exactly what he wanted to do. What he had to do.

His evening show was popular with kids. From 7PM to midnight, from Monday to Friday, he blasted his music and made his jokes to appeal to the 13-18 year old crowd in their town and the surrounding area. He knew their needs. He helped the ad representatives who sold radio time for commercials to focus on the advertisers who sold things that would appeal to kids. Sports stores, book stores, clothing stores, and many local restaurants were absolutely thrilled with the response they got from their wacky ads played by "Your Pal Cal".

So they kept advertising. And the kids kept listening. And the station owners kept getting good ratings and making good money. And Cal kept his air-wave vehicle for helping kids, which was his mission in life. Everyone was happy.

Paul picked up the first phone line. "What's happening man?"

"Hey, Paul," came a young female voice. "Can you play a song for me and my boyfriend? It's our first anniversary."

Paul smiled as she named the song. "You've been going out for a whole year?"

"Nope, a week," came the gum chewing voice. "It's our one week anniversary."

"Well, that's just fine." Paul said kindly. "Does he treat you good? With lots of respect?"

"Yep, I'm worth it!"

"Good girl!" he said, sliding her request into the pile before Cal, and hanging up the phone.

"This is Your Pal Cal," Cal said, his voice masterfully filling the airspace after Paul without missing a beat.

"Hey, Cal," came a young male voice, "No Indian jokes. It's not PC."

"You're right, fella," he said contritely. "It was done in the spirit of humor, sorry if it wasn't taken that way. You just gotta see Paul, man, and you'll know why I had a weak moment..."

The kid on the line laughed. "Ok man, it's cool. I'm black, man, and I guess I get bugged when anybody's picking on minorities."

"Good for you for calling instead of just getting mad at me and keeping it bottled up inside. State your case and clear the air. Because bottled up anger leads to violence, and that's what we DON'T need. Like I said, you're right. Are we ok now?"

The voice on the phone chuckled. "We're ok, Cal. All of us. Even Paul."

A few more calls, and then Cal played a couple of songs from the schedule the program director had made for the show. He slipped in the love song for the first call in, and crossed off one that had been scheduled on the list. The program director never complained about his changes. He kept his audience in the palm of his hand.

There was an ad for a new hamburger joint. They were giving out free soda on Friday night. Plus karaoke. Cal knew that that would go over big, and that the kids would keep the place high on their list.

He then played a segment from a Beethoven Concerto, challenging his audience to broaden their horizons, and remember that music "greats" lived in every age.

"Name the Concerto," he offered, "And you can come down to the station one night this week and laugh at Paul's hair."

Then the phone lines were open for requests, and comments.

The Concerto was named, almost instantly, by a high school violinist. Cal praised him, and the kid felt great.

The phone rang again.

"I think I'm pregnant, I don't know what to do," a young female voice said as Paul picked up the phone. "Hang on, Honey," came Paul's slow voice, as he transferred the call to Cal. "Cal's coming on the private line."

Then Paul threw switches to play music and announced the next two songs.

The "On the Air" light went dead as Cal picked up the phone. "Hi! What's your name?" He spent the next several minutes talking to a 17 year old girl named Delores. She was a nice kid, and he commended her for calling for help.

She was scared, totally terrified, actually, at the thought of telling her parents or even her friends. She was just about ready to head to a local abortion clinic.

"You need to talk to somebody about this. Are you sure about what you want? It's just really good to think hard about something as important as this." He spoke gently.

"I don't know what I want." she sobbed.

He talked to her then, about her parents, encouraging her to talk to them. He asked a few questions, but mostly, he just listened. At the end of the conversation, she told him she was going downstairs to talk to her mom and dad.

"Call me back, Delores," he said, and she knew he meant it. "Let me know what happens. And don't wait for a call-in time, when the lines might be full. Just call. I'll watch the phone." He gave her the number to his private line.

She was gone.

More songs, more commercials, more jokes and comments called in. The light on the phone flashed during an old Beatles song.

Paul nodded at Cal and pointed at the phone. Then he moved over took over the turntable. Cal picked up the phone.

"Is this Cal?" a shaky man's voice asked. It was Delores' father. "She told me about the baby." The man's voice broke and Cal just listened. "She told me what you said. I just wanted to thank you...She's our life, you know."

"I could tell she was a great kid. She made a mistake here, but she's got a lot of courage, and she deserves to know that people are behind her. Is she ok?"

Delores took the phone. "Cal?" she was crying. "There're going to help me decide what to do. Thank you for helping me...."

"You have great folks, Delores...Make sure you tell them." Cal had a lump in his throat for this unseen kid.

"Can I call again?"

"Any time, Kid."

He hung up the phone, and took off his glasses to wipe them. They were misty. Paul smiled, understanding. "Nice job, Man!"

"Aren't you glad you didn't scalp me yet, Tonto?" Cal jeered, taking over the mike and flipping on the on air switch.

"Hey, all you out there in headphone land, it's time for Knock Knock jokes! The worst one called in in the next two minutes gets a fantastic prize! They get to wash my car!"

He laughed and played a song, while the lights on the phone started to blink.

Chapter 6

A tired fog settled over Cassandra as she sat hunched over the steering wheel, looking into the black nothingness of the night. Far below the railing in front of her, the river rumbled by in the dark. She was just so tired of it all. Escape. Death beckoned her, like a black, misty promise. There would be no more pain in her shoulder, no excruciating headaches that made her eyes swim. No iron grasp of fear, making the sweat run down her back at the sound of Frederick's harsh voice. No feeling of panic so thick it welled up in her and paralyzed her, that overwhelming overpowering of problems that threatened to smother her. Nothing.

It's funny, she didn't fear death. It sounded easy, nothingness, compared to the hell she resided in on a daily basis. She felt almost resolved in her decision, almost peaceful with the next, seemingly inevitable step in her unproductive and pain filled life.

But there was one nagging emotion that didn't seem to be quelled with the escape of death. Guilt. She felt a flickering of guilt, drifting aimlessly through her depression.

She gave a deep, heartfelt sigh, and tried to think about her feelings, tried to focus on the random thoughts that ran through her mind. Her brain was full of fog.

Her boys. Duncan and Peter. Tears streamed down her face as she faced the thought of never seeing them again, never seeing what they were to become, never experiencing those heartfelt feelings of pride watching them grow. She loved her boys.

Frederick's wild accusations rumbled in her memory. "They're getting to be just like you." "You coddle them too much."   "They're better off without your interference."

The smooth faced doctor, ready to send her off to an unknown future locked up in a private hospital had said, "Your family and home will be fine without you."

Would they be better off without her?

Without her problems, without her personality that seemed to constantly send Frederick into a rage, wouldn't they be able to settle into a more comfortable and thriving existence? The life she dreamed of for them? She pictured the quiet in the house, the boys cheerfully doing their homework and taking part in their extracurricular activities without the stress and anger that seemed to permeate the very walls of the place she had called home. She would do anything... anything, if it would mean peace and positive living for her sons.

She started up the car quickly, and sat for a moment staring straight ahead. How did a person prepare to die? She had long ago given up on praying, and to pray at this point seemed hypocritical and ridiculous. She would simply hit the accelerator on the car, heading over the river cliff that loomed right before her. Gravity would take care of the rest. Yet she hesitated. The clock said 9:02. She had sat over an hour.

In a kind of final ritual, she flipped on the radio and turned the dial to KDRK, the station that Duncan was always glued to. This was the music he liked, this was the world that was his. She had never really listened, in all her fluctuating between pain and pressure of making everything in her life appear "normal" to the outside world. She took the time now, maybe as her last goodbye to her firstborn son. She couldn't talk to him, but this was a connection to him. She listened.

A rap song ended, and a gentle sounding man made a few jokes about the weather. She smiled. "Your Pal Cal", as she quickly learned he was called, had a voice that was easy to like. He played a song she recognized as one of her son's favorites, and she hummed the tune and thought of Duncan. He would be tall one day. He'd grow into those long arms and legs and fill out, and he would be a handsome man. Had she ever told him that? She pictured that he'd look a lot like her father, who had died when she was young.

A car accident had taken her parents. Instant death, the state troopers said when they came to the house, the car hitting a bridge span with full force, bursting into flames. She saw the twisted, charred car frame weeks later, and she still shuddered at the thought of it. Would her boys see this car frame, and be haunted about her feelings the instant before she died, have recurring nightmares about her violent death? Her stomach began to hurt.

The song was over, and the DJ's assistant announced that the lines were open for calls. She heard a variety of teens voices as they requested songs, asked for advice about friends, "My best friend is mad because now I have a boyfriend and she doesn't… What should I do?"

"Don't give up on your friend," had been the heartfelt advice. "Maybe she's having trouble adjusting to the change in your interests and availability."

"Yeah," agreed the sad girl.

"But make sure you leave time for your friends," Cal cautioned. "In a good relationship, you have the space to have a boyfriend, friends, good grades and your activities. Don't give up ANY of those things. You deserve them."

"You mean," she reflected, "That maybe I DO spend too much time with my boyfriend? Or do your mean that she just has to adjust to me being too busy?"

"Only you know that one, Jeannie," he suggested. "But if you are honest with yourself, you'll know what to do.   We're always adjusting and readjusting in relationships."

Kid problems.

The next call was a funny one. "I'm in hairdresser school and I wanted to volunteer to give Paul a haircut," a giggling voice offered.

"Gee, that's a nice offer," Cal said excitedly. "But I'm afraid that he may be a little like Samson, with his strength and organizational abilities in his hair. If we cut his hair, I may never get the songs on in the right order. But thanks for calling!"

What a nice man, Cassandra thought, listening quietly. She was inordinately pleased that this was the station that her son listened to every night.

"Cal, man", came the next voice, this one teen and male and obviously under distress. "I just can't take it anymore. I'm going to run away tonight."

The young man's sad voice pierced her heart, and she wanted to cry out, right through the radio to him. "No, no, young man, there has to be a better way. Don't give up."

"Sounds like you're feeling pretty bad," came Cal's soft voice, acknowledging the kid's pain.

"Yeah."

"What's your name?"

"Duncan."

Cassandra felt her heart drop to the region of her stomach. Her head spun.

"You wanna talk, Duncan? Because talk is what you have to do. When something is so unbearable, you have to do something about it. But probably running away isn't the best way out. That's kinda like giving up."

"It's the only way, Cal. Things are so bad here. My dad is just too much to take. And now my mom has run away, and my dad says it's because of us. If she's given up, why can't I give up, too?"

Cal sighed, and she could hear the care in his very breath. "Sounds like a bad problem, Duncan. I'm gonna have Paul transfer you to the private line so we can really talk, OK? Listeners, we're gonna take a little priority break here and play a few tunes."

His voice disappeared, and a rowdy rap sound filled the air.

"NO!" she screamed aloud, flicking the radio dial, as if the motion could make the voices return. "NO! Duncan!" But he was gone.

She turned the radio off abruptly. The luminescent light of the clock dial said 9:22. There was night time quiet around her, broken only by the smooth hum of the BMW engine, and the rumbling water on the rocks far below.

Her hands were shaking and she was breathing heavily. "God Damn that Frederick!" she screamed futilely into the darkness. "Damn him to hell for blaming this mess on my poor kids!"

She felt lost. She banged her hand on the dashboard, frustrated that she couldn't call her son. Or the radio station. Frederick had always made a big deal about denying her a cell phone. And she hadn't fought back. Self disgust flowed over her like a wave. She never fought back.

She lay her head back on the headrest and closed her eyes tightly. She could almost feel Duncan's pain as if it were her own. How could he possibly feel that his father's anger was in any way his fault? How could he possibly feel that her problems were caused by him? And if Duncan felt the depth of despair that she had just heard, what did poor Peter, younger, more sensitive, feel? She literally wanted to scream.

A vision of Frederick's face suddenly appeared in front of her. Suddenly, it was as if she could really see him for the first time, her eyes suddenly opened, stripped of the blindfold that had given her only glimpses of the ugliness behind his handsome facade in the past. He was manipulative, he was cruel, he was selfish and evil.

The face she saw in her mind's eye laughed suddenly, and it made her skin crawl. "I win, Cassandra," the face said in an elated voice, like a little spoiled boy who has gotten away with a prank. "I have beaten you. I have beaten Duncan and Peter. I can beat everyone. You gave up, and so I win." The ugly laugh echoed in her ears.

"Never!" was the answering voice that came from somewhere deep inside of her. The feeling was stronger by the second. She would not run away. She would not give up. And she would not allow her boys to, either. There would be no mangled mass of metal for her boys to regret. No dead mother who had given up. She would find a way to build a better life with her sons. Frederick would not win.

Her head was still groggy. She needed to focus her thoughts.

She opened the car door, deciding to stretch her legs and clear her mind. She needed a plan. She had to have a plan. She would find a way to make life better for her sons. And for herself.

Her right hand flicked the seat belt release button, but the belt didn't come loose. Aggravated, she used her left hand, too, but the contraption was stuck tight. In the murky shadows thrown by the overhead light from the opened door, she couldn't clearly see the silk of the pleated skirt on her dress was caught in the clasp. When she left the hospital upset, she still automatically attached the belt, her mind working on "automatic pilot" as it had so many times when she was upset.

The belt was jammed tight.

"I'm not going to be held back," she thought defiantly, frustrated by the belt. She bent her head and slipped the shoulder belt behind her. Then she turned her back to the door, raising her arms over her head to the door frame. She would simply pull herself out from under the belt. She wiggled and squirmed as it was a tight fit, still not aware that she was being held back by the silk of her skirt.

Her determination grew. Almost like a test, getting out of the car seemed like a feat that she must accomplish to prove her determination. She put her right foot on the seat and gave a hard push. It became almost symbolic. Her sons were going to know that you could get yourself out of your problems.

It all happened at once. With the hard push, the silk on the skirt finally gave out with a loud rip. Her body flew backward, out from under the seatbelt, just as the skirt ripped loose. The sudden movement made her body jerk as it came free, still half out of the car. Her right foot, now loose, swung up with reflex action, and came down hard, on the column gear shift. The car bolted into drive, and started forward, toward the cliff.

She was far enough out of the seat belt that her feet could not touch the brake pedal, and her hand could not reach the shift. The car was going over the cliff, and she was still half inside the car.

"NO!" she screamed, flailing valiantly, but totally unable to stop the car. With all the strength she could muster, she threw herself with all her might. But she felt only air whizzing past. Her last conscious thought was of Frederick, and it was filled with hate. She had thankfully blacked out before the sound of the crashing car echoed through the river valley.

Chapter 7

Twelve year old Peter was lying on the top of his bed in his room in the dark. The house was quiet for the moment. He was worried, real worried. Next door, he could hear the steady beat of a song coming from Duncan's radio. Duncan was listening without the earphones, which was weird. Peter wondered why, but didn't dare get up from his bed and check it out. He wanted to stay right where he was, in the safe, silent dark of his room, and wait for his mom to return. His father was quiet now, somewhere out in the living room, and for now that was good enough. He put the pillows over his head, and rocked. He wished he could go to sleep, anything, to make the time go by. "Where are you, mom!" his mind cried over and over.

****

Duncan also lay on top of his bed, but face down, his face pressed tightly into his pillow, occasional sobs escaping and muffled by the material around him. "Stop crying," he kept berating himself. "Only babies and toads cry." But no matter what insults he gave himself, he couldn't stop the flow of tears from escaping. No earphones. He hoped and prayed the sound of his music hid the sound of his crying, so no one would hear.

The radio played, and he listened as he stretched out on the bed. Cal and Paul were up to their usual thing. He wished he could laugh, but he just couldn't. His mind was too sad to think that anything was funny. He had even called Cal, on the last call-in, and told him that he was going to take a hike away from this place, and Cal had tried to talk to him. God, it felt so good to talk to someone who cared. His dad was a maniac, and didn't care about anybody but himself, and sometimes his precious students, and his mom...well, his mom had enough trouble dealing with his dad, and she didn't have much time to talk, to tell the truth. He couldn't imagine telling her how bad it all felt, anyhow, because it would only make it worse. And he didn't want to hurt his mom.

And he couldn't make it better. God knows he'd tried. But there was really no pleasing his dad. If you got a 98 on a test that everyone else bombed with a 75, he'd still berate you for the 2% you got wrong. If you scored a touchdown in a football game, he'd complain that you should have done it 10 minutes sooner. And on and on and on.

His mom. Nobody, even if he had the courage to tell somebody about it, would understand the anger and disgust and hate he felt when he saw his dad manhandle his mom. Sometimes with his hands, but mostly with his mouth. It was like he, the oldest son, should be able to protect her somehow. He should be able to stop what was going on. But he couldn't. He didn't even mind as much when his dad picked on HIM, like he did tonight. He grabbed his arms where his dad's hands had been. He'd have bruises for sure.

He'd come storming into the bedroom while Duncan was on the phone with Cal, screaming about his mother, and in one split second, the good feeling of having someone who cared was ripped away and replaced by fear.

"Get off that damn phone," his father yelled, slamming down the receiver. "Now tell me EXACTLY what your mother said when she left."

"She said she had some errands to do dad, that's all." Duncan couldn't stand the whiny sound of his own voice. What he'd like to do was to punch this man who was his father in the mouth. Instead he stood here, pulled to his feet by strong hands on his arms, and cowered like a baby.

"You must have done SOMETHING to get her upset," Frederick had roared. "Tell me!"

"Let go, let go," Duncan had screamed then, when his dad had begun to shake him. His father dropped his hands abruptly, picked up his radio headphones from where they lay on the bed, and twisted them into a mangled mess. He dropped them right where they had been, then turned and left the room. "Clean up this room right now. It's a pigsty," he said in an even voice as he shut the door behind him.

Duncan trashed the ruined headphones with a heavy heart, and dutifully put the clothes away that lay at the end of his bed, moving like a robot. Turning the radio on again, he listened without the headphones, silently cursing the man who seemed to have all the power in the world over him.

****

Frederick Ellington felt like hitting something. There was a seething, bubbling, burning rage deep in his gut. He clenched and unclenched his fists rapidly as he paced across the living room.

That damn Cassandra. It was one thing that he had been called out of his class, right at the very moment that he was going to begin a lecture. The call was from that dolt of a doctor at the hospital. God, he hated emergency rooms. Embarrassing and unprofessional. The class had had to be cancelled on such short notice.

It was just like that stupid woman to pick a time like this to blow a little thing out of proportion and go running off to the hospital. She'd cause him to get upset, and then have the nerve to be amazed when he hit her. You'd think she would listen by now. You'd think she'd have better sense than to bite the hand that fed her.

He thought he'd covered all the bases, being prepared for a time like this. Why couldn't it have been someone else on duty at the ER? Why did it have to be that young, idealistic do-gooder doctor? He'd bungled the whole thing, told her too much, and set her off. Now where the hell was she?

Just went to show how inefficient things were run with people who didn't have a "vested" interest in the results. Burns, Walters, McCormick....now all those doctors would have played it just right, and the outcome would have been a hell of a lot more discreet and effective than this...fiasco. But then, they would have had a lot more at stake...their own little asses to protect.

But that young goof Watson, there was absolutely nothing the man had to cover up, as far as the digging went. Approaching him with the "care for humanity" approach only went so far. He had been cooperative, believing wholeheartedly Frederick's impassioned plea to help his wife, but hadn't even a notion of what was at stake, and he had let her get away. Well, he'd take care of that guy. After.

After what? Frederick ran his hands through his usually perfectly styled hair, a subtle gesture that the pressure was getting to him. Where was that damn woman? His gut twisted.

Now, knowing his plan for her, she was bound to be really tough to deal with. And she had been getting tougher by the day, it seemed. Some strange desire to assert herself, to disobey, to go off on her own and make decisions had been gradually creeping over her, like a slow growing disease. It made him crazy. Cassandra had to be controlled.

One thing was for sure, he wasn't going to let the bitch ruin everything that he had so carefully concocted, so intricately planned. He sat himself down on a classy, stuffed armchair. One way or another, he was going to win and get what he wanted, what he deserved. He always did.

He just needed to keep a cool head, and steady nerves. He wouldn't get rattled, wouldn't get shaken.

He had been in tighter places before. Visions from his childhood slashed unwelcomed through his thoughts, unnerving him. The horrible hotels, his mother fondling the unending parade of strange men. He thought of being shut in the musty darkness of the closet, alone with the smells of dirty clothes and sweaty shoes, the nightmares. The shame haunted him until he learned to be focused, to set his face in a confident smile. He learned to look confident and in control. And pretending had worked. He had risen above it all. He WAS in control, and no one was ever going to control him again. He would let no one would interfere, least of all Cassandra, who he had molded and shaped into the perfect representation of a wife and mother, and as far from his own disgusting mother as she could be. He would find her and break her spirit, until she was obedient in her role again. Or there would be hell to pay.

The doorbell rang, and it made him jump. "Steady, Buddy," he told himself, rising and smoothing his hair. He straightened his shoulders, and crossed the room to answer the door.

Chapter 8

Marv Greenstein had been a cop in the suburban town of Sollington for ten years. Before that, he had put in another ten on the Philadelphia police force. He had hated working in Philadelphia, with its murders, armed robberies, and unruly gangs that sometimes terrorized the very neighborhoods that their own parents and grandparents lived in. It was like working in a zoo. It had been a glad day, a turning point in his life, when he had gotten the gumption to make changes in his life and move out to the suburbs.

The police force here was a totally different thing. Break-ins when people were on vacation, car accidents, and occasional domestic violence calls, as you would find anywhere made up the blotter. There were a few scattered car thefts, and an abundance of complaints for disturbing the peace, especially in the spring when the young people began their ritualistic coming of age parties. Light stuff, mostly, compared to the vicious crime and loss of life that he had seen in his early years in the city. There hadn't been too many things that had happened here in the suburbs that had made him lose sleep… just the ordinary, basic, ugly things that happen in regular society.

But tonight was a night he'd remember. It was a car accident. The details, while horrible on the one hand, weren't unique. A car had gone over the edge of the river cliff up on the river road, and had plummeted viciously down onto the rocks below before bouncing angrily into the river, upside down. The river was high, as it usually was in the spring, with all the melting snow in the mountains upstate, and the fierce and undaunted flow had evidently carried the body of the unfortunate driver away with its flow. The search crews were out, with bright lights and river dredging equipment. It was generally expected that the body would be found momentarily.

The driver had apparently been a woman, and it looked like she had been alone. Her purse was found still in the car, jammed between the seat cushions. One shoe was found in the wreckage of glass that had been left on shore after the vehicle's initial impact on the rocks. The shoe was a classy one, as was the purse. Leather and imported, and had cost a pretty buck. Just went to show, he thought gruesomely, that money makes no difference when it comes to tragedy.

The other thing that remained in the car had been material that was evidently ripped from the victims skirt or dress. It was expensive print silk, tightly clamped into the seat belt. The seat belt had been jammed tight.

It most probably hadn't mattered, Marv surmised, because the poor lady hadn't had a chance of surviving that impact on the rocks. Most likely she had died on impact, then, upside down in the water, the current had loosened her body and had taken her remains downstream. He felt kind of nauseous just thinking about it.

There were no skid marks at all, so she probably just misjudged the road and drove right off the edge. He cursed the thought that there was no guard rail on the site, but there just wasn't an abundance of traffic on this out of the way road, so the state had never thought it was necessary.

It wasn't the first time a car had gone into the river, though it was the first time one had gone from this far up, he was sure, since he arrived on the force.

Something about this one was really getting to him, though, and he had absolutely no explaining why. He had gotten into his patrol car after getting the preliminary information and left the accident squad to work out the details. He had the lady's purse on the seat beside him. He knew her name, and her address. All that vital information, stored in a bag, all that was left of her. Life was vicious, sometimes.

It was his unpalatable job to inform the family of what had occurred. He really wished that he had had some concrete information to give them, bad news such as it was. But too much time had already gone by, and he had to inform them about the accident as soon as possible. Because the news, being how it was, would blast the information everywhere as soon as they found out. When the body was officially located, that would be another step.

But a family deserved to know. They deserved to hear the news with dignity, if there was such a thing. Pretty, she was. Even in her license picture, which look like mug shots on most, this one was classy and good looking. Long brown hair, and big green eyes. She was 36, according to her birth date, and had a subtle hint of kindness mingled with sadness in her picture. Made you want to help her, somehow. He suddenly felt sick. She was beyond help, now, that was for sure.

He drove into a classy neighborhood and pulled up in front of a giant house, well manicured lawn, carefully planted shrubs. Spotlights gently lit the outside. A showplace. Well, he was going to ruin their night. How does a family deal with this? His footsteps felt heavy as he walked to the big front door. He was glad he had a day off tomorrow. He had a feeling he was going to need it. He rang the bell.

****

Frederick pulled open the front door with all the presence he could muster. Who was it?

A man stood at the door, wearing a well worn tweed sports coat and a tan pair of khaki pants. No uniform, no badge, but with an almost uncanny 6th sense, Frederick knew without a doubt that it was a cop. Shit. A cop. What had Cassandra done to him now?

"Yes?"   Frederick kept his voice calm, well modulated, and wished that he had re-combed his hair.

"Mr. Ellington?"

"Professor Ellington," he corrected. "Yes?" God, this eternal politeness was getting to him. He wouldn't let it show.

"Professor Ellington, I am Detective Greenstein from the Sollington police." Now the badge came out. "I need to have a few words with you."

Frederick thought quickly. The boys were in their rooms, probably asleep. They wouldn't hear what was said. He cordially asked the officer to come in, feeling a little like a net was tightening around him. God damn that Cassandra. What had she said about him? He was going to kill her when she got home. He kept smiling.

"What's the problem officer? Or are you collecting for the policeman's ball?"   His voice was charming, welcoming, but it made Marv's teeth ache. He didn't like this guy.

"I'm sorry, sir," Marv began softly, unhappy in his errand. "I have bad news. It seems your car, which we believe was driven by your wife, was involved in a serious accident this evening. The car went off the road and over the cliff on River Road. There do not seem to be any survivors." He stopped and watched the man before him.

The man was thinking. Frederick Ellington was shocked, that was evident. He was upset, that was also evident. But the most evident thing to Marv Greenstein was that this man was thinking...thinking. It wasn't horror, it wasn't despair. It was just...thought. Marv had driven to this house full of compassion and empathy, but those feelings were ebbing. He really didn't like this guy.

Finally Frederick began to speak. Now his voice was pained and caring and full of expression. "Cassandra?

An accident? Oh my God! Are you sure? Where is she? I have to see her! This can't be true!"

All the words came flowing out, all the normal, grief filled words that policemen hear when they bring tragic news. But for some strange reason, Marv didn't believe a word of it. A Broadway performance, right in front of him.

Marv had caught the guy off guard, somehow, and he had actually seen him THINK up his reaction before giving it. Very strange. In twenty long years with a badge, he had never seen anything like it.

He gave the rest of the details in a reserved, professional way. He told the husband that they were dredging for the body, but he had absolutely NO hope that she had survived the crash onto the rocks at the bottom of the cliff, let along being submerged upside down in a wildly flowing, cold river.

"Do you have children, sir?" Marv asked gently, still not knowing quite what to make of the man who stood before him.

Frederick sat down then, looking suddenly overwhelmed. That was a real emotion, Marv registered, and doubted his initial reaction to the man. "Two boys, officer. Duncan is fifteen and Peter is twelve. They are asleep."

"Just as well, for now, Professor Ellington. I'm very sorry. Is there someone I can call to be with you right now? I'm sure that you will need to do some things later, but for right now, it's a time to wait I'm afraid. Not a good time to be alone."

Frederick looked thoughtful again. Like his mind was racing. "I don't have relatives right nearby."

"A neighbor or friend perhaps? A doctor?"

Frederick had to see a doctor, all right, he thought brutally, but not the way the officer thought. But there was merit, perhaps, in having someone here for the boys.

"My neighbor, Mrs. Briggs, perhaps. If the boys wake up or I have to go out..." He pointed to the house next door. Mrs. Briggs was harmless.

"Certainly, sir. How about if I go next door and explain the situation. And then I will let you rest, until we need to be in touch with you later. Are you ok?"

Frederick nodded, and Marv went next door to get Mrs. Briggs.

****

Peter felt like he couldn't breathe. He had not been sleeping when the doorbell rang, as his father thought. He had been wide awake, lying in his dark room, and worrying his brains out. He crept out of bed at the sound of the doorbell, hoping that it was his mother, and that the worry of the last several hours was a bad dream.

But it was not a dream. His father let the man in the brown tweed coat in, and Peter crept from his room and sneaked down the hall to a spot behind one of the large chairs. He heard every blasted word the little dark haired man said to his father.

His mother was dead. His mother was dead. At first it felt like a sharp hot sword was being pushed right through his heart. His mother was dead. A car accident. Her last words on the phone rang and rang in his brain. "No matter what happens..." "No matter what happens..."

He pulled his knees up to his chest and squeezed tight, trying to hold back the sobs that wanted to escape. That was all he needed, to be discovered by his dad hiding behind a chair and eavesdropping. Scrunching up his face, and trying not to cry, he quietly and carefully crawled back to the hall, and then scooted to his room. He lay in the dark, conscious of the trail of tears that cascaded down his face. Mom. He could almost see her face before him, kind and sweet and loving. She had loved him, he knew. But she had an accident. His bright mind began to work. Was it an accident? Or had she killed herself? Was he ever going to know? The police said they had not yet found the body. Were they sure she was dead? That thought made him sit still. Was it possible that she was not dead? The policeman certainly seemed to think...But if there was no body...there was a doubt. He clung to it like a drowning man to a floating plank. He would simply not believe his mother was dead until he absolutely, positively, and without a doubt had to. He would just hope. And pray.

And if she WAS alive, his boyish mind went on, she was going to need his help. He heard his dad let the detective out, with a comment that Mrs. Briggs was coming over.

He peeked out of his room again. His dad went straight to the phone in the living room. Peter shut his door and crossed the phone to his extension, carefully hitting the mute button so that he could listen without being heard. As long as there was doubt, he was going to keep his eyes (and ears) open, and watch what his dad was up to. He lifted the receiver to his ear.

"Yes, she was distraught, Professor Ellington," came a man's voice, who was soon identified as a doctor named Watson. "I gave her a pain pill for her collarbone and to calm her down. The collarbone was broken."

Frederick sounded wild with anger. "And what did she say about that collarbone, Doctor?" he snarled.

The doctor sounded embarrassed. "She said that you had hurt her, Professor Ellington. She said that you had grabbed her and shook her."

"Have you talked to anyone else about this?"

"Why no, no one has asked. Will they?" The doctor sounded puzzled.

"You better believe it, Dr. Know-it-All. And you'd better have a very convenient case of amnesia when it comes to any insinuation of abuse."

"Amnesia?" countered the doctor, realizing that he was being told to withhold information, getting more aggravated by the minute. "I'm not in the habit of discussing my patients with anyone, Professor Ellington, unless there's a specific need. But when I do, I tell the truth."

"Truth?" snarled Frederick. "You'll tell the truth that I tell you to tell. And you're going to find that there will be a specific need to discuss this patient."

The doctor tried to maintain an even tone. "Why don't you tell me just what is going on here, Ellington."

"Did my wife, the alcoholic, come to see you today?"

"Why yes, of course she did. You and I have already discussed this."

"And did you give her a dose of painkiller for this supposed broken collarbone that you were just talking about?"

"Why yes, again, we already discussed this."

"Well, it is my STRONG suggestion, Dr. Watson, that you listen carefully to what I say. Are you in your office?"

"Yes."

"Look at the wall. Do you have any of those fancy Latin certificates there? You know the ones that I mean, those pretty little documents that show how hard you worked to become a medical doctor?"

"Yes...." drawled the puzzled man.

"Well, unless you want to say goodbye to them and all that they stand for, you will totally forget ANY reference to physical abuse that my dear wife may have erroneously spouted off to you in a drunken rage."

"Your wife was not drunk when she was here!"

"That's for you to say. I say she was. And if you repeat her accusation to ANYONE, I will pursue the fact that you gave a strong pain medication to an unstable woman who was obviously an alcoholic and under the influence. My wife drove her car off a cliff, Dr. Watson. She is dead. Dead."

"Oh my God!" gasped the doctor. "Your wife... I'm so sorry...."

"Not as sorry as you're going to be if you so much as insinuate that she came to you for ANYTHING but her alcoholism.

"But Professor Ellington, the medication I gave her was really needed...and she was definitely not drunk."

"Well, a major malpractice suit is just what you and the hospital need right now, Dr. Watson. You can prove it in court."

"Oh God," said the young doctor, "My reputation..."

"Will be gone to hell in a hand basket, sir. That's a promise. My wife was a drunk, asking for help, and there was nothing else wrong with her. No broken bones, no problems. Understood?"

She was already dead, the doctor thought. There was nothing he could do for her, anyway. "Understood," he said in a small voice.

The connection was broken. Frederick hung up and Peter knew he would have one of his nasty smiles on his face. He had won. His father loved to win, and Peter had heard the tremor in the doctor's voice. Frederick Ellington had won. Like usual.

Peter hung up the extension gently, sitting quietly in the dark. What in the world was going on here? He felt suddenly, very young, and very alone.

He crept quietly into Duncan's room, and tapped his shoulder to wake him up. "Dunc," he cried, "Wake up. It's me and I have something bad to tell you."

He crawled into bed with his older brother, and told him, between sobs, what had transpired, including his fervent resolve to believe that his mom still had a chance to be alive.

"Oh, man," cried Duncan, into his brother's shoulder, for once not caring if his younger brother saw him cry. "Poor mom. Poor mom." The two boys cried themselves to sleep in the same bed, holding on tight to each other, and wishing, with all their might, for a miracle.

Chapter 9

By the time Detective Marvin Greenstein had gotten back to the police station, it was well past midnight. He had driven back up the river road after leaving the Ellington house, back to the site where the river was being dragged for the victim's body. He wrote down the time in his notebook, as he always did. He was thorough, he was conscientious. He was organized and methodical. He certainly had not always been able to describe himself that way, but for today he could. He felt a sense of pride, of accomplishment in that fact.

When he reached the site, he quickly learned that the crew was just about ready to give up on their task. The river was flowing briskly, the early spring night was dark and getting cooler by the moment. They had not been able to find the body before it had been swept away downstream in the strong current.

"No good keeping up the search here," said one exhausted searcher. "The body is probably miles downstream by now. Maybe it'll turn up down river tomorrow. But I'm gonna call off my men for now up here. Nothing we can do for this one. Sorry, sir."

The man pulled off his well-worn work gloves and fished an ancient whistle out of his jacket pocket. The shrill sound filled the air immediately. Hearing the signal, the floodlights abruptly switched off, and the sound of starting motor boat engines rose over the sound of the rushing river. They were pulling the nets in, they were giving up.

Marv tried to push down the feeling of sadness that came over him. Putting his hand into his pocket for his notebook, he felt something smooth and square. He pulled it out and looked at it, puzzled for a minute, and then berated himself. It was the victim's license, the laminated card he had removed from her retrieved purse to get the address to inform her family. It should have gone back into the pocketbook that still lay on the seat in the police car. After finishing his report, and having the contents evaluated, the purse would be returned to the family.

He looked down at the picture on the card once more.

"Night, sir," said the retreating search organizer. "Sorry about not being able to find the body."

Something in Marv's controlled demeanor snapped for the flash of a second.

"It's not just a body, for God's sake," he roared, astonishing even himself with his raucous outburst. "It's a woman. Her name was Cassandra. She had kids..." He was horrified to feel his eyes fill up with tears. Him, a tough cop who'd seen just about everything. But this one had gotten to him.

"Oh, man," said the well-meaning young man, "I'm really sorry, sir. I didn't realize you were connected to the victim."

"Connected? No, I'm not connected," he answered, giving in to the tiredness he suddenly felt. "I didn't even know her. Maybe just connected as a member of the human race. It's just such a ...tragedy."

The young man nodded.

"Excuse my temperament," said Marv contritely. "I got carried away. Sometimes this job can just get to you, you know?"

"Sure, Detective Greenstein," said the young man with a smile. "Don't I know... It's nobody's best day when you have to fish someone out of the river like this. Maybe we are all, connected, like you say. I like that." He offered his hand in a handshake, and then strode quickly over to his truck, where the rest of the team were loading their search supplies, nets, ropes, and lanterns. Marv got into his car and drove quickly back down the river road, hoping that the bright glare of the police station would be able to wipe away some of the feeling of darkness that had fallen over him.

****

By the time Frederick Ellington III climbed into bed the sun was creeping up over the horizon. For once in his life, his handsome face was marred with lines of worry. Real worry.

"Shit!" his voice echoed in the large, gracious bedroom. The room was elegantly decorated in soft tones of grey and silver, the massive king sized bed dwarfed by the spaciousness of the cathedral ceiling and the large palladium windows. He usually loved this room. But not at the moment. He felt as trapped as if he had been back in those old hotel closets. At the moment, he didn't love anything.

"That stupid Cassandra," he murmured from his pillow. "That stupid emotional idiot."

He was crying, he noticed in amazement, from the dampness of the pillow. But it was not, as one might expect, tears from grief. He felt beaten. He was beaten. Here, in death, Cassandra had beaten him the way that she never could in life. Her death had ruined everything. She had ruined everything. She had won.

The thought stuck in his throat. He felt the anger and hate rise up in him like bile. He lay, stark naked, under the designer bed covers, not moving a muscle.

"Think! Frederick." he commanded himself. "You can find an answer to this. Think."

The house was absolutely quiet, the only perceptible noise was the routine ringing of the chimes of the grandfather clock that stood in the foyer downstairs, marking every fifteen minutes. The sound was distant, muffled. He lay perfectly still while the time ticked by. The clock struck the hour, then the quarter hour, the half, then the three quarters. Finally, a kind of euphoric peace seemed to come over him, and the corners of his mouth turned up in a kind of smile.

"That will work," he said to himself victoriously. He had a plan. It would be tricky, it would be dangerous, but the stakes were high. He could get away with it. Even with Cassandra dead.

"Bye, Cassandra!" he murmured into his pillow, as he let himself relax and began to fall asleep. He had thought through the problem and come up with a solution. As usual. He drifted to sleep, his last thought being, "I win, Cassandra, I win."

Chapter 10

Cal pulled out of the radio station parking lot with a heavy heart. It was 12:30AM. He was beyond tired, and his stomach was literally screaming with hunger. Belinda, the night owl DJ had arrived a little before midnight, ready to get her play list lined up for her show. She went on the air from midnight to four in the morning. The last hour of Cal's show had been a slow one. He and Paul had played their songs, talked with a few more call ins, and had played the scheduled commercials, weather, and news.

The rest of their shift had been relatively calm, no particularly exciting news, except for a bad car accident that had been reported up on the river road outside of town. The police had retrieved a car that had plummeted over the cliff and down into the river. Not a pretty sight. The driver had evidently been killed, but they were not giving out any specific details about the name of the victim, or the circumstances of the crash.

Cal pulled his aged Suburban wagon onto the road with a sigh. He was definitely upset. Finally he had to admit to himself that he was not handling the earlier call in from the kid named Duncan particularly well. The kid had really worried him. He had heard many a teenager in a fit of temper, anger or temporarily upset, and had been able to "talk them down" to think things over, or to go to someone for help. But he had definitely failed with this one. This Duncan had some real problems, and he had been long gone before Cal had been able to think of anything to say to help.

The boy was ranting about his father, and then about his mother, and was obviously at a very desperate stage. Abusive stuff. And then the father evidently stormed into the room, maybe overhearing the conversation, and the situation turned from bad to worse.

"Is that your mother, you sniveling brat?" a cold, angry voice yelled.

"Leave me alone, Dad. I don't know where she is."

"Get off that damn phone!"

And then Cal heard the sounds of a scuffle, right before the phone was unceremoniously slammed down in his ear. The kid had problems, that was for sure. Could he do anything about it? Should he?

The old suburban groaned a little as it traveled up the hill toward home, but it kept on going. There was literally no traffic in sight, and Cal had the road to himself. His friends took great pleasure in teasing him about his old car, but he happened to like it. Yes, it was old, had clocked over 180,000 miles so far, and showed a smattering of rust and dents that befitted a car that had seen a lot of life. Like Cal himself, smiled in the darkness. Nothing wrong with a few dents. It gave a guy character. A car too.

He turned onto River Road, and headed out of town, toward the mountains. Within a few minutes, just before reaching the turn off for his house, he passed a pull off at the crest of the road. Two police cars stood there, lights flashing, and spotlights pointing down into the river. They were packing up their equipment.

It was the accident on the news. He remembered the description, but he hadn't realized it had happened so close to his house. The car that had gone over the cliff had obviously been recovered, and had been taken away, but the officers were looking for something. Cal felt his skin crawl. The calm quiet night suddenly seemed ugly. They were probably looking for any bodies that had been in the car.

He couldn't wait to leave the sight behind. The single lamp post at the end of his drive beckoned him about a half mile further on, and he turned his car in with undisguised relief. Immediately, he was surrounded by trees along the winding drive. Quiet. Food, shower, bed. That sounded great. He hadn't slept a wink the night before, but he had a feeling that it had been worth it.

His house was dark, except for a small porch light. He let himself in and flicked on a lamp, savoring instantly the comfortable feeling of coming home. His house was a haven for him, and he was more than thankful for that. Cal took a deep breath, letting out the tension in his body.

The quiet was broken by the sound of insistent meowing coming from the vicinity of the basement door. He opened it to free his two cats, "Salt" and "Pepper", whose names were another source of teasing from his friends.

He loved his cats, and they were evidently the bosses of the house. "Hi, guys," he answered their cries. "Dinner time." He opened a few packets of food and poured the contents into their waiting dishes. They didn't wait for an invitation, and soon the sound of their purring filled the quiet air in the kitchen.

"I wish I could pour my meal out of a package," he sighed, tiredly. "What's to eat?" He opened the refrigerator, and surveyed the contents. Several meals to choose from, but all of them taking time and preparation.

He pulled out half a hoagie that he had left over from the night before. It was a little soggy, but he shrugged. "This'll do it, 'til I get some sleep. I'm bushed."

He poured himself a big mug of milk and sat down in front of the TV screen. An old movie was playing, and he watched it for a minute while he wolfed down the food.

The cats had disappeared, fed and full, back down the basement steps. He picked up his dishes and plopped them into the sink, eager to go to bed. God, he was exhausted.

As he passed the front door to lock it for the night, he heard one of the cats crying on the outside. Cal opened the door and let him in, puzzled for a moment, because he was sure he hadn't let him out. But then he remembered that he had left the basement window open to air the place in the earlier in the day. The cats had evidently decided the open window was their private entrance.

Grumbling good naturedly, and talking to himself, a harmless habit he had gotten into since living alone, he stumbled down the steps to the basement. To leave the window open, no matter how tired he was, was an open invitation to squirrels, mice or any other kind of wildlife to take up residence in his house. He really didn't need that.

He walked across the basement in the dark, and shut the window with a bang. Remembering he had left a load of clothes washing when he had left for the station, he pulled open the washer and quickly plopped the wet things into the dryer, right next to it.

His jeans. Good thing he had remembered, he realized, or he would have been without pants the next morning. The laundry. It was a thorn in his side. His housekeeping skills were simply not up to Good Housekeeping standards, and the piles seemed to build. Towels, jeans, shirts, sheets, underwear. Then when he was absolutely out of everything, he would fanatically go on a washing spree, as he had the past two days. At least the clothes were clean. But he knew, if he turned on the lights, that he would see no less than four baskets of now washed, but still unfolded laundry. He hated folding. Wrinkles were his forte. The jeans were the last of the bunch.

So now it was all piled in baskets, and if he looked a little crumpled around the edges this week, the world would have to forgive him. At least the clothes were clean. Right?

He laughed to himself, promising to fold the clothes tomorrow. Maybe. After he slept for a long, long time. He started up the steps, when he heard a sound in the basement. It was actually more like a movement than a sound, but it was certainly not graceful enough to be a cat.

"Shit." was his first thought. "I don't want to turn on the light and see all this laundry that I still have to fold."

Had some wild animal already taken advantage of his open window? Too noisy to be a mouse. He picked up the broom that stood against the wall at the bottom of the steps, where the light from upstairs filtered down, casting shadows next to the stairway.

One side of his exhausted brain was saying "Just go to bed, cowboy, and conquer the wildlife tomorrow in the light of day. A zoologist you are not!"

"Face it, get it over with, and get on with your life." said the other side of his mind.

He had learned the hard way to listen to that second sometimes quieter voice in his head. With a grimace, he flicked on the light to see what he was dealing with.

Nothing scurried, which he took as good news. He looked around the basement, and at first, saw nothing unusual at all. His tools and storage bins were lined up along the far wall, the washer and dryer sat along another wall, right below the window, the dryer working diligently on his load of jeans. The four baskets that he had come to dread were lined up next to the appliances, filled to the brim, as he knew they would be, with every article he owned that was made of cloth...sheets, blankets, clothes, towels. Like a mountain.

He looked again. Maybe they were even filled more than to the brim. He swallowed and rubbed his eyes, and a very uneasy feeling came over him. This was wildlife, all right, and much worse than a squirrel of a mouse.

Cal knew that occasionally there are little moments in a person's life when something happens in a life changing instant, assuring that your life will never be the same again.

This was, Cal registered with a lump in his throat, one of those moments.

Because lying across the top of all four baskets, half wrapped in his favorite patch work quilt, lay a very still, half naked, barefooted, bleeding woman.

Bleeding, mind you, all over his clean clothes. Was she dead? Where the heck did she come from? His eyes shifted to the window above the dryer. Was it possible? What, on God's green earth, was he supposed to do?

She stirred, which meant, he registered in his exhausted mind, that she wasn't dead. Yet. Was she hurt badly? He crossed the room slowly toward her, still carrying the broom in front of him. Suddenly, he thought of the picture he must have made, ferociously grasping the broom. What was he going to do, sweep the sleeping woman to death?

The broom clattered to the floor, and the sound made her stir. His mind started to accept the facts. She was hurt, she was bleeding. First things first. He crouched down next to her, and felt her pulse. It was fast, but steady. She didn't seem to have a fever.

"Hello. Hello." he said softly. "Are you all right?"

She stirred again, but she didn't open her eyes.

"God," he prayed fervently. "Please show me what to do. I'm not the hero type. I'm totally out of my element with this one. Do I call the cops? An ambulance? Do I take her upstairs?" His mind was racing. "God, give me a sign."

Her eyes started to flutter. "Duncan." she said in an almost whisper. He felt a chill travel the length of his spine.

"Duncan?" he thought.   Was it possible that this woman had just said the same name that had been haunting him all evening? Or was he just hearing things?

She was still again. He spoke. "I'm going to call an ambulance and get you to the hospital."

"No." the sound spewed out, full of terror. "No," she repeated, opening her eyes.

God, they were beautiful eyes, green and wide, but at the moment they held nothing but fear.

"Please," she whispered, looking right up into his eyes. "Please don't call anyone right now. I'll be all right. I just have to think." She shut her eyes again.

The look on her face made him feel instantly protective, caring.

"Well, green eyes," he said softly, picking her up off the baskets. "You don't have to think in the basement. Let me take you upstairs."

She certainly wasn't heavy, and she clung to his arm like a child as he toted her up the steps. She was wearing some type of a blouse, he could see, and a slip, but no skirt, and her shoes were gone. Her legs were black and blue, scratched and bleeding in spots, and there was a mean looking cut on her shoulder, where her blouse was torn.

Nothing seemed to be broken, though, he thought, as he lay her down on the couch in the den. He put a pillow under her head, and covered her with an afghan that he kept on the back of a chair.

She was conscious now, silent, and looking at him warily. He looked back, not having any idea what to say. There was simply no etiquette book that he knew of that handled the situation "How to Make Conversation with the Beat Up Almost Naked Woman Who Appears in your Basement in the Middle of the Night." He'd have to take this one step at a time.

****

Cassandra felt like she had entered another lifetime. In the moment the car went hurtling over the edge of the cliff, she was more than certain her life was done.

She had flung herself with every ounce of strength that she possessed in her tense body, freed suddenly from the restraining seat belt. The car plunged over the edge, the horrifying force of gravity making it drop without hesitation. She found herself freed from the car, flying in the air, falling all at once like a parachutist with no parachute.

She prayed then, really prayed. How long would it take to hurtle into the rocky river below? It was so far! Her mind flashed in panic. A scream rose up, but even before she could open her mouth, her descent ended as her body abruptly crashed into solid rock. Cassandra landed with great force on a rocky precipice that stood out like a shelf about eight feet below the edge of the cliff, saving her from certain death. The force of the fall knocked her blissfully into unconsciousness, and she didn't hear the sound of her car crashing ferociously onto the jagged rocks in the raging river far below.

Cassandra had no idea how long she had been unconscious. When she awakened, it was completely dark, and completely silent, except for the sound of the water flowing still far below her. She felt spasms of pain, lying flat, her cheek pressed hard against cold, unyielding rock.

It took many minutes for her memory to clear and review that moments that had passed. It took many minutes more for her to get the nerve to try to move her arms even in the slightest, to feel around the area that surrounded her. She moved her legs gingerly. She didn't think she had any broken bones, except for the already aching collar bone that now throbbed like crazy. Her head was very sore, and her entire body felt like it had been pummeled in a boxing ring.

As the minutes passed, she got braver in exploring her surroundings. She rose to her knees, she was on a rocky ledge that was about six feet long and three feet wide. She had landed on the very outer edge of that scant three feet, and it made her body shiver to think of the consequences if she had been thrown even six more inches from the edge.

She hurt all over. In the dark, she couldn't see the car at all, but she knew, even though she had lost consciousness, that must be resting somewhere far below. The roar of the river was the only sound that greeted her ears.

Frederick was going to kill her about the car, she thought disjointedly, and then she began to laugh. Ridiculous. She didn't give a damn about what Frederick thought anymore. Or did she? What would Frederick do to her? Suddenly she began to cry. She felt lost and hopeless and confused.

From up on the road above her, she heard voices approaching. A woman's voice first, followed by a man's.

"It went over the cliff, I swear," said an upset older woman. "I was driving by in my car, and I saw the lights go over. Oh God, I can't see a thing. We have to call someone."

"OK, ma'am, let's get to a phone. Nothing we can do here." The two voices receded down the road. She heard a car start up.

Cassandra sat frozen in position. Why hadn't she cried out for help? One part of her had wanted her to scream up to the concerned voices, to get help up off her treacherous cliff and into a warm, safe environment. But something in another primitive part of her held back. The thought of Frederick's angry face, the thought of the doctor's cool and detached voice, explaining to her that she was to be sent away held her bound to the spot. Being rescued meant being trapped. She hadn't uttered a sound.

But someone would soon be here, she realized, as soon as the call for help was placed. She gingerly stood up on the ledge and tested her bones. So far so good. She needed time to think, and she didn't want to think stuck up on this lonely, scary cliff all by herself in the dark. She put her hands up high over her head but couldn't feel the top of the cliff. Far above, she could see a faint difference in color, between rock and night time sky. Cassandra was more than eight feet down.

In the dark, she began feeling her way sideways across the expanse of rock wall. Sections were smooth, sections were broken and rough. It seemed like it took forever, but finally she found two places that were indented enough to use as steps. Gently she placed one shoeless foot into an indentation, and lifted herself up about two feet. Reaching upward, she still could not feel the top of the wall. Determined, and biting her lip with all her might to ignore the pain that was emanating from her broken collar bone, she lifted her other foot up to the next indentation. Again, she raised herself two more feet.

She could feel a difference in the air flow now, and knew that she was near the top of the cliff. If only it wasn't so dark! Typical of her bad luck, she chided herself, that she would be in this predicament without benefit of moonlight. She raised her hands up high, and was rewarded with the feel of cool grass along the edge of the cliff top.

She was almost there. The last two steps were desperate ones, as the toeholds she found were much smaller than the earlier ones. Her hands were shaking and her stomach was in a knot. One slip, one misstep would send her hurdling toward the river. Her legs rubbed viciously against the rocky wall as she climbed, the roughness ripping the nylon of her pantyhose from her feet and scraping her exposed skin.

When the edge of the cliff was almost at her waist, she flung one leg with all her might, while pushing up ferociously with her arms. The impetus hurled her over the cliff top, and she rolled away from the edge. She welcomed the scratches that the rough undergrowth gave her, because it signaled victory from her prison on the ledge. She had made it!

She tried to stand up, but her whole body was shaking at this point, and she didn't have the strength. She lay for a minute in the rough, rocky grass, smelling the pungent greenness mixed with damp dirt, and welcoming the aroma. She was alive. She was also very cold.

A few minutes passed, and she knew that she had to push herself to move, or face the questions and excitement of being discovered. Would it be Frederick? She could only imagine him graciously giving her a shove, helping her back over the cliff, laughing as she hit the rocks below. Or maybe he would look curiously over the edge, and SHE would be the one to give a little push....She almost smiled at the thought, and then was filled with self-loathing. Was she truly going crazy? She shook her head to bring herself back to reality and made herself stand up by sheer will power. She was shaky, but she was up!

Looking down the hill from the edge of the road, she could see three sets of car lights in the distance. Headlights and police flashers. The accident had been reported and they would be on the spot within minutes. She wasn't going to face Frederick like this. She needed a plan. She needed to think. Her mind was still cloudy from shock and the lingering effects of the pain medicine.

As quickly as her battered body could move, she took off stealthily in the opposite direction, moving farther up the road, hovering in the cover of the trees, mindless of the rocks that cut into her now bare feet. Her pantyhose were actually ripped to shreds, and hanging from her legs, while still fastened around her waist. The tatters kept catching in the undergrowth along the road, pulling briars and sharp grasses back to torment the bare skin of her legs. She quickly bent and slipped the remains of the panty hose off, tossing them back from the road toward the cliff.

Fearful that another car would come and she would be discovered, she kept close to the trees that bordered the cliff edge, even when the road turned and moved inland away from the river for a while. She determinedly felt along each step in the dark, knees weak but responding, shoulder aching, but still making progress. How had her life come to this?

Cassandra had absolutely no idea how far she had gone, but soon the accident scene was far behind her, hidden by the river's bend, and the trees and thicker undergrowth that existed the further she moved from the road.

She moved along , winding through the trees, each step torture as she worried about snakes and other wildlife that might resent being disturbed in the night air. And it was getting colder. The spring temperatures of the day had disappeared along with the sunset, and the degrees had plummeted. Her feet were freezing, to start with, and her body was trembling all over, with shock, cold, and fatigue. But she kept on.

Far up ahead, she could see the vague glow of a light through the trees. Like a beacon, she headed for it, hardly thinking of anything now except the excruciating effort of putting one foot in front of the other. Eyes locked on it, she aimed for the light.

It was a house. Nestled deep in the trees, and backing up to the river, it had a quiet, peaceful air about it, and looking at it made Cassandra feel warm. By the glow of the single porch light, she could see that it was a wood sided cottage, with a high sloping roof and cute square windows. Like a forest cottage in a fairy tale. The windows were all dark.

There was a long driveway that disappeared back up through the trees, evidently back to the road. At the end of the driveway, there was a rusted basketball backboard on a slightly tilted pole with no net. She strained her eyes to see more in the porch light, but could not.

There was no car in the drive, no one was home. She laughed at herself suddenly. Then tears filled her eyes. Her emotions and logic were all over the place.

What was she thinking? Would she walk up to the door, cut and bruised and barefoot, in the middle of the night and ask to come in? It was ludicrous, but it was exactly what she wanted to do. She had an undeniable urge to get inside that house. It seemed to symbolize warmth and safety and peace. Ridiculous really, she chided herself.

She sat down on the grass beside the driveway and tried to think, but her brain didn't want to work. She was tired, exhausted. Her muscles were aching with a strange burning feeling, and her head felt light. The pain in her shoulder was really getting to her, and she began to fear losing consciousness again. She would be found here, and returned to Frederick. Returned to what? She began to cry.

Suddenly she jumped, because something warm and soft rubbed up against her. After a second's panic, she realized it was a cat. A friendly cat. She reached out and pet his soft coat, and was rewarded by an immediate purr. The cat crawled easily into her lap, and nestled up next to her. It felt like heaven. She hugged the small, warm creature, and stroked his fur.

She had never had a pet, she realized. Frederick thought animals were dirty, bothersome creatures, and had never permitted one in his house. Her house. Their house. Boy, was she mixed up. But this kind gentle creature was showing her more love and care than she had felt in a long time, and she welcomed it.

The cat left her, suddenly, and she felt bereft. But he didn't just walk away. Instead he stood a few feet off and made a slight meowing sound. Then he moved a few feet more, turned, and meowed again. She stood up on her wobbly legs and followed his pitiful funny sounding cry. Whenever she hesitated, the cat stopped again, turning around and crying at her. It was almost as if he were beckoning her to follow him, and so she did.

In an almost dreamlike state, she moved toward the dark back side of the house, led by the persistent meows. She was light headed and dizzy now, and her eyesight seemed to be off. Was she in shock? Maybe she had a concussion. She had no idea. The cat moved toward the edge of the house, and she could barely see the dark outline of a basement window, open wide.

The cat disappeared into it, and meowed from the inky depths. Did she dare to follow him? Break into an empty house? With the night she had just experienced, nothing now seemed out of the ordinary. The thought of being warm, of being safe, was too much to resist. She put her bare leg over the window sill and pulled herself through.

Her foot banged against something cold and metal, which turned out to be a clothes dryer. She stepped down onto the top of it, and then climbed clumsily to the floor. It was warmer in the basement, but it was very dark. The friendly cat still beckoned her, and she tiptoed toward his voice. She tripped, stumbling over a mountainous pile of clothing. She lost her balance, and came down on top of the clothes basket with a grunt.

The clothes were soft and clean smelling and too much to resist. Feeling a little like Goldilocks in the Three Bears, she pulled herself up into a ball on top of the clothes, pulling a quilt over her cold and now vibrating body. God, it felt good. The cat leapt up on the basket, nestling in the curve of her body, and purring with all his might.

She began to cry again, stroking the loving little animal and thanking God for the feeling of warmth that was slowly returning to her battered body. She had to think. But like Goldilocks, she fell into a thankful sleep, her body still shivering with shock, but comfortable in the strange bed. She slept without even a thought of what she would say to the Three Bears when they discovered the intruder in their house.

She had drifted in and out of a kind of sleepy semi consciousness for a while, occasionally aware of the soft purring of the animal by her side, and once in a while aware of the sound of the river as it rushed by behind the cozy house, its sounds coming in through the open window above her.

After a while, she heard sounds from upstairs, normal people sounds like doors opening, the TV going on. Stirring in her consciousness was the fact that the warm, comforting bit of furry cat that had guided her had disappeared, and she missed his presence. She couldn't concentrate, couldn't think correctly. One moment, she felt in a panic, not knowing where she was or how she had gotten there. The next moment, she remembered the accident, the excruciating, horrible trip along the river's edge, and the cat guiding her in through the open window.

The next moment, she panicked about being found in her warm, safe hiding place, trying to will herself to rise from the makeshift bed she had collapsed on, and simply unable to command her legs and arms to obey. What was wrong with her?

Whose house had she entered, and what was the reaction going to be if she was found there? When she was found there?

But she couldn't fight the drowsiness, and sleep beckoned her again, gently persuading her to put her fears to rest and succumb to its pleasant escape. Sleep. Her head hurt. Her shoulder ached. Scratches and cuts on her body burned. Escape sounded more than good.

So she would start to drift, almost mindless again, and then suddenly find herself tormented by a fleeting flash of Frederick's cruel face, making her heart beat faster, and her head feel like it would explode. And then, she would be haunted by the picture of Duncan's face, scared, overwhelmed, and needing her so much. Was she crazy? Was this what it was like to have stepped over the brink of sanity into the incomprehensible? She slipped into the blurry grey cloud of retreat again.

When someone entered the basement, she vaguely heard him on the stairs, vaguely wondered if she should scurry and hide, but she was simply unable to do so. She opened her eyes momentarily and had seen a darkish figure, broom in hand, coming toward her. Another vision, a hallucination? Or would this be the end of her?

The light flashed on, and she closed her eyes again, hurt by the sudden increase in light. In the back of her mind, she could remember Duncan's tortured voice, and she had croaked out his name

."Duncan," she had called, and the man had stopped dead in his tracks.

Besides being puzzled by the broom, which suddenly had disappeared, Cassandra was willing to face the shadowy, blurry figure that stood before her. She tried valiantly to open her eyes. She had to help her son.

But then the voice had mentioned calling an ambulance, and she had wild visions of straight jackets, and Frederick's victorious smile as she was carted away, and she had objected with all the might left in her slight body.

The figure, which her subconscious had already labeled as kind, seemed to acquiesce to her plea. How did she know that? She had no idea, but again, felt safe and understood as she was gingerly lifted up from the pile of softness that she lay upon.

The man took her up the stairs then, and had put her gently onto the couch, covered with a warm blanket.

Even in her distressed, confused state, she knew she didn't know the man, had never seen him before. And yet, there was something about him, something hauntingly familiar, something friendly and comforting, as he spoke to her.

"No! Don't call an ambulance!" she had heard herself protest. She saw him nod, and she hoped desperately he would give her the time she needed to get her thoughts straight. She fought the recurring urge to go to sleep, fought the shadowy blanket of unconsciousness that beckoned her. She took a deep breath, forced her eyes open, and tried to focus on the man before her.

Chapter 11

Cal Johnson was baffled. And at this age and stage of his life, he didn't baffle easily. But this little slip of a woman lying so still on his couch, obviously struggling with all her might to keep her eyes open, had him baffled, for sure.

After a couple of minutes, she seemed to be able to hold her eyes open, and focused on him. God, they were pretty eyes. Green and expressive and full of emotion.

"I'm really sorry," she began, in a whisper-like voice, her eyes locked with his. "I crawled into your basement...the window was open, I was so tired and cold. I followed the cat..."

She seemed to drift off again.

"Well, just take it easy now," Cal said gently, still having no answers as to the woman's appearance in his basement, but drawn to the deep, troubled green eyes.

"How about a cup of tea?" he said, suddenly, and then began to laugh at himself. "I have no idea how on earth a cup of tea is supposed to help in a situation, but it seems like such a movie thing to say." He could feel himself blushing. Blushing?

"That would actually be wonderful," she said, with a shy smile. He marveled at the way that her eyes lit up when she smiled. He had a feeling that she didn't smile often.

Cal went off to the kitchen then, and soon the kettle was getting ready to boil, while he got the tea tray together. Tea? With an injured, half naked stranger on his couch? He shook his head. He had lived many days in his life, but he had a feeling this one day was going to stick out in his mind for a while.

He set the tea tray in front of her and added some sugar and milk, as she liked. She drank it slowly, closing her eyes as the warmth filled her.

He watched, mesmerized.

Finally he couldn't wait any longer. "What's your name?"

She paused for a minute. "My name is...Sandra."

Well, it could be, he thought, but his intuition told him that she was not telling him the truth.

"Sandra." He waited a minute, then he went on. "I'm Calvin Johnson. Are you OK? Should I call a doctor?"

Her eyes widened, and she turned white. He thought for a minute that she was going to pass out again, but she didn't. In fact, her voice seemed stronger when she talked, the words spilling out.

"I'm truly embarrassed to be in this position, Calvin. I got lost. I fell and got disoriented...I lost...my shoes. It was so very dark, and so very cold, that when I saw the cat and he went toward the house, I simply followed. I climbed in the window, and then I guess I passed out. But I'm ok, see?" She sat up abruptly, and the color left her face again.

He jumped to his feet and crossed over to her. "God Almighty, Sandra, just lay back. You don't have to go doing acrobatics to prove anything to me here. I can see that you don't want a doctor, but I can also see that you have been hurt. I'm not the pushy type, and I'm not going to press you tonight for answers. But I have a feeling that you've been through something really bad, and you ought to have some damn kind of help."

"Just let me stay here tonight," the glistening green eyes pleaded. "I'll be better able to think tomorrow. I promise, that's the best kind of help I can have right now."

Cal felt like a stooge, a gullible idiot, but he found himself nodding, in spite of all his better judgment.

"Don't get involved here, Cal," the quiet, sensible side of his mind was playing. "This gal, as adorable as she is, has obviously some serious problems that you just don't need right now. Keep it simple, man. Detach."

He had dealt with needy strangers many times in his life, but mostly they had been introduced or accompanied by a friend showing up at his doors. Never had there been a surprise like this..and through a basement window. And never did a set of eyes seem to capture him like the green ones he was looking into at the moment.

"Sure, you can stay here tonight, Sandra," he heard his voice saying. God, he must be more tired than he thought. His mind and his voice did not seem to be connected. Didn't his voice get the message his mind had sent?

"Can you walk now? Let me take you to the bathroom and you can get yourself cleaned up." He helped her to her feet.

"Those scratches need some antiseptic. I have some in the medicine chest. And you should have a robe. I don't know if you've noticed, and believe me I don't mind, but you're missing some of your clothes…"

He was babbling like an idiot. He was an idiot. Definitely. Without a doubt. Certifiable.

It seemed like an eon or two had gone by, but finally Sandra had emerged from the bathroom, clean now, her hair pulled back into a loose pony tail at the nape of her neck, her scratches disinfected and in some places bandaged. The robe was a mile too big, but it looked warm and soft on her small frame.

She looked better. Her feet were still bare, and so Cal brought her a pair of his thick red woolen socks.

She pulled them on, grateful for their warmth. They were big and bulky, and looked absolutely ridiculous. He looked down at them, and began to laugh.

He couldn't help himself, even though he worried about embarrassing her, but the socks looked so damn funny. The laugh started deep inside of him, maybe built up from the tension of the night, and exploded in a guffaw. She looked down at her feet and looked up at him, and burst into giggles herself. That made him laugh even harder.

"Sorry," he babbled, trying to control his chuckles but losing the battle. "It's just that they are so big...and red. They look like somebody else's feet. Or maybe clown shoes."

That made them both laugh even harder. She did a little jig in the socks, a sudden burst of energy making her kick up her feet, her antics proving that she wasn't offended with his laughing.

They laughed until the tears ran down their faces, and they collapsed on the couch, catching their breath. She held her one arm folded against her chest, wincing a little as she landed.

He could see something was painful, even through her giggling.

"Boy," she said finally, "That was better than any doctor. I don't know when I've laughed so hard. I feel so much better."

"I'll send you a bill in the morning."

"OK, you do that, but I'm keeping the socks."

That set them off again.

When they had settled down, she turned to him seriously.

"Calvin, I know you have to have so many questions about me, but I just can't talk about myself right now. I promise, I'll make it up to you."

"Don't talk now, Sandra," he said, holding her hand for a minute. "You're safe here. I don't know what plan God had in bringing you here, and through the window no less. But it's ok. I've come to pretty much trust fate. We'll worry about tomorrow, tomorrow."

She blessed him with a sad smile. "I don't know much about God, Calvin," she said quietly. "I kind of think I was brought here by the cat..."

As if on cue, the cat slipped into the room, grey and long haired, followed by a second cat, pure white. "Maybe." Cal said. "This is Salt, and this is Pepper."

Salt opened his mouth and let out a pitiful yowl. Pepper joined in. Then Salt jumped up onto the couch and settled himself in her lap. She smiled at his rough purr, remembering the comfort it had given her when she had been in despair.

"So there's two of them. That's nice. They're great. I never had a pet." There was something wistful and childlike in her comment.

The night had almost passed, the first rays of light were beginning to show in the sky, by the time Cal had settled her into a bed in the upstairs guest room. He covered her with the heavy crocheted afghan, the cat still by her side. She fell asleep immediately. He looked at her for a minute, amazed at the concern he felt.

With a heavy heart, he followed the hallway to his own room, knowing that his body craved sleep, having gone almost two days without it. But his mind craved answers, and he had none. Where had Sandra come from, and what had happened to her? She was so evidently under stress, and had been adamant about not calling for help. He thought of her torn clothes, her injured body, the look of desperation in her eyes when he had first seen her. Had she been attacked? Raped? Had she been kidnapped and turned loose on the road? His thoughts soared with possibilities, none of them good.

What was he getting himself into, he wondered. He had been in plenty of strange situations in the past fifteen years. He had spent time with some amazing people, and had heard some amazing stories, but he had a feeling that the one he was currently dealing with was going to be a doozey.

He shook his head. There was a beautiful, injured mystery woman in the bed down the hall in his house. And he was ok with it. Not exactly detachment.

Tomorrow. Tomorrow he would have to have some answers from the beautiful stranger. But for now, he would have to settle for sleep. He crawled into his bed, said a prayer of thanks for his day, and slipped into a deep, much needed sleep.

****

Frederick Ellington III awoke at 6 in the morning, after only a short sleep. He wasn't tired. In fact, his body feeling vigorous and alert. He had a lot to do.

The house was very quiet. He peeked out into the living room, and saw that Mrs. Briggs was asleep on the couch, curled up in a blanket. At first he felt a moment of dismay. He hadn't even taken her to the guest room, when she'd been so helpful as to come in case he had to leave with the police during the night. He had totally forgotten the lady. Not very thoughtful. He grimaced. What would she say to the other neighbors? It wouldn't look good. He had really been upset after the cop had left, and had let his guard down.

Then he smiled. The overwrought husband. Couldn't think. It was actually better this way. He had played the scene as the mourning spouse without even planning it.

He slipped back up to his room, and showered and shaved quickly. He heard noise down the hall. The boys.

For a brief moment, Frederick felt a lump grow in his throat. Duncan and Peter. He didn't want to tell them what he had to tell them, because he knew that they would take it hard. Cassandra. They had really been attached to their mom. Probably too attached. But nonetheless, it would make this hard for them.

But it would also make them tough. And they needed it, those two. They had been coddled long enough. Maybe they would learn something about the results of too much emotionalism. You had to keep your emotions intact. A good lesson to learn.

When he walked out into the living room, the boys had already seen Mrs. Briggs, who was now up and bustling about. They were talking in low voices, and Frederick realized that they had already somehow heard the news.

Both pairs of eyes were red rimmed, and they didn't look like they had slept much. Frederick put an arm around each.

"We'll get through this, boys," he said quietly.

The boys nodded, trying to keep a "stiff upper lip" as they'd been taught by their father.

Mrs. Briggs volunteered to stay with the boys when he said he had to go to the police station. He promised to call when he had some news, and left without looking back. He felt bad when he looked at the boys' lost eyes. And he didn't like to feel bad.

****

The sun was rising high into the sky by the time that Cassandra woke up. She looked around the cozy second floor room. Its dormer windows were curtained in fluffy white panels, the breezed ruffling their edges gently to allow the sunlight to peek into the room.

She gazed around. The furniture was made of oak, old and well worn, the bedposts thick and tall, the dresser top empty and smooth, except for the tell-tale scars of life that marred its top. The mirror behind the dresser was rather splotched,and cloudy, its silver paint deteriorating with age. A wooden rocker stood in the corner, with a crocheted blanket hanging over its back, not unlike the one she had wrapped herself in the night before in her quest for safety and warmth in the living room.

She felt safe and warm now. The house was totally quiet. From outside the window, the surrounding birds were putting on quite a performance of sound, but their noises meant peace to her and she cherished the moment. The rushing river sounded in the background.

She climbed out from under the hand quilted patchwork cover, pulling back the stark white sheets. Simple, she thought, feeling the soft cotton with her hand. The motion brought pain to her shoulder and collar bone.

Her bare feet hit the floor, which was covered by a simple braided rug, showing an expanse of random width hardwood floor at its edges. She looked at her face in the old mirror, surprised almost to recognize herself, while feeling that her life had changed so drastically since the day before. There was a big dark bruise on her cheekbone, probably from where she fell, and scratches on her forehead that had been treated with antiseptic the night before. Calvin. A nice man.

She smiled. She looked down at her now bare feet, remembering being playful about a pair of red socks..a dream? And then she saw them, sitting incongruously at the bottom of the bed, by the foot rail, carefully folded and waiting. Waiting for what?

The socks had been real. The night had been real. The car accident had been real. Calvin had been real. A million memories and fears and questions and doubts filled her head with the force of a great tidal wave. Reality. The feeling of peace evaporated. What, in God's name, was she going to do now?

Automatically, her hands began to shake, then her body. Fear. Shock. Panic. She wrapped her arms around herself, despite the sharp ache in her shoulder brought on by the action. Where was Calvin? What would she say to him, here in the daylight where questions had to be asked, had to be answered?

And even worse, where was Frederick? And what were his plans for her, when he found out about his wrecked car, and her panicked escape? A numbness slowly crept over her, and the shaking stopped.

Maybe she would simply slip away, run away from the pain of her life. But then she thought about the boys. The desperate, needy sound of Duncan's voice on the radio played again in her brain. She couldn't run from her boys, no matter what the personal cost. She had to let her boys know she was all right. And deal with Frederick. Whatever that would mean.

And Calvin? He was a strange, kindly man who had accepted her presence in his basement, in his house, and had offered her shelter and sleep and food and warmth, without badgering her with questions and doubts. He had helped her out, without calling the police, or an ambulance, when she had simply asked him to give her time? What kind of man was that, and what kind of answers did he have a right to expect? And did he deserve to be drawn into her ugly weave of problems?

She pulled her terry cloth robe around her, and pulled on the red socks. She couldn't even remember falling asleep, she must have been exhausted. Calvin must have taken off the socks. Calvin must have tucked her into the bed.

She found a bathroom right next door to her room, and saw that there were two more bedrooms, similar to the one she had slept in on the second floor. Both had the doors open, and both were empty. She went into the bathroom, and gazed at the claw footed tub that sat majestically along one wall. The other fixtures were new and shiny, but the tub made a statement about the past, like the comfortable oak furniture in her room.

On the counter in the bathroom, she found a neatly folded pair of grey sweat pants, and an oversized navy blue sweatshirt that said "University of Vermont", a pair of boxer short, a tee shirt, and a note written on a long yellow piece of paper torn form a legal tablet.

"Dear Sandra," it began, in a neat, artistic print, using all capital letters. "I hope you had a good sleep. You were sleeping soundly when I left, and I didn't want to disturb you. Here are some clothes you may want to try. I know they will be way too big and some of them of the wrong gender, but hey, they're clothes, and they're clean, and I finally got around to folding and sorting them. Bad thing is, there are no shoes in this place that will even come close. We'll work that out later.

"I'll be back around 4pm, and maybe you'll be ready to talk, or maybe you'll even be gone. Whatever. If you go, I hope things are OK, and I'll always remember you in the red socks. I'm probably crazy, and maybe you are too, but I play my hunches, and so you're welcome to stay and make yourself at home, and talk to the cats until I get home. Help yourself to anything in the fridge (check the milk before you drink it. I'm famous for letting it get too old), and have a good day. Your friend, Calvin."

She felt warm and safe again. Changed, and yet nothing had changed. She had a lot of thinking to do, but meanwhile, she was going to enjoy this short respite of safeness, while she got her thoughts together. God bless Calvin, whoever he was.

She took a shower, and brushed out her hair, and pulled on the soft, comfortable sweat clothes, smiling at herself in the mirror. Definitely a different look than Mrs. Frederick Ellington III, for sure.

She climbed gently down the steps a few minutes later, her body still under protest from all of its traumas the day before. But she was feeling clean and warm. She found the coffee pot plugged in, with coffee left over, so she helped herself to a cup. She added milk from the fridge (it was fine, so Calvin, shouldn't be so hard on himself) and made some toast with jam. She felt like she was living an alternative life, on a separate planet. It was hard to believe, or even imagine, the different life that was going on only a few miles away.

She sat down on the living room soft, admiring the beamed ceiling, the great stone fireplace, and the wall of windows that opened to an expansive deck above the bank of the river. Beautiful.

The clock on the wall said it was noon, which amazed her. She had really slept a long time. A large TV sat across the room, and she found the remote control on the cushion beside her. With a flip of the finger, the large screen came to life. A colorful commercial came to an end, and the noon news began. The carefully self-controlled anchorman looked directly into the camera, and delivered the top story of the day.

****

Frederick had a busy morning. After a brief stop at the police station, where he made an appearance as a devastated and concerned husband, he went quickly through his list of necessary appointments before arriving at his office at the university.

The police had had no additional news or information to impart, the general consensus at this point was that Cassandra's body had been taken rapidly downriver toward the ocean with the swift river current, and the odds of ever retrieving the body decreased with each passing hour. The search team was out again, with daylight, but hope was not high.

And so Frederick began his day, getting his facts and options in order, determined to see his way out of the mess that Cassandra's accident had produced.

He arrived at the University office building, its thick muted carpet muffling all sound, so that the atmosphere inside resembled the hush of a hallowed library hall. He had nodded curtly to the few professors or staff members that he passed.

By the sympathetic look on their faces, he knew that the ever present grapevine of the university had already begun spreading the word about what had happened to the wife of one of their esteemed faculty members. But he kept his head down, and his eye contact minimal, to discourage any questions or sympathetic comments from his peers. He simply did not want to answer or reflect on any questions they might pose until he had thought through the implications of what had occurred. He couldn't afford to make a mistake, with so much at stake.

His actions, as he knew they would, brought about the exact effect he had wanted. The people passed by, concerned, but not attempting in any way to break through the image he presented, the grieving professor who wasn't ready to talk. People were so gullible.

Once in his office, he sat down in the burgundy leather chair, and leaned back in a stretch, looking out the window to the green lawn below. He had a lot of thinking to do. A lot was at risk, and there was, he knew, only a short window of time before the answers had to be given. The press, the cops, the university, the boys.

Like maneuvering in a minefield, he had to plan every step. Cassandra's death had sent a tremor that could topple the "house of cards" that he had carefully constructed, and only the best of plans could save things now.

But that was his forte. That was exactly where he excelled. Planning. Thinking things through. He wasn't going to give up on his dreams now, not when he was so close. There was an answer here, a way to salvage things, and he would find it. He had planned for everything, he had thought. Except her death.

He closed his eyes, shutting out the vision of his handsomely wood paneled office, his rows of distinguished books, his elegantly framed certificates and citations. He thought.

Chapter 12

Hannah Mae March sat on her old back porch and watched the noon sun glistening off the river water as it rushed past behind her house. She loved this house. She had loved it since she came here as a bride, over fifty years before. Being close to the water had always brought comfort to her. She liked the sound of the river, the smell, the way the light at different times of day could make the water glisten in a million varied patterns and colors.

She especially like the sunset, when the ball of red in the sky gently dipped down below the horizon on the other side of the house. It shed its oranges and purples in rays that bounced off the river's surface with a mystic, shadowy beauty. She was 79 now, and had barely missed a sunset on this river in almost fifty years.

Hannah didn't think of herself as an unsocial person. Indeed, a good gossip or a zesty argument could make her day. But for the most part, she valued being alone, thinking her own thoughts, and sorting through her own memories. Especially since she had lost her husband, Herbert. She liked the seclusion she had enjoyed on the road by the river, no noisy neighborhood, no newsy people watching your every move. The people who lived out here pretty much kept to themselves, and that was just fine with her.

But something had happened the night before, and it was weighing heavily on her mind. She didn't know quite what to do with it, or maybe, whether she need do anything at all. But her conscience was nagging her, and she had learned a long time ago that the most annoying noise in the world was a nagging conscience.

She had been sitting in this very spot, on her favorite rocking chair, and looking out over the river as the sun set behind her last evening. Nothing new, nothing unusual. She had been deep in her thoughts, first thinking about her Herbert, who had passed a few years before, and then thinking about her first great grandchild, who had been born to her daughter's son in Michigan, just the day before. It's a big milestone, she had been thinking, becoming a great grandmother. A GREAT grandmother. It sounded pretty amazingly old. On the one hand, she just didn't feel that darn old. Her mind was quick, and her thoughts were clear. She could excuse the occasional twinges of arthritis, the wrinkles on her face that seemed to multiply daily, and still put on her favorite jeans and tee shirt and make it almost all the way through her Richard Simmons exercise tape each morning. But the term GREAT grandmother had pretty much floored her, and she had been thinking about her age. Maybe she had even dozed a bit (which she hated to admit, but it was probably true, and why she was a little unclear as to the exact minute of "the noise").

But the truth was, she had been startled to consciousness by a strange and frightening noise last night, and it was a little after 9 o'clock. She was not even sure as to which direction the noise had come from, seeing as sound had a way of reverberating and reflecting in the river valley. It was like a scream, but not exactly. It was like a yell, but not exactly. It had sounded like a woman, maybe. It had sounded like a woman, frustrated beyond belief, letting out a deep, heartfelt "NOOOOOO!" and the sound had chilled Hannah to the core.

It had been the sound of desperation, the sound of a human energy which has been pushed beyond its endurance, beyond its belief. It was the sound of a spirit in agony.

Hannah had been touched by the cry, because she had felt the cry. She had been touched by the cry, because it had, in one powerful instant, brought back the feeling of pain, of loss, of total devastation that she had felt when the doctor had turned to her in the emergency room a few years back, and had gently told her that her Herbert had died from a heart attack.

The cry was from a woman in much more than physical pain. The cry was from a woman in pain of the soul. Hannah had been there once. She had felt that pain, too. And though the years had passed, and her life was healed in so many ways, watching her river and growing her herbs and reading her books, a person doesn't forget a pain like that.

The sound had disappeared as soon as it had come, followed by an awful crashing sound, that she thought, instinctively, had come from down the river. But the river bent shortly below her house, and she had had no view of what had gone on.

She hadn't done anything about it, she had just kept to herself as was her way. But now, in the brightness of day, her conscious was on a rampage. Finally, after giving herself a good, stiff, talking to, she picked up the phone and called the police.

Her call was transferred around like a ping pong ball, first to the main desk, then to the complaint department, then to some limbo that they like to call "On Hold."

She was ready to hang up, when the voice finally came back and took down the information, her name, her phone and address, and the nature of her call. She estimated the time, told about the noise she had heard, beginning to feel a bit like a ninny. The clerk wrote down the information and thanked her for calling, all with a bored voice that made Hannah feel unnecessary and uncomfortable. She hung up feeling a little aggravated, but the nagging voice of conscience had quieted, and for that, at least, she was very grateful.

****

Frederick Ellington III was not having a good day. In the late morning, he had met with his attorney James Jenkins, Esquire, in the latter's high rise and high rent office in the city.

"What do you mean, we can't get around this?" Frederick had found himself screaming at the dour faced man who knew more about the problems he faced than any other man alive.

"This is absolutely the worst, the worst thing that could happen to us at this time, Freddy boy," Jenkins had spit out. "Leave it to you to have a wife that goes and dies at a time like this. We have no time, Frederick. No time at all. If we don't come through on this, the deal is off, man. SHE is the pivot in this whole complex fiasco you have designed. Without her...."

He paced the plush maroon carpet, head low, hands behind his back.

"She was a buffer, James, a buffer. She was just a way of keeping my name out of print until the time was right. But we don't need her," Frederick stopped for a minute, not liking the desperate tone of his own voice. He took a deep breath, and modulated his tone.

"We don't need her. As her husband, I'll inherit since there's no will. Anything for the boys will go into trust as they are minors, and I will be the trustee. Set it up, and we'll transfer the property. We don't need her, right?"

"Wrong, you clown."

Frederick's eyes narrowed to slits. He did not allow people to speak to him that way. There was a price to pay.

"Watch it, Jenkins."

Jenkins noted the flat tone, and knew he had crossed the line. Ellington was brilliant, that was for sure, but his brilliance came complete with a streak of narcissistic insanity. Maybe even a psychopath. He had seen what the man was capable of doing.

"Sorry for losing my cool, Frederick," he said contritely, cursing himself silently for getting involved with such a man, despite the profits that had come of it. "But we do need her. The point is, we need her dead or alive, but we need her. No body, no certificate of death. No certificate of death. No property transfer. The death certificate will be tied up for years. It's as simple as that."

Frederick felt the blood drain from his face, the problem suddenly becoming clear.

"But what if they don't recover the body? What if she's never found? How long until she's declared dead in this state?"

"Seven years. Seven long years is the standard time." Jenkins nervously cleared his throat.

"Come on, man, there has to be a loophole here! We have to be able to do something."

"Yes, we can do something. But it takes time. And time is what we haven't got. Our deal has to go through next week. The sales contract stipulates it. And if we try to renegotiate, we run the risk of losing everything. We can't run the risk of having anyone scrutinize the deal too closely. You know you're getting more for the tract of land than the normal market value. The city has to purchase the land for the new zoo right on schedule. The council members will do as you say, as long as everything is quiet and runs without trouble. One whiff of scandal, and the thing will fall through." He paced back and forth, back and forth as he talked.

"So we have almost no time. How do we get her declared dead? How can I get my hands on the assets?"

"There is precedent of this kind of thing." Jenkins was thinking hard, running his hands through his graying hair as he talked. He grabbed a thick green book off the shelf near his desk and started rifling through.

"Here it is. The statute is called "Exposure to Specific Peril". It's for cases when a person has died, without a shadow of doubt, but the body is unrecoverable."

"Such as?"

"Such as objective witnesses saw a person fall overboard on a cruise ship in a freezing storm, hundreds of miles from shore. Such as a daredevil photographer dangling with camera from a helicopter falls into the lava pit of a volcano...."

"Jesus, James..." Frederick paled for a minute, thinking of Cassandra plummeting to the rocky river. But his next thought was of the money at risk.

"When a situation like this occurs, a Trustee can be appointed by the court, who is empowered to secure dispositions of the witnesses and experts who can testify about the absolute certainty of death. The facts are presented at a hearing for the "Findings of Facts and Conclusions of Law". The decree is issued by a Common Pleas Judge."

"Can you get yourself appointed as the Trustee, James? We have connections, let's get this thing done."

"It still takes time, no matter how many judges you can blackmail and bribe. I don't think we can do it."

"NO!" Frederick yelled.

James looked suddenly at the excited man before him. Frederick's wife had died less than twelve hours before. He knew that Frederick had not been overly fond of his wife, but he was horrified at his lack of concern, his lack of loss. He had met Cassandra Ellington at many a social event. She was a darn nice woman, whatever problems they may have had. Shouldn't he care, even just a little bit? The fact that he obviously did not set off warning signs in the lawyer's head.

"It's not as easy as you think, Frederick. The hearings, the dispositions, the presentation, the conclusions all take time. And the courts really expect to wait nearly a year to be sure that there is no doubt. It's never been done in less than a few months. They don't declare death easily. It's a big responsibility."

"I'll tell you about a big responsibility, James." Frederick's eyes had narrowed to slits again, and James resignedly knew what was coming.

"Responsibility is keeping yourself a member of the bar, Jenkins. One breath of the deal you're involved in, and you can kiss your fancy legal career goodbye. I'm not going down on this one without a fight. If I go, I'll take you with me."

"If I try to push on this, Frederick, the odds are it won't work. The Trustee is held to a thorough and exhaustive search for details and verification. If anything crops up later, I could be personally sued for incompetence."

Frederick Ellington III gave a bright smile then, and James Jenkins knew for certain in that split second that he was insane.

"Well, the way I see it, you can either risk the chance of being sued to incompetence later, or you can rest assured that you'll be disbarred and then sued for divorce right now. Without a doubt."

James swallowed hard. Frederick had him by the balls and he knew it. Frederick had everyone by the balls. He always got his way.

Over a year ago, after celebrating the first deal that they had put together, he had taken one drink too many, which was an extremely rare occurrence in his disciplined life.

But Frederick had been there, and he had let his guard down, confessing to his so-called friend of a misalliance he had with a young secretary in the early years of his marriage. The girl, who later had his child, had been paid off, and lived comfortably in another city. She was a nice woman, and she had never made trouble for him. And he needed to keep it that way. The entire situation had been hidden from his wife. His rich wife. His rich, unforgiving wife.

And he knew that Frederick held the cards that could remove his career, his wife, his mansion and his children in one swift phone call.

"I'll give it a try, Ellington," he said, trying to keep the emotion out of his voice. We'll get a death certificate. We'll do whatever it takes to make this deal come off on time."

Chapter 13

As the TV news came on, Cassandra sat on the edge of the comfortable couch and looked around the room. She felt comfortable here. It was a far cry from the designer coordinated living room of the elegant Ellington house. No plush and well cushioned carpet here. No blending of colors and fabrics to "tie the room together" as the decorator who had planned the decor of the living room in the Ellington house had insisted.

Here, in Calvin's well-worn living room, the walls were lined with books...books of all sizes and in all conditions. Paperback books, encyclopedias, hardback books of a variety of topics were placed in absolutely no order at all. They just filled the shelves, and in some cases, overflowed into piles stacked neatly on the deep windowsills. The room had, despite the mixture of color and size of the books, a kind of unspoken order about it. A well-used desk sat against one wall, a green tinged desk lamp sitting upon it.

The couch she sat upon was a slate colored blue, and over the back a hand crocheted blanket with nearly of every cover in the rainbow was hung with care. A smaller crocheted blanket was draped over the back of the wooden rocking chair that she had noticed the night before.

A stuffed chair, comfortable and well worn, sat adjacent to the couch, also facing the TV. The room felt so good. It felt homey. Cassandra was touched by the thought. Never, in all her many years of marriage, had she felt "homey" in her own home. She blinked her eyes to settle the tears that threatened to form, willing her mind to focus on the TV before her. A commercial for laundry soap finished, and the news began.

The news always began the same way. They listed the lead story quickly, as if to pique your interest, then broke to a commercial. The commercial featured a fast food restaurant. The lead story featured Cassandra Ellington. She sat, frozen, rooted to the edge of her chair, and watched her own face as it appeared on the TV screen.

"Cassandra Ellington, well known society matron and wife of respected university professor and successful book author Frederick Ellington, perished last night in a single car accident on River Road north of Sollington. The car plummeted over the cliff at the edge of the road, smashing onto the rocks below, before landing upside down in the strong river current. Mrs. Ellington is believed to have been alone. Dredging for her body, which is believed to have been washed downstream by the current, is still going on at this moment. However, authorities seem to concur that there is no possible way that anyone could have survived the crash."

The blonde haired anchorwoman turned to another camera and continued. "We are going live now to the university to speak with Professor Ellington."

The screen blipped, and before her, Frederick appeared, at the side of a young, dark haired newsman. His lawyer, James Jenkins stood next to him.

"Totally unreal", was Cassandra's haunting thought, "Can this be happening?" People were actually on TV, discussing her demise, while she was sitting in an oversized sweatshirt and red socks watching them. She felt like she was having an out of body experience. She wanted to scream. What was she supposed to do?

****

"Professor Ellington," the earnest young newsman began, as the cameras were being set up. "We were distressed to hear the news of your wife's accident. Thank you for talking to us today."

The reporter, Charles Upworth, watched the man before him curiously, as he shoved a microphone in front of the man's face. Charles felt like a ghoul. He had a tight feeling in his gut. He'd be hearing complaints about this, for sure, before the hour was out, and it made him kind of mad. But his job was to be out on the street, "the reporter on the scene". He was about to interview the distressed husband of a brutal automobile fatality. This was how news people got a bad name. This was why people phoned, wrote, sent emails to the station to complain about the insensitivity and callousness of TV and the press, barging their way into people's private grief, and splashing it into the public eye. Ratings and tragedy. It made him sick. It left him cold.

News was news, but it could be done in good taste. It was not as if some of the big wigs at the station didn't agree with him about this point. They had received enough bad response in the past when they had gone over the line of what the public felt was acceptable, and policy, lately it seemed, had changed to please the public and the advertisers: Use good taste.

But this, he told himself as he looked at the well dressed, well-groomed man in front of him, was not in good taste. The problem was, in this case as a reporter, he was blameless. He hadn't pushed his way in anywhere. Charles had been assigned this job, and when he had protested that the assignment sounded crude and could bring about the reaction that the station wanted to avoid, he had been told, not in so many words, to "Shut up, shape up or ship out."

The crux of the matter was that the GQ guy standing and primping himself in front of the camera, the "grieving widower", as he had earlier cast him, had actually REQUESTED the press. He had DEMANDED the press. And whatever kind of connections the creep had, he was getting his way. It made Charles kind of sick to see him huddled with his lawyer one second, smoothing his hair the next. This was, in his opinion, not a man in grief. But when the cameras began to roll, the camera's eye would record another story. Whatever this guy was up to (and he had to be up to something), Charles Upworth, ANC News, was going to have to play along, and there'd be hell to pay with the public criticism. He could feel it in his bones.

"Five seconds, Mr. Upworth," said the quiet voice of his camera tech. "Four, three, two, one, roll…"

The red light glowed on the camera before him, and he was on live TV. "Good afternoon, this is Charles Upworth, ANC News, with a live noon report at Newton University. We are talking now to Professor Frederick Ellington, husband of Cassandra Ellington, who is alleged to have died in a one car crash last evening."

The camera included Frederick now. His eyes looked misty, but he kept his shoulders straight. His face now held emotion, visible grief, and his voice sounded ready to break. He appeared overwrought.

"A tragedy. A great tragedy. My Cassandra was a wonderful woman, dedicated to her family and her community. I am heartbroken." His eyes looked full of tears as he looked straight into the camera.

Charles felt like squirming. The guy now looked devastated, and minute ago, he had been smoothing his hair. But the public would only see the tears, and ANC (not to mention Charles Upworth) would look like a bloodthirsty news vampire. Life was not fair.

"We're all so sorry, Professor." he said gently, trying to take the sting out of the situation. "We don't like to intrude on your grief. But apparently the body has not yet been discovered. Do you hope that there's a chance that she may have survived?"

He barely got the words out.

"How dare you say such a thing?" Frederick Ellington croaked at the newsman. His face flushed and flashed anger for a minute. His lawyer reached up and touched his arm. Then the hurt returned. "I mean, it's cruel to get people's hopes up. Like my boys. They will have to adjust to living without their mother, and it will not help to have people throw the possibilities of miracles in their faces. My wife is dead. The police concur that anyone who went over that cliff had no chance of surviving. Her purse, her shoe, a ripped part of her dress were found in that car. As hard as it is to face, my wife is dead."

"It was a tragic accident, Professor Ellington," Charles added.

"And a needless one. For years, there has been discussion of putting more protective railings along the road along the cliffs, but nothing has been done. And now this. Perhaps now it will be taken seriously as a threat."

Charles Upworth nodded in agreement. "Thank you, Professor Ellington, for talking with us. You and your family have our sympathy at this difficult time. And now, back to the station, and Kathleen McGree, with the noon news. This is Charles Upworth, ANC reporter on the street."

The camera light flashed off. It was over. But it wasn't over.

Charles felt a strong hand grab his shoulder, turning him around abruptly. He was suddenly looking into the face of Professor Frederick Ellington again, only this time, there were no phony, tear rimmed eyes. This time there was rage.

"How dare you, insinuate that she could possibly still be alive like that on TV, Buster?" he yelled. The lawyer grabbed his arm.

"Frederick, let it go, man. Get hold of yourself." The attorney looked worried.

"I'm sorry, Professor Ellington," Charles said through clenched teeth. He automatically flexed his fist. He had played on the football team in college. He was no pushover and he had the sudden urge to haul back and toss this rude guy through a wall. But he didn't want to get fired. "The spot seemed so depressing. I was interjecting a little hope."

"Well, you better interject a little hope that you still have a job, buddy boy." He turned on his heel, and stomped away, back up the steps to the university building that housed his office. The lawyer followed him silently.

A small crowd had gathered as they did the spot, witnessing the outburst, but they scattered quickly when the action was over. Charles helped the tech crew to reload the van with the cameras and mikes. He was very thoughtful. He sure didn't like that guy. He sure didn't like this story. But he had a feeling, deep in his bones, that something was not quite right. His newsman's nose smelled trouble. And he felt very, very sorry for Mrs. Ellington.

      ****

Cassandra sat back on the couch as the newscast finished and moved on to the next story. According to the news, she was dead. In Frederick's eyes, in the police report, in the public eye, she had perished when the car went over the cliff. And yet, here she was, cut up and achy, but certainly alive as can be. It was the strangest feeling.

But even stranger was the realization that Frederick was insisting that there was no hope that she was alive. He was sure she was dead...and he was glad of it. She could see it in his face. She knew him. She flicked the TV off and sat quietly, staring at the blank screen. She had some serious thinking to do.

Chapter 14

Tired as he had been, Detective Marv Greenstein hadn't slept more than a wink last night. He had tossed and turned in his usually comfortable single bed, until he had finally given up in the early hours of the morning. He had risen, made coffee, and had settled himself at the coffee table in front of the couch, deciding to tackle his un-favorite job. He needed to balance his checkbook. With two months of cancelled checks and two aggravating monthly statements, he buckled down and tried to make heads or tails of the numbers before him.

It was a job he hated to do, but a job that had to be done. He had learned the hard way that avoiding the issues that bothered him would never work. You had to face your issues. So he faced the checks. He mumbled and swore under his breath, and twice got up and walked around the room in frustration. But he came back, and finally, when he was about ready to pull the hair he had left right out of his head, it balanced. He had done it, right on the penny. He allowed himself a moment of intense pride, sipping his now lukewarm coffee, before allowing his brain to identify the other murky areas in his mind that needed tending.

Cassandra Ellington. Her name kept rattling around in his head, and a vision of her face, which he had in truth only seen in her rigid driver's license picture, was haunting him. Such a tragedy. He sighed a deep sigh, right from the tip of his toes.

He had fixed his checkbook. He sure couldn't fix this situation with Mrs. Ellington. Life was like that. You roared around thinking about all the little problems, and blowing them all out of proportion. They were little, fixable problems. But then you got hit with the big ones, like death, or illness. Or a car going over a cliff. No matter how much you roar, you just can't fix that.

So the key was to appreciate the good things that you have while you have them. Things like your friends, your family, your coworkers. You had to just tackle the little things as they come, and not get too bent out of shape about them. But we all seem to learn that the hard way, he realized sadly. After a great loss....

Marv put himself back to bed, right about the time the sun was beginning she creep up into the sky, and when he awoke again, it was noon. He flipped on the bedroom TV, and watched the news, scowling as the report of Cassandra Ellington, with the interview with Frederick came on.

Something about this accident was really bothering him, and he just couldn't let it go. Maybe it was her face, which had really touched him when he had seen her picture. Maybe it was the jerk she was married to. He was a good looking, conceited, phony big shot who had really had, Marv would swear, no true grief upon hearing of Cassandra's death. Cop's intuition.

He didn't like jerks like that. Didn't like them at all. The main reason was that it came too close to home, reminded him of his own life and things he would rather forget. Well, he was sure of two things for himself. One being that he would never forget his past. Two being that he would never repeat the mistakes he had made as long as he had those memories. But Professor Frederick Ellington...he just had a bad feeling about the guy.

There were kids, too, Ellington had said. Two boys. Marv shook his head. Really sad, the whole thing. It would be much simpler, he thought, if they had actually found the body. He watched Ellington on the news at noon, simpering, phony sadness, and a belated community awareness about the necessity for railings along the river road. There was just something deep inside him that didn't buy it. Was there any possible other scenario for this accident? What if Mrs. Ellington had NOT been in the car when it went over the cliff?

What if Frederick Ellington had a very good reason for knowing that his wife's body would NOT be found? What if she had met with foul play at some other location...and the car pushed over the cliff to make it look like an accident. There had been no identifiable skid marks, as far as anyone could determine, at the cliff's edge. And if that scenario was true, what had happened to Cassandra Ellington's body? The husband was always investigated first in a case of a dead or missing wife. But in this case, Marv knew he felt no resistance to casting Frederick Ellington in the role. Which wasn't exactly justified, and not exactly fair. He just didn't like the guy.

Marv shook his head in an attempt to ward off a headache that was rapidly making itself known.

He showered and dressed and drove the short distance to the police station without incident.

"Marv", greeted the desk clerk in the station lobby, "So how come you're here when it's your day off?"

"Hi to you too, Jesse. Couldn't stay away. I have some loose ends to tie up. Anything new around here?"

"Pretty quiet morning."

"No new developments in the search for the Ellington woman?"

"No body, if that's what you're getting at. But wait..."

Jesse, the clerk shuffled through some papers, then plucked one from the pile and handed it to Marv.

"This one is supposed to go to you. It might be nothing, but some lady called in a little while ago with a report of unusual noise in her vicinity. She lives up on the River Road, near that Ellington accident you were investigating last night."

Marv grabbed the sheet and read the words of the complaint. An elderly resident was startled by loud, long, anguished cry of "NO!", followed by a crash. It sounded female. The time matched. Marv noted the name and address of the witness, his stomach sinking like a rock. It looked like Cassandra had been in that car after all. He'd follow it up, for sure, but it seemed like his theory of pushing an empty car over the cliff was dead in the water. Bad pun. His headache was escalating by the minute. Poor Cassandra. He wished like hell that they had found the body so he could put this thing to rest. He also wished like hell that he had known this woman, for some strange reason. The way he was reacting to the death of someone who was an absolute stranger was getting on his nerves.

He went to his office, downed two Tylenol for his headache, and picked up the phone to call the witness, whose name was Hannah Mae March. An elderly but spritely voice answered and affirmed that she would be home and would welcome talking to him.

He got into his car, and headed back up to the River Road, past the pull off where the accident had occurred, and pulled into the second driveway on the right, marked "March". The house was back off the road, in the trees, and perched right along the river's edge. Very pretty.

His shoes crunched on the gravel as he got out of the car. A big cat was startled by his appearance, and made a hasty retreat from the side of the house, running off to the right to a neighboring house that was barely visible through the trees.

Hannah greeted him with a smile, and offered him a glass of fresh lemonade, which he readily accepted. They say on the back deck of the house, where there was a slight breeze, but in the light of the spring sun. The river ran by below, peaceful and beautiful today. He tried to forget the thought of Cassandra Ellington being swept away in its path, and to concentrate on the little woman in front of him.

She had been sitting on the deck the night before, much as they were here. She liked to watch the sunsets. It had occurred soon after sunset. She had dozed a little, she admitted. A loud, bone chilling cry had awakened her.

Hannah Mae described what she remembered the best she could. She liked the wise and caring gaze of the young policeman before her.

He was a nice man, she could tell. Probably Jewish, by his name. Marv Greenstein. And not from this area originally, she would bet.

"Are you from the city?" she asked suddenly, curiosity getting the best of her.

He smiled. "Yes, Ma'am. Can you tell?"

"Not really, you just seem a little more formal than folks who've always lived out here. And maybe the accent."

"Accent?"

"I've found people from Philadelphia have a slightly nasal way of pronouncing their A's and O's."

"Very observant." He nodded.

The lady was sharp.

"Tell me again about the cry you heard."

And so she did. She said it sounded "female", as it was high pitched. It had gone on for several seconds. It had been full of fear, and pain and emotional devastation.

"Aren't you reading a lot into a single cry, Mrs. March?"

She looked at the man, directly into his eyes. "It was emotional devastation, Detective Greenstein. You may doubt it if you wish, but there is not an inkling of doubt in my mind." She went on to describe the feelings, the rage and fear that had twisted up in her when her husband had died. " It was that kind of pain. It was the pain that comes deep from the soul when you have to accept an awful truth."

Marv swallowed hard.

"I read the papers this morning, Detective, and I read about the accident down the road. It was probably that lady that I heard, before going over the cliff, and it hurts my heart to realize it. I had that kind of pain, and it was the worse and I have been able to work my way through it for the past few years. That poor woman had to die with that kind of pain on her soul. That's really sad."

"Most probably it was the fear of impending death, Mrs. March," Marv said gently.

"No, I just don't think so, Detective Greenstein. I don't think it was the fear of death. I can't help but thinking that it was the fear of life. That cry made me think the poor woman was in pain over life, not death."

Her words made him thoughtful, as he said goodbye and thanked her for her information.

"Thanks for listening to what I had to say," the grey haired woman with the twinkling eyes said. "And come back by one day soon for another glass of lemonade. I love my solitude as a rule, but it is a treat to have a visitor every once and again."

"I'll consider it an invitation," the kindly man said.

He started out the door to his car.

"Detective," Hannah Mae said softly. "I'm sorry about that Mrs. Ellington. Did you know her well?"

"Funny thing," he replied. "I didn't know her at all."

"Sometimes it's like that," she said quietly, looking at him with the wisdom of age. He smiled a sad smile, and left quickly, his mind reviewing the things he had heard.

Chapter 15

Many minutes after watching the noon newscast, Cassandra was still powerless to move off the couch. She sat staring at the blank screen of the television, seeing instead, flashes of memories coasting through her mind, memories of her childhood, memories of her early life with Frederick, memories of the boys. Tears flowed silently down her cheeks as her mind traveled through the past.

She had been only thirteen when her mother and father had been killed in a plane crash, leaving her and her eleven year old sister, Diana, without any family but their spinster Aunt Claire, and literally not a penny to their names. When the horror of the tragic accident had initially passed, the two girls had been left with literally nothing. The family home had been sold, the debts had been paid, and Cassandra and Diana had found themselves tenuously perched in a stuffy house filled with resentment and antiques, and a formidable Aunt Claire.

To say that Aunt Claire was not fond of children would have been an understatement. But her father's elder sister had made the commitment to raise her homeless nieces, and she was bound by it. For her, it was a monumental sacrifice of her time and space, and she had not let a day go by without reminding her young charges of her benevolence.

Cassandra, being the oldest, and realizing the precarious position that she and Diana were in, spent her time trying to please the bitter older woman, trying to "earn her keep" to make up for the nuisance and expense that she could sense that they were. And the more she had tried, the more Aunt Claire had found to complain about.

Diana, on the other hand, had been born a free spirit, and had not let Aunt Claire's complaining and martyr's sighs restrict her in any way. While Cassandra had been studying her brains out to achieve honors in high school, Diana had been slipping out to practice singing with a teen aged rock band, causing consternation and reprimand at every turn.

While Cassandra had won an academic scholarship to the state university, Diana hadn't even finished high school, finally taking off with her long haired boyfriend for New York City, and a chance to find fame and fortune in the theatre.

At almost the exact minute that the girls first left Aunt Claire's house, Cassandra for college, Diana for footlights, Aunt Claire declared her job complete and done, and wanted nothing more to do with them. She passed away soon after. Despite her crusty temperament, Cassandra felt a great loss. Determined to succeed, she had done well in college.

Her sister Diana never looked back. She was glad to be free of the oppression of Aunt Claire, and took a certain kind of pride in the hand to mouth existence she led. She got her GED, and took acting courses in New York City, and lived her life by her wits, personality and nerve. She got small acting and singing parts in a succession of moderately successful shows. The long haired boyfriend had been replaced many times over, but her lifestyle hadn't changed.

Cassandra and Diana kept in touch a bit at first, but the differences in their lifestyles made it difficult to be close as adults. Tears filled Cassandra's eyes as she thought of Diana. The truth was, Frederick hadn't cared for Diana. It was mutual. In fact, it wouldn't be totally incorrect to say that they hated each other. And over the years, it became easier to let the time lapse between their contacts than to fight Frederick's moods at every turn. She missed Diana.

Cassandra met Frederick at the University. Not merely another student, he had been a graduate assistant at the time, and his worldliness and self-confidence attracted her like a moth to the flame. He had ideas and opinions about everything.   Whereas, Cassandra sometimes felt undefined and unfocused, feeling her way through life by asking for other people's advice and direction about which way to go. Which suited Frederick well.

He was so in control of things, and at first, that was like a gift. But the gift dimmed over the years, through marriage and children and professorships, and books. Frederick liked to be in control of everything, of everyone in the sphere of his life. He not only liked it, he demanded it.

And so, she had gradually adapted, as she had to Aunt Claire's demands. She spent her time and energy foreseeing his needs, and planning the events and details of the day to his specifications and needs and demands, relieved when things went well, and feeling guilty when they didn't.

And somewhere, in this web of fear and guilt and anxiety, she lost herself. She forgot the Cassandra who was so intelligent and well-spoken that she had been president of the National Honor Society and had been granted an academic scholarship to college. She had forgotten the Cassandra who had given up her dreams to be a writer, in order to please her husband.

She had forgotten the Cassandra who had felt the pain and loss at her parent's death, the pain and loss at Aunt Claire's caustic reprimands and eventual desertion, the pain and loss at Frederick's constant criticism, control and abuse. She could feel the guilt and frustration she had felt for years, not knowing how to protect her own children from Frederick's cruel words and actions when they needed to express an opinion or need that did not fit with his plan.

Cassandra saw herself clearly, all of a sudden. From the needy, distraught child who had struggled to find acceptance in her grief, to the insecure and immature young woman who had married a demanding, neurotic man, making futile and soul killing attempts to find approval and acceptance in his world. The painful clarity of her realizations enveloped her.

Visions of her sons' pained faces raced before her eyes. Duncan and Peter, already manifesting the same look of fear that she recognized in her own eyes, trying valiantly to please and placate man who would never be pleased. Trying valiantly to live a happy life in an unhappy environment.

She thought of Frederick. She thought of his calculating plans to try to have her committed to a hospital to control her, rather than to face the repercussions of his violent actions. He was, she realized with a shudder, capable of anything. Visions of his once handsome face, distorted with rage and hatred, tormented her. And now he thought she was dead, and was glad of it.

Suddenly, sobs racked her body. The deep, heartfelt sobs shook every cell of her body. She could hear herself making painful crying noises, sounding like a wounded animal. She couldn't stop. She cried and cried until she was all cried out. She cried for the little girl who had been so alone, and for the adult woman who had had to face that fact that her life meant absolutely nothing to the man she was married to. She cried, then, for the fact that her life had meant nothing even to herself.

Then she thought of her minutes on the edge of the river's cliff, when the world had seemed black and forlorn, when she had seen no option at all but to end the pain that had racked her for so long. Never again. Cassandra sat up straighter and took a deep breath, eyes dried now.

She had been weak. Suicide had been a weak option. Never again. She had been given another chance for life. She was still afraid, and alone, and had absolutely no idea of how to change her life, but somewhere, deep in the innermost part of her she knew she would find the answers. There was a ray of hope, a glimmer that she was strong enough to salvage her life and the life of her sons. And that ray of hope was enough to keep her going.

She was going to live in a different way. She was going to save her children, and allow them to value life, too. But she hadn't a single clue as to how to accomplish this.

Curled up in a ball on the comfortable, well used couch that belonged to a stranger named Calvin, Cassandra Ellington had run out of tears. She gently drifted off to sleep. Somewhere in her subconscious mind, she had a memory of a kindly voice, the voice from Duncan's radio DJ the night before, telling a little desperate pregnant girl that things would be all right, that things had a way of working out. The girl had believed that voice and Cassandra did too. She slept, curled up in a little tight ball, tear stains on her face for the rest of the afternoon.

****

That's the way that Cal found her when he arrived home, with two contented cats curled up at her feet.

He looked down at the woman, who looked more at the moment like a child than an adult, and felt an unexpected protective urge run through him. He gave a worried glance at the newspaper he held in his hand, then tossed it gently on the coffee table by the couch. With a deep sigh, he let her sleep, creeping to the kitchen to put on a pot of tea. This was going to be another one of those days.

Calvin studied Cassandra as she began to wake up. He sat in a stuffed chair, across from the couch, where he had marked time quietly read his paper, and reviewing a few magazines. He let her sleep. She apparently needed it. She needed something, that was for sure.

She began to stir and move a little. Cal was amazed at the childlike quality of her face in sleep. Her face showed no worry, no fear. When he had first found her, fear and worry had been paramount. But in the fleeting moments the night before, when she had dared to dance in those horrible red socks....when the smile that lit her face had felt like a punch right in his stomach. Such an expressive face.

She was an attractive woman. He smiled, looking at her. Even in those oversized sweats, and still wearing the famous red socks, her beauty was evident. He saw the tear tracks on her face. She had been crying. What was going on here? What was she thinking?

She had opened her eyes, and it took a minute for her to orient herself. She froze in fear. She was on a couch, and gazed right into his eyes.

He could see her body begin to relax, once she had recognized him, and that made him feel unjustifiably good.

"Hi, Sandy," he said gently. She watched him warily.

"Hi. Thanks for the clothes. They're..comfortable."

"How are you feeling?"

"Kind of bruised and sore. My collar bone aches. I have a broken collar bone."

"Did you want to see a doctor?"

She made a laughing sound, but there was nothing funny about it. "I already saw a doctor yesterday. It didn't work out too well."

The two stared at each other for a full moment, each wondering what to say, where to begin. Honesty?

Simultaneously, they said, "I have to tell you...."

The sound of their voices in unison broke the tension and they both laughed, this time, a real laugh.

She began again, "My real name is not Sandy."

He nodded and opened the newspaper. He spread the front page before her. Her picture graced the page right under the headline, "Respected Community Service Matron Perishes in River Cliff Crash."

The color completed left her face. She was so white that Cal was sure that she would pass out. But she didn't.

"God, it looks even worse in print than it did on TV."

So she had seen the TV transmission, too. He watched her carefully, instinctively knowing that there was much more to the story than the TV or newspaper touched upon. There was more to the story than the fact that Cassandra Ellington was indeed alive and sitting in his living room.

There was more to the story than the fact that this lovely, gentle lady was married to the pompous buffoon he had seen on TV at noon. His intuition didn't usually fail him. He had so many millions of questions for this lady, and yet, he knew that it would be a mistake to barrage her with questions...he had to get his answers at her pace.

"I...I wanted to thank you for letting me stay here last night, I was pretty much in shock, I guess. That IS me, in the paper. Except I'm not dead."

"Small detail. The press is often wrong in small details."

She smiled at that.

"But you're alive," Cal said. "And you're more or less well. I thought maybe you had amnesia or something."

"That would be convenient at this point, maybe. Amnesia would be helpful. But not true."

"Do you want to call your husband?"

"No." It was simple, quiet, definite.

He thought of the self assured, pompous guy on the television screen. He had certainly accepted the fact that his wife was dead without delay. In fact, he had insisted upon it, resisting any suggestion that she might be found.

His gut knotted again. Listen to your gut, Cal. Let the woman talk.

"Do you want to tell me about it? What's going on here, Sandy? Cassandra?"

His voice was gentle. It was understanding. She opened her mouth, and the story came out. She told about her early life, and her early marriage to Frederick. She told about the fear and control and worry that she lived with. She told about trying to find help, and finding only road blocks and embarrassments. She tried to explain about Frederick's ability to coerce people to do what he wanted, his need to control and make decisions. It was hard to put her relationship with Frederick into words, but she tried. And he listened. He was a very good listener.

She told about her concern for her sons, and how she felt powerless to help them. She told him things she had never before dared to say or acknowledge to another human being. She told about the collar bone, the visit to the emergency room, the time spent on the edge of the cliff. She confessed wanting to end it all.

"But you lived, Cassandra. You lived."

"I had to live. I was listening to this radio station. It's one that my son listens to all the time. The guy helps people. Maybe I was trying to say goodbye, in a way, to my boys. But then, right at that very moment, I heard my own son's voice on the radio, and he was in such great pain, and wanting to give up. Just like me."

A sob emerged from deep in her throat.

"And all of a sudden, I saw everything clearly, Frederick, and me, and the boys, and I knew that I had a job to do, that I had no right to give up and leave my boys. And I wanted to live again."

She was crying now, and he instinctively moved to the couch and wrapped his arms around her, stroking her back. She talked through her tears.

"So I tried to get out of the car. But the seatbelt was stuck, and I couldn't get out. It was like another roadblock in my way. And then I got mad. Really mad. And I pushed and pulled and got myself halfway out the door, when the darn car started rolling...I think I kicked the gear shift or something. I just heaved myself with all my might, and went flying in the air. I landed on the ground, on a ledge. It was so dark. The car crashed and went into the river. I was so afraid. Frederick loves his cars...he would be so mad...and he wanted to have me put away. I just don't understand what's going on, but I know I have to help my boys. Peter and Duncan."

Cal nodded at the sound of Duncan's name.

She rambled through her tears, and Cal held her, his heart seized with emotion. He had heard a lot of life stories. He had helped a lot of people, but never, never, in all his life did he want to help anybody as much as he wanted to help this woman. The feeling was intense. It was personal.

He truly believed in destiny. He truly believed that people were connected to each other in strange and sometimes unnerving ways. And this was one of those times. The boy he had spoken to on the phone , Duncan, had been in great pain, and it had sent a message to his heart. He had felt it. This distraught woman had ended up in this spot by a series of coincidences that he was simply not going to argue with. She was here. She was supposed to be here. And he was going to help her. Whatever that meant, whatever the cost. Her crying had lessened to an soft whimper, and he stroked her back, his mind racing with more questions.

"It will all work out, don't worry. It will all work out. It will be ok." He said the words quietly, but with the gentle conviction of one who speaks the truth. "Just relax, these things have a way of working out. We'll find the answers. You're not alone."

She pulled her head back and looked up into his eyes. The voice, the words? She thought of her minutes on the cliff, listening to the radio and the gentle, humorous DJ who had calmed the frantic teenager. The one who had spoken to Duncan, and then switched to his private line. The voice...

"It was you," she said in wonderment and confusion. "On the radio...it was you...you're.."

"Your Pal Cal," he supplied with a soft smile, tucking his arms around her with a chuckle. "You, little lady, crawled into the window, and, if I may add, bled all over the clean clothes of Your Pal Cal."

"Oh my God," she pulled her head up with a jerk. "I'm so sorry, I didn't mean..."

"Cassandra, I'm kidding. It's all right. I don't understand all of this any more than you do, but I have a feeling it's just meant to be."

She sat beside him, staring now into space. "I don't know what I'm supposed to do."

"Don't worry, little lady, we'll figure it out. But first things first. I don't know about you, but I'm starving. How about some dinner. I think better on a full stomach."

She shook her head in amazement, as if to wake herself up, then followed him to the kitchen to see about dinner.

Chapter 16

Jenkins, wearing one of his conservative, grey pin striped suits, walked into the judge's outer office wearing his "charming" lawyer smile. Mary Ellen, the judge's secretary met his smile, and rose to her feet.

"Mr. Jenkins, Good Morning," she said brightly. "Is the judge expecting you?"

"Not really, Mary Ellen. I was taking a chance that he may be in, since court isn't in session yet. I had a question."

"Let me check." She sat down at her desk, and swiveled her chair a few degrees, so that her back was to him as she spoke into the phone. She turned around again with a smile.

"That's just fine, Counselor," came the same bright smile. "He has a few minutes and he'd love to see you."

She pushed a button that opened the door behind her desk with a buzz. "Go right in."

Jenkins straightened his tie, and his shoulders, and stepped into the judge's chambers to make his request. He would try the friendly, good old boy approach first, to get a quick hearing on the Cassandra Ellington's death certificate. Every bone in his body prayed that it would work.

Because if it didn't Frederick would attempt to get the job done his way, and his way was scaring Jenkins more and more every day. He had the sickest feeling that Frederick was crossing the line, becoming unpredictable and therefore extremely dangerous. He rued the day that he had spilled his guts to the man, giving him a hatchet to wield over his head whenever he chose.

This had to stop. He'd get through this crisis, and then concentrate on a way to get out from under the snake's power. A thin sheen of sweat broke out on his brow.

The judge rose from his chair at his entrance, and greeted him heartily. Jenkins declined a cigar, and seated himself in the red leather chair that faced the judge's desk.

"Lovely, to see you, young man," said the judge, puffing away. "What brings you here this morning? Everything well with your wife and her father and those charming children?"

"They are fine, Your Honor. Thanks for your interest. I'm here to make a request and to get your advice about a problem a client of mine is having. Frederick Ellington."

"The writer/professor?" said the judge.

Jenkins nodded.

"Dreadful business about his wife, I hear. Very unfortunate loss for the community."

"It's that loss I'm here to speak to you about. We are interested in petitioning the court for a declaration of death. They have not been able to recover the body."

"Of course. Such a tragedy."

"The usual seven years would be a travesty in this case. The finality of a death certificate would be a positive step for the family at this time. The pressure on the boys..."

"Quite. I see the path that you are following. There is a statute, about the Exposure to Specific Peril. You could apply that."

"Exactly, your Honor." Jenkins clenched his fists, and found his hands to be sweating, the clamminess extending to his body. Could the judge go along so easily? He wet his lips.

The judge continued speaking, blowing smoke into the air. "A hearing would be scheduled, after all of the necessary paperwork has been assembled. Depositions from witness, experts, that type of thing."

"How soon can we have that hearing, your honor?"

The judge looked at him questioningly. "These things, while important to proceed with, should not be rushed. It's customary to follow the procedure, and to avoid any look of impropriety."

Jenkins sat quietly, watching the judge think.

"A year perhaps," the man went on. "I would approve of it done in a year. That would give ample time to gather..."

"A year!" A red flush was creeping up James Jenkin's neck, coloring his face. The sweat was heavier now. "It must be sooner than that. Much sooner!"

The judge looked at the lawyer disapprovingly. "Mr. Jenkins, you know as well as I that the system of law in this country was designed to protect and preserve. Sometimes the time element is inconvenient, I will grant you that. But there you are. That's the way it is. We can talk again, when more pertinent information has been gathered." He stood, a signal that the interview was over. "It's only been a day, sir. Surely it's a time to mourn, instead of a time to plan."

Jenkins nodded miserably, taking his leave. His smile to Mary Ellen was much less bright, much less self-assured as he left.

"Ellington isn't going to like this," he thought dismally, as he punched the elevator buttons on his way to the ground floor.

"That young man is under some sort of strange pressure," the perceptive old judge remarked from his doorway. "We'll have to keep an eye on him," he said quietly to Mary Ellen. "Take a look around, and see what you can hear about him. That Ellington fellow as well."

Mary Ellen nodded, and picked up the phone.

****

Duncan and Peter spent the morning quietly at home, where Mrs. Briggs cooked breakfast and kept things as relatively normal as possible with a grandmotherly air.

She kept the boys home from school. She had no idea what was the proper thing to do, but there was no way, she stated profusely, that they would be able to concentrate on their lessons. There were occasional phone calls, which Duncan ignored, preferring to hibernate in his room and listen to the radio. Peter, on the other hand, kept a silent vigil over the phone, unashamedly listening in on every phone call that Mrs. Briggs picked up on the kitchen phone. He wanted to know what was going on. He simply had to know what was going on, and it was obvious to him that no one was going to tell him.

Someone from the newspaper called, and Mrs. Briggs got him off the phone in a flash, calling him a bloodthirsty nincompoop. Peter smiled through his continuous tears. She was a spunky lady. Then the police officer, Officer Greenstein called, looking for Dad. Dad wasn't home. No message.

Then Mr. Jenkins, his father's lawyer, called. He was usually very friendly and polite on the phone. But today, he sounded upset, and was actually quite curt with Mrs. Briggs when she didn't know his dad's schedule. She took a message for him to call back, which she posted on the board in the kitchen. They hadn't heard from dad since he had left in the early morning hours.

Mrs. Briggs made a few phone calls, too. One to her husband, next door, who was a semi-retired accountant. She told him she would be staying with the boys. He sounded like a very understanding man, offering to bring her a suitcase with her necessary things.

"I just can't go and leave these poor boys right now, Charles," she said brusquely. "I just can't understand what's going on in Mr. Ellington's mind right now. I'm sure he's distressed, but these boys need someone. They really need someone to care. He should be here with them."

"Well, I'm glad they have you, dear," said her resigned husband on the phone. "I'll bring your things."

She was a really nice lady, Peter decided, blowing his nose. He had developed a whopper of a headache, and he meandered out to the kitchen to find her.

"Can I have a Tylenol, Mrs. Briggs?" he said, a frown creasing his freckled brow. "I have a headache."

"I'm sure that's fine, Peter," she answered. "With all that's happened around here, I'm sure you're justified in having a headache. I have one myself." She handed him Tylenol and a glass of water.

"Thanks for staying with us. I really feel...sad."

Mrs. Briggs could feel tears coming to her eyes. "I'm sure you do, young man. It's a tragic thing. It's normal to feel sad when you lose someone special like your mother."

"She's not really lost, Mrs. Briggs. You'll see." He gulped down the Tylenol and drained the glass. "She'll be OK. They didn't find the body. She's alive, I know it. I can feel it."

She looked at him sadly, and not for the first time, wondered who she should be calling to get some help with the boys. She really wasn't experienced in these things. Children and grief. She had never had children, but if she had, she would have wanted boys just like this. Her heart felt heavy for him in his denial.

"I'm not sure that that's so, Peter," she said softly. "Sometimes we have to accept things that we don't want to accept."

"Well, I'll never accept this," he said, raising his voice to almost a yell. "I KNOW she's not dead, and nothing anybody says is going to change that!"

She watched him run from the room, shaking her head. He disappeared down the hall and into Duncan's room. She was glad the boys had each other. There were no other relatives that she had ever heard of, and they certainly weren't getting much support from their father.

She looked at the clock again, and went back to work in the kitchen. It was almost time to start dinner.

Chapter 17

James Jenkins hadn't looked forward to telling Frederick about the judge's reaction to a quick hearing on the death certificate, and the look on Frederick's face was evidence that his anxiety was well founded.

"You're an ass, Jenkins," Ellington spit out, his face only inches from the lawyer's. Jenkins didn't move.

Frederick started pacing back and forth across the lawyer's office. He ran his long fingers through his hair, an indication, Jenkins had learned, that the man was deep in thought. He waited. He felt awful about the whole thing, awful about his whole life, as a matter of fact, and how it hung in limbo because of this one extremely clever and equally as vicious man. But he had played along for too long, trying to escape the consequences of his actions. He should have known, he chided himself silently, that succumbing to a blackmailer is a form of living death. He had told plenty of clients that in his day. He should have taken his own advice.

Frederick started talking to himself, not even acknowledging Jenkins' presence in the room. "Got to get something on that guy. We have to get him under control. There has to be something. This is too important to let it slide. I'm not going to lose here."

He turned and strode out of Jenkins' office, not even bothering with the courtesy of a goodbye, passing the receptionist without a glance and banging the button on the elevator door with his thumb.

The door opened immediately. "Tell Jenkins I'll be in my office after lunch." He spoke without even turning around, stepped into the elevator, and was gone with a swish.

The receptionist turned to Jenkins, who had appeared at her side. "He couldn't tell you that himself?" she said sarcastically.

"Bad day, Mrs. Barker," the lawyer said with a tired sigh.

"If you don't mind my saying so," offered the efficient, middle aged receptionist, who had been with Jenkins for years, "That one is missing a few buttons, if you ask me. I don't know why you put up with that."

Jenkins sighed, and gave the woman a pat on her shoulder. "We do what we have to do, Mrs. Barker." He felt suddenly, like the weight of the entire world rested on his shoulders. He felt tired.

Actually, it wasn't the weight of the entire world, but it WAS the weight of HIS world, and he had the sneaking hunch that it was about to come crashing down on him. He turned and went back into his office, shut the door, and poured himself a stiff drink.

****

Frederick spent a busy afternoon on the phone. Drastic situations deserve drastic measures, and this was, in his never humble position, a drastic situation of the highest degree. He was calling in his markers for this one. He had too much at stake.

Through the years, he had developed a cast of players for his activities, mostly people who had succumbed to his blackmail and who were more than willing to take part in his little plans to keep from paying him money. Like a pyramid game, those people then worked for him to find the messy details he needed for his further blackmail schemes. Like clockwork, the web was drawn.

Others, he had found had a penchant for fast money, and a seemingly lack of values as to how they earned it, and could be "hired" to do a necessary job. So if he couldn't find the "dirt" on someone he needed to control, he had several paths to follow to create the "dirt" himself.

He knew several women who were more than willing to put themselves (or at least their bodies) on the line to entice a historically straight character into a situation that could be photographed and used to threaten his marriage.

He knew of several others who were more than willing to use their employment access to computer files and bank records to find information that a target would be willing to negotiate a nice price to keep hidden. Etcetera, Etcetera. In his opinion, you could always find something on somebody. Nobody was perfect, and the fear of the world discovering their imperfections was the leverage that had learned to use at an early age. Doctors, lawyers, clerks, fellow professors, students, they all had their quirks.

He was going to find this damn judge's quirk. He was going to pull out all the stops, digging deeply as necessary, or manufacturing the situation if need be. But he would get the job done, and the judge would listen to reason. And he needed it to happen very soon.

After he made his preliminary phone calls, he waited for the results. The phone began to ring within minutes. He didn't like the initial response he was getting.

Financially, the judge was clean. No exorbitant expenditures, no gambling, no visits to Switzerland or the islands to open secret accounts. The guy didn't take bribes. Family wise, he came up empty handed, too. A hard working widower, his wife had passed away several years before of cancer. No current women in his life, no errant children with behavior patterns that could be embarrassing to his career.

His career seemed to be everything to him. He took his job seriously, and was known for being fair and thorough. Shit. The worse kind of guy to bring down. But he had to do it. He made some more phone calls. One way or another, he was going to get Cassandra declared dead so he could sell the damn property on schedule.

Not only did he have most of his own funds locked into the property, but he had borrowed the rest, very short term and at a very high rate, from some people who were anxious to get the return on their money on time. And they were not people to mess with. They tended to get a little physical when upset, and he had better uses for his body than to have it ensconced in a body bag. Damn that Cassandra.

He got back on the job, determined to set up the judge. If you stared at even Mother Theresa long enough, you'd catch her slurping her soup. Nobody's perfect. Everybody has an Achilles heel. The trick was, he had to find the judges Achilles heel, before the guys in the black suits found his...The land deal had to go through.

Chapter 18

Marv Greenstein had a pretty normal day off, which meant that he still spent about half of the day on the job. But he did it by going at his own pace, and interspersing such things as a trip to the cleaners and a visit to the library to pick up a movie or two. His job was more than a job, really, it was more like his life. But he still liked his day off. It was like he could choose what to do and what not to do.

He was having trouble relaxing though. Even after talking to Hannah Mae, up on River Road by the scene of the Ellington woman's accident, he couldn't put the case to bed. He had to face the fact that she evidently HAD been in the damn car when it had tumbled over the cliff. But he couldn't accept the fact that it was a simple accident. Some trigger, deep in his mind kept nagging at him that Frederick Ellington wasn't what he appeared.

But when he checked things out, he learned the man was standing in the front of a classroom when the "accident had occurred. Ellington had been in front on about 35 bright eyed witnesses. Since the a neighbor had heard the "primal scream" as she had gone over, the time of death was pretty clear. So he hadn't been physically responsible for her death, even if his grief didn't ring true.

Suicide? The thought came to him like a blinding light, and instantly, Hannah Mae's even voice played back to him in his brain, "It was the sound of a woman agonizing over life...not death."

Shit. What did that mean? He tossed the steak sandwich down on the plate in front of him, his appetite gone in a flash. Suicide. Double shit. It literally made him sick. He reached into his shirt pocket, and pulled out the license that he had accidently held onto at the accident scene the night before. It had been an oversight that he had taken the license, but it hadn't been an accident that he had kept it. Even while at the station earlier in the day he had a chance to return it to the clerk who would catalog and hold any effects. He'd forgotten, "accidently on purpose", again.

He looked into the eyes of the woman in the picture. Could this attractive, intelligent looking woman, respected in the community, married, with children, living in a goddamn mansion and wearing real silk and suede have committed suicide?

He had been around the block long enough, both in his job, and in his personal life, to know that many, many times, things were not as they seemed. People were not always what they seemed. Cassandra Ellington may not have been what she seemed. The thought made him depressed, and he chided himself for allowing himself to be emotionally involved in a case. It was very unlike him. People would be less surprised if he announced he had taken up ballet!

But there was something that drew him to the face in the picture, and he sighed in resignation. Like it or not, he was going to ask a lot more questions. He was going to dig around and find out if there was anything in that lady's life that would drive her "over the edge", both literally and figuratively. Because if that lovely lady committed suicide...somebody or something had to have driven her to it, and there was going to be hell to pay.

Marv was amazed at the strength of his own convictions. He had surprised himself, he thought with a smile. Marvin Greenstein does have feelings! Marvin Greenstein is a human being who can care and grow! He chuckled at himself and picked up his steak sandwich again, wolfing it down and following it with a diet soda. Who knows, maybe next thing you know, he'd be wearing a leotard and learning ballet.

****

"But you are alive," Cal said insistently to Cassandra. They stood in the middle of the kitchen, drying dishes together, as the late afternoon sun crept in through the many paned window, casting a grill like shadow on the floor. "You can't just pretend you are dead. You can't just disappear."

"I know," she said softly. "But I have to think. There is something horrible going on with Frederick. Something worse than usual."

"Some guy."

Cassandra shook her head. "I'm looking at my life from a different angle, and honestly, it scares me to death. He was always mean. Like wanting to control everything I thought and did. And I always went along with it." Her voice broke. "I guess I inherently thought there was some truth to what he said. You know, I was stupid, had dumb opinions, couldn't make good decisions. So after all, I just left it up to him. It was safer that way."

"You were so afraid of him?"

"Yes...No...In the end I was afraid of him. In the beginning I guess I was afraid of myself. That I was inadequate, and the world would find out. And of course, he was only too happy to reinforce that opinion. Look where it got me. I could kick myself."

Cal smiled. He had heard the story before. Different faces, different actions, but the story was the same. There was this shame that so many people had planted deep inside, like a stubborn, hearty destructive weed with roots that would continue to grow under the most amazing circumstances, gradually taking over the lives and thoughts of those infected with it. It was called shame. He also knew that the only way to keep the weed from growing was to dig out the root, once and for all. You had to really face yourself and your issues. He looked into the gentle face of the woman who stood before him, clutching an old plaid dishtowel like it was a security blanket.

He guessed she was going to have to face it, come hell or high water, with the pickle of a situation she was in. He had helped many a person, but never a woman whose husband was totally ready to write her off as dead, instead of following his original plan to have her hospitalized against her will for a non existent case of alcoholism. Like a bad movie. Only it was real.

"Cassandra," he said softly. "Do you have a problem with drinking?"

She looked him dead in the eye. "No."

"Sometimes it's hard to admit a thing like that, but believe me, it's no sin. Alcoholism is a disease."

"Believe me," she cut him off. "I know the damage that alcohol can do. My father was a drinker, and he died in a car accident. That crash took both my father and my mother, and I'll never forget it. He was driving that car, Cal, and the autopsy showed that he was drunk at the time. I've never abused alcohol in my life, and I never will."

He watched her carefully. She was telling the truth.

"Ok, Cassandra."

She smiled at him.

"But what are we going to do here?" he asked. "Like I said before, you just can't be dead and that's that."

"I have to find out what Frederick is up to, why he would want me out of the way like that. He could have divorced me if he wanted. I mean people do it every day. Why this grand plot to have me hospitalized?"

"Maybe it was the ultimate control. He could control you mentally, physically, and legally, once you were declared incompetent. But a doctor would have to give the prognosis, and a court would have to agree with it...seems like a tough act to me. Do you really think he has that much pull over people?"

Cassandra could feel a prickling at the back of her neck. A chill made her shiver. She remembered the doctor, the minister, the staff at the hospital. "Yes, I'm afraid that he does. But I'm going to find out what he's up to, and I'm going to stop him. I'm going to find a way to get my boys out of there and away from him, once and for all. I think I'm finally growing up."

He could see the determination and strength in her face, and it was hard to imagine the battered woman who had sat on a cliff contemplating death the night before.

"Probably it was coming for a while. But last night, when I heard the sound of my son's voice on the radio, how broken and distraught he was, I saw red. Maybe I couldn't see or feel the damage he had done to me, but I sure as hell could hear the damage the whole situation had done to my son. It was like a curtain had risen, and I could see the setting clearly for once. It's Frederick who has the problem not me. I'm not going to be intimidated again. Nobody should have to live like that, not me, and certainly not my kids."

"So what are you going to do, Wonder Woman?" Cal teased gently, and she could feel the approval in his words.

"I'm going to use my God given brain and figure out what the bastard is up to, why he wanted me out of the way. And if he thinks I'm dead, he won't be looking over his shoulder, right? I mean, I'm not hurting anybody or breaking any laws, right?"

Cal looked at her carefully. His conscious self was telling him that he should steer clear of this unusual woman, that what she was proposing was both dangerous and deceptive. But the same subconscious voice that had bid him to protect here and allowed her to sleep in his house the night before had taken over.

"You can stay here, Cassandra. I'll try to help you. God knows, I don't know or understand what you are going to do, but you can take the time to figure it out. OK?"

The smile she gave him made the risk almost worth it. Almost.

"Thank you."

Her simple words twisted his gut. He looked at his watch. It was almost time for him to go to the station for his evening show. "I'm going to have to go to do my show, Cassandra. Do you want to come?"

"To the radio station? With you?"

"No, to the movies, with Clark Kent. I hear he has a thing about secret identities."

"I'd rather go with you. Flying with a man in a cape can be such a drag."

God, he loved the way her eyes crinkled when she laughed.

"But I have no clothes," she exclaimed, looking down at the worn sweat suit she wore.

"We'll do something about that tomorrow. Wearing that to the station tonight is fine. But we'll have to get you some shoes. I just don't feel comfortable having you stay here alone at night."

"But what if somebody recognizes me?" she whispered softly, suddenly afraid for a moment.

"There's nobody much there at night except me and Paul...and I'm lucky if Paul even recognizes me!"

"Paul sounded really nice on the radio last night."

"He's the best...but don't ever tell him I said that. It would wreck my reputation. But honestly, I think you'll be safe there. It's practically empty, and no one even suspects you're alive, let alone looking like that!"

She laughed and danced in the sweat suit and red socks. Her collar bone hurt only a little bit.

She looked like a little imp, in the oversized clothes, with her hair straight and clean and pulled back into a pony tail. No makeup, no expensive coiffure, no Cassandra Ellington like the picture in the newspaper. This was the real Cassandra, and she was great. He reached in a drawer, and pulled out a red Philadelphia Phillies baseball cap.

"This will complete the outfit. And it matches the socks. "

She put it on, and looked in the mirror over his desk. Her face looked solemn, and he instantly felt bad. He glanced at the picture on the front page of the paper, still sitting on the coffee table. She was used to such elegance. Silk clothes, suede shoes. Maybe this was just too much.

"Sorry, Cassandra. It's all I have. Hopefully, in no time at all, you'll be back to looking like yourself."

She turned, and gave him a soft smile, and he could see the tears glistening in her eyes. "Don't you understand yet, Cal? For the first time in years, I feel like I AM myself. Thank you."

Without another word, they left the house for the station, both deep in thought.

Chapter 19

"The judge isn't buying, Frederick. We're sunk."

Jenkins collapsed into a leather chair in Frederick's university office.

Frederick looked at him with disgust, but not surprised at his statement. He had spent the better part of the afternoon on the phone, making and receiving phone calls. Jenkins was, for once in his pampered life, saying the truth. He himself had tried to get to the judge from a myriad of angles. The judge was clean. Nothing could be unearthed that even hinted of alcohol, infidelity, financial mishaps. He showed no indications of falling for any of the usual scams that would get him in a bad light.

Besides that, the judge looked like he was becoming suspicious of all the questions, a sure indication that they had to back off. And Frederick didn't like backing off.

"Shit, man. I'm telling you, I'm not going to be defeated by this thing. How about another judge? Why are we stuck with this one? If the case could be heard by one of my judges..."

"No deal, Frederick. This is his bailiwick, and he's not budging. You're not going to get a death certificate in time."

"That bitch Cassandra. I wish she were here right now."

He made a violent wringing motion with his hands.

"I'd get a death certificate in seconds flat."

Jenkins shuddered at the look on the man's face, and rued his involvement with him one more time.

"Well, better find a different solution, Professor...the clock's ticking. And if your "investor" gets a hint that the deal is threatened, there's no figuring what he'll do."

Frederick's fist pounded the desk. "Damn it all. Why did I ever put that property in Cassandra's name? There was just a little risk of my name being recognized and calling attention to the deal. Now the whole thing is shot to hell. Going off a cliff. Incompetent bitch. She couldn't even die without screwing things up."

Jenkins narrowed his eyes, a thought racing through his head. Besides the point that the man in front of him was nuts, he had a glimmer of a way out of the mess they were in.

"Incompetent. She was incompetent," Jenkins said softly.

Frederick looked at him blankly.

He went on.

So the court says she's alive. And since she's incompetent… There's no doubt that you should be the one to handle her affairs. It happens all the time. You know, old age, Alzheimers,..."

"How about alcoholism? That was the gist I was going to use to get her out of my hair for a while and keep her from interfering with the boys. She put too many ideas in their heads."

God knows, Jenkins thought bitterly, people should not have ideas around Frederick Ellington III. But the plan might work.

"Alcoholism is considered a disease. And the courts look at it pretty much as something you can recover from. The only time they would really interfere is if there were real danger to kids or something. But if the person GAVE away their rights...say with a Power of Attorney, where you would act and make binding decisions in their behalf, well the court would look on that differently."

Frederick's eyes were opened and bright. "Go on."

"Well, say that Cassandra had realized she had a problem. Say she had written a letter saying she wanted to receive help. Say she had signed a Power of Attorney form with me as her lawyer, naming you as the person in charge of her affairs, as she was preparing to go away to receive that help for alcoholism....and then she had the tragic accident.....a judge would buy that. Poor thing. Poor kids. You'd be in the driving seat."

Frederick stood up. "Go for it, Jenkins. I'll forge her name to the letter and the form. Date it a few months ago, so the accident doesn't look too coincidental. We'll say you held it and I didn't act on it until she actually went away, so as not to embarrass her in the community. You know I'm a sensitive kind of guy..."

Jenkins was on his feet and out the door. "I'll be by the house with the forms tonight so you can sign them. I'll file them tomorrow morning, and you're in business again."

Frederick was sitting in his desk chair, head tilted back, hands in front of his with fingers forming a pyramid, eyes closed. "God, I love it when I win," he said in a vain voice.

"I'll be over about 8 tonight, Frederick."

"And don't forget, the memorial service for Cassandra is at 10AM tomorrow. I set that up right away, to make a point of the fact that she is accepted as dead, even without discovering the body." He sat up suddenly. "God, do we still have the Memorial Service with this Power of Attorney thing?"

"Sure, legally the memorial service it doesn't mean a thing. It'll just look… respectful. And maybe it will help the boys. Frederick, you've got to think about Duncan and Peter. They must really be upset over this."

"They'll get over it. They have me. Don't forget to send flowers. A big bouquet of flowers."

James Jenkins left the office quickly, that nagging burning pain beginning again in his stomach. An ulcer, probably, brought on my Frederick Ellington III.

****

Duncan and Peter were both home when Frederick arrived. The house was as silent as a tomb. Mrs. Briggs had fed the boys, and had put a plate of food in the microwave for him.

"The boys have had a quiet day," she began. "They were wondering where you were. I wasn't sure when you'd get home."

Frederick's nerves were shot, and the last thing he needed was a busybody neighbor reprimanding him for his coming and going. His words came out clipped.

"For your information, I wasn't sure myself when I'd be home. This has been an extremely frustrating and painful day, and I've had a lot of devastating things to attend to. I'm not in the mood to be scheduled on a time clock." It sounded like a snarl.

Her face showed her contrition, mixed with shock, and Frederick had a flash of conscience. The lady had probably done a world of good for the boys, and she had been available when he needed help. He could very well need her again.

"But I'm sorry," he went on smoothly, this time his voice kindly and like syrup, "And I really appreciate having a neighbor like you. Please forgive my bad mood. It's been a day."

The woman nodded understandingly then. "I'm sure." She warmed up his plate, and he ate it silently.

"Thanks," he said, when he was finished. "It's fine for you to go home now. I'll spend some time with the boys. Tomorrow we're having a memorial service, just a little service at the church. I thought it would help the boys..."

"Very good idea. I would love to attend. Perhaps flowers?"

"Flowers would be great," he said. "Cassandra loved flowers." He forced his face to go tight with grief, and he could see the reaction on the woman's face.

"I'll go then, and see you at the church in the morning," she said, her eyes filling with tears. "Meanwhile, if you need me, please call, and afterwards, just let me know what I can do to help." She gathered her things, and walked to the boys room to say goodbye. He saw her to the door.

"Nice lady," he thought. "And a great cook. But I'm glad she's going home." He wanted no witnesses when Jenkins arrived with the papers. He went to his room to change his clothes.

The boys had eaten a quiet dinner, and had retreated to Duncan's room. They kept together, not even talking much, but needing to be together. Peter sat at the desk, with his back to his brother, working on a puzzle book. Duncan lay on his back, hands behind his head, eyes closed, listening to the radio. The house was quiet.

They had heard their dad come home, and figured he had closeted himself in his room. They heard the shower running. He'd be in to see them soon, they both knew without saying.

Duncan broke the silence. "What's the French word for ticket?" he asked, eyes on his puzzle, pencil in his mouth.

"Billet."

"Great." Peter had an analytical mind, logical and complex. He was famous at school for solving riddles, winning word games and puzzles, and out-maneuvering teachers. Duncan was a few years older, but had heard of his little brother's reputation, his nicknames ranging from

"The Wizard", to "Brain Buster" to "Computer Man." It was the weapon he used to rile him when necessary, like when he stole his favorite tee shirt, or "borrowed" his new CD.

"How can you sit there doing those dumb puzzles, Peter?" he asked. "How can you concentrate? Aren't you upset? I can't stop thinking about mom being dead."

"First of all, mom's not dead, and if you keep saying things like that, I'm going to break your face. Second of all, when I concentrate on this stuff, I can keep the pain away. I feel bad." His voice got squeaky. "Don't go giving me a hard time here, Dunc. It's going to be hard enough to deal with dad."

"You better believe it."

The sound of the shower had stopped.

Duncan sat up on his bed and looked at his younger brother. He really looked at him. And he was embarrassed to find his own eyes were filling with tears to match the eyes of his brother across the room.

"What are we going to do, man?" It came out from the back of his throat, broken and gravelly, full of anguish.

Peter stood up. "We're going to do whatever we have do to get by, Dunc. We're going find out what happened to her. And we're going to keep an eye on him." He jerked his shoulder in the direction of the hallway.

Duncan stood up and the two boys stood looking at each other, one tall and lanky and showing all the signs of full blown puberty, broken out face, angular body, a whole range of emotions on his face, the other still soft and childlike, his freckled face and chubby cheeks framing a pair of intelligent eyes, wise far beyond their years.

"But what if she's really dead, Peter? What if she's never coming back?"

"I'm never going to believe that, Duncan, never." His chin was set in a determined way, in the look that Duncan knew meant he had dug in his heels and was not going to change his mind. He looked at his little brother with a feeling of amazement and respect. And he was very glad that they had each other.

Behind them, the door opened, and their father entered the room.

"Hi, boys. Tough day."

They nodded silently.

"Eh, listen guys. We are going to have a Memorial Service for your mother at the church tomorrow. 10 AM. You guys have clothes for it?"

Peter spoke up. "Did they find her body?"

Frederick's face tightened for a split second, then his "calm" face reappeared, but Peter and Duncan had seen the initial reaction.

"No. No body yet."

Peter tried to hide his smile of satisfaction. To him, no body, no death.

"Maybe we should wait on the service dad. Maybe she's all right..."

Frederick cut him off in clipped tones. "Nonsense. It's best to get this over with, difficult as it is."

Duncan found his stomach beginning to swirl, reminding him of a movie he had once seen about a tornado. He felt his insides were being ripped up.

"And we have to get a few things straight. There may be some inquiries. By the press, by the police. I want you to listen carefully to what I say."

Peter's eyes narrowed.

"What kind of inquiries?"

"About your mother. About her mood and behavior before the accident. About our life here."

He hesitated, carefully selecting the right words. Duncan looked kind of shell shocked, and he was pretty sure that he could steer him in the right way. But Peter's eyes had a look that was too bright, an inquisitiveness that was unsettling. This one liked to think for himself, instead of following directions. And the directions needed to be followed here.

Frederick wasn't going to allow any slipups at this crucial time. He had to pull this thing off without any more roadblocks, and the last thing he needed was someone getting the wrong idea about Cassandra.

"Boys, there are....legal complications here. It's important that no one think badly of your mother. We're going to be honest and open about her drinking problem."

"Drinking problem?" interrupted Duncan and Peter simultaneously. "Mom didn't have a drinking problem."

Frederick's face turned to stone.

"Your mother had a drinking problem. I can only thank God that you have been spared the pain of it, if you have been unaware. You know how sad and withdrawn she has been lately. She had confessed to me the trouble she had been having with drinking. She was very depressed about it."

"Maybe she was depressed because you threw her down the stairs. Maybe she was depressed because you knocked her around!" Peter yelled, words spilling out of him like a dam bursting.

Frederick's hand flew out, clipping the boy on the side of the face. Hard. The force threw him sideways onto the bed. Duncan lunged forward, but his dad was too fast. He caught him by both arms.

"That will be enough of that." His tone was low and menacing. Peter sat on the bed, rubbing his jaw and cheek. Duncan's eyes looked haunted.

"Let me lay the groundwork here. There will be no more comments about my behavior with your mother. There will be no more outbursts like the one I just witnessed. You should be ashamed of yourselves. You are worthless, disgusting, selfish children."

The boys looked at the floor. They had heard it before.

"Your mother had a drinking problem. A drinking problem. She had been planning to go away to get medical help for the addiction, but this terrible, tragic ACCIDENT interfered. Do you hear me?"

Duncan raised his eyes first. "I'm not going to lie about mom. Even if you hurt me." Defiance and fear emanated from him, but he stood tall.

Frederick smiled. The effect of the smile was more devastating than a growl would have been. Duncan found his knees shaking. He swallowed hard.

"I won't hurt you, Duncan, if you don't obey me." He crossed the room, and grabbed Peter by the ear, jerking him to his feet with a yelp. "I'll hurt him instead."

The color left Duncan's face in a flash.

"Let him be. Let him be."

Frederick dropped his arm, and Peter collapsed back onto the bed, breathing hard. "Fine. Fine. I thought you'd see reason."

He turned to leave the room. "And of course, the same arrangement goes for you, Peter, if you have any wild ideas of defying my instructions. Duncan will pay."

He left quickly and silently, shutting the door behind him.

The two boys stared at each other in stunned silence, each trapped in their own thoughts. It was going to be a long night.

Chapter 20

Marvin Greenstein bit into a huge sandwich, and washed it down with a hot gulp of coffee. He was sitting with a fellow cop, George, in a busy diner in the shopping district in Sollington. He had a good day, for a day off. His errands were run, the cleaners, the bank, the drug store and the post office. He cleared up a couple of extraneous piles on his desk at work, and at home. He liked days off like that, no time pressure, just time to play catch up with all of life's messy little details.

George popped a hot French fry into his mouth with his fingers.

"So what is it about this accident that has you frazzled, Marv? Seems pretty routine from what you say." He talked with his mouth full, moving his hands all the time. He was a robust, lively Italian, larger than life, and Marv really got a kick out of him.

"Can't exactly say, George, but I guess it's the husband. I just don't like him. He exudes sneakiness and I just don't trust what he says."

"But if I got the story straight, someone heard her go over the cliff, and he was teaching in front of a class at the university at the time...doesn't sound likely he's involved."

"Yeah, I know. Strange isn't it, that I can't put it to rest?"

George stopped chewing for a minute, hands still, and looked at his friend. They were surrounded by diner sounds, but neither spoke for a while.

"You wanna know what I think, Greenstein?"

Marvin nodded slowly, their eyes locked.

"I think you're the best damn cop I ever saw. I think you have a kind of sixth sense in your soul. And if that sixth sense is telling you to follow up some more on this...well, I'd put my money on you, that's for sure. If you think there's more to this than meets the eye, go for it."

"Thanks for the vote of confidence, my friend. I'm not sure, though, that the chief is going to see things that way. You know how tight things are with the budget, how cramped we can be in the department. He's the last one to smile while I spend extra time on this when it looks so open and shut. I have no evidence. Not a single clue. It's just a feeling. The chief's not so into feelings, you know?"

"That's because the chief is an asshole. I think it's in his job description. It's a prerequisite for the job.

That made Marvin smile.

"But go ahead and ask him. Maybe something will crop up. Some little thing to check out. The last thing you are is a time waster, that's for sure. You even use your day off to clean out your desk. Actually it's rather disgusting, if you think about it."

George stuck almost half a steak sandwich in his mouth, and started to chew vigorously. But he didn't stop talking.

"No, you gotta follow your instincts and ask for time to go over the case."

Marvin smiled in amazement as the big man swallowed. "You're some eater, George, you know that?"

"We all gotta do what we all gotta do!"

They finished, left money for the check and a good tip for the familiar waitress and headed out the door.

George left the lot in his black and white police car, and Marvin got into his own Chevy and drove to the station to corner the chief. Like George said, he had to ask. Maybe a miracle would happen and he would catch the chief on a good day.

He parked in the lot and walked in the front door, where he immediately ran into one of the young cops who had been on phone duty for the day shift.

"I was just going to your mailbox, Detective. I had a call you might be interested in. Some lady called from the housekeeping staff at the hospital a few minutes ago. Seems she noticed a bronze colored BMW in the hospital emergency lot the night of the Ellington woman's accident. Maybe about an hour before. She was cleaning up, looked out the window, and noticed it because of its unusual color. Then she read about the accident in the paper, and the car was described. Might be a coincidence, might not. Thought you might like to follow up on it, since no one seems to know what she did before the accident. Here's her name and number." He waved a white sheet of paper.

Marvin grabbed the sheet with a smile. "Thanks, Buddy, this is just what I need."

He headed directly for the chief's office, note in hand. Miracles do happen. He had a question that needed to be answered. Just exactly why was Mrs. Ellington parked in the Emergency Room lot shortly before going over a cliff? Now even a guy like the chief was going to want to know the answer to that one.

In two minutes, he was back at his desk, grinning ear to ear. He had been given carte blanche to investigate the Ellington case. Even an asshole had their moments of sanity. He picked up the phone to call his lead.

The woman from housekeeping was named Colleen. He made arrangements to meet with her on her shift break in the next hour. He drove to the hospital, parked in the ER lot, and was met by her at the door.

"There's where it was parked," she said and pointed to a nearby space. The sign above it said "Emergency Patient Parking Only". He nodded, making notes in his notebook, and thanking her for her observance and care in making the call to the station.

Next he tackled the patient records department, who referred him to the Public Relations Director. They weren't overly used to police inquiries at the Sollington

Community Hospital. But his badge, and a few questions about search warrants got him the clearance he needed, and Cassandra's medical history was checked. She had seen Dr. Watson in Emergency on the date in question, but evidently left before treatment was given.

"What was she being treated for?" he asked.

"Why, that's strange," the grey haired clerk replied. "It's not officially documented here. The doctor always puts down a code for treatment, and we type it into the computer for the records. But in this case, it was left blank."

She was thoughtful for a moment. "I suppose because she left before any treatment was given, perhaps before a diagnosis was made..."

"That's a little unusual, isn't it?"

"Well, I'm sure there's a reason for it. It's Dr. Watson you would want to see. He could answer any questions, I'm sure."

He thanked her for her assistance, and armed with a note giving the doctor permission to speak with him, he found himself face to face with young Dr. Watson, wanting answers about the last hours in Cassandra Ellington's life.

The doctor was nervous, that was apparent. He was hesitant about speaking, and his reaction made the knot in Marvin Greenstein's gut a little tighter.

"So there is no notation about why she appeared in the emergency room, but there is evidence that she had checked in. Insurance numbers, and the like. And you were the attending physician. All I'm asking is if there could have been extenuating circumstances to her death. Was she sick? Had she been injured?"

The doctor's mouth was moving, but nothing was coming out. He showed a faint sheen of perspiration on his upper lip. There was a nerve being hit here. Marv's pulse rate increased, but showed no outward sign of it. He appeared steady, questioning, unemotional. A cop doing his job.

Watson felt like he was going to throw up. In this one instance, he felt like all his years of training, longing to be a doctor, were perched on the edge of a precipice. And they were ready to go over with the slightest shove. His mind was racing with Frederick Ellington's threats..."You gave strong pain medication to a woman who was a known alcoholic. Mixing alcohol and drugs probably caused her death. Not a word about the injury. No complaints of physical abuse. If this emotionally unstable woman drove off a cliff, perhaps because of you...."

Dr. Watson had spent the whole night since the accident tossing and turning, hoping against hope that the questions would not be asked, that he would not have to lie. He had omitted information on the chart, hoping it would be considered an oversight and that the spotlight of truth would not shine on him. But the moment was here. There was no escaping it. He had seen no evidence of alcohol with Cassandra Ellington. She had been abused and had been hurt. But the staff had alerted him that night that they had been informed of her alcohol problem, and of her husband's concern for her, planning her hospitalization for help.

Alcoholism, as Frederick had said, would get him off the hook. So what that he doubted it, after seeing the woman? So what if he had prescribed the pain medication because he had seen NO evidence of alcohol, and she had been in terrible pain? It would be his word against Frederick Ellington's. And the public and the courts tended to prosecute doctors like wildfire. She was dead after all. And he was alive and had a medical career to worry about. The smart eyes of the cop bore into his, and he opened his mouth to speak the lies that would save his reputation.

"I hate to speak ill of the dead, Detective."

"Speak."

"Cassandra Ellington was an alcoholic. She was drunk when she came in here. She wanted help."

Marvin Greenstein was so stunned he stepped backward, and plopped into a chair. His mouth hung open.

"Drunk?" It was the last thing he had expected. He, of all people.

"A lot of people have trouble with alcohol, Detective. It's not a crime. It's a disease."

"I know damn well it's a disease. I just didn't expect you to say that."

"She came for help. For her alcoholism." The doctor's voice was stronger now. More sure.

"But she ran away as soon as my back was turned. I guess she drove off. Changed her mind. It was probably because of the alcohol that she went over the cliff. A shame. A real shame."

"You are telling me that she came to the emergency room because she was drunk? The emergency room?" His voice showed his disbelief.

The doctor was angry. "I'm telling you what happened. If you want to blab it around and ruin a woman's reputation in the community, I guess I can't stop you. But there was nothing else wrong with Cassandra Ellington that night. And I couldn't do anything to help her."

Marvin left him then, a feeling of defeat in his bones. He had nothing against alcoholics. It wasn't a crime, but it just didn't fit. He kept thinking of the woman's eyes in the license picture, and shaking his head. It just couldn't be that simple, something told him.

He ran into Colleen from housekeeping as he neared the back door. She was emptying trash cans, and reinserting clean trash bags into the cans.

"Hi, Detective Greenstein," she said, her freckles shining as she blushed. "Leaving now?"

"Yep. Let me ask you something. You saw Mrs. Ellington park her bronze BMW the day of the accident, right?"

"Right into the space I showed you. It sure was a nice car."

"Was she driving funny? Steering straight? Driving fast or slow? Did you notice if she had trouble parking?"

"I'm not sure what you're getting at, Detective." she said slowly. "She just drove like normal. I didn't even notice her driving. Drove right in, into the space and got out of the car. That's all I saw. Except maybe she was holding her arm up across her chest. Like this." She demonstrated. "Like maybe she was hurt. But she drove just fine. Just fine. I only even noticed her because it was a nice car."

"Thanks Colleen." His adrenaline was flowing again. Something was going on here. When the pieces of the puzzle don't fit, they don't fit. You just go looking for more pieces. That was what he was going to do. He headed for home, determined to come up with answers.

Meanwhile, back in the emergency department, Dr. Watson was upset. He had listened believingly to Frederick's laments on the golf course about his alcoholic wife. He had heard about the plan to help her conquer her addiction at Hillmeadow House. It had been common knowledge at the hospital. Frederick had seen to that, in case there had been an accident, or a problem.

His stomach turned over. But that was before he had met Cassandra Ellington, and had heard her complaint that she had been abused. That was before she had overreacted to the plan about the hospitalization, and had run away. To her death.

He swallowed hard, because the bile in his stomach kept wanting to escape. He knew that the woman who had stood before him had not been drunk. She showed no signs of drinking. She had been hurt. He had not had the opportunity to take x-rays yet, but he had felt the injured area in her shoulder. She had at least a broken collarbone, to be sure. And Frederick Ellington had threatened him about telling the truth.

So what if Frederick Ellington had a thing about not telling the truth? What if the woman was NOT an alcoholic? What if she HAD been injured, and her claim that he had hurt her was true? He knew she had not been drunk when she drove over that cliff, and the medication he had given her was simply not that strong. But what if her emotional state had caused her to drive over the cliff? What if she had committed suicide? His stomach turned and turned.

He had spent his life wanting to become a doctor. He had just lied to the police about a patient. He had succumbed to an evil kind of blackmail. He may have contributed to the emotional collapse and death of a very nice lady. He closeted himself in the bathroom, fighting the panic that welled up in him. Next thing he knew, he was throwing up in the toilet, as if purging himself could remove the evil and guilt he felt inside.

Chapter 21

Cassandra's heart was pounding as Cal pulled the aged Suburban into the radio station lot. The station was located on the outskirts of town, on the south side; a single level, freshly painted white building that sprawled in a grassy field. Next to the station, two tall towers reached into the sky, and a giant satellite dish graced the side of the building.

They had stopped at a discount store on the way to the station, where Cal had run in and purchased a pair of inexpensive tie sneakers for her, size 7. She hadn't dared to leave the car. Cassandra wore the sneakers now, feeling the crunch of gravel as she stepped from the car.

"Come on, Sandy, don't be nervous. It's quiet here at the station at this time of day. No one expects to see you, no one is looking for you here. Just relax." He smiled, and took her hand, and instantly she felt safer.

The corridors were dim inside. The clock read 6PM, an hour before Cal was scheduled to be on the air. They walked by a glass wall, and Cassandra saw the current DJ sitting behind the glass, earphones in place, placing cassettes and records in order, speaking softly into the mike, pushing buttons for commercials and songs with a precision that amazed her.

Cal saluted as they passed, and the DJ looked up and waved. "First stop is the office. The staff has left by now, but the program coordinator has made a schedule for each DJ's show. I have to review mine."

"A schedule? You mean your time is all laid out, and you just follow a schedule? That doesn't make sense. I heard your show. You have call-ins, and take time to talk. You play kids' requests..."

"Ah! A fast study, I see. Very good, Cassandra. To explain," he began, slipping a pack of papers out of his mailbox and guiding her through the room to the next corridor, "My schedule is a little crazy. My special needs are slotted in, and I fill them as I may. But still it's a schedule..."

They sat at an empty desk in a small office, and he turned on the desk light. The schedule sat before him, and she perched on a stool beside him. The paper looked like a time grid, listing records and commercials, time checks, weather and news updates. Scattered here and there were open blocks, saying "Call-ins" or "requests".

"You see, I'm given a lot of license here, which is why I love this antiquated station and this show. It gives me a chance to work with the kids. That's worth a lot. So as long as the advertisers are happy, I get a long leash. Now, the advertisers. This is the part that's carved in stone."

He pulled a yellow highlight marker out of the drawer and began marking certain time slots.

"These time slots I don't mess with. The advertisers have contracted to have their ads played a certain amount of time in a certain time frame. I just follow the program director's schedule, to make sure no one gets gypped. Also these."

He highlighted time checks, station ID's and weather and news updates. Paul watches the teletype and puts together a short news broadcast and weather each hour. Those are dictated by station and FCC regulations. The rest," he moved his arm in a flourish, "I can monkey with. And I do. You'll see! Come on, I have to pull my ad tapes."

Next he took her to a crowded room holding shelf after shelf of tapes. He quickly went down the rows, plucking tapes as he went. When his hands were full, he turned to her with a laugh, and started loading her down.

"First I select the ad tapes that are scheduled. Everything needs to be handy and organized before we go on the air. The rest of these are songs that the program director has listed, plus a few of my own creations. I like to add different types of music, to make kids stretch their brains. You can only listen to so much rap before you start biting your nails, in my opinion!"

He whistled as he worked, his natural exuberance and enthusiasm filling the small studio and flowing over to her. Cassandra felt her mood lighten, felt her mind focusing on the growing pile of songs in her arms. It was actually fun.

It was almost 6:45 PM by the time they were finished. She was introduced to Paul at the news teletype machine, where he was pulling the latest transmissions and highlighting the things of interest to report. He did the same with the weather.

Paul didn't blink an eye or react at all when Cal ,introduced her as "Sandy Rivers", which made Cassandra relax a bit. She liked the quiet, gentle long haired man who seemed to know Cal inside and out. They complemented each other's actions, instinctively handing each other tapes and materials, and finishing each other's statements with a laugh. She felt a warm glow as she watched them get ready for their show.

And before she knew it, the light over the booth was blinking, a signal that they could enter, as Ken, the evening drive time DJ finished his show.

"Have a blast, Crazy Man," he joked comfortably as he gathered up his tapes and turned the controls over to Cal. A song played gently in the background, and the mikes were turned off.

"Later, Ken!" He saluted the DJ as he left.

He turned quickly to Cassandra, pulling her into the booth next to him and Paul. "One rule, Sandy. Never talk when the red light up there is on." He pointed over his head to a red bulb that was now off. "That means the mike is on, and anything you say will go out over the air."

"And that means Cal just wants to hear himself. What an egotist!" laughed Paul as he entered the booth to begin the show.

****

Although Paul had asked no questions about Cassandra's presence at the radio station, Cal and Cassandra had eventually told him the whole story, in bits and pieces, between songs and call-ins and commercials. In his usual laid back way, he had simply nodded, asked a few questions as the story went along, and punctuated their tale with occasional comments like "Wow, man", "Awesome", "Bummer", and "Bad scene!". And then it had been business as usual in the transmission booth, with Cal and Paul doing their usual stint, playing off each other, and off the teens who called in.

Cassandra felt a strange sense of peace as she sat in the background, listening, absorbing, watching the men at work. She listened intently to the kids who called in, sharing in their problems, their excitement, and their pain. Maybe, in the back of her mind, she hoped to hear Duncan's voice once again, but he didn't call.

Which was probably, she told herself, for the best. She still had no idea how she was going to approach Frederick, how she was going to leave her old life to begin a new one, with her boys. She only knew, deep inside, that she had to have a determined plan to beat the man that she had been so afraid of for so long.

But she longed for her boys, and she prayed silently that they were OK. How did they feel, thinking she was dead? The thought made her very sad.

Her collar bone had been aching her, but she still refused to get any medical attention, so Cal and Paul had devised a sling using the materials in the station's first aid kit. The sling took the pressure from the weight of her arm, and she felt a little better.

"It's time to play the Genius Hunt, ladies and gents," said Cal in a character voice. He sounded a little like an old southern colonel as he spoke, and Cassandra giggled.

"Here are the magic numbers....call in when you have cleverly deciphered their relationship: 617,413,508." The prize for the lucky and brilliant winner is a trip to the radio station, where you will get to sing your favorite song on the air!!! No, seriously, the prize is two free tickets to the WDRK radio station Super Box at the stadium in Philadelphia, a chance to see the Phillies as they start up what promises to be a most excellent season..."

"Whoa, man," interrupted Paul. "Some of us out there are not jocks who want to see grown men in pajamas chase a ball with a stick. What about if the winner isn't a baseball fan?"

"Ah, Paul, you don't know what you're missing in life. But just to be fair, we'll give the winner a choice, OK?"

"Radical, man!"

"A choice of the baseball tickets, or two free tickets for admission to the art museum, day of your choice. Will that keep you from complaining, O Hairy One?"

"That's buffo, Baldy! Truly beats pajamas. I never did understand why those guys wear pajamas to play baseball. It's so... weird."

"Looks who's describing weird! But to appease Paul, the lines will now be open for anyone who cares to call in and describe what THEY think baseball uniforms should look like in the future If the line is busy, just keep calling, 'cause we'll be right here. And of course, waiting for the correct answer for tonight's Genius Hunt. Now, a song I know you'll love..." The red light went out, and the next tape began.

The next few hours went on the same way, with easy banter and frequent phone calls. Listening to the teens' comments, and how the callers related to Cal and Paul, she felt a deep ache for her sons. She could easily see why the station, and Cal's show, were such a hit. She enjoyed every minute of it, from listening to teens who were struggling with first relationships and questions about life, to the young girl with a raspy voice who won the Genius Hunt... correctly identifying telephone area codes of Massachusetts.

The girl told Paul apologetically on the phone that she preferred the Phillies tickets, because she was going to take her grandfather to the game, and Paul laughingly admitted to her that he really was a baseball fan, too, pajamas or not.

It was all so alive and intense, and Cassandra found herself exhausted but disappointed when the time flew by and a woman DJ named Cindy arrived to take over for her late night show. Cal signed off with a joke, and gathered his papers and tapes while his last song played.

She was introduced to Cindy briefly, who didn't seem to question her presence at the station. It made her wonder a little if Cal had often brought women friends to work with him. She pushed away the thought, embarrassed by the flash of jealousy that such a thought evoked. She didn't own Cal, she didn't even have a relationship with him. For all practical purposes, she was still alive and married to the angry, cruel man who had been her husband for years. Even falling off a cliff wasn't going to change that one easily. She had a long road to go before she found herself out of the woods.

They were quiet on the way home, pulling into the long, wooded drive off the River Road in silence. A single light burned at the end of the driveway, a single light burned on the small porch by the front door. She found herself warmed by the sight, a beacon in the black night beckoning to peace and home.

"It's so peaceful and gentle here," she said, almost in a whisper as she left the car and followed him to the door.

He reached behind and took her hand in the dark. "I like that, peaceful and gentle. It's a good description. I feel the same way when I come home." He smiled at her in the dark, but she really couldn't see him.

He opened the door with his key and they were greeted by two rambunctious cats, meowing and rubbing their legs.

"I know, I know," he spoke to them. "Time for dinner."

She watched quietly while he emptied a few packets into their bowls, changing their water, talking gently to them all the time. Such a nice man. He was such a nice man.

Soon he came and sat on a chair across from her seat on the couch. "You ok? Shoulder hurt?"

"It's better with the sling. I guess I'm tired."

"I bet." She really did look tired, circles under her eyes, a slightly haunted look about her. "Why don't you go get some sleep, and we'll talk more in the morning about what should happen here. I think you'll think better after some sleep. And tomorrow's probably going to be a tough day."

She looked at him questioningly.

"Cassandra, I saw it in the paper." He motioned to the newspaper still sitting on the coffee table. "Your funeral service is tomorrow at 10AM. That's enough to depress anybody."

She looked back at him with eyes filled with pain.

Chapter 22

Frederick pulled up to the church with the boys a few minutes before ten the next morning. The three were dressed in dark, well pressed suits, white shirts, subdued ties.

"Remember what I said, boys. The press may be here, or people may ask well meaning questions. I don't want you to give me any trouble over this. There are legal implications here that you don't understand. You have to trust me. Your mother had a drinking problem. She was going to get help."

His voice sounded concerned and caring, but the effect didn't quite reach his eyes. Those eyes were as cold as stones as he turned to look at the two boys, and they both visually shuddered.

"I know this is a tough day for you. I know you cared for your mother. This service is a way to show respect to her. Now put your chins up, and make me proud of you."

They got out of the car without a word, and followed him silently into the church. The church was filled. Duncan and Peter could see neighbors and friends, schoolmates and families, as well as many people they did not recognize. Solemnly, they walked up the aisle with their father, taking their places in the first row. Neither boy was able to stop the tears that welled up in their eyes, trying to focus on the brilliant display of flowers that filled the front of the church, but their tears flowed silently. They didn't make a sound. Neither boy was willing to risk the wrath of their father, if he disapproved of their behavior.

The service was brief. The congregation said prayers, and there were a few Bible readings and a few songs, but for the most part, it was a blur.

"She's not dead. She's not dead. This is just a joke..." Peter's mind ferociously and silently chanted the words over and over as he sat stoically in the pew. To him, no body, no death. He would not believe his mother was dead and gone. Unconsciously, he raised his hand to his right cheek, where he had been struck the night before. The cheek bone was bruised and tender, and he knew his eye was a little blackened from the blow. "She's not dead. She'll be back. She's not dead. We're not alone."

Duncan felt dead himself. He sat in the pew, trying to imagine what it would feel like to have no life left inside. No pain at all, no grief, no fear. He felt almost jealous of his mother, for what she had escaped. He glanced quickly to the right, at the hard profile of his father. God, he hated the man. Death seemed like a relief.

But then he glanced over to the left, where his freckled younger brother stood, coming only to the top of his shoulder. He could see the discolored area by Peter's eye, and could see the tears escaping like a river down his brother's cheeks. He wasn't going to let anything happen to this little genius of a brother of his. Peter may be the biggest pain in the neck in the history of the world. But he was going to find a way to protect him, to get him away from this.

"I won't let you down, Mom," was Peter's silent prayer. He wished he had as much hope as his little brother, who would not give up the dream that his mother was alive. But hope had been smashed out of him a long time ago. The best he could do was make a solemn promise to the memory of the gentle lady who had been his mother that he would take care of, no matter what it took.

The service was over, and they had to endure the long and painful moments of friends and neighbors offering condolences and sorrow. Frederick's voice was low and controlled, and the boys weren't expected to talk much.

Duncan was horrified to see a TV camera in the parking lot when they left the church, and to see his father talking to a young newsman as they walked to the car. The man was always ready to be in the public eye. His father made him sick. He had probably, Duncan thought, asked the press to come, himself.

Feeling depressed and alone, the two boys scurried away from the camera, and waited in the back seat of their father's long black car. Finally, the cameras left, the crowd dispersed, and they were on the way home.

One lone man stood on the walkway by the church, watching their retreat. The man's heart was burdened with a number of emotions; anger, fear, frustration and sadness. He had not spoken to anyone, though he had nodded to a few familiar faces in the crowd. But most didn't recognize him. He wore a simple grey suit, and had tamed his unruly hair out of respect, even though suits and ties were definitely not a part of this stage of his life.

Calvin Johnson had just attended the memorial service for Cassandra Ellington, and had seen the pain and fear and loneliness in her sons' eyes. She had not overestimated her enemy. Cal was a good judge of character. Frederick Ellington was a dangerous man. And those boys needed help, as did their confused, wonderful mother. He was going to help her to find a way to get her life back, her life and the lives of her sons. "Your Pal Cal" was going to have to do his best performance ever. There was a lot at stake, but he had the distinct belief that it would be worth it.

****

Charles "Charlie" Upworth went back to the TV station after covering the funeral of the Ellington woman with a sick feeling in the pit of his stomach. It was the second time that he had come into contact with Professor

Ellington, and it was the second time that it had made him sick. Not a good indication of the quality of the man. But it wasn't just the man himself that had given him a kind of physical reaction.

It was his boys. Two regular, pimple and freckled faced teenagers, one lanky and lean with arms and legs that didn't quite know how to move with fluidity, one short and still sporting baby fat, his hair complete with stubborn cowlick. The area around the young one's eye had a greenish/purple tinge to it. The kid had gotten a black eye. But he didn't look like the type who found trouble on the playground. The boys had been dressed in conservative, basic suits, shoes shined, shirts pressed. Their father's sons, probably both to be good looking when their bodies evened out, and adulthood set in.

But the eyes. Feelings swarmed over him again, as he sat in the back of the news van, not even hearing the easy banter that went on with the driver and camera man in the front, as they munched on slightly stale donuts. Like thick, dense clouds being blown by an evil wind, the feelings descended on him where he sat.

In an instant, his hands felt clammy, and his body began to sweat. It had been a while since he had had an episode like this, he thought, trying to be rational. Flashes of memories ran across his mind. He could see himself as a little boy, then as a young man, not so very different from the younger chubby Ellington son. He felt his mind slip momentarily back to those early days, and felt again the fear, the anger, the confusion and the overwhelming self doubt.

He had seen the look in their eyes, the furtive, darting glances, the stiff upper lip that came from years of control. He could see the way their faces monitored their dad's...watching for his reactions...and, he was sure, his temper.

He consciously calmed himself down, thankful, once again, for the years of self- investigation and realizations that had helped him to cope with his past. The flashes of memory faded slowly, and the physical fear reaction began to pass. Pulse more normal, the sweats stopped. Crappy post traumatic stuff.

"This is today," he told himself. "He can not hurt you anymore. You are a good, worthwhile person. You did not deserve what happened to you as a child. You were not the cause of it, and you couldn't have stopped it. Today, you have choices about how you live your life. Today you are strong and fine."

Charlie went through the litany of affirmations that never failed to bring him back to the present, away from the abuse and ugliness that he had known in his childhood. He had been a physically and mentally abused child, with a maniacal, power driven father who had taken every opportunity to "knock some sense" into his kid.

A train accident had taken his father away for good one night. He had been hit when an engine had jumped its track, and had bled to death on the way to the hospital. The unsettled years that had followed, foster homes and unwilling relatives, which might have been a nightmare for some kids, were a blessing to him.

And then Charlie had finally ended up with his father's cousin, late in high school, an aging ex-hippie who had gently and lovingly taught him to accept his past and to grow from it. A lifetime of nightmares had stopped then, as he had begun the work of building his life, leaving only these occasional panic attacks when his memories were triggered.

And they had been triggered today. Charlie could see himself in that younger boy, standing stoically, black eye and all, beside his brother and father at his mother's memorial service. He had seen the quick way he had escaped as soon as humanly possible, seeking the asylum of the dark black car, out of the watchful eyes of his father. He was an abused child. Charlie had no doubt. Probably the brother too, with that distant, desperate look in his eye. Different from pure grief at the loss of his mother, it looked like the light of life had been knocked out of his eyes long before his mother's car went over the cliff.

He wished he could help those boys. But what could he do? His impressions were just that, impressions. The news director at the station had assigned to come to the funeral because Frederick Ellington had requested it from the station. Ellington had stated that he wanted coverage of his wife's funeral. So they complied. Fancy caring about a thing like that. He repressed a shudder at the thought of the man. He hadn't liked the man from the first, and his opinion went downhill from that point. He really felt bad about the dead wife, but most of all, he felt bad about the boys.

He pushed his thoughts of the Ellingtons from his mind as they pulled into the next stop on their roving schedule, the opening of a local Art Museum. He spent the rest of the day filming, and then editing his clips for the evening news, still feeling bad when he reviewed the footage of the Ellington family. It was as if the kids' faces were burned into his brain, like he was somehow supposed to help them. Which was a ridiculous thought. Their paths probably wouldn't cross again, and they weren't even connected in any way. It wasn't Charlie's job to help every struggling kid. He shook his head at himself and went back to work.

****

Cal drove back from the funeral with a heavy heart. He was feeling unsettled and confused, like a mouse caught in a maze and simply not able to find the path out. What a mess.

Something had to be done here. Here he was, hiding a beautiful and emotionally scarred woman in his house. She was petrified of her husband, and had failed in several normal attempts to get help for her abused family. She simply refused to come forward. She had what was probably a broken collarbone, no clothes or belongings, and he had just attended what the rest of the world assumed was her funeral. This was insanity.

It was probably even breaking some law or other, though for the life of him he couldn't figure out why. But even if it wasn't illegal for you to allow people to assume you were dead if you weren't, it didn't exactly sound ethical or healthy, and so it had to be faced. He had learned the hard way that when things didn't set well with him, he had to thrash them out or pay the penalty. And the penalty was too high. He needed his serenity and peace of mind.

But the other side of him understood and could read, totally, her pain and reasons for remaining under cover. She was afraid for herself, and she was afraid for her sons. And with a husband who had been threatening, and amazingly very successfully, to convince the world that she needed hospitalization to get her out of the way, it was easy to see why she felt she needed a plan to face him and come out unscathed. The guy was some kind of a nut.

Cassandra needed help, that was for sure. But he wasn't sure that he was the one who could give it to her. She was going to need help psychologically, and well as legally and medically. He was an amazing guy, he laughed to himself. But he simply wasn't able to provide all those things. So he had to convince her to get the help she needed, and he had to help her to find it. Whew. A tall order.

Cal pulled into the driveway, amazed at how eager he was to see her. Problems and all, she had touched something in him that he hadn't felt for a long time. It wasn't just a sexual thing, despite the fact that he thought she was sexy as hell, even wearing his so-becoming sweat suit. It was her sense of humor, her mannerisms, the way her eyes connected to him. It just made him feel good. Very good. But that was neither here nor there. She was married. And according to the world, she was dead. He had to find a way to help her to come back to life.

Cassandra stood from the couch when he entered the front door, and smiled shyly at him. Both cats were lounging on the couch with her. She had evidently been reading.

"Hi!" she said softly.

"Hi, yourself!"

"I wasn't sure when you'd get back." She had gone right to sleep when they had returned from the radio station after midnight, and he had already been gone when she woke up in the morning.

He sat on the couch, moving one disgruntled cat, and pulled her down next to him. The cat immediately jumped into her lap.

"I can see who these fickle beasts are warming up to," he said with a false frown. "Feed them for years, and they still turn on you when they get a chance."

She laughed. "Not these guys. These guys are just fine. The best." He rubbed the fur under the cat's throat. His purr could be heard across the room.

"Cassandra, Sandy.." Cal began, not quite knowing what to say.

But he had to talk. "I went to the memorial service today. At the church."

Her face paled, but she didn't say anything.

"It was nice." That seemed like a dumb comment, but he said it anyway.

"Did you see my boys?" she asked in a scratchy whisper. It was as though she didn't trust her voice to speak aloud.

He nodded. "They were all dressed up."

"Did they look ok?"

Cal stammered then, not quite knowing what to say. "I mean, they were dressed fine. But they looked really sad. Upset. But remember, they think you are dead, so of course they are upset."

"Frederick?"

"Dressed up, too. In control of himself. Charming before the TV cameras.."

"TV cameras?" she squawked.

"A TV crew was there. They spoke to Frederick after the service. Publicity, you know."

It made her sick to her stomach. God, would he love being a widower. "Tell me, honestly Cal. How did the boys look to you? How did they really look?"

He swallowed. "To me, not good, Cassandra. We can't play around with this. It's not fair for them to think you're dead, especially when he's so tough on them. It's just not safe."

Tears began to cascade down her cheeks. "What am I going to do?"

"If you'll let me, I'll ask a friend or two for advice. You know, legal and all. There's people I can trust with my life." He knew the words he said were true, because he DID trust them with his life. "Is it OK if I ask?"

"Yes," she whispered, stiff afraid. But she'd risk anything for her sons.

"Listen, Cassandra, I have a slightly embarrassing situation here. At 4PM today, some friends of mine are coming over, they come every week. I can't really call it off. But with you here...."

Her face turned red. "Please, I'm sorry I'm in the way." She stood up.

"For Christ's sake, lady, you're not in the way. It's just a little hard to explain until we know what to do." She could tell by his eyes that he was telling the truth and she felt a little more relaxed.

"Maybe I could stay upstairs? They wouldn't even have to know I was here."

He thought for a moment. "I guess that's ok for now. I have a portable TV I'll put up there for you. This sounds so dumb, but I don't want to upset anybody." He knew she didn't understand what he was talking about, but she was going along with it.

Cal could tell that her feelings were a little hurt as he moved the TV into her room a little before four, but they didn't talk about it any further. Actually, he felt like shit, as he headed downstairs when the doorbell rang for the first time. Maybe he should have just included her. But people might not like to be surprised, and he didn't want to tell any lies to this group. It meant too much.

But once people began to arrive, sitting casually in a circle around the living room, on couches, on windowsills, on the floor, his uncomfortable feelings faded, and he got into the business at hand.

Upstairs, Cassandra sat quietly in her room, trying not to listen to the activity and noise from downstairs. Cal had said "a few friends" but to tell the truth, she was sure an army had moved in since she had come upstairs. Out the window, she could see one side of the driveway, and it looked as if cars were lined the entire length. The doorbell rang incessantly for a few minutes, and peoples' voices drifted up to her. She could decipher no words, but could hear the "crowd". A party? There had been no food, no fuss. Cal had put on a pot of coffee, she knew, she had smelled it as it perked.

It got quiet suddenly, and the absence of noise made her nervous. Had they all left suddenly? What exactly was going on here? She tiptoed to the steps. What did she know about this man, anyway, she thought? Was he some kind of kook? A cultist? A religious nut? Her heart said no. But what was going on?

At the top of the stairs, she halted, trying to peer down to see if the room was vacant. She saw the backs of some heads, a few folded feet on the floor. There was a group in the living room, and they were all very quiet. She swallowed hard.

But then they spoke, together. Their voices were soft but forceful, full of meaning. "God, grant me the serenity to accept the things I cannot change, the courage to change the things I can, and the wisdom to know the difference."

Silence again, and then a lone voice spoke. "Hi, I'm Alan, and I'm an Alcoholic".

She tiptoed silently back to her room and shut the door behind her, a lot of things suddenly making sense. She was sorry that she had snooped. She would respect Cal's privacy and needs as he had respected hers, and be thankful for his friendship. It had nothing to do with her.

She turned the TV on low, and curled up on her bed to pass the time, not feeling resentful or neglected any more.

****

Most of the gang had left soon after the meeting was over. With the meeting held late in the afternoon, several of the AA members came from first shift jobs, or were on their way to evening jobs in restaurants, hospitals, or factories. A small core group hung around, finishing their coffee, and helping Cal to straighten up his living room.

Cal loved having a weekly meeting at his house. He attended several meetings a week, as he had for many years, many held in church basements, hospital meeting rooms or empty schools. But having his AA friends in his home was symbolic to him. It was an important part of his life, and it felt good to meet in the haven that was now his home.

Home hadn't always been a haven.

Years before, caught up in the whirl of success and pride and a never ending drive to achieve and shine, he had taken to alcohol like a moth to a flame. Having grown up in a home where his father believed that being propped up in front of the TV set, one six pack in hand and another ready in the fridge, was about as close to heaven as a man could get, Cal had imitated his dad and had begun a downward spiral with alcohol that had nearly ended his life.

First, in a high pressure college, competing for grades, he had used his booze on the weekend to "unwind" and to have fun. The next step was picking up the bottle to get himself going on Monday morning. A few drinks before a date made him much more fun to be with, hysterically funny and without inhibitions. And then there were the drinks to help him forget what he had done or said the night before. And the drinks to help him get to sleep. And so on. Successful in school, and then in his career, he had never run out of booze, and he had never run out of excuses or "reasons" to drink it.

Some alcoholics panic and reach their bottom when they begin to "black out", having periods of time where their memory had totally failed after drinking. They honestly didn't know where they had been or what they had done, often waking up in strange places or with strange people and absolutely no recollection of the process they took to get there.

But it hadn't been exactly like that with Cal. He had been a functioning drunk, for the most part, doing well at his job, accumulating wealth and fame in the circle in which he had lived. He had been in the hospital when his life had fallen apart, having suffered an attack of appendicitis. The emergency surgery had been difficult, complicated by his poor condition from all the alcohol, and an intelligent doctor had kept him in the hospital while he had dried out, feeling sick and having the DT's, and probably feeling the first feelings or pain he had felt since his downward spiral of drinking in college.

And he had felt horrible, for sure.

The door of the hospital room had opened, and two strange guys had entered, asking to talk to him. He had felt like an open, festering sore at the time, sick from coming off the alcohol, pain in his gut from the surgery, and pain in his heart from guilt and self disgust. The guys were George and Bob, and they were from a local group of Alcoholics Anonymous. The seeds they planted that day had fallen on fertile ground, so to speak. His new life had sprouted in those minutes, and he would never forget. Bob had become his sponsor, the person who had held his hand as he learned to live again, this time without booze, and had been his sponsor until he had died two years later.

When he had moved to Sollington to take the radio show a few years ago, he had found his AA groups before he had even found a place to live. First things first. His new sponsor, Craig, had been one of the first members he had contacted in the area.

He could live one day at a time without alcohol now, and he was thankful and humble about the change. The twelve steps of the program were an everyday part of his life. He went to his meetings without fail, and spent many an hour talking to newcomers who were struggling with the effects of alcohol in their lives. It was always worth it. The AA program had taught him many things, not the least of which was the fact that you have to share what you have with newcomers. He remembered where he had been, and he simply did not want to go back there.

He loved his home now, it was a place to think and relax and be happy, rather than a hiding place to hole up in while pickled in booze.

But at the moment, he was feeling a bit of turmoil, with Cassandra waiting upstairs, unknown to his friends. He needed to explain her to them, and then explain them to her...and with his promise to keep her identity secret, and his pledge of anonymity to the group, he was in a bind.

He cornered Marv, a longtime friend who he knew was a cop. After years of friendship within meetings, most of the members had extended their friendships in the outside world, too, and shared many aspects of life together. He needed to know what was legal and what was not with Cassandra, so she didn't cause herself any more ugliness than she had to face. Everyone else had left, except his friend Janie, who was sitting on the back porch, petting the cats, and Marv.

Marv was standing in the kitchen, drying cups.

"Marv, I have a problem. You have time for some advice?"

"Shoot."

"I have a...friend. She doesn't want someone to find her. Is there a law about using another name instead of your legal one?"

"Depends." Marv had turned to look him full in the face, looking curiously at his friend. "What kind of a girl are you getting messed up with, Calvin?" He said softly. "AA?"

"No, this one doesn't even drink. It's something different. What does it depend on?"

"The court would basically say "intent". Is she trying to make money or sign contracts in an illegal way? Is she trying to commit a crime? Is she avoiding prosecution or questioning by the law? It's a grey area. There are people who change their names all the time. For marriage, divorce, career reasons. It's a simple legal procedure." He watched Cal's eyes. "But I have a feeling that that's not what we're talking about, is it?"

Cal shook his head, his eyes not breaking contact. "She's afraid of someone. Very afraid. She has her reasons."

"Cal, my friend, that's what the law is for. She's better off facing the issue and getting rid of the problem. If someone's threatening her, there are steps she can take."

"You know the system as well as I do, Marv. When threats are innuendos and vague, when past abuse can't be documented, and the victim has no money or connections, the wheels of justice can really get a kink in them. "

Marv was silent, wanting to disagree, but knowing what his friend said was true.

"Just how special is she to you, man?" Marv asked quietly, suddenly afraid of the intensity in Cal's eyes. Cal had never, in all the time he'd known him, gotten more involved with any woman other than a casual and short time friendship. And it sounded like she was trouble.

"I just met her. Weird circumstances. But Marv, there's something about her. She's special to me. Or maybe it's just that she could be. I can't define it. She just hit me like a ton of bricks."

"Can I meet her?"

"I hope so. She really has to find a way out of the mess she's in, and I don't know where to start. It's kind of complicated. But I'm going to ask her to talk to you. She's upstairs."

"Upstairs?" Marvin croaked. "You are hiding a woman upstairs? Here?"

Cal took a deep sigh, ready to begin what would probably prove to be a lengthy explanation of Cassandra's existence in his house. He was cut off, though, by a sudden noise from upstairs, an anguished, heartfelt scream.

"Oh, God, NOOO!"

Cal leaped up the steps, two at a time, Marvin at his heels, Janie bounding in the door, following.

Cal rushed into Cassandra's room to find her collapsed into a heap on the floor, passed out cold. The little TV was playing on the dresser where he had placed it. On the screen, a colorfully dressed newsman was cheerfully giving the weather forecast.

"Sandy!" gasped Cal, kneeling beside her and placing her head gently in his lap. Janie had run to the bathroom, no questions asked, and he could hear the water running. She tossed a cold wet towel at Cal, and he softly stroked her face. Marv stood behind him, upset for his friend and his obvious concern, and worried for the woman on the floor, whose face was blocked from view by Cal's back. Was she sick?

What exactly had Cal gotten himself into here? He looked around the cheerful little room. There had been many a night when he and Cal had sat up with an alcoholic friend, either easing them out of a binge or listening to their plight as they tried to reenter the world sober, then putting them to sleep in this room. Cal's house was really like a "safe house" for so many, and Cal had always opened his home, and his heart to AA friends who had a problem. But this was different. Cal felt differently about this woman, and Marv could tell it right away. Who was this woman, and what was going on here?

Her breathing was uneven, shallow at first, then punctuated with little gasps, like cries. "Sandy," Cal said again, "It'll be all right. It'll be all right." His voice was soft and soothing, and within seconds, she began to move a bit. "Cal," she said softly.

"What happened? What happened?" he asked.

"The TV, Cal. I saw them on the news. He hit the boys, Cal. I can tell. They showed the funeral, and a shot of Frederick and Duncan and Peter. Peter has a black eye! A black eye! I've got to find a way to save them..."

She sobbed then, and Cal held her tight to his chest, filled with anger.

Marvin Greenstein stared. He felt his head began to swim a bit, almost like an out of body experience as he stood in the small room.

Feelings gripped him as they had two nights before when he had stood on the bank of a black and cruel river, a river that he thought had claimed the life of the woman whose picture had touched him so. He moved his hand, as if in a dream, and touched Cal's shoulder.

Cal pulled Cassandra gently to a sitting position, and turned to Marvin. Marv felt like he had a lump in his throat as he looked down into the already familiar face before him. Her hair was straight and pulled back into a rubber band, and the clothes she wore did not even resemble the silk and suede he knew she had worn when she had been in the car, but the eyes were the same, soft and green and haunted. He was looking into the face of the supposedly dead Cassandra Ellington.

Chapter 23

Marvin Greenstein probably should have been stunned that she was alive. He had been at the scene of the accident, he had seen the smashed car lifted clumsily out of the river. He had filed his reports saying that there was no indication that Cassandra Ellington could have lived through the impact. But here she was. Alive and basically well. He could see partly healed scratches on her face, he could see her arm was in a sling. She was upset, she was dressed like a bum (in fact, she was dressed just like Cal), but she was alive.

The thing that stunned him the most was his reaction to that fact. His heart swelled with thanks and happiness at the sight of her, looking fragile and upset in Cal's arms, but breathing and whole. The funny thing was, he had had a strange feeling in his gut the whole time, just not accepting the evidence that had seemed undeniable. But his cop's mind had honed in on "why" she had died, instead of "if" she had died.

His face probably showed recognition, but of course, she had never seen him in her life. So this was the lady who had turned Cal's life around, the mystery lady who was using a false name. Did Cal know who she was? His mind had registered the fact that Cal had called her Sandy. He decided to do the same, for the moment.

"Are you ok, Sandy?" he asked quietly.

She nodded, looking terrified when she saw that there was someone in the room besides Cal. Then he saw guilt flash across her face.

"I'm sorry, Cal," she stammered. "I didn't mean to interrupt your group. I was really trying to be quiet. But seeing Peter with a black eye on TV..."

Cal met Marv's eyes over her head, and their eyes locked, Cal transmitting the fears that he had alluded to downstairs when he was trying to explain her presence. Cal had no idea that Marv Greenstein had been the cop on the case, and that he knew the true identity of the woman in his arms.

But Marv's cop mind had started turning when the facts had started to fly at him, and he was beginning to figure things out. He had, perhaps, been more on the right track in his investigation that it seemed. There was something wrong with Frederick Ellington. He had gone to the Ellington funeral in the morning. He had arrived just when it had begun, and had been quick to make an exit at the end. He had not seen anything but the backs of the Ellington man or his sons, and he had evidently left before the media had arrived.

But if Cassandra Ellington said that her son had a black eye, and she was hiding in fear of her life, it didn't take a genius to deduct that the creep was abusive. It didn't take a genius to know that this little woman had a big problem on her hands, and needed help. Had Ellington tried to kill her? Or had she tried to stage a disappearance to escape him? She had obviously been injured, but had it been at Frederick's hand, or had she actually miraculously survived the accident? He had a lot of questions to ask, but he knew that first, he had to win her trust, and make sure she was all right.

"Sandy," Cal said, "This is my friend Marv. He's a cop." He hugged her reassuringly as the fear flashed in her eyes. "He's ok, Sandy. I'm hoping he can give us some advice."

He turned and saw Janie standing in the door. "And this is Janie, another good friend. You can trust her, too."

Cassandra looked down, scared. Panic flashed in her eyes.

"Sandy, I trust these people with my life. You can trust them with yours."

She looked up then, into the face of the dark haired cop, with intelligent but compassionate eyes. He wore a striped dress shirt, opened at the collar, and a crisp pair of jeans. He smiled a crooked smile, and Cassandra smiled back.

"I don't know who you are, lady," piped up Janie, "But any friend of Cal's is a friend of mine. How about we get this girl all the way off the floor?"

Her open cheerfulness broke the tension, and Cal helped her to her feet. "Let's go downstairs." Cal stated. "I could use a drink."

Everyone stopped dead and looked at him.

"Coffee, clowns.   Just coffee." he said in a Groucho Marx voice.

When Cassandra was seated on the couch, feet pulled up under her, and coffee had been served all around, they all sat and stared at each other, not knowing where to begin.

Cassandra broke the ice. "I think I'm just going to be honest here, Cal, if that's all right. Seeing Peter on TV has me crazy, and I feel like there is no time to lose. I think Frederick's gone over the edge. I have to do something, anything, to end this. No matter what happens to me."

"Go for it, lady," said Cal with a gentle smile. He admired her courage, because he could sense how terrified she was.

"My name is not really Sandy. That's kind of a nickname my sister used to call me. My real name is Cassandra. Cassandra Ellington." Marv Greenstein didn't blink an eye. Janie looked shocked.

"The woman who went over the cliff. I saw it on the news. But you're supposed to be dead!" she said, her red curls bouncing unmercifully as she shook her head. "Far out!"

Cassandra turned to Marv, who still didn't say a word. He was just watching her. She started to feel the panic return, but when she looked into his eyes she saw understanding there.

She took a deep breath.

"You knew who I was, didn't you?"

He still didn't say a word, instead, he reached into the breast pocket of his shirt, and flipped something out, placing it on the coffee table in front of her. It was her license.

She swallowed hard. "Are you going to turn me in?"

"Have you committed a crime?"

"I pretended I was dead when I wasn't."

"Why?"

Her eyes showed anguish, and he instantly wanted to comfort her. But he knew he had to let her grapple with the truth.

When she didn't answer, he asked another question.

"Did you plan this whole thing?"

"Not exactly."

He rolled his eyes and looked at Cal. "You want to help me here, buddy?"

"Go ahead, Cassandra, tell him the whole story."

The dam burst then. She told him about her life, her fears, he thwarted attempts to get help, and the depression that followed. She told him about the unfounded but paralyzing guilt she had carried that her behavior was causing her boys to get worse treatment. She confessed being fearful of Frederick's escalating violence, verbally and physically, and how she had finally taken herself to the emergency room at the hospital to get medical help and to turn him in.

She told about her shock in finding out that Frederick had laid the groundwork for the staff to suspect that she suffered from severe alcohol abuse, that her judgment was faulty and clouded, and that he had been planning court ordered hospitalization for her. She explained her confusion, her feeling of betrayal, and her worry about her boys. She spoke about how she loved them, and how she had decided in her panic, however unwisely, that they would be better off without her, and how she had felt that she herself was the cause of Frederick's unpredictable behavior.

They all listened without a word. She told about the momentary desperate desire to drive over the cliff to end it all, and then she stopped speaking, her voice breaking.

"So what did you do?" asked Janie spontaneously, unable to control herself.

Cassandra smile. "I turned on the radio."

"You what?"

"I turned on the radio. I guess it was a kind of symbolic gesture, a way to say goodbye to my sons, who are always listening to the radio. I heard Your Pal Cal."

Cassandra smiled the first genuine smile they had seen from her, and it lit up the room. "He said such supportive and understanding things to kids, and then suddenly, it was my son Duncan on the call in line, saying how he wanted to give up...Cal told him he couldn't, and I felt that he was speaking to me, too." The smile had disappeared.

She was crying now, and Cal handed her a handkerchief. "So all of a sudden, instead of being scared or worried or guilty about upsetting Frederick, I was MAD for the first time. I mean really mad. That was the end of trying give up on my life. But when I tried to get out of the car, my seat belt was jammed, and the car started going over the cliff."

"Holy shit!" whispered Janie.

"I just leaped with all my might. I pulled and I leaped. My skirt ripped. The next thing I knew, I was on a little ledge a few feet down that broke my fall, and the car was plummeting onto the rocks and into the river with a bang. It was horrible. Terrifying."

"She wandered to my house in the dark, and climbed into my basement. When I found her, I didn't know who she was. The next day, she found out everyone thought she was dead."

"Marv, there's something about this Frederick guy, something about how he can get to people and get what he wants. You know how hard it is to get a court order to get someone hospitalized against their will for alcoholism, even when there is every indication that they can not even function? Well, this guy got it done...court order and all, and Cassandra doesn't even drink."

Marv's eyes narrowed, and he looked at her for a full minute. He knew enough about alcohol to know about denial. More than not, drunks denied their drinking until they hit bottom. "You don't drink, Cassandra?"

"I swear to you. I don't drink."

For some crazy reason, he believed her. He believed her whole crazy story. And he also believed that Frederick Ellington would be a formidable opponent.

"So why did he want to get you committed? Why did he want to get you out of the way? What would he gain?" His cop mind was working overtime.

"You believe me?" Her voice sighed in relief.

"Amazing, but I do. Again, what would he gain? He could have just divorced you." They sat and discussed far fetched theories, but they couldn't come up with any motive that would justify the lengths he had gone to control his wife.

"Why don't you just reappear, and file abuse charges against him? I'd enjoy taking the sucker out." Marv's jaw was set, determination showing.

"No," she cried, "I just can't risk it. Even in two days' time, I have a twelve year old son with a black eye. He'll never willingly let go of the boys, and I can't bear to think of what he'll do to them if he thinks I'm fighting him for control. He's connected to too many people. He knows doctors, judges, lawyers, and they all do what he says. I have no proof. It would take too long to fight for the boys. I have to find a way around him."

"What can we do here, man?" asked Cal quietly. He knew Marv's quick mind, and he was counting on him.

"Well, for starters, we have to find out more about Frederick. I want to investigate the hospitalization he had planned. I want to find out what he would gain with Cassandra out of the way. Do you have any assets, or money that you own separately from him? Do you have any life insurance?"

"I've had to beg Frederick for every penny I've ever had my hands on. He would shower me with things, clothes, cars, furniture, when he thought I was being "good". And deprive me when he didn't like my attitude. I had to account for every penny I spent for running the household, I don't have a dime to my name. I guess he liked it that way. It gave him a feeling of control. Once, when my sister was visiting, years ago, I opened a joint account with her, she was so determined that I should have more independence. But when Frederick found out about it, he had a fit, and that was the end of that. He sent my sister away.

To be honest with you, I'm sure it never crossed his mind to insure my life. I don't think my life was worth much to him." She started crying gently again, and Janie bounded over and sat by her.

Cal felt like he had fire in his gut, he was so angry at Frederick Ellington, III.

Marv ran a hand through his hair. His stomach, too, was in an uproar, but for a very different reason. The words he had heard, and the pain in the voice that had shared the story had sliced him like a knife, right to the core. He knew he had to help this woman, he knew this challenge had been presented to him for a reason.

"Give me a day or two to come up with some information. Keep a low profile, and we'll find a way to take care of those kids."

He left quickly, leaving behind a group of anxious, but hopeful friends, including his new one, Cassandra Ellington. He was simply glad she was alive.

****

Marv pulled away from Cal's house with his adrenalin flowing. Cassandra Ellington was alive. And Cassandra Ellington needed help. He whipped into his apartment complex, jumped in the shower, and pulled on his clothes for work. He was scheduled to work on the 11PM to 7AM shift, but he had a lot to do, so he was going in early.

In his bedroom, he paused for a second and looked at the picture that sat on his bedside, the only knick knack in an otherwise undecorated room. A pair of dark eyes, straight dark hair looked back at him from the frame. He swallowed hard, amazed at the way things worked out. Then he said a short prayer.

In his early life, he had never been a religious man. He had been born Jewish by nationality, but had been taught very few of the traditions or customs, and had had practically no religious training whatsoever. With him and his dad, the issue had been getting enough to eat to get by, not worrying over whether the food was Kosher or not.

But as of today, he had learned to pray a lot. The AA program had taught him that. He still knew little or nothing about Judaism, and that didn't really matter anymore, though he thought maybe someday he would find the time to study a bit, just to know. But the spirituality he had found had nothing to do with rules and customs, and the God he knew didn't wear a yarmulke or jiggle rosary beads. He was just God, a higher power, and the things he could do could be mind boggling at best.

He said a prayer of thanks, and asked God to watch over him, and to watch over Cassandra Ellington. Then he looked at the picture again, and asked God to watch over Marcia Greenstein, where ever her spirit may be.

"OK, Marcia," he said to the picture on the table, "This one's for you, lady." Then he was off to the precinct, where he was going to find some way to help Cassandra Ellington, and to put a stop to the diabolical abuser who was her husband.

Marvin Greenstein had been born to a youngish couple 45 years before. His mom had died when he was a baby, leaving his father, a tailor, in the bottle, and Marvin with practically no memories of her whatsoever. His early life had been a hectic one, with his dad alternately working his ass off, or drowning himself in the bottle. Dr. Jekyll and Mr. Hyde personified. But Marv, with a philosophical look at life, had kind of just rattled on, accepting the insanity in which they lived as normal, and becoming a master at dodging his father's angry fists when he was drunk.

He had graduated high school, and had entered the police academy, though at the moment, he didn't realize exactly why. He had already started experimenting with alcohol and found that it dulled the pain and depression that living with his dad seemed to automatically provide.

But by the time he had become a cop, his father died, because of problems with his liver and a bad bout of pneumonia. For the first time Marv was on his own. He had pretty much always provided for himself anyway, so that was no big deal. He was working for the city of Philadelphia as a cop with a good salary. He was one of the only "Jewish boys" in a sea of cops, mostly Irish, Italian, Polish, or black. He was pretty tough, and he got along fine. But since he was "on his own", and didn't have to deal with the ups and downs of his father, he didn't really have a need to keep dulling his life with drink. But he didn't stop. Today he knew he couldn't stop. But he used to pretend it was an option.

He met Marcia one night down by Penn's Landing, the wharf area by the Delaware River, where gentrified clubs and restaurants were a favorite "hang out" place for the upwardly mobile young in the area. He was 22 at the time. He got his first promotion, had been taking sporadic college courses at the community college, and generally was feeling pretty darn good about himself.

Marcia caught his eye. She wasn't beautiful, but somehow Marv found her striking, and decided to pursue her after they met over drinks one night. He had been on his best behavior for months, and wooed both her and her parents to the best of his ability. They were married six months later.

They moved into their first apartment about the same time that Marv had moved to the Homicide Department. Marcia was quiet, and worked as a clerk for the city. He remembered those early days with a fond heart. Even though he had been a bit of a jerk, to be honest, it had been a pretty good time.

But working Homicide in the city had taken its toll on him. It was hard to see the victims of gunshot wounds, often teen aged kids, and then come home and care about the meat loaf recipe. It was hard to run around trying to ID a homeless man who had been killed by a hit and run, and then come home and discuss draperies.

But no matter what the difficulty, what evolved hadn't been Marcia's fault. He took the blame: hook, line and sinker.

He got into the booze, heavy time. He would come home, anxious and tired, and down a six pack while waiting for dinner. And then, with the first provocation, question, or complaint, he would "turn into his father" and start on Marcia. At first, it was with cruel words and insults, later it was with his fists. It made him sick to his stomach, but he had to face the facts. He made himself face it every day. In his drunken rages, he had violently abused his wife.

He would wake up the next morning, after each episode, fuzzy on what had happened, but feeling overwhelming remorse. It felt so bad, he had to have a drink to deal with it. And so on and so on. It went on for two years.

And then one day he came home, and Marcia hadn't one single complaint or question. She didn't say a word. That was because she was gone. Cleared out. She had left him. Looking back on it now, it was the only choice she had, but at the time he had felt betrayed and abandoned, and he had needed a drink. Then another. You get the picture.

The divorce had been quiet, handled mostly by her father. Now he realized he was lucky they had never pressed charges. Now he realized it was a miracle that his bout of drinking had not openly affected his career as a cop. He had been in the booze for a whole year after that, his mantra had been "Poor me, Poor me, Pour me a drink", to be sure. It amazed him how he couldn't see the forest for the trees, but alcohol is like that, it kind of puts a hazy glow on things, and you just don't see right.

But then one day, he reached his bottom. He went on a case where a child had died, a little scrawny black boy of about six or seven. His name was Lucas, he remembered that. Lucas' father had boldly and brazenly beaten the kid to death with a baseball bat. Seemed that the darn kid hadn't finished his chicken. Shouldn't waste food.

So he whacked the kid, and a neighbor, hearing the noise, had called the cops.

Marvin had arrived. He was still in uniform then, and a black police woman named Claire was his partner. They had entered the apartment, guns drawn, not knowing what they would find. But they didn't find bullets. They found a chubby black guy, shiny face and shiny head, seated at a wobbly table, calmly eating the remains of a chicken dinner, and guzzling a bottle of cheap red wine. At his feet was a dead and bloody child, and a blood soaked baseball bat.

"Just a minute, guys," the man said affably, wiping his mouth on his sleeve. "Shouldn't waste good food."

It was Claire who pulled him through that one. She kept her eye on the guy while Marv had run to the bathroom and lost his lunch in a grungy toilet.

They called an ambulance, even though it was much too late, took the guy in, booked him, and the system took over. Marvin Greenstein's life had never been the same. He could see his potential self in that disgusting man, that poor excuse for a human being. He had never taken a drink again.

That long ago night, sitting in a greasy spoon and desperately wondering how he could change his life, he struck up a conversation with an elderly gentleman from his neighborhood. The man's name was Oliver, he had been 77 years old. With the wisdom of Solomon, he had introduced Marv to the principles of AA. It was the support and love and safety net he had been yearning for, and it changed his life forever.

As he learned about the AA program, he had to make a list of people he had harmed in his drinking...and then try to do something to make it up to the people on his list. They called it making amends. He had listed and taken care of nearly everybody on his list, like the partners he had risked by senses dulled by alcohol, landlords and creditors he had stiffed along the way, things like that. But the biggest name on the list, and the one he left for last was Marcia.

He owed a big giant amends to Marcia. At first, it was hard to track her. Her parents had evidently moved several times in the past year. He thought that was strange, but he kept pursuing. He finally found them when they moved to a little neighborhood in West Philadelphia, getting help from a friend in the electric company, who alerted him when the name cropped up to connect service. He had gone quietly to their house, positive that he would now find Marcia, and willing to do whatever it would take to make his amends to the girl he had hurt.

But he hadn't been able to make the amends. Her mother wouldn't talk to him. Her father, face now with a grayish tinge that comes from a broken heart, curtly informed him that Marcia was dead. Dead. After leaving Marv and moving home, she had gone on a whirl of activity and craziness. Wild friends, wild cars, and maybe drugs. Marcia, the calm and striking Jewish girl had been in a bright blue Corvette that had wrapped itself around a tree going about 80 miles per hour. She, and the driver, had been instantly killed. And he hadn't even known.

There wasn't much more to say that day. Marv left the little stone house with a heavy heart. What kind of pain had Marcia been trying to dull, to forget, in her wild quest for fun and excitement? How much was he to blame with the events that ended a young and valuable life? He hadn't used a baseball bat, but he had killed her spirit, as much as that crazy father had killed Lucas.

He had driven away with a solemn promise in his heart, praying hard to the God he had just been beginning to know. Someday, somewhere, he would get the opportunity to help someone, in Marcia's name. Since he couldn't help her, he would make his amends through someone else, no matter what the price, no matter what the risk.

He remembered the wave of emotion he felt two nights before when he looked at the license picture of Cassandra Ellington on the river's cliff. He hadn't known what it meant at the time, that rush of feelings. But it had been God talking to him, to be sure. This was it. Cassandra Ellington had a friend here, and he was going to make his amends.

"This one's for you, Marcia," he said aloud as he parked his car in the station lot. He had a lot to do.

Chapter 24

Frederick Ellington III had come home from the funeral in a pretty good mood. Jenkins had whispered to him, right before the service at the church, that there had been no difficulties or snags with the phony power of attorney and forged letter he had presented. No one seemed to question that Frederick was to be the one to represent her in all her affairs.

Next to an actual death certificate, this was the next best thing. He and the boys returned to the house, which was filled with concerned neighbors and members of the church. Casseroles had been warmed in the oven, and the many smells of baked goods permeated the air. Mrs. Briggs, from next door presided over the kitchen while people paid their respects.

The boys looked sad and withdrawn, and accepted people's condolences with a heavy heart. At the first quiet opportunity, they slipped away to Duncan's room together, lying on his bed in identical positions, feet stretched out, and hands folded behind their heads. In the background, the radio played with sounds of WDRK, volume low, so as not to attract attention. They didn't even talk to each other, but stayed together, needing the warmth and comfort of each other's presence.

Frederick spent the afternoon solemnly nodding his head and agreeing with the many comments about the tragedy and Cassandra's death. He couldn't wait until it was over.

"She was a beautiful woman," he would state softly, bringing tears to bystander's eyes. "Life will not be the same without her." It was a long afternoon for him.

Later, at his request, Mrs. Briggs began suggesting that the visitors take their leave, to allow the family to rest and spend quiet time together. She assisted with the mess left behind, reorganizing the food and putting leftovers in the refrigerator. Duncan had stated he didn't want to eat, but Peter had come out to get some food, staying to help the kindly neighbor as she put things back into order in the house.

"Your dad says that it's OK for me to leave you guys this evening. You sure you're OK?"

Peter nodded. Emily Briggs hadn't really known the Ellington boys, but she had seen them come and go in the neighborhood since they had moved in a few years before. Cassandra had more or less kept to herself, but had always been kind and friendly, saying hello here and there when their paths had crossed. Frederick, she had barely known.

But in the past few days, watching out for the boys at this terrible time for them, she had grown very fond of them, especially Peter. Her eyes actually got misty as she watched him wrap the remains of a cheesecake in cellophane, with a methodical, almost mathematical precision, he did the job well. He was a nice boy, as was his older brother, and she was really, really sad for them. She supposed their father was just caught up in his own grief, trying to handle his life and the details necessary, just too busy to pay much attention to his sons. Or to worry about how they felt. Hopefully, she sighed to herself, that would come in time.

The kitchen in order, she gave Peter a hug and hurried next door to her own husband who would be patiently waiting for his dinner. In her hands, she carried a still warm casserole, that Peter had suggested, and then insisted that she take to share with Mr. Briggs. Such a nice boy. Such a smart boy.

Mrs. Briggs made him promise he would call if he needed her, and then she was gone.

Peter stood in the living room, turning around slowly in a circle, as if looking at the room for the first time. Not a thing was out of sight. The furniture gleamed, no dust, no clutter. He couldn't help the tear that escaped his twelve year old eye and ran in a path down his freckled cheek. The room was ugly. It was empty. He missed his mother with a fierceness that flowed from the top of his head to the tip of his toes.

His father had excused himself earlier, when the last of the guests had gone, and had gone to his room. Duncan had fallen asleep on the bed. Peter felt very alone.

He went back into the kitchen, contemplating the cheesecake that he knew was sitting in the fridge. The telephone was on the counter, sitting in its cradle, black and sleek. It possessed the ability to program the telephone numbers for 10 frequently called people, automatic redial, and a little golden light that lit to warn when the line was in use from another extension. The light was lit. Duncan was asleep, and so Peter knew his father was on the phone.

Silently, with the skill of a surgeon, he pressed the mute button, and rendered the mouthpiece silent. When he turned on the phone, there would be no warning or indication that someone was listening in on the call.

He heard his father's voice right away.

"What a boring load of crap that was. Neighbors drooling and whining all day. People are amazing, you know that?"

Peter felt nausea building up in him, anger and all the hate a twelve year old could muster for the man who was his father. He had lost his mother, the only person who had ever really loved or understood him, and his father was making fun of it. Staring blankly at the phone in front of him, he absently noticed the little answering machine sitting on the counter next to it. On the machine was a small black button that said "Call Recording". He pushed it, and the tape in the machine began to silently turn.

He recognized the next voice as James Jenkins, his father's lawyer friend.

"Maybe people are just being nice, Frederick. Don't be such a shit. It's a shame about Cassandra, really."

"Of course it's a shame.   Look at all the aggravation it caused.   It's too bad about the death certificate delay, but I'll get that bastard judge back yet, when all this is said and done.   But the power of attorney is going to work, isn't it?   No chance for a snag with this, right?"

"The letter and form seemed to work like a charm. Not even a question.   You're an artist, Frederick, I have to hand it to you."

"The closing on the land deal is next Tuesday," his father said. "Nothing can go wrong. I won't let it. I heard from our "friends" today, and they were more than nervous about the deal coming off. They are very worried about their investment.   I told them things were OK.   They assumed I got a death certificate, and I didn't tell them otherwise."

"You didn't tell them about the power of attorney?"

"They're not mental giants, Jenkins. They're overgrown hoods. Organized crime. I didn't bother with the details. We'll keep a low profile from now on."

"Low profile?   What was that little bit with the press at the church today? Calling in the TV news doesn't smack of low profile to me.   What are you up to, Ellington?"

"Keep your shirt on, Perry Mason. Do you know a better way to transmit a message to our dear little "friends" who are worried about a screw up? A funeral is final. It means it's over. They see her dead and buried, and they won't be worried about me handling the estate.   It all looks very above board.   They don't know we can't get a death certificate."

"You're an ass, Ellington. They know. You should have turned on the 5PM news a few minutes ago. Nice shot of you and the boys, and of your caring words to the press. Nice touch. Very final. But after you walked away and got into the car, the little jerk of a newsman looks at the camera and says, let me quote, "Even though both family and authorities know that it was inevitable that Cassandra Ellington perished in the river road crash, since her body has not been found, the courts have not officially issued a death certificate. In a case like this, it can be quite a while before legalities settle down, but meanwhile, the Ellington family, surrounded by the comfort of many friends, must go on with their lives. This is Charles Upworth ANC, TV news."

For once, Frederick Ellington was silent.

"You still there, Frederick?"

"Shit. What's the matter with that little bastard newsman and his interfering tag lines? Who does he think he is, Barbara Walters? Why can't he just report the damn news and stop his infernal editorializing? I'm screwed on this one."

"You can say that again."

"We have to find a way to tell them about the power of attorney now. If they think I'm playing games with them. I wish there was a way we could contact them."

"Can't be done." Jenkins said. "You have to wait for them to contact us. That's the way they do it."

"Shit."

"Chances are, you'll hear from them pretty quick," Jenkins said. "But it won't be a social call. You'd better be ready for some fast talking."

"Fast talking is my strong suit, Jenkins." Frederick sounded full of bravado, but the truth was, he was sweating.

His father hung up the phone, and Peter quickly returned the phone to the cradle. He stopped the tape, and flicked it out of the machine, replacing it with a new tape from the counter drawer. He marked it with the date and time, and slipped it into his pocket.

"Wait until Duncan gets a load of this," he thought, his emotions running wild. He slipped down the hall to his room, and hid the tape under the mattress of his bed. He had no idea at all what was going on, but he knew his dad was up to no good. He wished fervently that he had someone to help him.

****

By the time evening came, Cassandra was exhausted. Janie had stayed, and they had a quick dinner of tuna sandwiches and soda. When Cal had to leave for his radio show, Cassandra decided to stay home and rest, promising to be part of his "radio audience" while he was on the air. Janie volunteered to stay and keep her company for a while, and the two put the dishes away, before taking up residence on the back deck, overlooking the river.

They put the radio on the railing, tuned in to WDRK, where the last few minutes of the afternoon show were playing. The air had a bit of a chill. The sun was beginning to sink in the sky, but they still had some daylight left.

The river looked beautiful from where they sat, and for a while the two women were quiet.

Janie was a spunky, humorous young woman, in her late 20's, with bright red hair and a mass of freckles on her face. Her eyes were large and brown, and she had a look about her of someone who had seen a lot, and could still laugh about life. Cassandra felt herself drawn to her friendliness.

"You know," Janie stated thoughtfully, staring out at the river, "I thought I had heard a lot of crazy stories in

AA, but I have to admit, yours is a doozie. You sure you're not a drunk?"

Cassandra's laugh came bubbling up naturally, and it made Janie smile.

"I don't drink, Janie. I have a lot of other problems, but that is one that I don't have. But that doesn't mean that I think any less of you and Cal and the others in AA. I just don't drink myself."

"Thanks for that. Sometimes people are skittish, when they think you have a drinking problem. They're sure you're going to start slurring your words, or seeing pink elephants, or doing some other bizarre thing." She changed the subject abruptly. "What do you think of Cal?"

Cassandra smiled. "What's to think of Cal? He's great. He's been a lifesaver for me, that's for sure. I can't believe I crawled in his window, but there you go. I did. Actually, I can't believe a lot of what's happened to me lately."

They talked for a while as the sun went down, the radio playing softly beside them. They paused to listen to Cal and Paul as they went through their nightly antics. On this show, they were zeroing in on country music. Paul was for it, Cal against. Which Cassandra knew was funny, because she had seen the whole rack of tapes that Cal had in the living room, and country music was definitely one of his likes.

It made the show lively, though, with their adversarial comments, and the wild country songs they played in between bouts of rock and roll and mind deafening rap.

As the two women talked together, Cassandra learned of Janie's early life, a tough childhood followed by wild teenaged years filled with alcohol, drugs and bad relationships. She had been in recovery for six long years, and was now married to a calm and gentle plumber, Bernie, who made her feel like a million bucks even though they didn't have two cents to rub together.

Janie did clerical work with a local real estate title insurance company several days a week, and worked part time in a small hair salon to make some extra money. She and Bernie had no children yet, but they were hopeful that they would begin a family soon. She was honest and open and funny, and Cassandra liked her a lot. Cassandra talked a lot about her life, too, about the years of tyranny with Frederick, so obvious to her now, but so paralyzing when she had been immersed in them. Janie understood, and it felt really good.

"It's not just where you've been, Cassandra, that makes you the person you are. It's what you learned from it. That's what I've learned from life. I don't look at my past drinking as a horrible experience any more, but as one I can share with someone else, and maybe they will see their way a little clearer from seeing my mistakes. You have a good life ahead of you," she commented quietly as the sun began to dip below the horizon. "You just have to believe that things can be better."

About three hours into Cal's show, the women left the now dark deck and moved to the living room. After a few more life stories, including Cassandra explaining the last violent episode she had had with Frederick, about getting her hair cut, Janie disappeared into the bathroom and came out with a pair of scissors and a comb.

"Wanna go for it, Lady? That was just a trim. We could REALLY change that hair," she teased, snipping the air with the scissors.

Cassandra looked at her in open amazement, as the thought settled over her. Then she grinned widely. "I'm game if you are!"

A few minutes later, years of hair growth decorated the floor in Cal's kitchen, and Cassandra was sporting a short, carefree hair style, the soft wisps framing her face gently. She looked with absolute amazement at herself in the mirror, excited and delighted with Janie's work. She jumped up and danced around the room.

"I can't believe it's me!" she exclaimed to Janie's continuing laughter. Cassandra's enthusiasm and childish excitement was contagious and fun. She would bring out the smiles in the biggest grouch around, Janie decided.

"The hair looks great, toots," Janie giggled, "But the clothes have to go. I'll be over tomorrow with some jeans and things. We're about the right size, at least closer than Cal is."

Cassandra felt a surge of hope. Janie left a short time later to go home to Bernie, and Cassandra felt like she had made a good friend. She fell asleep curled up in a chair, listening to Your Pal Cal and his wild friend Paul on the radio.

When Cal let himself in the door well after midnight, he found her there, sleeping peacefully, her short hair glowing in the lamplight, her face relaxed and contented for once. He couldn't resist placing a soft kiss on the top of her head, before he woke her up.

****

Frederick said a quick goodnight to his boys, who had been holed up in Duncan's room for most of the afternoon and evening, listening to that infernal radio. The radio business was going to come to an end, that was for sure, but tonight he was just too tired to make and enforce new rules in the house.

But new rules there would be. He wasn't going to have any more of this simpering or goofy behavior in his boys. They were totally in his control now, and couldn't go run and hide behind their mother's skirts.

Damn Cassandra anyway. Why did she have to go and pull a stunt like this? Why did she have to mess everything up by dying? If she had only realized that he knew what was best for them. For all of them... she wouldn't have gotten all riled up and gone over the cliff. Women were stupid, that was for sure.

He went to his room, took a shower and got ready for bed. He had a headache, thinking about what he was going to say to those creepy loan guerrillas when they realized he hadn't succeeded in having Cassandra declared dead. And that was the damn judge's fault. He and his high and mighty principles. He'd bring him down sooner or later, and enjoy doing it. But for now, he had to be able to convince the goons that the power of attorney was registered and sufficient, and that the closing could go on without a snag on schedule.

God, he wished he hadn't gotten involved with those guys. Frederick rubbed his temples, trying to release the pressure he felt in his head. But he had trouble putting together the last bundle of money for the land purchase. He had counted on money from a book advance that he hadn't gotten, and so he had run short. And the last parcel of land was the most important. The owner had held out and held out until the last minute. But then he had been ready to deal on Frederick's terms.

He snickered. Funny what a little scandal about a college age daughter could do to a man. Suddenly he was able and willing to sell his farm for a bargain price. And, of course, the negatives to a few well focused pictures.

But he had still been a hundred grand short for the deal, and so the loan had looked good at the time. Short term deal, and he could afford to give the grease balls a nice return on their money. All had been well until Cassandra's accident. Now they were as nervous as little old ladies. But rumor had it that they played very rough when they were nervous. He wasn't looking forward to seeing that.

He got into bed and planned what he would say to them, knowing that sooner or later, the phone would ring. He was right. He picked it up on the first ring.

****

Duncan had fallen asleep on his bed, and Peter had left him there, turning off the radio and light, stopping in the kitchen to get a soda before turning in. The house was as silent as a tomb.

But then the phone gave a short piercing ring in the nighttime quiet, and Peter saw by the light on the phone that his father had picked it up.

It was late, and the call was evidently expected. Peter swallowed hard and repeated his phone procedure calmly, muted the phone, and flicked on the button to tape the line.

"Ellington...You trying to screw us man?" The voice was low and gruff.

"No way, my friend. Things are right in order. No problem," Frederick said, voice smooth.

"No death certificate sounds like a problem. A big problem."

Frederick laughed, sounding relaxed and in control. Reality was, he was sweating hard, and his heart was beating so fast he was sure the creep on the line could hear it. "Maybe a problem for some, but not for me."

"Go ahead."

"We've registered a power of attorney that my wife had signed. It gives me the ability to conduct all her business in her absence, or whatever. It's been officially registered, and recorded, and it's as good as gold. Dead or alive, this deal is going to go through."

"Nice you sound so assured, Mr. Big Stuff."

"I am assured, Sir. Things will go according to schedule."

"Sorry, Ellington, but the schedule has been changed. You know how schedules are. The boss has decided that dealing with you is a little shaky. He wants his money back. All of it. You have 48 hours."

"48 hours!? Are you crazy? The money is tied up in the land. You have to tell him to be patient. A few more days. The closing is next Tuesday..."

The guy on the other end of the phone laughed, and the sound was low and grating, like a laugh that had had very little practice. "You don't tell the boss to be patient. He sets the schedule. The only patient around here is going to be you, if you don't fix this mess. Get the message?"

The phone line went dead, and the dial tone rang endlessly in Frederick's ear. After a moment's thought, he hung it up, and headed for the bathroom. He was sweating like a pig, and he needed another shower.

In the kitchen, Peter put the phone back together again, his chubby fingers shaking this time. What exactly was his father up to? What was going on here? His stomach felt upset and he was more than worried. He wished he had someone to help. He had a fleeting thought of his Aunt Diana, his mother's sister, who he hadn't seen since he was a little boy.

He remembered her as being wild and crazy, smart and strong. His dad had hated her, and his mom had been a little wary of her too. He remembered she said what she thought, and sometimes made people mad. They had tried to contact her when his mom had died, but the last number they had had for her didn't work. Evidently, she had moved and the phone had been disconnected. Dad said she didn't want to be found.

She and mom hadn't been close in the past couple of years, probably because Diana had always thought his dad was a jerk. When he was a kid that used to hurt his feelings. But right now, he pretty much saw her point, and he'd give anything to have somebody like her to talk to.

He silently changed the tape again, and added the used tape to his hiding spot under the mattress. He climbed into bed, but he couldn't fall asleep. He was still staring out the window, deep in thought, when the sun crept back up and brought the new day.

Chapter 25

By noon the next day, Marvin Greenstein was frustrated and puzzled. The effect that those feelings brought about could be vouched for by any number of employees at the Sollington Police Department. He had spouted off about the quality of the coffee (which was not an abnormal complaint, as it had often been compared to liquid mud), the lack of paper towels in the john (also business as usual), and the crumby maintenance department who still hadn't gotten around to fixing the wheel on his desk chair.

No matter that the repair order had been written over six weeks before, and that he had been putting up with the wobbly wheel ever since, his mood today had erased the word tolerance from his vocabulary.

Since Marv's demeanor was for the most part considered easy going and polite, the staff simply resorted to tiptoeing around him and praying that the black cloud over his head would soon pass.

Madge, one of the telephone operators, actually stopped at a convenience store on her way back from her break, and brought him a steaming cup of "real coffee", complete with handy little packets of "real cream" instead of their usual powder stuff, to sweeten him up. It didn't change his mood, but he was touched with her effort and made a concerted effort to be a little more pleasant as he sat in his crooked, squeaking chair and air dried his hands after visiting the men's room.

It was the Ellington case that was irking him, of course. Now, with secretly knowing that Cassandra was alive, he felt he should be able to answer the questions about the case in easy order. He had listened to her story, and had believed her testimony totally. He had truly thought that pegging the creep who was her husband would be an open and shut thing, and that she would be able to quickly reclaim her identity, take custody of her boys, and begin a new life.

But the more he dug, the more questions he asked, the murkier the whole thing was becoming. He could see, finally, the overwhelming doubts and fears she had had when dealing with this man. Because nothing he was finding out made sense. Either the picture that was developing in the evidence he was finding was a carefully, fraudulently painted masterpiece, or Cassandra Ellington was out of her mind, and incapable of telling the truth.

He had cornered the doctor from the hospital again. The guy SWORE that Cassandra had not been injured, that she had been drunk as a skunk (not using his street wise terminology, of course) and that she had requested help for her alcoholism.

He had talked to the family doctor, an older practitioner who enjoyed a fine reputation in the town, and had been told that he had often counseled Cassandra about her drinking, and that Frederick Ellington was nothing but a caring, concerned, overwrought husband.

He had spoken to the minister of the church where the funeral had been held, and had been lectured for over twenty minutes on the evils of drink....real fire and brimstone stuff. The man had shaken his head and offered a prayer for Cassandra and her drinking, which, he was certain, was responsible for her death. He had gone on to praise Frederick Ellington as a religious, caring man, a good husband and father, and a generous benefactor of the church.

He had called the Hillmeadow House, the hospital that Frederick had evidently contacted regarding his wife, and was told by the administrator that Mr. Ellington had nothing but concern and care for his wife, that he had been extremely worried about her deep seated emotional problems, along with her severe alcoholism, and that they had been more than willing to help her "when she was ready". The doctor he had spoken to was not available, as he was attending a conference out of state. But Marv had little hope that his testimony would differ.

The chief of police had been no help at all. Marv had gone to him, considering taking him into his confidence about Cassandra's survival and asking his help. Since his reports about the accident (and supposed death) had been filed before he knew Cassandra was alive, he hadn't actually filed any false information. But sooner or later, he would need to update what he knew, to keep the case legitimate.

"What would happen, Chief, if this Ellington woman were to show up later, say, with amnesia or something? How would that be handled?" he asked.

Instead of drumming up interest or questions about possibilities, the chief had, in fact, shut Marv off. A flash of distress crossed the man's face, gone as soon as it appeared. His reaction was puzzling. But then, with his usual huff, he had reprimanded Marv about wasting too much time on the accident. Suddenly, he was being told to write the case off, to stop asking questions and muddying the water about what had been a tragic, but unremarkable accident.

Marv hadn't argued, but he had ignored that request, feeling a strong responsibility to Cassandra. But he had decided, at that moment, to keep his knowledge to himself. When he had the answers, he would decide what to do about the whole thing.

Later, he had even dared to call Frederick himself, to ask him about his wife's drinking, and had been met with subdued anger.

"Of course she was a drinker, Detective. Everyone knows that. I don't see what bearing this has on the case.

Most probably she was drunk and that was why she went over the cliff. Drunk or sober, I don't see what difference it makes. My wife died in a horrible accident, Detective. What's this all about?"

"Routine, just routine, Sir. We always have to tie up the loose ends like this. Especially in a case where the body can't be found. Have to have the facts straight, that's all." Marv kept his voice low.

"Waste of time, in my opinion. It's all very upsetting."

"I'm sure it is, and I apologize for that. That's why I'm trying to finish this up. Do you happen to know where she usually bought her liquor?"

"How the hell would I know that? I didn't buy the damn stuff for her." Frederick Ellington's words were clipped, disgusted.

"I guess not. That makes sense. But maybe you have found some in the house. Is there any clue as to where it was purchased?"

"Detective, there is no alcohol in my house that I know of. You are getting on my nerves. If you can't put this to rest, I'm going to talk to your superior, and you'll be reading meters next, and worrying about where people got the nickels to put in them."

Marv had gulped over that one, not that he had any fear of being put on the parking detail, but because he had been asking questions in direct defiance of the chief's command, and that was not something that would set well with the man. Marv had already heard fire and brimstone from the minister, he didn't need another sermon.

So he apologized, sounding meek and agreeable, while all the time his mind was spinning as to where he would investigate next.

When he got off the phone, after a very unfulfilling morning, he decided to go to lunch at the deli down the street.

He snagged a young patrol man who was also on his lunch break, and the two of them hustled down the street together, where within minutes, they were huddled in a red leather booth, enjoying hefty roast beef sandwiches and cold iced tea, and discussing the upcoming baseball season for the Phillies. It gave his mind a rest.

When he returned to the station a half hour later, he found a cryptic message on his desk. "Call Don at 215-555-1435 about purchases."

He dialed the number, having no idea at all who he would be speaking to.

"Mid Town State Store," said an efficient male voice.

"Is Don there?"

"You got him."

"Detective Marv Greenstein, Sollington Police. I'm returning your call." That funny electric feeling was coming over him again, the same creepy feeling that had followed him everywhere on the Ellington case.

"Yeah, I thought I should call you. It's about that Ellington woman. The one who had the accident." He paused, but then went on. "She bought a lot of booze here. Constantly. She liked Johnny Walker, and also Port Wine. A good customer. Paid cash."

He kept giving small details, his voice was choppy.

"Why are you telling me this?" Marv asked, calmly. But in his heart, he knew there was only one reason the man had called.

"She bought a lot of stuff," he said, defiantly. "But she wasn't drunk when she bought it. I'm careful about that, sir. I don't sell to people when they look like they had too much. I just wanted you to know that. It's against the law to sell liquor to someone who is obviously drunk, and I don't want to get in no trouble."

"Thanks for your information, Don," he said slowly, then took the time to write down the man's full name and number in his notes. He hung up the phone, and sat sitting at the wall in front of his desk.

Frederick had been annoyed when he had asked the question. He had claimed total ignorance to his wife's source of liquor. He had claimed it wasn't important. Yet, in less than an hour, he had evidently discovered the supplier, and convinced him to call the police to report the information. He felt, suddenly, like a pawn in Frederick Ellington's chess game, and he didn't like the feeling a bit.

Cassandra Ellington didn't drink. He was sure of it. He had seen her, heard her, and he believed in her. He also knew she had been hidden in Cal's house for almost three days. Cal's house, the bastion of defense against alcohol. She had had nothing to drink, and hadn't suffered or complained in the least. No craving, no shakes, no withdrawal. He had known a lot of drunks who had decided to give it up, and some had had an easier time than others with the physical withdrawal. But no one had ever done it like Cassandra Ellington. No, he'd bet his buttons on the fact that the lady didn't drink. There was just no sign of it.

So what kind of man was this, and what power could he have over so many people, that doctors, lawyers, ministers and even liquor sales clerks were ready to swear on a stack of Bibles to a lie like that? The man really scared him, and he didn't scare easily. But no matter what the Chief had said, he wasn't going to let go of this one until he had the answers. Frederick Ellington wasn't going to win. Marvin Greenstein might be just a pawn in the chess game, but even a pawn could call "check mate" and bring down the king. He was going to win. He was pretty damn good at chess.

****

The next day dawned sunny and hotter than it had a right to be at this time of year. The preview of summer was welcomed and celebrated, however, as lighter clothing and sun glasses made their appearance in Sollington.

Janie had hurried to work, almost late, as usual. She had spent the early morning hours pulling together a bag of women's "essentials" for Cassandra. Shoes (real ones, instead of the dime store variety. Then socks, panty hose, a simple linen dress, two pair of jeans, a few colorful tops, a navy blue button down sweater, and assorted undies had made their way into the bag. An assortment of makeup followed. (Cassandra was a fall and winter color, she was sure, and so she had selected makeup to suit. She had a knack for these things, Bernie always bragged.) A few necessary toiletries finished the package, and she had hurriedly driven to Cal's house, and left the parcel on his front porch at 7:30 AM. She didn't dare to ring the bell. She knew Cal well, and admitted to herself with a giggle that Cal would do just about anything for anybody with a smile on his face. But wake him up early in the morning and you might just have a riot on your hands.

So she left the things where they were sure to be found, and drove her Toyota at break neck speed into town, parking in a municipal lot, and practically jogged into the office, which was located right across the street from the county court house.

She ignored the tight, judgmental smile of the receptionist, Agnes, as she galloped to her desk, sitting unceremoniously in the brown vinyl chair just as the door to her boss's office began to open.

With the skill of a Broadway star, stared with avid concentration at the file that sat before her on her desk. Any observer just arriving on the scene would be certain to believe that the intent redhead had been perched at her desk just about forever, working her tail off.

"Oh, good morning, Mr. Sloboski," she said in a chipper, competent voice to her boss. She threw a daring glance at the busy body receptionist, nonverbally promising to do her bodily harm if she interfered. The receptionist took the hint and turned back to her phones.

"I must have missed you coming in, sir. I bet you'd like a nice hot cup of coffee!" She acted like she had been slaving for hours, and he bought it, hook, line and sinker.

Mr. Sloboski, preoccupied and pudgy as usual, smiled at her thankfully. "Thanks so much Janie, you always know just how to start my day. I can depend on you."

Janie smirked at the sullen Agnes as she passed to get the coffee. Mr. Sloboski was a bit of a jerk, but she really didn't mind getting him coffee, though she knew that many women with "consciousness raising issues" had declared it a no-no. She had learned for herself, though, that certain simple things were worth the reward. She had consciously decided that her "consciousness" had already been risen to a suitable level to allow her to pamper a silly man with a cup of coffee, especially if he was the great boss that Mr. Sloboski was.

By that, she meant that he was in a fog half of the time, and out to lunch the rest. Like this morning, for instance. Late and off the hook. It was worth a cup of coffee. She made it just like he liked it, lots of sugar and cream, and stole a donut out of the box by the coffee maker for him, too. That would get her a longer lunch hour, in case she needed to see Cassandra.

"Thanks, Janie. As usual, you have made my day." She closed the door to his office, after watching him munch hungrily into the sugary, creamy donut with a dreamy smile on his face. It had been a good morning, so far, even if hectic. She had gotten the clothes for Cassandra, and she had made Mr. Sloboski's day. Actually, she had made

Bernie's day, too, she blushed to herself,. Though in a different way, when he had awakened early in the morning for an emergency plumbing call.

She had gracefully and enthusiastically climbed on top of him, not allowing him to get out of bed until they had both been smiling and satisfied. Powerful, wonderful stuff. God, she loved that guy and the things he did to her. And he accepted her just the way she was, sometimes crazy and frantic, and always into causes. Like the clothes for Cassandra. They were always counting pennies, just trying to get by, but he didn't even question her when she started dumping her clothes into a bag. If she had a reason, that was good enough for him!

"You're the best, Janie," he had called from the shower, where she had heard him whistling as the sun had begun to come up. "You really made my day."

Donut and coffee for Mr. Sloboski, honest passion for Bernie. Making someone's day was very relative, she decided philosophically, as she plunged into the file on her desk.

Suddenly she laughed, glad once again that Mr. S. didn't pay much attention to the world around her. The file she had been studying to impress him was upside down.

She turned it around, stuck her tongue out at Agnes, who was giving her another snake like look, and got to work.

*****

Duncan had wakened at the break of day, finding his little brother Peter curled up in bed beside him. He felt a little better. Yesterday had been the pain of all pains, he had felt so alone, so scared, so tired and so overwhelmed.

It made him feel good to look at his little brother's face, as much as the twerp made him crazy at time, he was really fond and proud of the little wizard. He tried to turn over without waking him. His arm was stiff from the position he'd slept in. But with his first movement, Peter's eyes popped open, looking directly into his.

"Hi, Dunc. Hope you didn't mind sharing the bed. I couldn't sleep in my room. It feels too...creepy."

"Yeah, I know. It's ok, man."

"Dunc, we have real problems."

"No kidding."

"No, I mean REAL problems. Dad's into something bad, and something awful is going to happen. I can feel it."

"What more awful can happen, Peter? The worst already did. We lost mom."

"Well, if you think you know everything, you better listen to this." He climbed out of bed, and popped the tapes into Duncan's tape player. Duncan's eyes grew larger with each moment.

"Damn."

"See what I mean? We gotta get some help here. I may be smart, but I'm too immature to deal with this."

Even through his fear, Duncan smiled at the intensity of his brother's face. He thinks he's "too immature". Too much.

"I was thinking, maybe we could find Aunt Diana. You know her, she's not afraid of anything."

Duncan thought for a moment, remembering the outspoken, off beat woman who had visited them years before. His father had hated her, and the visit had made his mother nervous and upset. But she HAD stood up to him, argued with him. It was true what Peter said, she wasn't afraid of anything.

"Dad said he tried to call her about the funeral, and that she had moved. But really, maybe he didn't try too hard. Maybe we could find her. I mean, detectives do it all the time in movies, look for missing people and stuff."

"This isn't a movie, Peter. This is real life and it sucks."

"Don't talk like that Duncan. You know mom says you shouldn't talk like that." All of a sudden, he started to cry, showing his mere twelve years, despite his brainpower.

Duncan put an arm around him, feeling strange and awkward. He wasn't used to comforting his little brother. He was used to driving him crazy, and keeping him out of his stuff. But then Peter hugged him back, and it felt good. He didn't feel so alone. He had Peter, and Peter needed him. He had to make sure that nothing happened to his little brother.

"OK, Peter. I'll watch my mouth. And we'll make a plan. Just don't cry. How are we going to go about finding Aunt Diana in New York?"

Peter smiled. "I love you, Duncan."

"Jeez, don't be weird, Peter."

"You love me too, don't you big brother?"

Duncan paused for a minute, then ruffled his brother's already uncombed hair. "Yeah, I do, little brother. Come on, let's get to work."

They were interrupted a few minutes later, as their father came to check on them, and to tell them that he would be gone for several hours on business appointments. He looked tired and stressed, and was more than a little cranky. The boys acted pleasant and obedient, not daring to push his buttons when he was in "a mood". They were relieved when he left.

For the next two hours, the boys were busy. Peter did a search on the internet and found thousands of hits for "Diana Clark", but nothing he found pointed to his aunt. Duncan retrieved his mother's address book from her desk drawer, and began the search for Diana. They called her prior numbers, finding them mostly disconnected. Diana had moved a lot. She had also lived with several guys, mostly artist/actor types. Cassandra had kept track of her numbers in the earlier years, drawing a line though each number that had changed, and adding a new one. The list was seven numbers long. They started with the most recent, and worked their way backwards.

At two of the numbers, men answered who swore they hadn't seen Diana in years. Peter calmly asked for any information they might have, any other people who might know her whereabouts. But he got the distinct impression that the guys couldn't care less, and just wanted to get off the phone.

But finally, when they got to the end of the list, the number that was actually the oldest number in the book, they had luck.

After ringing and ringing, the phone was picked up by an answering service. The operator had a Spanish accent, and was young and polite.

"Grant Holdings' service." She answered. "Would you care to leave a message?"

"Um, yes, ma'am," began Peter. "I'm trying to find my Aunt, and I thought maybe I could get information at this number."

The operator was sympathetic to the young voice on the phone.

"What's your Aunt's name, honey?"

"Diana Clark. She's an actress."

"Well, we don't have anybody with that name listed here. How did you get this number? Do you know Mr. Holdings?"

"Um, actually no. I... think maybe Aunt Diana lived with him a while back .Or something. She moves alot. But I have to find her. It's really important."

The operator laughed, a kind, understanding chuckle. "Well, people move around a lot these days. That's life, right?"

"Yeah, I guess so."

"Well good luck. I hope you find her."

"I think I just ran out of numbers." The disappointment in his voice touched her.

She paused for a minute. "OK, you sound like a nice kid. How about if I give you one more thing to try. Have a pencil?"

"Go ahead," he said hopefully.

"Well, if she really is an actress, there's a way you can probably find her. This number is for Actor's Equity. It's like a union for people in the theater. If she's in this town, and she wants to work, she'll be registered with them, and they would have her current address."

She rattled off a number, and Peter wrote it down, repeating it to make sure he got it right.

"Do you think they'll give me information?" he asked the woman.

She laughed again. "Probably they won't want to, but then, you got this out of me, right? It's worth a shot. You sound like a nice kid. I got nephews, too. I hope you find her."

He thanked her and hung up the phone.

Their next call was to Actor's Equity in New York. It was Duncan's turn on the phone.

"I need to get in touch with an actress who I believe is a member of Actor's Equity," he said in his most grown up voice.

The clerk on the phone wasn't buying. He sounded tired, and overworked, and in a bad mood.

"What the hell do you want, kid? I'm busy here."

Duncan wouldn't be deterred.

"I need to find my Aunt. Diana Clark. It's very important, a matter of life or death."

"Yeah, right." The guy sounded like he was yawning.

"Well, can you help me? Please, Mister, this is important."

"Everybody's important around here, if you ask them. If you ask me, I don't care much. Leave me your name and number, kid, and if I have time, I'll look her up."

"Oh, God, please, could you?" Duncan's voice broke and he was horrified that he was going to cry.

The guy on the other end of the phone had a human moment. "Hey kid, I said I'd try, OK? Don't freak out on me. You said it's important, and I'm gonna treat it important, OK?" He wrote down Duncan's number.

"Thanks, mister," Duncan said, his voice tight.

"You got it," said the guy, hanging up abruptly.

They hung up the phone, looking silently at each other for a full minute. They had no idea at all whether the man would find anything, or if he would call back. But it gave them hope. And if there was one thing the boys needed, it was hope.

****

When Cassandra opened her eyes in the morning, she found herself in her cozy room in Cal's house, with absolutely no memory of getting into bed there. Her last conscious thoughts had taken place when she had been down on the couch, determined to stay awake to talk to Cal when he came home.

When she looked across the room, she found him sitting in the chair in the corner, elbows on his knees, chin resting on his hands, just looking at her.

"You had to put me to bed again, I see," she chirped, trying to hide her embarrassment.

He smiled, and it lit her heart. She was determined not to show it, though, feeling like a needy child, an orphan, a charity case. She had felt that way before in her life, and the feeling was as ugly as it was familiar.

"Here's some stuff," he said gently, pointing to an overflowing bag by his feet. Cal seemed to be able to read her discomfort with no effort. "Janie dropped it off early this morning. Knowing Janie, it has everything you need and then some."

"She's very nice."

"Yeah, I think so, too. She's rather nuts, but nice."

A panicked thought crossed her mind. Was he involved with Janie? It was followed by a wave of guilt and self disgust. Just what business was it of hers WHO he was involved with? You don't crawl in someone's window in the middle of the night and take over their life, right? And hate it or not, she was a married woman, with children who were in a crisis and a husband who was cruel and vindictive, to say the least. Her stomach curled into a tight knot as the remonstrance and self criticism whipped through her mind.

"I'm not involved with her, goof," he said softly, with a twinkle in his eye. "She's very, very married to a nice guy named Bernie, and they can't keep their hands off each other. She's a friend. A very good and very crazy friend."

She was quiet for a moment, amazed that the demons in her stomach had gone away.

"Just how do you do that, read my mind and all?"

"Maybe I don't really read your mind, I read your face. I like your hair, by the way."

She tossed her head, still amazed at the lightness and difference. Despite all the problems, there was something deep inside of her that felt good. A ray of hope.

"Let me get dressed, Cal. I'll be right down."

She met him in the kitchen a few minutes later, after a quick shower and perusal of Janie's donations. The clothes fit great, even to the shoes. She glanced at herself in the mirror on the way down, watching the way her hair bounced a little when the air hit it, or when she moved abruptly. Her eyes seemed larger, her smile seemed brighter. Was it just the hair? Maybe it had something to do with that feeling of hope.

They baked some cinnamon muffins that came in a tube, and made coffee. They sat on the back deck with their coffee, waiting for the muffins to be done, the tantalizing smell of cinnamon escaping even outside.

"This is as close as I ever get to baking," Cal admitted. "I even prefer just picking it up from the bakery, except for the smell. There's something about the smell when they're cooking."

They sat quietly, then ate the muffins. Finally Cal began to talk. "You didn't seem too out of sorts about Alcoholics Anonymous. I didn't know how you'd react to that."

"You thought I'd be horrified? Me, the woman who climbs up cliffs and into unsuspecting windows? Me, the woman who is afraid to claim her own name and identity out of fear? Hey, a little booze problem, I can handle."

"Don't minimize it, Cassandra. It's my life. I spend a lot of time and energy in helping other people stay sober. It keeps me sober, keeps me facing reality. Not everyone can handle that."

He looked so somber, so helpless all of a sudden. She put her hand on his arm.

"I didn't mean to minimize it, Cal. I just meant to let you know it was OK."

They looked into each other's eyes for a long moment, both unable to deal with the emotions they saw there. They looked away at the same time.

"I really want to hear from your friend Marv. I have to find a safe way to get those boys from Frederick. I have nightmares of him playing legal tricks for the rest of my life."

"He's just a man, Cassandra. He's not invincible. We'll find a way."

Then he voiced a secret, painful doubt that had been plaguing him, especially as he watched her peacefully sleep. She was a kind and loving woman, he could tell, and she had spent a lot of years with the guy.

"What if he were to want you back, Cassandra, when he finds out you're alive? What if the shock of everything has brought about changes in him? What if he makes promises, wants to go into counseling or something? What exactly does your marriage mean?"

He held his breath, watching her carefully for any glimmer, any spark of emotion that her eyes might hold. He had known many women, even having gone through hell and back, who took up again with their errant spouse.

Something was happening to him here, and his nerve endings were alert. Somehow, in a very short, crazy time, this woman had gotten under his skin as no one else ever had, and it was scaring him to death. Why did her answer matter so much?

Cal saw more than a glimmer in Cassandra Ellington. He saw the fire of rage.

"What does my marriage mean? What marriage? This is the man who hits my kids, who has beaten me, broken bones. Married to him, I have actually contemplated taking my own life. Here I sit, unable to go to my boys, because I'm afraid of what he'll do to them if he fears they would be out of his control. And to me when he sees how I've changed. And I've changed. There's something about going over a cliff that makes a bit of an impression on you. I saw my life flashing by. In technicolor. And I didn't give the show great ratings. I don't know how I'm going to do it, but I know I will. I'm going to have a life again, a real life, and I'm going to bring my boys up with love and self-respect and peace."

She had been standing before him, her voice so forceful she was almost yelling, her eyes filled with tears. He believed her. His heart started beating again. He stood, automatically, and wrapped his arms around her shoulders, pulling her close. She nestled her head in his chest, and started to cry.

"I'm crying all over your shirt," she babbled.

"You're kind of tough on my clothes, you realize that?"

She pulled back and smiled up into his eyes.

"You're such a nice man, Calvin Johnson."

He pulled her close again, embarrassed that she wouldn't think he was quite so nice if she knew what kind of thoughts that were firing him as he held her close. His hormones were raging, his nerve endings on fire. He felt like an inept teenager on a date. He cleared his voice, praying for sanity. His body calmed down, if only a few degrees. Self-discipline was vital here. She had a lot of more important things to tend to.

"You've got a lot to get through here, Cassandra. One step at a time. But you'll make it."

He was actually talking to himself, as well as to her.

"You're handling a lot, Cassandra," Cal said thoughtfully, "You want to get some objective help for this, help in sorting out the past, and getting ready for a new way of life?"

"I know I have a lot of work to do, a lot to learn about myself, but I don't know who to talk to." Her mind drifted to the men she had once tried to confide in, like the doctor, the minister. She shivered involuntarily. Not exactly helpful.

"I could introduce you to a friend...a woman. She's a very competent psychologist. You could just talk about whatever you're ready to talk about."

"Thanks. Maybe I should try that. I like talking to you, though."

"Objective, that's the key here. And objective I'm not, at this point. I think I'd better keep in the friend role, if it's ok." She smiled, and he ruffled her short hair.

They went back inside, just as the phone began to ring. It was Marv, and the news wasn't good.

"What is it about this guy, that people lie so effortlessly for him? Do they like him that much? Does he have some kind of charismatic power? How can a guy who spends his time teaching and writing books get so many people to do what he needs? I've got doctors and lawyers, and preachers, and even wine sellers all swearing that Cassandra is a drunk. We're not missing anything here, are we buddy?" He asked Cal desperately. "Tell me there's NO chance the lady is an alcoholic."

"There is no chance," Cal said succinctly.

"Then something's going on here, and this guy is more manipulative than I imagined. I have a bad feeling in my gut. I'm going to need a little more time. I have to find out some more particulars about this guy. Tell Cassandra I said hi."

Marv hung up the phone, stroking his chin. It was dark and prickly with a day's worth of beard. He hadn't taken the time to shave yet. He strode to the bathroom, picking up his electric shaver and getting to work.

He had to be in by 3PM today, and he had a lot to do before then. He was a good cop, an honest upright guy today, and it was grating on him that he was hiding the news about Cassandra being alive from the chief. But his gut was obstinate about it, and he obeyed his gut. He wasn't going to tell anybody. It just wasn't safe.

The chief wanted the case closed, though, and the paperwork in. To put the paperwork in, he would actually have to put things he knew to be untrue in his reports. Which he couldn't do. Wouldn't do. So the only way out was to hurry up and find out the answers, so he could file a true report, and reveal Cassandra as alive. He would use his own time to do that. He felt like he was out on a limb. He never did have very good balance.

"Only for you, Marcia, only for you," he chanted to himself as he started his car and headed for the office.

Chapter 26

"No stalling, Ellington," said the menacing voice on the phone. "The money comes back, now, or else." The line went dead.

Frederick swallowed hard. He was up against the wall. God, he rued the day he had gotten involved with those bloodsucking creeps. His office felt too hot. He got up and opened the door, noticing that his secretary was not at her desk.

One of his students, Pamela Gravely, sat on the couch in his waiting room. She had been in his writing class for the past two semesters, quiet but competent.

"Pamela?" he asked politely. He really wasn't in the mood to counsel writing students. It was the last thing on his mind at the moment, but he couldn't very well avoid her. Damn the secretary.

"Do you have a minute, Professor Ellington?" she asked shyly. She was hugging a thick brown envelope tightly to her chest, as if afraid that it would run away.

"Certainly, Pamela," he said with a cordial voice, hiding the frustration he felt at being cornered by a student when he was under such pressure, with time being so short. He had mobsters on his tail with an impossible deadline, and a sniveling student wanted advice. Shit.

She followed him into his office, sitting in one of the brown leather chairs that faced his desk.

"I finished my manuscript, Professor," she said shyly, with a kind emotion in her voice that belied both relief and amazement. "It's a mystery. If you would read it, let me know your opinion. I mean, with you being a famous author and all..."

Anything, anything, he thought, to get rid of her.

"I'd be honored, Pamela." He took the offered envelope with a gesture of reverence. "It will take me a few days."

"Oh, that's just fine, sir. Just take care with it, which I know you will. It's my only printed copy."

"Your only copy?" he said surprised. "Don't you have a backup?"

She reached in her oversized purse and held up a computer disk. "Here's my backup. But I just printed it once, so far."

"Fine, fine, Pamela. That's fine. I'll be looking forward to enjoying this." He put the manuscript on the corner of his desk and shepherded her to the door. She left quickly, knowing he was a busy man, a look of hope in her eyes.

He shut the door behind her, sweating suddenly. Manna from heaven? Not from heaven, maybe. But a miracle of sorts. He flew to his desk and ripped open the envelope, beginning to read.

The story was a mystery, with a female detective in the spotlight. It was clever and well written. He read the first five chapters, his hands getting sweatier and sweatier with each page. Finally, he reached for the phone, his heart in his throat. He could pull this off. He would pull this off. He wouldn't let himself think of the risk or the consequences.

****

Frederick opened the front door of his house, several hours later. He had left the boys alone for the day, which they had said was fine with them. His nerves were shot. He really needed a drink.

At first he was puzzled. He could hear a man's voice in the background. He followed the sound to the kitchen.   Coming to the entryway, he found Duncan and Peter by the kitchen counter. A bag from the convenience store a few blocks away sat on the table.   They were evidently just coming back from a trip to the store.

The voice he had heard had come from the telephone answering machine, which they were in the process of playing at the moment. They hadn't heard him arrive.

"Hey, little buddy, this is John from Actors' Equity, calling you back like I promised. I told the boss it was a life and death matter, just like you said. Anyhow, I checked things out, and I think I found your aunt Diana. At least I think I found her agent. His name is Zachary Yolandblock, on 6th Avenue. His number is 555-1987. Area code 212 of course. I hope he can help you out, guy. Good luck, little buddy." The tape went dead, followed by a beep at the end of the message.

"What the hell is going on here?" Frederick's voice cut the air like ice. The boys spun around. Peter reached behind him, popping the tape out of the machine and palming it. He didn't know how long his father had been standing there, or how much he had heard, but he didn't want him to get the tape. But it was too late. Frederick had heard every blessed word, and he was not happy about it.

"Uh, hi dad," stammered Duncan, trying to diffuse the situation.

It didn't work. Frederick advanced on the boys, his right hand in a fist. "No one told you to stir up a bee's hive and find Diana. What do you mean, telling people you need help?" He reached over and pushed the erase button on the phone cradle.

He was close to Duncan now, almost eyeball to eyeball, but he had quite an advantage of weight and strength on his son.

"Sorry, dad," he croaked, fear in his eyes.   "It seemed like the thing to do. She should know about mom."

Frederick pulled his hand back, and swung it hard, backhanded, striking Duncan across the jaw. The boy bounced back a few feet, colliding with the counter. "Sorry, Dunc," he said with blazing eyes, his voice sarcastic and cruel. "It just seemed like the thing to do." He pulled Duncan to his feet.

Peter jumped between them, his voice squeaking with fear.

"No, dad, no," he tried to holler, but with the fear, very little sound came out. Frederick grabbed him by the shirt.

"Get out of my way, Peter, now!" He pushed the boy away. Duncan had regained his balance and was standing by the counter, his hand on his jaw. He was trying his damnedest not to cry.

Frederick started to lunge for him. Peter closed his eyes, unable to stop him, but unable to watch.

But instead of the sound of impact, he heard the sound of the doorbell. Frederick froze in place for a minute, then turned abruptly toward the door, all anger seemingly gone from his face. Smooth and calm, like a deceptive mask.

"Boys, I have an important business engagement right now. I have to go out. Please go to your rooms. We'll discuss this later this evening when I come home." His voice sounded controlled and normal.

The boys looked at each other in confusion and disbelief. That reaction lasted for about one second. In the next second, they were high tailing it down the hallway, both cascading into Duncan's room. They had escaped, and that was all that mattered for the moment.

"Well, hello, Pamela! I'm so pleased you could meet with me on such short notice. Once I began reading, I simply couldn't stop." His voice was professional, relaxed. "Let's take my car, dear, there's someone I want you to meet. I'm so excited about the manuscript." They could hear the door shut behind him, as he left the house.

"He's crazy, man," said Duncan, still rubbing his jaw. It wasn't broken, but he could tell he was going to have a heck of a bruise. He reached over and turned on the radio. His favorite show, "Your Pal Cal," was just about ready to begin. The familiar voices were comforting, seeping down through his depression and pain. He laid down on the bed, closing his eyes.

Across the room, Peter touched the tape he had snuck out of the machine. He had the number for Diana's agent. Maybe they would be able to find her. He didn't dial the phone though, a wave of paranoia flowing over him like an incoming tide. What if his father found out? Or if he realized Peter had swiped thee tape from the machine? He sped to the other room, and put in a blank tape. He stopped in the kitchen, grabbing an ice pack for his brother's jaw. Then he plopped in the chair next to Duncan's desk, not able to take any action for the moment. He listened to the radio with Duncan, praying silently for some way out of the deep dark hole that he felt his life had fallen into. Mom. He missed his mom.

****

Cassandra had accompanied Cal to the radio station in the evening, not wanting to spend the evening hours alone. She sat in the corner of the booth, helping Cal occasionally with paperwork, but mostly just observing Cal and Paul at work.

"Well, things have a way of working out," Paul had said in a philosophical voice when they were talking.

"You sound like Cal."

"I learned that from Cal, ma'am. I won't ever forget it."

She nodded, at peace for the moment, as the show grinded into gear, songs, jokes, occasional puzzles and call-ins forming the intriguing mixture that the young listeners seemed to love.

"....the greatest tire sale in the history of Sollington," screamed Cal excitedly at one point. "Run (or drive) right down (or up) to the best dealer in the region, "Midland Motors!"

Paul flipped some switches as Cal spoke into the mike, and the sound of screeching tires and revving motors filled the background with noise. "Tell them that you're there on account of Your Pal Cal, and the manager is going to give you two free passes to the movie theater in town, courtesy of radio station WDRK! Make a deal for your wheels!" The car noises started up again. "But drive carefully, ya hear?"

"And now, it's call-in time in Sollington. Tonight's topic is "What kind of parent are you going to be when you grow up?" The Lines are open, here at Station WDRK, so call in and give us your thoughts...."

Another commercial went by, as the phone lines began to light. "Your Pal Cal," he answered the first line. On the air, he chatted with a bubbly young girl about not using too much grade pressure with kids. Cal agreed. Paul spoke to a quiet young man who said he didn't ever want to have kids. His folks had always told him what a pain in the butt kids were.

"A lot of folks say that, Sam," Paul told the young man in his gentle voice. "Sometimes because they were told that themselves. Maybe you'll have kids, and then have the courage to break the chain. Having relationships can sometimes be a bit of a pain, but most people are worth it. Except Cal, of course. He ain't even worth the stool he's sitting on..." said Paul with a laugh, breaking the tension. The young man laughed. "Thanks for calling," laughed Paul as he hung up.

"I'm afraid," said a young voice next, on Cal's line. "I'm really afraid of my dad, and I feel so alone."

Cassandra gasped involuntarily in the corner of the booth, and Cal's ears perked up instantly. He looked at her. The color had drained from her face.

"What's your name, Buddy?" he asked.

"Peter."

"What's the problem?" The voices filled the air in the sound booth, Cal locked his eyes to Cassandra.

"It's my dad. He's a mess. I think he's in some kind of trouble. He gets meaner every day. Today he hit my brother, really hard. I think he has a loose tooth."

"Peter, shut up man," said Duncan's voice in the background. "No one cares about my tooth. You better get off the phone."

"Well, if I was a parent, I wouldn't die and leave my kids alone. And I wouldn't hit my kids. Especially not for nothing." His voice was strained.

"Peter," said Cal softly, "Maybe there's an answer here. No one has to endure getting hit. Maybe someone can help you. Can I talk to you on the private line?"

He motioned to Cassandra to come closer.

Peter sounded panicky. "No, No, I don't think so. My dad might come home any minute. I gotta go." The connection was broken, and right along with it went Cassandra'a heart.

"I have to talk to him. Call him back." She wrote the phone number on a piece of paper. Paul dialed it quickly, handing her the phone. It rang twice, and then there was a click as the phone was picked up.

"You have reached the office of Professor Frederick Ellington. I'm not in the office at the moment, but I'll be happy to return your call. Leave your name and number at the beep. BEEP!"

Cassandra hung up the phone, dread pooling in her stomach. She couldn't call the boys. The phone wasn't even ringing in the house anymore.   Frederick had forwarded all calls to his office number. She lowered her head, and began to cry softly.

****

Miles away, Frederick's hands were shaking. "Think, man, think!" he commanded himself, trying to control his body's reactions. He had made the right moves. He had stopped, immediately after leaving the house, and had had all phone calls forwarded to his office machine at the university.

Now that the boys had stirred the waters in New York, he couldn't afford having that arrogant Diana getting wind of what was going on. He had thought it was a blessing that her last number had been disconnected, when he had called her out of obligation for the funeral. But that was as far as his obligation went.

The last thing he needed was another problem to solve. He looked down at his hands, and had a fleeting feeling of sickness in his stomach, before he gathered his emotions, tucking them away safely, deep inside.

He had taken care of business tonight, that was all. He always did just what he had to do. A person couldn't be blamed for that. When people got in the way, that was their fault, really. Some people didn't have the sense to make a deal. So they got what they deserved. No sense belaboring a point.

He got in his car and drove home.

Chapter 27

"We can't get through. The bastard's had all the calls transferred to his office." Cal slammed his hand on the counter in the sound booth, making the lights on the console blink.

"Cool, it Cal. You knocking down the station isn't going to help matters. Use your head man. Use your head." Paul's voice was firm.

Cal nodded, knowing what the man said was true. Cassandra's eyes were still wet with her tears, but she had stopped sobbing, and was watching Cal intently.

"They just called us. They can make phone calls, they just aren't receiving them." Cal said thoughtfully.

"How about calling the cops, man," said Paul, his pony tail bobbing as he shook his head.

"There's a cop working on this, Paul," admitted Cal. "He said he needed more time."

"I want them to know I'm alive," said Cassandra softly, but with determination in her voice. "They have to know that they're not alone."

"We'll get them to call again," said Cal in a raspy voice, amazed at the emotion that he felt. His mind started to work. "Cassandra, quick. What's Duncan's social security number? Write it down here." He pushed a tablet in front of her, and she wrote furiously.

"Does he have a student number at school?" She nodded, not having any idea what his plan was, but she added the number to the sheet.

"How about a locker combination? His basketball shirt number? Highest number of points he ever scored in a game?"

When they had completed the list, it was over 20 digits long, each series of numbers separated with dashes.

"What is this for, Cal? I don't understand?"

Cal smiled at Cassandra. "You said these guys are smart, Cass. We're gonna see just how smart they are. We're going fishing! We're going to get them to call us."

He flicked on the microphone as a noisy rock tune came to a finish. "Now, listening audience, it's time for tonight's Genius Hunt...get a pencil and get ready to play. The prize for the winner is a great one..."

Cal paused and looked at Paul. They both shrugged their shoulders. Then Paul took the mike with a gleam in his eyes.

"Yeah, Man, Wow," he said in his slow drawl. "Cal's really got a great one for you guys out there in radio land...."

Cal looked at him threateningly, but Paul just laughed. "Winner gets 2 tickets to next week's concert at the Civic Center. You'll be the envy of ALL your friends."

Cal covered the mike. "You idiot," he said in a whisper. "That concert has been sold out for weeks. I'd have to give scalped tickets. We're talking about a couple hundred bucks here..."

Paul kept smiling. "Yeah, well man, if you want to catch a good fish, you have to use good bait!!!"

Even Cal had to grin. Paul was a nut, but it would be worth it to get in touch with those boys.

"Here we go folks, write this number down." He proceeded to dictate the number, saying each digit carefully into the microphone. "First one to call to tell me the significance of this string of numbers is a winner." He repeated the number chain again, and repeated the phone number for the private line.

In a minute, another song request was playing on the air, and the mike was off. The three waited in silence in the booth, but the phone didn't ring. He repeated the number string into the microphone. Cal reached over and took Cassandra's hand, which was cold and clammy. "Give it a chance, Cass, give it a chance." She nodded, and the three of them sat glumly waiting for the phone to ring.

****

At the house, Duncan and Peter were still in Duncan's room, feeling anxious and knowing that their father would be returning soon. The radio played softly in the background, but neither of them was listening, both lost in their own worlds of fear and depression. "I want to run away, Dunc," said Peter miserably. "You know he'd find us. Besides, where would we go? We can't even find Aunt Diana."

"I have the tape, Dunc." He pulled it out of his pocket. "We have the number. We could call the agent."

Duncan rubbed his jaw, which was aching like crazy. "Sure, make a long distance call, Peter." His voice was sarcastic. "Just be sure to duck when dad gets the bill."

Peter's eyes misted again. "Don't cry again, you twit," Duncan admonished. "There's no sense crying. Just go find something to do."

"I'll call Tommy. I'll find out what was going on in school this week while I was out. God, it's been a horrible week. I'll be glad to go back to school Monday."

Dunc nodded without speaking. School seemed like another lifetime away. Peter called Tommy, who picked up the phone on the first ring.

"Peter, did you figure it out?" Tommy said excitedly. "Wouldn't it be awesome to get tickets to the concert? It's been sold out for weeks, at least that's what my sister said."

Tommy's sister Susan was pretty much the last word in coolness at the high school. She was great looking, a cheerleader, and could dance like somebody on TV.

Duncan was so petrified of her, Peter knew, he couldn't even talk to her. He would start stammering and blushing all over the place. But if Susan said that the tickets were a catch, they were a catch. Case closed.

"So how do you win these tickets, Tom?" said Peter, glad for the minute to have something to think about other than the back side of his father's hand.

"What kind of a Geek are you, anyhow? Aren't you listening to the Radio? It's Cal. He's giving away tickets if you can solve this puzzle he put on. It's a bunch of numbers."

Peter could hear papers rattling in the background. "Get a pencil, Doofus, and I'll read them to you, said Tommy. "I'm not having a lot of luck here, and you're pretty good at puzzles. But if you win, you take me, hear?"

"Sure Tom, sure," he complied, picking up an old envelope and a pencil from Duncan's desk. "Shoot."

The list was long, but Peter wrote it down. "I'll call you later, man. Or you can call me."

"Better call me. I think there's something wrong with your phone. I tried to call you at suppertime, but the phone kept ringing at your dad's office or something."

"That's weird."

"That's what I thought, but anyway, you call me, OK?"

"OK."

Peter hung up the phone thoughtfully.

"Duncan, Tom says when he calls here, the phone rings in Dad's office. Did you hear the phone ring at all tonight?"

"Not since this afternoon. The last call was the one from New York..." He stopped talking and the boys looked at each other solemnly, realization creeping up on them.

"He fixed the phone. He fixed it so we can't get any calls."

"Shit." said Duncan.

Peter opened the phone book. "It's called call forwarding. I think I can change it if I read about the codes."

Duncan reached over and slammed the phone book shut. His jaw was still aching, and now he had a headache. "Leave it, man. It's not worth getting him any madder than he already is."

"I feel like a prisoner, Duncan."

"Me too."

"If only mom were here. I know she's not dead."

Duncan's eyes softened and he mussed his little brother's hair. "I know how you feel, little brother. Best thing is to find something to do."

He flopped down on the bed and closed his eyes, and Peter turned his attention to the number puzzle in front of him. He reached over and turned up the dial to hear Your Pal Cal. At least Cal and Paul could make him laugh.

The puzzle was tough. Cal came on the radio again and repeated the numbers. No one had called in yet. This was one tough puzzle. He kept concentrating on it.

"Duncan, does this number make any sense to you?"

He gave out the first five digits. Duncan had his head on the pillow, arm over his eyes. "Sure. Duncan repeated the five, and then said 4 more numbers. That's my social security number. "

Peter stared, puzzled, at the list in front of him. The four numbers Duncan had added were the next on his list. "How about 02498?" he asked. The hairs on the back of his neck were standing up, and he felt like he had the chills.

"That's my student number. Stay out of my desk, twerp."

"How about 23-34-12?"

Duncan jumped up, finally. "That's my locker combination number, you snoop. Where'd you get that?"

Peter stared at him, opening his mouth wide, but words wouldn't come out. The radio was playing in the background, and suddenly Cal's voice filled the room.

"Here's the list again, folks." He repeated the numbers on the air. Duncan was frozen on the spot. "We need a winner for these concert tickets, or else Paul is going to get them, and you know how hard it is for him to get a date. Have mercy here, and solve this puzzle! Call my private line…" Cal recited the number twice.

"Dunc?" asked Peter hesitatingly.

"Give me the list, Peter." His voice was shaky, but determined. The numbers were there, in black and white. His social security number, school ID number, book locker number. Then there was his basketball shirt number, then the highest number of points he ever scored.

"This is me, all right. This list of numbers is me. "

"Call the phone number," said Peter, staring at the list, chewing on a pencil eraser.

"How did he get these numbers, Peter?" He looked fiercely at his little brother. "Did you give him these numbers when you called before?"

"No, Dunc. You heard every word I said. I didn't even talk about you. I don't even know your stupid locker number."

Duncan was thoughtful. He knew that that was true. Who could have given Cal these numbers? And why? There was only one person who could recite a list like this, besides himself. And that person was dead.

He remembered the day that his mother had sat patiently at the kitchen table when he had started high school. He had been in a panic, having locked his books in his locker, and forgotten the combination. "23-34-12," his mother and he had chanted over and over and over, until he knew it in his sleep. Just knowing that combination had given him the courage to face school the next day.

His body was tense all over, and he was finding it was a little hard to breathe. He was tingling all over.

"Give me the phone, Peter."

He dialed the private number at the radio station.

"Your Pal Cal, here," said the voice of his favorite DJ.

"You're listing my numbers. It's me in the contest. This is Duncan Ellington. What's this about, man?"

Cal smiled, and pulled Cassandra to his side. "I'm sorry to trick you like this, Duncan, but I had to get you to call. I have to talk to you about something important. It's about your mom."

Peter had scrunched over next to him, trying to hear in the receiver, too.

"I know." His voice sounded older, somehow, like he had suddenly grown up in the course of a few seconds. "It was the locker number. No one but my mom knows my locker number. Peter was right. She's not dead."

"She had an accident, Duncan, but she's very much alive. Ready to talk?"

And then Cassandra was on the line, talking to her boys, one then the other, and explaining to them about the accident, about her fears for them.

"I knew you were alive, Mom," Peter said through his tears. "I could just feel it. But don't come back, mom. Don't come back. Dad is really...."

"Shhh. I know that things are bad with dad. That's why I'm calling you now. I heard your voice on the radio before, and I couldn't stand not talking to you."

Cal took the phone. "Are you boys OK for now? There is a policeman named Marvin Greenstein who is trying to help us. He is trying to get some information to bring an end to this. We want you to know that you're not alone and that your mom is trying to make a new life for you. You can call this station number 24 hours a day, or you can call me at the house or on my cell. He gave them his numbers, and Marv's number at the station. Just don't do anything crazy, or put yourselves in danger, while we unravel this thing."

There was noise in the house, sounds that meant that Frederick had come home.

"Dad's home. We gotta go."

The phone went back on the hook just as the bedroom door opened. "You boys still up?"

Frederick looked tired, his shirt was open at the collar, and there were dark circles under his eyes.

"Just going to bed, dad." The monster light that had been in his eyes earlier was now gone. He would act as if nothing had ever happened, and would expect them to do the same. They knew the drill well.

"Take showers. Then get some sleep."

"OK."

"You're listening to Your Pal Cal on Radio station WDRK." boomed the radio. Duncan reached over and turned off the radio and they hustled obediently off to the bathroom.

Too obediently. Frederick narrowed his eyes, looking around the room. The phone sat on Duncan's bed. Had they been on the phone? He knew that they couldn't have received calls, but had they made any?

He reached for the phone. He hit *69, automatic return call. The phone rang once, and it was picked up at the other end. "You've reached Your Pal Cal on WDRK. Can I help you?"

Silently, Frederick replaced the receiver on the hook. The damn DJ. They had been talking to the damn DJ. Harmlesss but aggravating. He had heard sections of the man's show, the show his boys idolized. A bunch of rot. Tomorrow he would look into finding out a little more about Your Pal Cal. He wasn't going to have some radio nut messing with his kids' heads.

But meanwhile, he was going to bed. It was late, and he had had a hell of a day. But then he smiled. Tomorrow would be better. The worst was over now. Finally, things would be going his way. No one could stop him now.

Chapter 28

Marv Greenstein got into work early the next morning, and it was a good thing. First, after checking in with Cal, he found out that the Ellington boys had been told that their mom was alive, and that Cal and Cassandra believed that more extensive abuse was going on in the house. He was going to have to put an end to that, or blow the whole whistle on the whole thing. The kids had to be protected, first priority.

But then, the chief had come to the door of his office, stack of papers flapping in his hand. "This will finish off the case, Marv. Add this to your report, tie up any loose ends, and get the report on my desk by tomorrow."

He was gone in a flash, leaving Marvin to look over the reports he had been handed. He sat in his chair with a plop, spilling coffee all over the front of his nice clean white shirt. A grainy black and white photo stared back up at him, a picture of death.

The photo showed the half clad body of a drowned woman, her long dark hair streaming over her face, and blocking the view of her features. He felt as if he had been punched in the solar plexus. Cassandra?

He took a deep breath, reading the short report followed that followed.

"Young Caucasian woman, body retrieved from the river early this morning when it was spotted wedged between rocks near the river's edge, far south of town. From the battered condition of the body, it was suspected that the victim had entered the river far north of town, and had been bounced along the rocks as the current flowed to where she had been found. An early morning fisherman had spotted her and had called the police.

Initial expectations were that it was the missing body of Cassandra Ellington, whose remains had not been recovered from the fatal car wreck north of town some days before. An autopsy and proper identification were being done at the moment, results ASAP."

He grabbed the phone and called Cal's house, his reflexes tense and his mind awhirl. He woke Cal up.

"Is she there? Is she OK?" His imagination was running wild, like Frederick finding her after she told the boys she was alive, and deciding he was better off if she was dead. His stomach was churning, as if he were on the river himself.

"Waking me up, copper? This better be good."

Cal and Cassandra had stayed up talking and talking until the wee hours of the morning. He felt like his eyelids had bricks on them.

"Go check Cassandra. Tell me she's ok."

Cal was awake now, and he didn't question the authority and fear in his friend's voice. He bounded up the steps with his heart in his mouth. What was Marv talking about?

Cassandra was sleeping gently in her bed, curled up on her side, which was becoming a familiar sight. His heart rate returned to normal. He ran back down the steps.

"She's fine."

"Thank God."

"What's going on, Marv?"

"A female body was pulled from the river this morning. Of course, the force assumed it was Cassandra. I got scared. Took 20 years off my life, at least."

"She's OK, Marv. I'm not going to have anything happen to this lady."

"I'm going try to help the kids today. I'll be in touch."

"Marv," Cal asked, as the phone call was coming to an end. "But who is the woman in the river? Coincidence?"

"I've been a cop too long to believe in coincidence when it comes to crime."

Cal nodded as he hung up the phone. He was still exhausted, but he knew he wouldn't sleep, worrying about Cassandra. He took his pillow and crept into his room, taking his spot in what was becoming his favorite chair in the house. He leaned his head back, against the wall, hearing the soft rhythm of her sleep. She was safe. He drifted into sleep himself, not even caring about the stiff neck he was going to have from sleeping in the chair.

****

Janie let out a big sigh. Work at the realty office had been incredibly busy since she had stepped in the door (for once on time). Even Agnes was getting a workout. The phones were ringing, and papers were flying. Members of the town borough council were in and out. Nothing like a lot of local politicians to screw up a day.

The gist of the confusion was a land purchase the town was getting ready to settle, concerning land for the new zoo. The closing was set for Tuesday morning, and since it was already Friday, and there was still a lot of paper work to do for the big event, tempers were flying high with all the little details that had slipped through the cracks. Bankers were calling with mortgage information. It seemed when a town gets a mortgage it's a bigger pain than even for an individual. You'd think the banks would realize that the town wasn't going anywhere fast, and their money was safe...but what did she know about high finance?

To her, it meant a lot of work, toting more donuts and coffee for the assorted bigwigs who were scurrying around, and having to come into more contact than usual with the ever non-effervescent Agnes. Forms, forms and more forms. But the worst thing was Mr. Sloboski's early morning pronouncement that they would be working late (and on a Friday, to boot), staying until every "i" was dotted and every staple was properly implanted. Mr.Sloboski wasn't used to closings of this magnitude, that was evident. And he wasn't about to leave anything undone for the last minute.

It was a command performance, so of course she'd stay. But it did mean missing out on the new Country Western band that was playing at the Oaks, and of course, telling Bernie she'd be late.

She had called him right away, catching him at the plumbing office before he went off on his customer calls.

"It's ok, honey bun," he said in that cute little voice of his. "You do what you gotta do, and I'll see you when you get home. We'll catch that band next week if they're still around. And if they ain't, then they probably weren't that danged good, and we didn't miss much, right?"

What a guy.

"How about dinner?"

"I'll call and order us a pizza, so it'll be here whenever you get home, too, OK?"

How could she argue with that? A handsome guy and a gourmet meal, too.

"Just tell that Mr. Sloboski with all the dag-burned money he's gonna be making, he oughta let me come in and give him an estimate to replace that infernal plumbing and inferior fire sprinkler system he has. Like a blasted dinosaur in this day and age! It's trouble waiting to happen."

"I'll tell him," she laughed, knowing it wouldn't do any good. The only thing Mr. Sloboski would get excited about was if his coffee pot went on the blink. He didn't care if the water pipes howled a bit, or if the fire sprinklers were a little teensy bit old fashioned and couldn't be turned off once they were activated. As long as his coffee was hot, and the donuts had nice gooey cream...

She got off the phone still feeling put upon for having to work overtime, especially at the typewriter, which was one of her worst enemies. But she at least felt great about Bernie, as usual. She went back to work, humming "He's My Kind of Guy," a hit from the country western station she loved to listen to...when Agnes wasn't around to complain.

****

It was almost noon when Marv Greenstein left the station, driving toward the Ellington house. The coroner's report had come in about the drowning victim.

Female, Caucasian, approximately age 21. 5'6", about 120 pounds. Not Cassandra. No evidence of drugs or alcohol. The autopsy stated that she had been dead by the time her body hit the water. There had been no river water breathed into her lungs. Death had probably been caused by a severe blow to the head, though the number of blows the body had received from the trip through the river rocks had made it virtually impossible to give details about the fatal blow itself.

Her identity hadn't been established yet, but Marv knew that it probably would be discovered soon. After the word about the discovery of the body leaked out, people would start coming forward and inquiring about missing relatives and friends. Horrible stuff, losing a young life like that. But it hadn't been Cassandra. And sympathetic as he was to the young woman on the slab in the morgue, he was glad it wasn't Cassandra.

He pulled up to the Ellington house, and was in for a surprise. A TV news van was parked in the driveway, a few people scurrying to and from carrying light meters, spotlights, and camera cords. Did this have to do with the river victim? Those poor boys. Did they think it had been their mother? He threw the car into park with a jerk, apologizing to the older but reliable Ford that was his only mode of transportation, and bounded up the sidewalk to the front door.

He didn't have to knock, as it opened right in front of him. He recognized the young man who stood there from TV. It was Charlie Upworth, the local TV reporter who appeared almost daily on his television screen. Funny, the guy was a lot shorter in real life. And he looked like he was wearing makeup on his cheeks. Yuck.

"Upworth?" he questioned, getting the reporter's attention. "Greenstein, from the police." He flashed his badge. Now he really had the reporter's focus.

"It wasn't her," Marv said to the reporter. The reporter looked at him blankly. "It wasn't Cassandra Ellington pulled from the river. We don't have an ID yet, but we know it wasn't her. No need to upset the family here." He felt so protective of those boys. They had been through a hell of a lot, and he had a feeling there was a lot more to come.

"Sorry, Detective," said the reporter easily. "I'm not sure what you're talking about. I'm here about the book contract. Ellington's agent called the station first thing this morning and we're having a live hookup with the noon news." He glanced at his watch, and snapped to attention. "Gotta go, sir. I'm on the air in two minutes and this makeup dude has me looking like Madonna in this indoor light makeup. I've got to get some of it off."

"OK, kid. See you later. And I agree about the makeup. Understatement is so much more.... elegant, don't you think?" His eyes sparkled with a bottled up laugh. Usually, he didn't have much time for the press. In his city experience, they were always a pain in the ass, harassing and upsetting people to get a story, adding grief upon grief to every tragedy, just for ratings.

But this kid had a light in his eyes that he liked. Despite the too red cheeks.

"Thanks, copper," Charlie laughed. "Maybe I'll get you on staff as my makeup consultant."

"I'll take it!"

Charlie disappeared into the van, and Marv turned and walked into the front door, which was standing open. An assortment of people stood around Frederick Ellington, attaching a microphone, fixing his hair. An elderly man, evidently his agent, stood to his side. Nobody noticed Marvin in the chaotic crowd, so he just stood to the side, and watched with interest as the different technicians did their thing. The boys, dressed in suits, stood off to the side, looking silent and pensive.

Charlie Upworth barged back in the door, took a microphone in hand, and stood next to Frederick Ellington.

"You know how it's done, Ellington," Charlie said easily. "Just look into the camera, and be yourself."

Frederick smiled, but the smile didn't reach his eyes. Charlie just didn't like this man.

"Three, two, one...Camera," said a black woman with close cropped hair and wearing an African Dashiki over a pair of jeans.

"This is Charles Upworth, ANC News, bringing you a live noon report. Today we are at the gracious home of Professor Frederick Ellington, noted and esteemed writer and professor at the University. It has just been released that Mr. Ellington's newest novel, entitled "Intimacies", a mystery thriller, has just been scheduled for publication with Aardvaark Books."

He turned to Ellington. "Professor, are you going to let us in on the details of your new contract? Rumor has it that this will be the most successful novel yet in your long line of successful books."

"I'm not about to spill the beans, Mr. Upworth," said Frederick, in his most charming manner, "But let us say that this will be one of the highlights of my writing career so far."

"We're most pleased," piped in Robert Austin, his agent, when introduced, "With Professor Ellington's superb work. Again, he has pulled off the magnificent magic of presenting us with a work that has a different style, a flair all of its own. He's a multi-talented writer. The book will be a smashing success. Hopefully, it will hit the shelves by Christmastime. We're even discussing a possible movie option already."

The interview had gone well, smoothly and positively. It was only at the very end that Frederick's eyes traveled the room, and came to light on Marvin Greenstein standing in the corner. For a split second, Frederick's face registered a flash of dismay, of panic. But it was gone as quick as it had come, replaced by a serious, professional look as he finished with the newscaster.

"We'll be looking forward to reading this new masterpiece by our local resident author." He turned his body a little after that sentence, as if ending the interview with Frederick, but still on the air.

"It's a wonder, with all that Frederick Ellington has had to deal with in the past week with the tragic accident of his wife, Cassandra Ellington, that we can share this great piece of positive news. Hopefully, the publication of a new book will be able to replace some of the joy lost in this household in the recent tragic death of his wife. This is Charles Upworth, ANC news."

The flurry of activity began again, this time removing the photographic equipment to restore it to the truck. People drifted away, and Frederick turned to Charlie Upworth with hate and rage in his eyes. "You say one more blasted thing about my wife on that TV camera, and your next report will be on the wonders of plastic surgery. Your own."

Charlie looked back at him coolly. "Maybe we'll get a group deal. Me and your boys. Maybe you could hit us all on the same day, make it easy for scheduling the OR."

"What the hell are you talking about?"

"I've seen the black eyes and the bruises, and I've seen the fear. I know that fear when I see it. No matter how big a celebrity you are, Ellington, you aren't going to get away with beating your kids," Charlie sneered. "Where are they anyway?"

He turned and looked at Duncan and Peter, standing across the room. Duncan's jaw was bruised, and his eye was a little swollen. The discoloring in Peter's eye had begun to disappear, giving it a slight greenish tinge.

"Nice work, Professor," growled the newsman with his teeth clenched. "Boys, you ever need any help, you just let me know," he said to the boys standing in the corner. Then Charlie Upworth stormed out the door.

Although the two men had turned their faces away from the crowd, and their angry words were uttered in low tones, Marv had heard the exchange. He tapped Frederick on the shoulder.

Frederick spun around, immediately flashed his public smile. "Why, Detective Greenstein. Trying to get a little publicity, sir?" he said with charm, looking like he was on top of the world.

"I guess this is the place to be if that was my goal. Actually, I came to give you a little news. Before it hit the news, so to speak."

Frederick listened to him cautiously.

"They found a body in the river this morning."

Frederick stiffened.

"But it wasn't Cassandra. I just wanted to let you know. She was too young, a Jane Doe at this point. But definitely not Cassandra."

Frederick's eyes looked stricken.   "Thanks, Detective. I hadn't heard. The boys..."

"Well, that's what this is about. I didn't want the boys upset. I'm going to make it a personal quest that those boys don't get any more upset by this stuff."

"Hi, guys," Marv said, turning to Duncan and Peter who stood quietly nearby. "I'm Detective Greenstein."

His eyes bore into theirs, and he knew they had heard his name from Cal. Smart kids. They didn't react.

"I was telling your dad you are going to hear that a body was pulled from the river today. But it wasn't your mother's body, and I wanted to make sure you knew that. I knew how hard all this has been on you guys. Duncan, isn't it?" He addressed the taller boy.

"Yes, sir."

"What happened to your face?"

"I, er, walked into the door."

"Bad thing, doors. Take care."

"Go on to your rooms now, boys, the newscast is over. Start on your homework."   Frederick's voice was tight. Did he know Greenstein had heard the reporter's remarks? He was definitely uneasy.

"I'm sorry to cut this short, Detective, but I have to get back to the University."

"Certainly. I just wanted to bring you up to date on the latest. And to make sure the boys were ok. Like I said, the most important thing is that the boys are ok. No more doors, right?"

"Kids can be so clumsy under stress."

"Lots of people can be clumsy under stress. And not just about doors."

He turned and left the house, content that his message had been heard and received. Frederick Ellington would think twice about striking the boys again, with both a cop and and a news reporter snooping around. He liked that Charlie Upworth. A pain in the ass newsman, but a bright kid. And he seemed to care about the boys. That was good. Marv started whistling as he climbed into his car and headed back to the station.

Chapter 29

Marv put in a long day. At supper time, he slipped out of the station and went to the diner. He ate a steak sandwich, smothered in onions. He didn't have to worry about his breath, he thought with a small sigh of dismay. There was no one to complain that he smelled like an old onion, no one whose eyes lit up when he appeared.

Funny, that hadn't bothered him for a long time. A really long time. He had put all his energy into recovering from alcohol, adjusting to his new small town life, and being the best cop he knew how to be. Also the best human being, he added as an aside. He had good friends, a good job, a good life. But all of a sudden, sometimes in the middle of the night, or maybe just when ordering a steak sandwich, there was this inner yearning that someone cared. And that he cared for that someone. Another phase maybe. God, he was always going through phases.

He returned to the police station and was greeted with the somber news. Jane Doe of the river had been identified. The chief had decided to assign him to the case (mostly, he thought, because he had already been handed the initial paperwork when it was assumed the body was Cassandra's).

The guys at the front desk were already calling him the "River Renegade" and "Marv Water-stein". They thought they were hilarious. He thought they were certifiable, but he let them have their fun.

He didn't mind the assignment, really. He had a lot of questions about the woman, who he now knew was named "Pamela Gravely". Her parents had reported her missing, and had called when they heard that an unidentified body had been found. Nice people, the chief had mentioned. They had been in to identify the body, and he was scheduled to stop by their house at 8PM. Not the best part of his job.

He drove to the modest bungalow, on the west side of town, far away from the river. He pulled into the driveway, noticing the house showed a bit of wear. There were cracks in the driveway, where already spring weeds were making their appearance. The house was aluminum sided, so it didn't need paint, exactly, but it had an air about it that was crying for a good sprucing up.

Marv rang the bell and was admitted by a woman in her late forties, slight and blonde and tired looking, eyes red from crying. She was wearing an apron. She asked him in right away. "You're the detective who's going to help us find out about Pamela?" Her voice was soft and kind, and she was evidently in great pain. He didn't doubt it.

"Yes, Ma'am. Marvin Greenstein. I'm going to do whatever I can to find out what happened to your daughter. And I'm very, very, sorry." He was sincere, and she nodded at him.

"Come on in, Bruce is in the living room. He's a bit upset."

Understatement, that. Bruce was practically a basket case. He was sitting in his chair, feet propped up on a faded ottoman, the TV was on, but screen was just solid blue. Tears were running down the man's face, and a half empty bottle of scotch stood at his elbow. Marvin couldn't blame him a bit. Some things were just too damn hard to handle. He remembered the feeling.

He crossed the room, and subtly turned off the TV. Then he pulled a chair up next to Bruce Gravely. Bruce finally raised his eyes and looked at him.

"There was none like my Pammy, you know. She was the best."

"That's what I'm hearing, Mr. Gravely. I'm very sorry."

To Mrs. Gravely, he said, "Do you have other relatives, Mrs. Gravely? Maybe a brother or sister or someone who could help you out here? Family can be a big help."

"My sister is coming tomorrow, Detective. From Pittsburgh. But it's a long drive. And first she had to get the car ready..."

He nodded, understanding. A lot of little details got stuck in the sea of pain. "That will be good. I'm sure she'll be here soon as she can." His voice was quiet, understanding. "Maybe it's better if I come back tomorrow, when you've had a little time to adjust." He looked at the half empty bottle of scotch and the man in the chair.

"No, stay," said Mrs. Gravely quietly. "The longer we wait, the less chance we will have to find out what happened. I need to know how my daughter ended up in that river. Somebody killed her, and I mean to know who and why."

It was obvious who had the strength in this house.

"OK," he said simply, pulling out his notebook. There was a lot of truth in what she said, but he hadn't wanted to push.

Bruce put his glass down. "Take this bottle away, Emmy. No sense me drinking myself into a stupor. We got a lot to do. And we got help here."

She removed the stuff in one swift, coordinated movement. He rubbed his eyes. "It's tough, accepting this."

"I believe you." said Marvin simply.

The next hour, he heard and wrote every fact and impression that he got of Pamela Gravely. They all painted the same picture. She had been a lovely girl, and excellent student, shy and hardworking. She had not had many friends, and had spent much of her time in her room, working on her writing project. She wanted to be a writer, her parents said with pride.

They had taken him to see her room, a neat little cubicle where she had slept, dreamed and had written. Her father flicked on her computer. "That's funny," he said in a bit of an alcohol stupor. "Her disk isn't here in the drive."

"Now, now," said Pamela's mother. "I'm sure it's there somewhere. She was very protective about her work, detective. Sometimes I think she was afraid we wouldn't approve of it. I have a feeling it was a bit....sensational. But I'm sure it's a good book. When I find it, I'll show it to you. She was so excited. She had just finished it. She was sure it was good and that she would get it published and make a lot of money." Her words caught a little in her throat as her eyes filled with tears.

"I'd like to see it. Did she have any boyfriends?" He got a negative answer, but he knew he'd have to pursue it further. Sometimes parents were the last to know. The autopsy has stated that she wasn't pregnant, and there was no evidence she was molested or raped. In fact, it appeared she was a virgin. A miracle, in this day and age. He didn't mention it to her parents.

Still, there may have been a boyfriend somewhere, and some kind of conflict. The whole thing didn't make sense yet, but he had only begun to investigate. He was trying to organize his mind, trying to decide what track to go off on first.

"She was such a good student, Detective. She loved school. She was in Professor Ellington's class at the college. He was such an inspiration to her writing."

Marv blinked. He blinked again. He knew what track he'd go on now, though he still hadn't quite figured out why. Call it a hunch. Call it his gut. He had the stinking feeling that the eminent Professor Frederick Ellington might play a part in all of this. He took his notes and thanked the family for their assistance, telling them he would be checking in soon to let them know what he had found.

Nice people. He pulled away from the squatty little house with its weedy driveway and felt very bad. Pamela Gravely had nice parents, and the odds were, she was a nice girl. Much too nice to end up lodged between rocks on the riverbank. He was going to find out what happened to her.

****

Marvin went over to Cal's house in the late afternoon, to talk about the discovery of Pamela Gravely's body, and how and if it could be tied into Cassandra, or more precisely, Frederick Ellington.

"Are you sure you never met this woman?" Marv asked gently, for about the fourth time. "Is there any chance that she was involved with Frederick? She was in his class."

"If she was in his class, he knew her, of course," she said without emotions. "His writing classes and his students were the focal point of his life. He would often talk to students on the phone, or read their compositions. Sometimes they would even come over to the house. This one, that one. But no Pamela Gravely that I can remember. No one who fits her description, either. Different ones would come and go over the semesters." She was thoughtful for a moment. "I really didn't pay much attention, I guess. I wasn't really welcomed or comfortable in that sphere of his life."

"Did he spend a lot of extra time at the university? You know, writing his books and stuff." Marv wrote down little thoughts as she spoke and listened to her responses. "Did he write mostly at home, or at his office at the university? It must take a lot of time, on top of his class schedule."

"Well," she began, "I guess he must have done a little of both. I mean, he didn't stay at the University until all hours or anything, but then he didn't hang out a lot at the house, either. He was on the phone a lot when he was home. Then he would play golf a bit, as long as the weather would permit it."

"Play golf with who?"

"Oh, I guess a lot of people. From the University. Or lawyers that he and his friend James Jenkins knew. Or doctors from the hospital." Her voice sounded a little bitter. "He knows everybody. He always bragged about his "connections". He said that it was important to develop a "network" of people. At least, that's the great advice he would give the boys..."

"He sounds like a busy guy. Classes, writing, golf and "networking." He's got a lot of energy," Marv said. "But no memories of Pamela, huh?"

Cassandra shook her head. Cal sat quietly by, just listening and watching. Marvin had shared many of his thought and feelings about Frederick Ellington, and Cal agreed, hands down, that he was a worm. But he didn't quite understand Marv's persistence in linking Ellington to the death of the poor girl found in the river. Who was this girl?

In fact, there was a lot he didn't understand here. He believed that Frederick had been manipulative and cruel, in trying to get Cassandra removed from his life by having her institutionalized. He could have divorced her, but he didn't. He had evidently spun quite an elaborate web to discredit and humiliate her, planning to hospitalize her against her will. But he didn't understand why.

Why? Marv could see nothing that Frederick would really gain with Cassandra committed and out of the way. It just didn't make sense. The whole thing didn't make sense. And they had to figure it out if they were going to help the boys. Just what were they up against?

The phone rang, and Cal picked it up automatically. "Cal here."

"Hi Calvin!" said the peppy voice of Janie on the on the end of the line.

"To what do I owe this honor? Are you calling me to brag about going to hear the country western band tonight while I'm stuck on the air?" He laughed as he said it.

"I wish. I'm working late. What a bummer," exclaimed Janie.

"What a miracle."

"Shut up, Mr. DJ. Actually I'm calling about something very strange and weird that is sitting on my desk at this moment."

"Is it alive?"

"No kidding, Cal. This is serious." Her usually cheerful voice was somber. "Remember asking Cassandra if she had any valuable assets? If there was any way that anyone would financially benefit from her death?"

"She said no."

"BZZZ! Wrong answer."

"What are you talking about, Janie? Give it to me straight."

"Here on my desk, I am typing the papers for a big real estate closing that is going to take place on Tuesday in this very office. Big stuff. That's why I'm working late, which you know how much I love. Confidential now, as this is not public information yet, and I'm risking my job here..."

"Which I know how much you love..."

"Right. Well, the city is the buyer in this deal. It's a total of 30 acres of prime land, originally residential and farmland, up on the west end of town. It's comprised of about 15 separate parcels, rolling hills and lots of green. The purchase of said land has been a big darn deal in the newspapers here."

A light went off in Cal's mind. "The new zoo."

"Bingo. Add cages, a few assorted animals, and a few peanuts, and presto...one Sollington Memorial Zoo."

"Sure. The city's been collecting money forever for that deal. Even on the station, we've been holding raffles and accepting donations for the past two years. A zoo is a good thing, Janie. What are you so hopped up about?"

"You belong in a zoo," snarled the frustrated redhead. "That's what I'm trying to tell you. About Cassandra. The deeds are right here in front of me. All 15 of them. They were purchased at various times over the last 18 months, at prices way under their market value. They will all be transferred to the city on Tuesday at 11AM, rain or shine, right in this office. The selling price is over three million dollars."

"Whew! That's alot of peanuts! We're getting a zoo, but somebody is getting quite a bank account."

"Now you're catching on, my almost bald one. It will be paid for by certified check. Monday, I have orders to do the financial arrangements for said money with the mayor at the bank. The check, my dear one, is to be made out to the person who is selling the property, the name on all fifteen deeds, a certain Cassandra Ellington."

Cal felt the color leaving his face. He turned and looked across the room at Cassandra, who was talking amicably with Marv, not paying attention to the phone conversation at all.

"Cat got your tongue, Buster?" Janie broke into his shock. "First time in the history of the world someone was able to shut up Calvin Johnson, I bet."

"Second."

"What?"

"It was the second time, Janie. You still win a prize. Tell me more about this deal. How can the city buy land from a supposedly dead woman? This doesn't make sense."

"But she's not dead."

Cal felt his temper flare. "Are you saying she knows about this? Are you saying that this is part of a plan?"

He had raised his voice, and Marv and Cassandra looked over his way, listening now, to see what had riled Cal.

"Keep your shirt on, Oh music master." Janie went on. "I'm not saying anything of the kind. Be it stupid, or naive or what, I think that Cassandra has been telling the truth. She probably has no idea about this property. But it exists, right here in black and white. The parcels were purchased over the recent past, all in her name, and all for cash, obviously planning this major resale to the city for the zoo. Looks like Freddy Boy Ellington has been up to a little trickery, and put the deals in his wife's name."

Cal was thinking fast. "So when she started to get testy, he thought up the alcoholism and emotional disturbance as a safety net...in case she did something exactly as she did...snap and go for help. If she complained about his abuse, he had already damaged her credibility. With whatever pull he had, he had arranged to get her committed, if necessary. If nothing had happened, he would have brought her along to obediently sign papers."

It was all making sense now. Ellington had put the land in her name for some reason or another, and he had been getting nervous as the selling time came close. But then there was the accident, and Cassandra supposedly had died.

"Isn't the sale off then, if she's considered dead?"

"But the courts have not declared her dead. There is a legal letter to that effect in this file. The courts will not declare her dead, without the body, for probably at least a year."

"Without the body?" Cal's stomach was starting to turn. Was it possible?

"I wonder if someone thought that Pamela Gravely's body would be mistaken for Cassandra's. If someone was desperate to have her declared dead..."

"Not that desperate, buddy. There's this one other little piece of paper in the file. It's called a power of attorney. It's legal, notarized, and recorded with the county. In the case that Cassandra Ellington is unavailable, incapacitated, or whatever, one Frederick Ellington is entitled to manage all her affairs. That includes real estate transfers, bank accounts..."

"Holy shit."

"Cal, I hate to cut this short, but here comes glorious Agnes in from her dinner break, so I can't talk. How about if I stop over later and we continue this interesting discussion out of range of Agnes' nosy little ears? Something stinks like old fish."

"Sure, Janie."

"Assemble the cast of characters there, and we'll figure this thing out. I'll bring copies. Bernie has pizza. You get dessert!"

Cal had to laugh. "How can you think about food at a time like this?"

"I can think of food at any hour of the day or night."

"Apple pie?"

"Perfect. I'll be there as soon as I finish this typing. Which may be a while. Typing isn't one of my finer talents. I think I'm going to need a new job."

"Your talents are being wasted at that one, that's for sure. See you later. I'll call Bernie."

"Thanks, Ciao!" The line went dead.

By now, Marv and Cassandra were staring at him with anxious curiosity. He took a deep sigh, turned around, and began to give them the details that Janie had stumbled upon.

"I don't know anything about that land, Cal," Cassandra said steadily, after hearing that story. "And I never signed any power of attorney form in my life."

"I believe you."

"There would be no way that he could believe Pamela Gravely's body would be identified as Cassandra," Marv said solemnly. "But it has to be tied in somewhere."

"Maybe not." Cal looked at his friend. "Maybe it's not even connected."

Marv frowned, looking out the window at the river rushing by. "It's connected. It's all connected."

In the end, Cal ran out for the apple pie, after putting in a quick call to Bernie to tell him about Janie coming over. Then they all just sat quietly, all lost in their own thoughts, while they waitcd for Janie to arrive with some of the missing pieces of the puzzle.

****

Jenkins was sweating, even though the air conditioning was running in his law office. He hated working nights. He hated the work he was doing, period. He hated Frederick Ellington. He had put down the phone with more force than necessary, the bang reverberating in the silence of the closed office.

It seemed to him that they were under enough pressure as it was, with the land deal hanging by a thread. Frederick had pulled a rabbit out of a hat, and had sold his manuscript to get a quick advance. He had given Jenkins the money...a wad of cash in a cheap briefcase to pay off the shiny shoed loan sharks earlier in the day. It was like something out of a bad movie, dealing with those guys.

And just when the dust was settling, he felt like he could breathe again. He had to concentrate on making sure the ducks were in a row for the real estate closing. But then Frederick had gotten a bee in his bonnet about some damn radio DJ he felt was "negatively influencing" his boys. "Check him out," he had said. The translation of that was, of course, "Find out something on the guy so that he can be controlled." Frederick believed that everyone could be controlled, sooner or later.

"I want to bring this guy down," Frederick has said with the snide tone he only showed Jenkins. "Guy thinks he can give all kinds of advice to kids, contrary to what their parents may say. Practicing psychology without a license. Get him, James. My kids are going to listen to me, and not some crazed quack. I don't want them complaining about me to some bleeding heart do-gooder."

Jenkins sighed, a long frustrated breath from deep inside. Could just about everyone be controlled? He feared that Frederick was pretty much right. Look at himself, James Jenkins, successful attorney, considered strong and upstanding in the community. He was a family man who had the world by the tail. Well, he might have the world by the tail, but the problem was, Frederick had HIM by the balls. So he spent his time at his beck and call, not just for these shaky business deals, but for any damn thing that crossed the man's punitive little mind. Some days, it just made him sick.

But he had done the job on the radio DJ, "Your Pal Cal", calling a few very sleazy but very productive private detectives who were used to doing Frederick's "research". They had been able to dig up a bit on this guy without too much trouble...He lifted the phone and called in his report.

"Frederick, you're not going to get anything on this guy for practicing without a license. They guy's a certified shrink. Credentials all over the place. Dr. Calvin Johnson, originally from Chicago. He wrote several books, mostly textbooks for college. He was a speaker on the intellectual circuit for several years. He had a big time radio show in Chicago, made lots of bucks, and got lots of coverage. He gave advice on his show, and was like a local guru. He's been on Dr. Phil, Oprah. Big time stuff."

"Why are you sounding so amazingly cheerful as you give me this garbage. I thought I told you I wanted something to shut this guy up. I didn't know you were his PR man."

"Keep your shirt on and think, Frederick. From big time to a tiny station in Sollington? The chink in the armor? The guy's a drunk, Frederick. He cracked under the fame pressure in Chicago, and ended up breaking his contract. He disappeared, spent time in one of those secret detox hospitals that aren't supposed to ever verify that you were there. Of course, like you say, everyone has their price. I have a fax here of his records."

"You're a good man, Jenkins." Frederick sounded like a predator, salivating for its kill.

Jenkins did not feel like "good man" aptly described the way he felt about himself. He felt anything but good. But he went on.

"He's been at this station for a couple of years, nothing much to report on in this location. He's popular with the station, the advertisers, the kids, the schools, the whole works. Keeps to himself. No dirt. But the past is a different matter, and he isn't going to keep his job if the public doesn't trust him."

"OK, Jenkins, I'll take care of him from here on. Talk to you tomorrow."

The phone went dead. A little part of James Jenkins went dead too. Every time he did the dirty work for Frederick Ellington, a little more of his soul seemed to be destroyed. Pretty soon he wasn't going to have any soul left at all.

He opened the desk drawer and pulled out an expensive bottle of scotch. Nestled with it was a crystal glass. It sparkled in the light of the desk lamp. Only the best. He filled the glass and gulped it down, repeating the action several times before he slowed down. His throat burned, his stomach felt fire for a minute, but the effects of the alcohol began to work quickly, and he welcomed it.

In a short time, he would be home at his magnificent house, probably to find his strong minded wife already asleep in their magnificent bedroom, right down the hall from his magnificent children. It was a life any one would envy. Anyone with a soul, anyway.

In a rush of emotion, he picked up the crystal glass, and threw it across the room. It crashed against the marble of the fireplace, smashing into smithereens. It was hard on a man, living without a soul.

He put the remaining scotch back in the drawer of his elegant desk, stopping at the fireplace to carefully pick up the glass shards, hiding the evidence of his ineffectual tantrum in a large brown envelope that he slid into the bottom of the trash can. And then he closed the door to his office and went home.

Chapter 30

"I swear if I ever meet the man who invented the typewriter, the guy is dead meat."

Janie literally fell into Cal's living room at about 9PM. Cal was off for the night, as the radio station was broadcasting a high school baseball game live. The local team had made the state playoffs.

Cassandra and Marv were sitting on the floor. Bernie was stretched out on the couch, reading the paper, and finishing the crust of a piece of pepperoni pizza.

Janie carried her purse, 2 three liter bottles of soda, and had a large donut box under her arm.

"Donuts!" exclaimed Bernie, wolfing down his last bite of the pizza, and grabbing for the box.

"Get away, you beast!" she laughed, dramatically rescuing the box from his clutches. "I've had it with macho donut-eating male chauvinists for the day. For the records, this box does not contain donuts. It's full of legal documents."

She put down her load, and opened the box, pulling out a roll of papers held with a rubber band.

"Ta Da!" she exclaimed, handing the roll to Cassandra. "Here are copies of the closing papers. Cassandra, you're a land baron, did you know? And I took my life in my hands, making these copies and smuggling them out under the ever watchful eyes of Agnes."

She shook the empty donut box. "Nice touch, eh? Agnes would never look in a donut box. She thinks that you can "catch" calories by just looking at carbohydrates. Boy, I'm some kind of detective. I could star in my own TV show."

Janie dug into the remaining pizza, warming it up in Cal's microwave and pouring a big cup of soda. The five of them huddled around the kitchen table, where Janie explained the plot plans and deeds for the land that was currently held in Cassandra's name.

The plots had been acquired, the dates showed, one at a time, paid for by cash, over the past several years. Cassandra's name was on every deed.

"Look at all that cash," wondered Cal, adding up the figures. "Seems like it is much more than a professor could come up with, even with successful book sales to his name."

"You sound like you're a writer, Cal." Cassandra looked at him with inquisitive eyes.

Cal laughed. "Yep. In my past life, I spent a bit of time at the keyboard, plugging out a few books. Heady, academic stuff. Not sensational, like Frederick's fiction. I hate to admit that he's a talented guy, especially with the variety of styles that he uses. But it's just that even in my most successful days, I could never pull in money to cover a deal like this. But maybe fiction sales are much bigger..."

"Well," considered Cassandra, "The book sales were occasionally good, but it costs a lot to live the way we lived. It took a lot of money to buy this land. Too much money."

"Well, it has to be from the book sales. He must write his tail off to get royalties like that."

"To tell you the truth," Cassandra said softly, now deep in thought, "I don't think Frederick spent much time at all on his writing. He spent a lot of time preparing for his classes, and then he spent time with his writing students..."

"Well, when we find out where he got this money, it'll answer a lot." Marv shook his head.

They turned their attention to the power of attorney. It was dated about a month previously, and contained a statement that it superseded any prior power of attorney assignments.

"That is not my signature," stated Cassandra emphatically. "I did not sign that form, or any other one."

"He must have been getting nervous that you would find out about this, Cassandra. He must have worried that you were getting more strong minded, not getting along with him, and he had too much at risk if you got wind of this deal before it took place. You could have ruined what looks like an intricate plan here."

"So if I made trouble, he'd have me locked up in a hospital somewhere, where I wouldn't see papers or any of the publicity of the sale, and he'd teach me a lesson, as a bonus." She shivered at the prospect.

"There's something that scares me in this," Marv explained. Marv explained about his investigation at the hospital, and the liquor store, and how people who were credible and established were ready to swear on a stack of bibles that they agreed with Frederick Ellington's description of his wife. They reported that she was a hopeless alcoholic who was a danger to herself and to her children.

How could the man get away with it? And how were they going to stop him? Even if Cassandra appeared "from the dead" right now, she would have a heck of a time establishing her sanity and her stability, against the witness of these supposed reliable experts.

They were deep in their thoughts when the phone rang, sounding like an explosion in the quiet night.

The call was for Marv. "Funny thing, Greenstein," said a young cop who was working the front desk at the police station. "A few minutes ago, a strange thing happened. A little kid, maybe 11 or 12 years old, curly dark hair, comes up to the station door, on his bicycle. In one hand, he's carrying a gallon of milk. In the other, he has this little package. He parks the bike, comes into the station, still carrying the milk, and presents me with this other package. And it's 9:30 at night. Weird. The package is addressed to you, and it's marked personal."

"He had dark curly hair? Age 11 or 12? Did you get a name?"

"Naw, I tried, but he bolted. All I got out of him was that his first name was Tommy, and that he had to hurry home with the milk."

Marv felt his gut relax. It wasn't Duncan or Peter. But why was a kid delivering packages to him? He turned to Cassandra.

"Do you know any kid named Tommy?"

Cassandra's eyes grew large. "Well, yes. There's Tommy who's Peter's best friend in the world."

For the first time since he had heard the name of Cassandra Ellington, he felt like he was going to get answers. His adrenaline was flowing, and he was excited. If Peter's friend Tommy had snuck to the station to deliver something to him, it was bound to be damn important.

"Hold it right there," he told the cop. "I'm coming to get it."

With a few words of explanation, he left the others at the house and drove his car to the station, pushing the speed limit as much as he dared. Answers. He was hoping to get answers.

****

Marv Greenstein made it to the station in record time. The traffic was light at that hour. His adrenaline was flowing.

The package was waiting for him at the front desk. He grabbed it, mumbling a rushed thanks to the man at the desk. He flew down the hall to his office, shutting the glass door behind him.

The package was small, and almost square, maybe about three inches or so in diameter. It was secured with a couple of rubber bands, wrapped around a plain brown bag, a brown lunch sack, he correctly guessed. He ripped off the rubber bands, noting the words that had been hastily written on the sack. "To Detective Greenstine, Police. Private. From P & D" He had to smile, despite his excitement. They had misspelled his name, but they had remembered who he was. Smart boys.

He ripped the paper, and three cassette tapes fell out. He removed them from their plastic protective boxes, reaching simultaneously into his desk drawer with his left hand. He pulled out a small cassette player.

The cassettes were labeled with dates, and he put them into date order, plunking the first into the player. Tapes from an answering machine? He pushed the play button. It was blank. There was no recording on it. He turned it over and played the other side, willing his body not to panic. He pushed the play button again. Pay dirt.

He listened carefully to the first conversation that the boys had recorded, probably from the phone at home. Frederick's voice....and James Jenkins, the man who was his attorney. They had been speaking on the phone. He heard them reference the phony power of attorney form, and heard about the land deal that was scheduled to take place. He took in the comments about people putting pressure on him for their investment. In the second tape, he heard the threats that a loan shark had made, and the ultimatum of 48 hours for a payback. That fell far short of the scheduled land deal. What was going on here? It sounded like Frederick had gotten in over his head.

The third tape was a puzzling one. It was from a guy with a spaced-out voice, probably long distance, by the sound of the static on the wire. He had been calling back, giving information about locating someone named Diana...What did that have to do with it all? At first, he thought that the tape had been included by mistake. But after the final beep on the message, there was a short blank space, and then a young voice came through. He was pretty sure it was Duncan, Cassandra's son.

"Detective, we don't know what this all means, but we know our dad is into something bad...he gets meaner and scarier every day. I hope you can use this to take care of our mom. We know she's alive, and we want to keep her that way. Maybe Diana can help."

The tape was blank from that point on.

Marv sat, rubbing his jaw. Five o'clock shadow had long since made an appearance on his cragged face. He felt the prickles of his beard as he tried to think. The information, of course, wasn't usable as any kind of evidence, but it did reinforce a lot of the facts that they had been able to come up with about Frederick. The last tape was a bit of a mystery, but he felt certain that it was connected.

Two things ran through his mind. The first was that this cry of help from the boys was not going to be ignored. They had to be protected. They had to be removed from the care of the man who had instilled so much fear in them. Marv was no stranger to the system. He knew from experience how crazy and ineffectual the court system was when it came from protecting kids from abusive parents. He needed to break open this case, and to remove the boys from Frederick's control once and for all.

The second, parallel thing that crossed his mind had to do with Cassandra. Cassandra's instincts were right. This was not a man to be taken lightly. Frederick was in deep water as it was, with a history of abuse. If he were to find that Cassandra were still alive, there was no telling what direction he would take. After he had so carefully constructed his profitable land deal, going to great lengths to hide his involvement behind his wife's name, he would undoubtedly go to great lengths to be sure that no court or legal representative doubted his right to act in her place.

And if the carefully constructed deal began to crack, there was no guess at how unpredictable he could be.

Marv believed every word of Cassandra's story. Though Frederick's cruel and humiliating actions had been the catalyst for the fear that had almost driven her to consider suicide, he did not believe the man had taken any direct action to put her car over the cliff. That had been a cruel trick of fate. But Frederick Ellington had used the accident to his benefit. He was a callous and greedy man.

If Cassandra surfaced and was seen as a threat to the real estate deal, he had no doubt that he would take ANY means to protect the web of lies and deceit he had woven. ANY means.

He stuck the cassette tapes into his jacket pocket, and headed back for Cal's house, and his friends. Cal's house felt like it was a ship of tranquility and peace, but Marv was very clear that that ship of peace and calmness was tossing on an ugly sea of evil. If Cassandra and her boys were to be safe, he had to find the pieces to the convoluted puzzle, and stop Frederick's manipulation forever. It was a tall order.

Chapter 31

Cassandra sat curled up in the oversized armchair in Cal's living room. They had spent over an hour reading and rereading the details of the land sale documents that Janie had copied. The parcels had been purchased, one at a time, in a seemingly tedious and well planned way over a period of time.

Purchases spaced out, dealing through separate realtors, different title insurance companies, it would have taken a genius to catch on to Frederick's plan. Time after time, innocuous little lots, some with buildings of little or no value, had been added, like pieces of a puzzle. One parcel included the remains of a burned down barn. The sellers had been varied. They included the elderly, young couples, families with children, a few small farmers.

But there were three common denominators. In each case, they had sold at far under the market value, and the purchase had been made in cash. The new owner was listed as Cassandra Ellington. And the lawyer who had handled the deal was James Jenkins.

Added together, the parcel was a large one, and its location at the edge of the town line made it valuable. But it seemed, compared to the very low prices paid for the plots, that the price the city had contracted to pay was far beyond its worth. Frederick would be selling the land for more than three times what he had paid.

The first lot purchase had been made just as the City Council had begun its quest for the new zoo, a little less than two years before. The last purchase, a ten acre farm that was located right in the middle of the parcel, had been acquired just a few months ago. The cost of this lot had been more substantial. Evidently the farmer must have realized his power position and demanded a little more for the sale. He had also been paid cash.

Frederick, or in reality Cassandra, as the deeds clearly stated, stood to make quite a profit at the sale of the land next Wednesday. The thought made Cassandra's throat feel tight. No wonder Frederick had been panicking at her attempts to assert herself in the last few months. No wonder he had concocted his intricate plan of making her seem incompetent to doctors, lawyers, and other people in positions of power. Alcoholism. Neurosis. A simple little label to pull out to assure that he could manage the funds without her interference. Not only did his claims cover up her attempts to get help to avoid his abuse, it gave him a free hand at silencing her if necessary, even if he had to go so far as to hospitalize her.

No wonder he had been less than broken up about her accident, and the thought that she was dead. That would solve a lot of his problems. And how he must have reacted when he found out that her body could not be located, and that she could not be declared officially dead! But if he found out she was still alive, she would not put it past him to try to make her death a reality.

The thought gave her the chills. She was finally looking clearly at the man who had been her husband, the man she had listened to and had allowed to beat the spirit out of her for so many years.

The deviousness, the manipulation, the cruelty.... She could feel her anger rising up inside her like bile, but even in her anger she still felt helpless and stupid. How could she remove her boys from his influence? How could she protect them?

She closed her eyes and her consciousness sunk into memories. The face that came to mind was that of her sister Diana, on her last visit to their house, several years before. Diana had been living a frantic and driven life, trying to find a way to break into a career in the theatre.

Her spontaneous, vocal personality and avant-garde approach to life extended to her varied hairstyles, her outlandish wardrobe, and her constant support to ethical and sometimes unpopular causes. Whether campaigning to "Save the Whales" or "Ban Styrofoam", Diana's opinion would be guaranteed to be heard.

She hadn't spoken or heard from her exuberant sister in several years. An argument about the boys had been the cause.

Cassandra felt her heart ache at the thought, but forced herself through the memories.

Diana had been vocal and disapproving of the way that Peter and Duncan were being raised. Instead of being complimentary about the way that the boys were obedient and controlled, Diana had been horrified. Duncan had been about ten at the time, and Peter had just been starting school.

"They're like goddamned robots, Cass," she had said with an outburst on her last visit. "They're not even allowed to think unless their thoughts are first approved by his Highness." Diana had never hidden the fact that she thought that Frederick was overbearing, opinionated, and controlling. She had constantly told Cassandra that she should stand up for herself, be more independent about her thoughts, her life, her money...

Cassandra remembered the way Diana had looked on that day, her long hair flying, wearing a multicolored gypsy styled dress and little black cotton shoes with a strap across the instep. She had flipped out when she had asked Duncan a question about his opinion, and he had responded that he'd have to "discuss it with his dad."

"Frederick is a good father, Diana," Cassandra had retorted, feeling hurt and criticized. "He's a good provider, very reliable, and the boys and I have a very good life."

Diana's eyes had been full of pain. "It's not about shelter and food and belongings, Cassandra. It's about freedom, and the right to be and think for yourself. Even animals in cages in the zoo are fed and housed, but it's not exactly a good life..."

"Are you comparing my family to creatures in the zoo?" Frederick's voice had boomed suddenly from behind them. His face had looked smooth and controlled, but his eyes flashed anger and hatred. Cassandra was familiar with that look.

"If the shoe fits...."

"Cassandra," began Frederick, his voice quiet, but allowing for no disagreement. "I think that it's time that your SISTER leave our home."

His face was hard. No disagreeing. "My wife and I have no time for anyone who does not approve of our family. Is that not right, Cassandra?"

"Yes..." she said in a meek voice. Diana had packed within minutes, a cab standing at the door. Diana was not one to take a lot of grief. Cassandra watched her go, wild clothes and hair flapping in the wind. She stopped at the door of the cab.

"I love you Cassandra, but I feel sorry for you. And for the boys. No good can come of this. Someday you're going to wake up and see what's going on here. Let me know when that happens."

The door of the cab slammed, and she disappeared around the bend, leaving the well manicured neighborhood that she had always voiced contempt for. That was over five years ago, and Cassandra hadn't seen or heard from her since.

She thought of her fiery sister, and now realized the truth and wisdom in her words. Diana had a strength of character that Cassandra always envied, a drive to be herself at no matter what the cost. Of course, it had sometimes made for a rocky road, and a lot of ups and downs. She moved constantly, as she bravely faced the world. Valuing personal possessions very little, Diana valiantly grasped her freedom. Cassandra could do with a little of that freedom right now, for herself and for her boys. She wished with all her might that she knew where her vibrant sister Diana was, somewhere in the labyrinth of the unsettled theatre world of New York City.

Cassandra had always been trying to win the approval of the people who mattered to her, while her younger sister laughed off the criticism and judgment and followed her own path.   As a child and teen ager, Cassandra often wished that she could "teach" her younger sibling to handle her life, to do what was expected of her, and to avoid the wrath of her superiors.

Today she realized that her little sister had the answers all along. By having the confidence to develop herself and not needing to depend on others, she had no "superiors", and was free to be who she was. Suddenly, she missed Diana with a wave of emotion that was almost painful, and realized that she would give just about anything to be able to have her little sister "teach" her about her confident approach to life.

****

When Marv parked his car in Cal's driveway and entered the house, he found the group waiting for him. Succinctly, he explained the tapes, and played them on Cal's stereo system.

Cassandra sat quietly listening to the first two, hearing more of the damning evidence that painted an environment that was not safe for her boys. Tears flowed freely down her cheeks.

"I've got to save my boys," she concluded silently, even if it meant giving up her own freedom, and taking her chances with Frederick's manipulation and control. She had friends, now, connections to the human race that gave her strength.

But then the third tape played, and she heard the message about finding Diana. Her heart felt lighter, hearing the information she needed.

"I have to find Diana," she said aloud, and they all turned to look at her. "She's my sister. She can help." She went on to explain the history she had had with her sister.

"It's true, if we can find her," mused Cal, running his hands through his thinning hair. "She might be just the one to keep an eye on the boys, if there was a way to get her into the house. But if Frederick hates her so much, what are the odds of that?"

But Cassandra's mind was spinning, as it had been for hours, since hearing the details of Frederick's treachery and lies. Fight fire with fire, was the message that soared across her mind.

"The money. She will be welcome in the house because of the money. If there's one thing I see clearly here, it's that Frederick will go to just about any length to make this land deal a success."

She crossed quickly to the table, rifling through the pile of forms, exultantly holding up the copy of the power of attorney she had supposedly signed, naming Frederick as her representative. Cal, Marv, Janie and Bernie sat watching her curiously, not knowing where her thoughts were going.

"This piece of paper is the key. It's a forgery. I didn't sign it. I never made Frederick my representative, and that land is in my name."

"No, Cassandra," Cal said loudly, almost in a yell. "You can't just waltz in there and declare that you're alive. I have a feeling that Frederick is really desperate, really out of control. God knows what would happen to you if you suddenly appeared. We need more time. We have to bring this guy down before he can get at you. Marv," he turned to the detective, a frantic and worried look on his face. "Talk her out of this, man, before she gets hurt."

Marv was thinking hard about Cassandra's words, and watching the determination that had grown in her face. She was coming out of the shell shocked condition she had been in since the accident, since trying unsuccessfully to fight the abuse. She was coming alive again, and he liked what he saw. He also liked the idea she had brought up...with a few alterations to her plan.

"You know you can't let him know you're alive, Cassandra. Not just yet. Let me have a little more time to gather more information. I'm missing a big piece of the puzzle, the piece that will tell me where he gets his power from, how he is able to control so many people in this town. Give me a chance, and we can bring him down once and for all."

"I know that I have to stay in the background right now, but I have to save my boys." She waved the power of attorney form again. "This is the answer. Get me a blank form. I'm going to file a new one. Frederick is going to find out that Diana has been given the power of attorney. He'll need her to go to the closing, he'll have to let her in the house and she can protect the boys."

Cal still looked panicked, but Marv and Janie were grinning. "Beautiful," complimented Janie. "What a con."

"It might work, Cassandra." Marv was thoughtful. "You can fill in a new form, dating it AFTER Frederick's form. Each new filing supersedes any prior assignment of representation. We know the date that this was filed, thanks to Janie. Checkmate!"

Janie beamed.

Cal was beginning to understand. "So we fill Diana in on the situation, and she appears and presents a new power of attorney. If Frederick wants the closing to happen, he'll have to charm her right up to the moment it happens. That will put him on his best behavior. He wouldn't dare be anything but the model father for the boys."

Cassandra was filled with a ray of hope.

"That will give you your time, Marv. You have until Tuesday to gather your ammunition. But then we have to get the boys out of there, no matter what the cost." Cal was elated at the plan, but still worried about Cassandra. He was amazed at the importance she had gained in his life in such a short period of time.

"Let's find Diana." Marv called a detective he had worked with in his days on the city police force, before transferring from New York several years before. Within an hour, his friend had called back, having called the number left on the tape, and having scanned the City information computers, giving Marv the number of Diana's agent, her apartment, and her office. They were making progress. It was time to let Diana in on the plan.

Cassandra dialed her apartment number, her heart feeling lodged in her throat. Diana's self-assured voice answered on the second ring. It was 11 PM.

****

With a shaky voice, Cassandra talked to her estranged sister, Diana. In a long and tearful telephone conversation, she told the story from beginning to end. After an emotional reunion, she spoke about the abuse, about the set up to get her hospitalized, about the boys fears and bodily injuries, about the car going over the cliff, about hiding from Frederick. She told about the land deal, the phony power of attorney, and about Frederick's cruelty to her sons. She told about their plan to ask Diana to get into the house to protect the boys with another power of attorney that would give her power over Frederick's real estate deal. Diana listened to every word.

"Can I at least have the luxury of saying "I told you so?" came Diana's spirited voice so strongly over the line, that the others who were huddled around Cassandra could hear her. Cal winced.

"I guess you can," said Cassandra humbly. "As long as you are willing to help me."

There was a minor vocal explosion on the other end of the line. "Willing? I have to say, you are some kind of idiot, Cassandra. Not only would I be willing, I'd welcome the chance to bring that pig to his disgusting knees. And, may I add, as long as you would allow me to say, "I told you so, " I can really refrain from saying it. Though I must say I could never see why you couldn't see through that overbearing, manipulating, critical bastard."

"Do you think she likes him?" asked Marv with a sarcastic grin, eavesdropping on the conversation, and loving every minute of it.

"Can I talk to the gentile lady on the line, Cassandra?" His face was still lit with a grin. "I kind of like her."

She handed him the phone.

"Diana?" he began. "My name is Marvin Greenstein, and I'm a detective who is working with Cassandra to try to bring this situation to an end."

"You're a cop?"

"Guilty as charged. And I'm a friend."

"Something new. A concerned cop. Well, let me tell you, this guy is a real sleaze, and if he has something or somebody standing in his way, he's going to roll right over them, with not a second of remorse. You've got to protect Cassandra from him. We've got to protect the boys."

"That's what Cassandra is talking about. But she's asking you to stand in the way of that steamroller, in order to protect the boys and give us some more time to build a case against him. You'll be right in the line of fire, Diana, and I have a feeling that this man is close to going over the edge. It's dangerous."

Diana's crystal laugh came over the phone lines, clear and true. "They haven't invented a steam roller that could do in this doll, yet, Mr. Concerned Cop."

Marv grinned again. He REALLY liked her. "Call me Marv."

"Mr. Concerned Marv."

"You're tough."

"I heard that that's what you guys need, right? Tough."

"Will you do it? I have to tell you I don't have all the pieces of this puzzle yet. You'll be operating in the dark."

"In the THE-A-TER," she said in an exaggerated affected tone, "We call that Improvisation. I'm RATHER good at it, DAHLING"

"Well, baby," he said, changing his voice to sound like a movie gangster, "In my world we call that rushing in without covering your butt."

Diana laughed again. "Now there's a visual I'd like to see! A bare butt, concerned cop."

He shook his head, and smiled at Cassandra, handing her back the phone. "You talk to her, she scares the shit out of me." But he was smiling broadly, and the rest of them were grinning, too.

By the end of the conversation, the details had been set. Diana would contact Frederick in the morning, acting concerned to have learned of Cassandra's death through a comment by a friend who had seen her obituary in the paper. She would discuss the power of attorney that she had, being willing to come immediately, to handle Cassandra's affairs.

There was little doubt that Frederick would go along with her suggestion, though he would be in a panic. She would fly in tomorrow night, which was a Saturday.

By the end of the night, Marv had gotten his hands on a blank form, and they had carefully fill it out, to void

Frederick's responsibilities and rights to handle Cassandra's assets.

"I don't even have a problem with my conscience notarizing this," said Janie, pulling out her notary stamp that she used in the real estate office during property transfers. "I saw Cassandra sign this with her own hand, and I'm happy to swear to it, if I need to."

The power of attorney would be taken to New York by special messenger, who would meet Diana at the airport prior to boarding her flight, so that she could carry it with her when she disembarked from the plane. Marv was sure that Frederick would be watching her carefully, and be wary of any suspicious actions, or signs that he was being set up. Diana would be throwing quite a kink in his plans, and he would be watching for any signs that she was up to something.

It was late by the time that Janie and Bernie and Marv left Cal's house. Cassandra was exhausted but much more peaceful than she had been for quite a long time. Frederick would be on his best behavior, she knew without a doubt, once he had heard from Diana. Her boys would be safe.

She and Cal sat quietly on the couch for a long time after the others had left, listening to some quiet strains of classical music and drinking tea.

She was relaxed and much more hopeful, talking suddenly about her past, about her early life with Diana, her fears, her failures and successes. Cal was a good listener. When she broke for thought, he told her a little about his early life, about his drive to be successful, his earlier radio show in Chicago that had made him rich and a media hero, and where his drinking escalated to the point where he became dejected and alone.

AA had taught him the right way to live his life, listening to his inner values and accepting the world around him. He followed directions, and he changed.

As the hour got later, and the temperature dropped, they snuggled closer on the well worn couch, huddled under one of Cal's ancient crocheted blankets. She listened and talked, alternately, as her body relaxed against his strong shoulder, his arm around her, her feet curled up under her.

He loved the smell of her, the gentle fragrance of her hair, the clean, natural woman smell as she curled up close to him. He could feel the moment she fell asleep, leaning on him, trusting him. It made him feel damn good. He kissed the top of her head, and signed a deep sigh.

They had a long way to go in this dark valley of pain and problems. The way out was going to be a tough and arduous climb for Cassandra. But she would make it, he could feel it. She needed time. She needed confidence. She had the rest. She would do it.

As she slept, he allowed himself the luxury of kissing the top of her head once more. He could not show the depth of his emotions for her. The feelings had begun the minute he had met her, and had grown wildly, out of control for the past several days. He knew he had to give her time to grow, to climb for herself out of the pit of problems, to reclaim herself and her life as a whole individual.

Cal smiled, pulling the blanket more closely over them. But when she finally climbed out of that pit, he'd be there waiting for her, ready to voice his love. But meanwhile, he'd just be her friend, a connection to sanity, and cheer her on her journey.

He closed his eyes then, too, and fell asleep.

Chapter 32

"Damn it, Jenkins! Is there another single thing that can go wrong here?" Frederick's face was beet red. "How the hell did this happen? Why the hell did Cassandra do a fool thing like that?"

It was early Saturday morning, and Diana had just made her contact by phone. She had called, sniffling appropriately, and whining angrily, having just heard about the death of her sister.

Why didn't you tell me, Frederick," she whined into the phone. "Do you know how simply devastating it was to hear about my own sister's death from a person who read her obituary. Oh, God, " she wailed, "I can't believe it. Poor Cassandra. You all must be devastated!"

He said appropriate things, his mind working rapidly, just wanting to get the woman off the phone. He didn't need this kind of complication right now. But then she dropped her bomb.

"I'm coming, Frederick, it's the least I can do. I have this silly paper that Cassandra sent me, saying that if anything ever happened to her, I was to handle her affairs. Imagine that...me handling her affairs. But she insisted, you know. I guess she thought you'd be much too broken up to handle things if she was ever incapacitated..."

"You have what paper?" Frederick's voice had been loud and incredulous, for once, not masked behind his smooth demeanor.

"Let's see, it's called a "Power of Attorney". Let me read it to you." She spouted off the date, the terms, the fact that it voided any prior assignment.

Frederick actually thought he could hear his heart beating, his blood pressure had skyrocketed. He took a deep breath. This was the kind of thing that gave people a heart attack.

"I don't believe it."

"Yes," she gushed, being obtuse. "It's so hard to believe this about poor Cassandra. But I can help you, Frederick, and I will. Those poor boys. I can help you with those boys. My lawyer said…"

"You spoke to a lawyer?"

"Well, sure. I don't know anything about these things. And he said that I should go to be with you. Like I have to be there, but you would know better what needs to be done, so you could advise me and all. You could advise me, couldn't you Frederick? I don't know too much about business matters..."

Frederick fell for the bait. "Oh, sure, Diana. I see. Yes, that would be good. You should come here, and I'll show you what needs to be done."

His mind was working furiously, realizing that she would be a kink in the plan, but not an insurmountable one, if he played his cards right. He could just lead her. She would follow his advice. He was good with women, after all.

And so he wrote down the details of her arrival and promised to meet the plane.

"Can I talk to the boys?"

He was glad, suddenly, that he had caved in and let them go over to Mrs. Briggs house for the day. She said they were spending too much time alone, and he had gone along with it, since it would free him up for the day. "They're next door with a neighbor," he said truthfully. "I think they're baking something." He had thought it was a ridiculous and sissy plan at the time, but he was glad now, it sounded good for Diana.

"Say hello to them for me," she said determinedly. "And tell them that I'm coming. How are they, Frederick?"

"They're ok, Diana. They're ok."

"Good. That's the most important thing, that the boys are OK."

She hung up, and Frederick sat staring at the phone for a minute. That seemed to be everyone's concern, that the boys were ok. Well, he'd make sure they were OK, and he'd get this bitch to do what he wanted, but he wasn't happy about it. He wasn't happy at all.

His next call had been to Jenkins, where he was spouting off about the constant problems he was having getting his neck out of a noose with the land deal.

What he didn't know, was that a certain young man, Charles Upworth, from the TV news, was meandering up his front walk, ready to knock on the door.

Frederick's voice was loud, and uncontrolled, and Charlie could hear every word he barked into the receiver. Whoever was on the other end, Charlie thought, had better hold the phone a foot away from his ear, or risk the possibility of deafness from exploded eardrums.

"Get everything you can on this bitch, Jenkins, and I mean fast. She's coming in tonight, and I want to make sure that I can control her if she decides to be difficult. No one is going to stand in the way of this deal, do you hear me? No one! And take care of that damn DJ tonight. I'm sick of his influence over my sons."

Charlie stood at the front door, watching him. He looked quietly in through one of the small windows that graced the side of the door. He saw Frederick hang the phone up with a bang, and run his hands through his hair. The pressure he was under showed on his face.

Yep, Frederick Ellington didn't look good. And the phone conversation had been interesting, if confusing. He stored the information he had heard in his memory. This guy kept popping up in his life, irritating him more each time.

Now, a leak had spouted the information that the city's purchase of the land for the zoo, a beautiful and very expensive 30+ acres outside of town, was owned by none other than Cassandra Ellington. Figure that. So the station had sent him here to ask a few questions, primarily about the possibility of interviewing him about the zoo acquisition on next Wednesday. Public interest stuff. Would the deal still go on, with Cassandra Ellington missing, presumed dead?

The station viewed Ellington as a kind of local hero, big time author, and so they had sent him to get permission for the publicity. Upworth didn't share their opinion of the man. Every time he saw him, saw Ellington's kids, he got the same gut reaction. But here he was, needing to talk to the creep again. He reached out and rang the bell, ready to face the lion in his den.

The reaction was pretty much what he expected, but he had to admit, he was impressed with the way the guy had pulled himself together in less than a few seconds. When he opened the door, his handsome face had been poised and relaxed. He had been charming and interested in what the newscaster had to say, and then he had politely and succinctly informed Charlie that he was not interested in coverage at this time, out of respect to his late wife. Yes, the deal would hopefully come to fruition, as it was for the benefit of the city and its citizens, but it was not coming at a time when Professor Ellington felt celebration was acceptable.

The man's voice was calm and controlled, the voice of logic and concern. It might be appropriate, he concluded, to interview the city council AFTER the land was purchased. It was a great public interest story, after all, but he steadfastly declined to be interviewed about the land deal itself.

Charles watched him carefully, seeing him weigh his words, make appropriate gestures, and listen attentively. This was the same man who had just hung up the phone with fervor, cursing and out of control. Amazing. He thought of the boys again, and the black eyes and bruises he himself had seen on them. He had known a man like Frederick Ellington once, long ago, when he was a kid.

That man was his father. He was a two faced, lying, hypocrite, too, and he beat his son so badly, that Charlie was hospitalized three times when he was a kid. The courts sent him back, over and over, to the smooth faced, handsome man who stood before them in the courtroom, professing his love for his son, and denying any part in his injuries. And the abuse had gone on, escalating in degree with each occurrence. That man was his father, and he had been relieved of him only when a train mysteriously jumped its track, and hit him when he was standing on a station platform, waiting for a train home, killing him instantly.

The papers called it a tragedy, Charlie called it an answer to a young boy's prayer. While others could complain of foster homes, he found them a blessing. A little negligence, a few extra jobs, these were welcomed attractions after dealing with traction and rewired jaws. He had survived, and he was ok, but that was because the abuse had been put to an end. He hoped the two Ellington boys were as lucky. It would take more than a train, he thought depressed, to take down this wealthy, popular professional who knew how to cover his tracks.

He politely said goodbye, saying that he would relay the professor's wishes to his news editors, and quietly walked away.

****

The minute he was gone, Frederick was on the phone to the station. "Keep that little jerk away from me," he said ferociously to the station manager. "You keep him out of my face, or you're going to be the lead story in tonight's news, you hear me? Your past will make quite a splash in this community."

"Please, Professor Ellington, I meant no harm," the man begged. "That's why I sent someone to speak to you BEFORE you were approached for an interview. You know I always take your wants and needs into consideration. There's no need to threaten."

"There's always a need to threaten, buddy, when people start to forget who their friends are. I don't like that guy, and I've told you that before. Believe me, pictures of your little gay episodes in your early life are going to plastered all over the news on your competitors' stations if I get hassled at this real estate closing."

"Please, Professor, I have a family now, a wife, little children. Leave the past in the past."

"Just do what you're told to do, sir, and things will be fine."

He hung up abruptly, knowing that he had hit his mark, feeling drained and tense. He didn't feel the same rush of adrenaline he usually felt when he controlled someone. This was all just too much, this land deal. After this was over, he'd pull back for a while, and relax. God knows, he'd have enough money. He'd spend time with the boys...straighten them out. Maybe he'd enroll them in military school. Learn some discipline. It would only take a little time he felt, to toughen them up, to get rid of the softness that Cassandra had allowed. Kids should be obedient. They should be tough. Yes, that's what he'd do when the closing was over. He'd straighten out the boys.

He went to his room for a nap before he made the drive to the airport tonight to pick up that interfering Diana. Diana had always been a pain. A big pain. But he'd control her. He'd win. He always did. He closed his eyes and went to sleep.

****

Cassandra opened her eyes at the first light of day, embarrassed at first to find herself tucked in Cal's arms, asleep on the couch. But then a feeling of wellness settled over her, a sense that life was going to be all right. She looked at the gentle, clever, sleeping man beside her. His mouth was relaxed and open a bit, his head leaning back on the corner of the couch. He wore jeans and a college sweatshirt, obviously his favorite "uniform", and his feet were bare. Comfortable. Honest. Open. Kind.

She thought about the things that they had shared the night before, a deeper kind of emotional intimacy than she had ever experienced with another human being. Deeper even, than sex, she thought with a blush, at least with her experience with it.

This had been more like a communion of souls, a sharing of minds and ideals. It had made her feel so real, so alive. An unfamiliar, achy sensation came over her as she looked at the man beside her. Not handsome, like Frederick's eye catching profile. Not well groomed, or dressed in the latest styles, like Frederick insisted was his trademark, but rather unpretentious and functional.

His thinning hair needed a trim around the edges, and a sprinkling of grey had crept in along his sideburns. His clothes were rumpled from sleep, but she knew that if the phone rang, and someone needed him, he'd be out the door in a flash, his mind on helping someone instead of on his wardrobe. The thought made her feel warm inside.

He made her smile. He also made her feel strangely wobbly, which she was beginning to realize, with a little bit of horror, was stemming from a flow of sexual attraction that was very new for her. She thought of the thoughts they had shared the night before, in the quiet of the dark, with the sounds of the night and the chill of the river air flowing in through the window. What would it be light, she wondered, to be physically intimate with a man like this, too? To be skin to skin, body to body? To be holding and held, to care what another person felt, to make them feel good, secure in the knowledge that they wanted the same for you? To trust?

God, for a minute the feelings were threatening to overtake her, the yearning to be intimate with another human being in that way. This human being. But the time wasn't right, she knew. She had problems to solve, children to claim, and a new life to build. She would build a life far away from the cold, calculating man who had fathered her children, but who had a heart of stone. And someday, someday, she would be strong enough to love a man like Cal on that level, a man who could love her in return. The thought made her hopeful. And maybe a little bit scared.

He opened his eyes, suddenly, looking deeply into hers. His smile was breathtaking, and she could feel the sensual feeling rising inside of her again.

"Hi, stranger!" he said gently, not moving from where he sat, holding her.

"Hi, yourself!" They communicated with their eyes, more than with words.

They were interrupted by the phone, and Cal grabbed it after the first ring. It was Diana.

"I'm in like Flynn!" she said lightly. "Sir Frederick will meet the plane, and I'll be with the boys before you know it."

"Take care, Diana," Cal said seriously. "The boys really need you." He handed the phone to Cassandra.

"Thanks for being a guardian angel, Di," she said into the phone, slipping into her childhood name for her sister. She felt close now, closer than she had been in all the troubled years of her marriage.

"It's going to be ok, Cass. The boys and I will be fine, you'll see." Her tone was serious, but then she lightened up. "How about that cute sounding cop, Cass? Is he married?"

Cassandra smiled, turning to Cal. "She wants to know if Marv is married."

"Married? Who'd be crazy enough to marry him?" Cal asked with amazement, laughter in his voice. "Not only is he not married, he is also definitely not cute!"

Diana laughed out loud. "So much for a reference. I'll go by my own opinion, thank you very much. Beauty is, remember, in the eye of the beholder."

They were still laughing when they hung up the phone, full of excitement, and hope. Cal reached over and pulled Cassandra into his arms, it was a natural, spontaneous thing to do. Cassandra felt a tingling rush through her body.

"Yes," she thought with amazement, "Beauty is in the eye of the beholder. Diana is right."

****

Saturday was a long day for Marvin. Hearing that Diana would be soon airborne and on her way made him feel good, except for a creeping uneasiness about the danger of getting her involved with a man he truly believed was really on the edge. More than a little unhinged. He knew that Frederick was someone he couldn't afford to underestimate. Everywhere he had looked, he had found people ready to swear to the man's lies and manipulations. He seemed to be able to paint whatever picture he chose, and there were always people to do his bidding. How do you control people like that?

It was obvious that Cassandra Ellington was not an alcoholic. God knows, he and Cal and Janie had seen enough of them, in every shape and size, and telling every story imaginable in the past several years. And he would bet his sobriety that Cassandra was not one of them.

And yet? He could see Frederick's convoluted plan...to have the property deeded over to his wife, a seemingly generous gesture, except for the fact that she never even knew about it. The action served only as a blind to keep his name from being publicized. He had gone to exorbitant lengths to assure himself that he could have her legally incapacitated, for her own health and well being, of course. If she got in his way, there would be no court in the world who wouldn't have given him the responsibility of caring for her business duties and obligations. Sure, Mr. Nice Guy would be glad to handle his wife's closing. He would be glad to be the trustee of his dear wife's profits, Marv mused.

Cassandra, perched on a high river bank that night, had unwittingly thrown a kink into his plan. He had pushed her too far, has miscalculated in his complicated efforts. Her supposed death (sans body) had almost jinxed his plan.

Ellington never intended to keep the land. That was obvious. He had knowledge very early on about the needs and interests of the city council. Ellington knew the land they wanted for the zoo, he knew the council's timing and budget. How had he known that? How had he acquired the knowledge that had been so closely guarded in those early days, sure enough to methodically purchased the land in question?

Obviously, he had a pipeline to the board, someone who answered to him in the same way that he was finding doctors, lawyers, judges, even store clerks dedicated. He bought the land at unbelievable, rock bottom prices, far below the market. He was selling the plot at far over the market value, if the appraisals that Janie dug up were to be believed. He would be making a giant profit, and at the expense of the taxpayers, plus the many organizations who raised funds to help with the purchase of the future zoo. The most amazing fact was he was getting away with it. Almost.

Cassandra's idea about the power of attorney had been a brilliant, if dangerous one. They had a chance of making his manipulative plan backfire. It was a good chance, but Marv wanted to increase the odds. How did this man manage to control so many people? And to what lengths would he go to make his plan successful? He was worried about the boys. And now he was worried about Diana.

Chapter 33

When Cal had to leave to go to the station for his evening show, Cassandra went with him. They had the calls to the house forwarded to Cal's private line, in case Diana should call.

They had heard from her right before she had taken off, hearing that the power of attorney had been directly delivered into her hand, signed, notarized by Janie, and witnessed by authorities (and friends) who had been willing to assist Marv in his "sting" operation. She had it safely tucked in her jacket pocket, and she was "ready for battle." Within minutes, Frederick would be meeting Diana as she disembarked from the plane.

It was a waiting game now. Diana would be with the boys, and Marv would have a few days to try to bring the case to a close. At the station, Cal's assistant Paul had heard bits of pieces of what had been going on, and during the show, when tapes were playing, and they were off the air, they filled him in on what had happened.

The show was a lively one, with several call-in contests, and a lot of rap and rock. Saturday night was a big night for their listening audience. The show was piped into several local teen-type restaurants, and was played at many parties. The time went swiftly, and was pretty much uneventful, until Paul turned to Cal suddenly, having picked up the private line.

"This one's for you, buddy," he said quietly, and the seriousness of his face spoke volumes that his voice did not.

Cal picked up the phone with trepidation. Was it Diana? The voice that greeted him was not Diana's however, but a voice he didn't recognize.

"Your Pal Cal?" the voice sneered into the receiver.

"This is Cal." He kept his voice light, with no reaction noticeable. With one finger, he flicked a switch that began to tape the call.

"This is a warning, Calvin. You are going to stop messing with kids, namely the two Ellington boys, or you are going to find your name smeared all over the news here."

"Who is this?" his voice was still calm, but he could feel his anger rising.

"Just a friend. A friend who knows all about your life in Chicago, Mr. Big Time Doctor. Mr. Big Time Drunk. The people in this town aren't going to take lightly to having a drunk on the radio, filling their kids heads with garbage."

"I am not a drunk."

"Who's to say? There's plenty who will say you were drunk. There's plenty who will say you ARE drunk."

"Would one of those plenty be Professor Ellington himself?" Cal said firmly. "Or would Professor Ellington just convince slobs like you to do his bidding by make threatening phone calls, or testifying to lies?"

"You leave Ellington out of this, if you know what's good for you." The voice was still aggressive, but Cal could tell he had found his mark.

"I'm not afraid of my past coming out. If it needs to come out, so be it. At least I'll be able to sleep at night, knowing no one pulls my chain. Can you say the same?"

"Mr. Wise guy. We'll see how wise you are when the rumors start flying about you and your cohort Paul there. You like guys with long hair, Cal?"

"I'm not gay, but it wouldn't matter if I were."

"Says you."

"Here we go again. Same old tune."

"Rumors are bad things, Doctor Johnson. Maybe no one quite believes them, but then no one quite forgets them, either, know what I mean? I mean, if you think a guy even MIGHT have a liking to young boys, you wouldn't take a chance, you know. You'd keep your kids away. Not let them listen. You know, keep them away from bad influences...."

"I'm going to hang up now," said Cal, his voice still even, but his face tight. "I don't suppose you'd like to leave your name. You know, to be on the mailing list..."

"Mr. Wise Guy. Think about it, Doc. Stay away from the Ellington boys. Far away."

An abrupt click sounded in his ears.

Cal sat, quiet and still for a minute, then played the taped conversation to Paul and Cassandra who sat in the booth, only able to hear his side of the phone call.

"Cal, that's horrible!" exclaimed Cassandra. "It's disgusting. Whoever that is, Frederick had to put him up to that. He could ruin you in this town. He could wreck everything you've built here, everything you've stood for."

"That doesn't matter, Cassandra." He reached out and stroked the side of her face, touched by the concern she showed. "He can't hurt anything that matters to me. He can't hurt my belief in myself, and I've learned the hard way, that that's the only thing that counts. Everything else is expendable, fixable, dispensable. I'm not afraid of what I was, I'm not afraid of what I am, and I'm not afraid of kooks who want to slander me and say that I'm things that I'm not. I'm sure of me, now, and that's enough."

She looked at him with awe, knowing that he meant every word of it.

"Gotta call Marv," he said quickly, motioning to the mikes and tapes to Paul. Paul moved over effortlessly and talked into the microphone, announcing the next few songs, and congratulating the local basketball team for their victory in the finals the night before.

Cal dialed Marv's office. He picked the phone up on the first ring. "It's me, Marvy boy. I've got the piece of the puzzle you've been searching for. It's called blackmail. It's called bribery. It's called extortion. Whatever it takes. Ellington had somebody call me and threaten to ruin me if I didn't stay away from the boys. Somehow, he's onto the fact that the boys have called here."

"What did he say? Did you recognize the voice?"

"Tough voice, I didn't recognize it. The gist was that someone has done extensive looking into my past in Chicago, and the time I was hospitalized for detox. Getting that information, which is more private than private, takes digging in high places. He's got to have a network, man. He digs up dirt on people, and threatens to expose them. Next thing they know, they are singing his tune. They probably don't ever have the whole picture, just the one little lie they are supposed to swear to. I taped it for you. Neat, huh?"

"Delightful. So...you are going to be exposed, Cal. How does that feel?"

"Just another day, Buddy. You know I can't bow down to that type of thing. I'll take my chances, and do whatever it takes."

"Strong guy, Cal. That's why I like you."

"It is? And all this time, I thought it was my fashion sense."

"The latest word in worn jeans and crusty tee shirts. Every woman's dream."

"Is this going to help, Marv?"

"You bet. You just take care of Cassandra. I have a few doctors that I'm going to shake out of their tree, for starters. Thanks for the tip. Hold onto the tape." He was gone.

He slid over, and took Paul's place at the microphone. A song was just ending. "Thanks buddy," he said to Paul. Paul nodded.

He said a few words, and another tape began to play. When the mike was off, he turned to Paul again.

"This concerns you, too, Paul. If he starts rumors about me, and brings you in, it's going to hurt. How do you feel about that, man?"

The long haired man smirked, tossing his hair like a fashion model. "Gee, Cal, I didn't know you felt quite that way about me...of course, my girlfriend Gina is going to be ticked to hell."

Paul smiled, and then he got quiet again. "You do what you have to do man. I've never lived one day of my life worrying what folks thought about me. Let them talk."

Cal clapped him on the shoulder. "You're one in a million, Paul."

"I know, Your Pal Cal. About those hair jokes..."

The next song was ending, and Cal flicked the mike on, the red glow filling the booth. "Boy, you guys and gals should see this Paul here. His hair looks even better than ever. Long and smooth, not a single split end in sight. How do you do that Paul? Are you going to let us in on your grooming secret?"

"Well, Cal," the familiar voice drawled, "I for one am surprised that you'd even care. I mean, looking at that almost chrome dome you got going there, I'd think you'd want dusting and shining tips, instead of hearing about my shampoo."

"Well, Paul, you got me there. Could be I'm just jealous. Let's have some call-ins with stories about what happened to you on your worst "bad hair day", or calls from people who have some good hair secrets to share. Heaven knows, Paul needs them."

"And if," interjected Paul, "You have any secrets about reestablishing hair growth...vitamins, creams, or even a phone number for a hair loss support group...Cal would be mighty grateful for it."

A new song began, and the phone lines began to ring.

****

Marv called the airport, and so he knew that Diana's plane arrived on schedule. He had to assume that she had been on the plane, because he didn't dare go to the airport to see for himself. She would be in Frederick's hands by now, and he'd have to relax and let the scene unwind by itself. She couldn't be in touch with him at all tonight. It would be simply too risky. Ellington was ready to crack, he figured, and he had too much at stake. They couldn't give him anything more to worry about. They had to trust that she'd keep the boys safe.

He had met, earlier in the day, with the chief, and several other cops about the Pamela Gravely death. They had exchanged evidence (there wasn't much) and details (nothing conclusive) about her demise, trying to come up with some lead or investigation that would give them answers. So far, it was not known where she had entered the river, and whether she had ended up there accidently, as a suicide, or as a murder.

Her father and mother were understandably anxious. The press was constantly sniffing around, and tempers were starting to fray about the lack of progress they had made.

Reports showed she had been a charming, well mannered, well behaved young lady, a good student with no discoverable ties to any troubled friends, no dangerous or questionable habits. She had been a quiet young woman, spending a lot of time alone, dedicated to her parents, to her college career, to her writing. There had been no sign of depression, or of overt stress. She had simply been a good kid. And now she was a dead kid.

The thought really bothered him, but what bothered him even more was the fact that he felt guilty. He had become, more or less, obsessed with Cassandra Ellington, her boys, her plight, and he knew that his mind was less than focused on finding the answers to Pamela's demise. Sometimes, he just couldn't think straight, and all that occurred to him were the similarities..two women in the river, the only person they had in common.. Frederick Ellington. One had been married to him, one had been a student.

But he didn't want his obsession with one case to overpower the other. Frederick had had thousands of students in his career. Coincidence might be coincidence. And just because he personally hated the man, didn't mean that he was a part of every unfortunate occurrence that was uncovered.

Frederick had evidently developed the network needed to ferret out unsavory information about people, and then to use it against them in order to control them. That was disgusting, that was illegal. But he hadn't put Cassandra in the river, (even though he had caused her horrible stress) and there was no evidence he had had any part or reason to put Pamela into the river either. Why? It just didn't fit. She had been a simple, innocent student, and there had been nothing to blackmail her about, and no reason to control her.

It was frustrating to him that his mind kept trying to connect the two. He would have a bit of waiting to do now, as Diana settled in and the facts about Frederick's activities were collected. He promised himself he would spend a little more time on closing the case of Pamela Gravely's death. The poor girl, and her nice parents, deserved it.

He picked up the phone, and requested some more assistance for his investigation. First, he was going to try to find out where the girl's body had gone into the river.

He left a message for Cal and Cassandra on Cal's home line, so that they were able to find him if necessary, and telling them that he would be talking to them after the radio show.

He took a local topographical map of the area out of his bottom drawer, refilled his plastic lidded coffee cup with more of the strong bitter brew that passed as coffee. It tasted horrible, but it was like medicine. It had a job to do, and that job at the moment was to keep him awake and alert. Marv knew he had a long night ahead of him.

His requested assistants were waiting for him in the conference room, and they wrote notes about the river banks, and made suggestions as to the locations where Pamela had gone into the river. Marv was going to assume, for the time being, that her death was not an accident. He was going to assume that it was not a suicide. He was going to assume that Pamela Gravely had been murdered, and that she had been thrown into the river by someone else.

The phone rang, and the autopsy results confirmed his suspicions. There had been no water in Pamela's lungs. She had not drowned. She had been dead when her body had hit the water.

Half an hour later he was scratching his head, and running tired hands over his face. He looked at the two men next to him, men who had no axe to grind, men who had no connection to the Ellington case. They had gone over the facts again and again, and all three had concurred. If Pamela Gravely had been thrown into the river, the current had hurtled her down stream to the place where her body had lodged in the rocks and been found. The only logical place for entry, was the same secluded pull off where Cassandra Ellington's car had gone over the cliff. It was quiet, had little passing traffic, and it was a straight, convenient drop to the rocky riverbank and the rushing water below. Another coincidence?

Marv shook his head. He wasn't crazy. Somehow this all had to be connected. But how? In the beginning, he had suspiciously built the scenario in his head...Frederick murders an unknown female, tossing her body into the river, hoping that it would be found and identified as Cassandra. He gets her declared dead, and goes to his precious closing without a care in the world.

But the theory wasn't a good one. It was too easy to prove and identity. Pamela's disappearance had been noted almost immediately, and Frederick obviously hadn't needed his wife's body to get what he wanted. A phony piece of paper had done the trick. So what was the connection? Why would another body be thrown from the same spot? Assuming, of course, that he was correct. His famous gut was talking to him, though, and his gut was almost always right.

Marv sat at the conference table, his head in his hands, his assistants respectfully sitting quietly. They knew Marv's crazy thought processes, and waited him out.

So if he had put her in the river and he didn't delude himself that she would be identified with Cassandra, what was the point? What was the reason? Why, if a man had murdered someone, would he put her in the same place that his wife had supposed met her death?

His fuzzy mind was beginning to see a little light, a tiny little pinpoint of truth. He kept thinking. Frederick Ellington truly believed that Cassandra was dead. He believed that in desperation, or by accident or whatever, she had gone over that cliff in his BMW, and had perished without a trace. Without a trace.

Marv's adrenaline began to flow, and his gut was practically applauding. If Frederick Ellington had thrown Pamela Gravely's body into the raging river at that same point, it was for one reason and one reason only. He had never thought that she would be confused with Cassandra. He had simply wanted her to disappear like Cassandra. He had thought (and a logical thought, since he thought Cassandra was truly dead) that a second body might follow the same torrential path as the first, to disappear without a trace. And he had wanted that body to disappear. Why? He didn't yet have an answer to that one. First things first.

He excused his assistants, after directing them to meet him at the river's edge the next morning, complete with equipment to do a serious search. If Pamela had gone over that cliff, there may be a trace. She may have hit the rocks on her way, she may have dropped something identifiable. He was going to prove that once again, his gut was right.

Chapter 34

Diana held her head high, her blond streaked hair wild and flying free as she stepped from the plane. She kept her emotions under control, at least from showing on her face as she approached Frederick at the gate. He didn't have to know how hard her she was trying to keep her knees from banging together as she walked, the fear in her making her body react in many strange ways. Her knees felt weak. Her stomach was in a knot. Her neck felt positively stiff with tension. But she looked great. She knew it and was satisfied with that. Frederick didn't need to know the furor, the hurricane of emotions that raged inside of her.

She stepped toward him, making her face turn downward in sadness, the sadness she would have felt if Cassandra's death had been real. She was a trained actress, for God's sake, and even if she didn't grace the stage much in this day and age, she would give the performance of a lifetime.

"Frederick!" her voice broke, and she flung herself into his arms. He didn't expect it. He took a step backward, but then recovered.

"Diana. So great of you to come. It'll mean so much to the boys."

"The boys," she wailed. She looked around, not seeing them. "Where are the boys?"

"They're at home, Diana. You'll see them soon. I thought it best for me to meet you myself."

Frederick didn't tell her he had decided to look her over on her arrival, and intuitively decide if she was up to anything. And if he felt she was, he was going to send her back on the next plane, and not let her near the boys. He didn't need any aggravation. But the power of attorney, he needed that. He wanted to be sure she had it. He wanted to be sure it was real.

Diana was good at reading people, and she knew what was on his mind.

"Oh, here, Frederick," she exclaimed, sounding slightly breathless, tossing her blondish head, as she presented him with a long envelope pulled hastily from the inside pocket of her trench coat. "Here's the power of attorney thing. Here's the thing Diana sent me."

He reached into the envelope, pulling out the piece of paper and searching it with quick eyes. The date, the names, the notarization...it was real. The knot in his stomach tightened a bit, but he looked at the woman who was his sister in law calmly.

"Very good, Diana. We can have this checked and registered on Monday. I'll hold it for safekeeping." He stuck it into his pocket.

He took her overnight bag, and directed her toward the doorway, putting his hand in the small of her back, familiar, too intimate. It made her skin crawl.

"I'll be glad to have your help with this, Frederick. I mean, you were her husband and all. My lawyer said.."

"You said your lawyer reviewed the form?"

"Sure. He copied it and registered it in New York. He said it was important to do that, in case it got lost, or anything."

Her big blue eyes looked blankly innocent, but she could hear the silent voices in her head. "Of course it's registered, you creep. And I want you to know that so that you don't have any bright ideas of getting rid of me. I'm here to stay. I'm here to protect my sister's sons."

"Come on, Frederick," she said impetuously. "I'm really anxious to see the boys."

"Sure." They were exiting the airport terminal to the parking lot. "The car is right over here."

She hated the close confines of the car, it felt far too personal and intimate with the cruel and controlling man who had been her sister's husband. She had seen the weakness in him from the start, the need to be the boss, the need to control and to criticize. But she had never realized the depth of ugliness that had surrounded the Ellington house in the recent past, and she was truly sorry for the decision she had made several years before to stop interfering in her sister's life. She had thought that it would mean more peace for Cassandra. Instead it had probably been a break in the last link to sanity and normalcy for quite a long time.

But she was here now, and the past was the past. She would help her sister and her boys to pick up the pieces and build a new life. They would build a new life away from this awful, self-willed man.

She had heard the disjointed story from Cassandra, her friend Cal, and from Marv, the cop. She knew she was thrusting herself into a snake pit of deceit and corruption. She'd heart about the shady land deal, a forged power of attorney, the suspicion that funds had been raised by extortion and blackmail, and the abuse that Cassie and the boys had suffered at Frederick's hand. She would deal with much worse than snakes for the opportunity to stop the man in his tracks.

She leaned back in the seat of the car, and tried to appear relaxed. She watched the scenery speed by, listening to Fredericks occasional comments as he pointed out interesting landmarks that had grown or been developed since her last trip to see her sister. He was trying to act normally and cordially, and she would do the same. As long as he didn't try to touch her. She couldn't stand the thought of it. A single touch would make her shudder with the hate and revulsion she felt, and she feared that no acting ability would make her able to hide the way that she truly felt about him.

The ride passed quickly, all things being considered, and they pulled up in front of the impressive, well kept home in a very short time.

****

The boys had been, of course, delighted and surprised to see Diana walk in the door with their father. He had not told them she was coming, later stating that he did not want them to be disappointed if she did not show up. Diana knew instinctively, though, that he had been hoping against hope that her arrival, and power over his transactions, would not be real. But it was real, and she was here, and she had felt only the deepest love and concern for the two boys who welcomed her with opened arms. She ignored the sternness in Frederick's face, it was obvious that he resented his boys wanting or needing anyone or anything but himself.

But one thing he seemed to love the same as, or maybe more than, his power and control was money. And she had him over a barrel with her legal rights as Cassandra's representative. His hands were tied, and she could give the boys the love and interest that they so needed, and so deserved.

Catching up on several years was a whirlwind, but they all enjoyed it. Frederick had excused himself and had gone to his room to do some work, leaving them alone for a short while.

"She's OK," they had whispered conspiratorially. "She's with Cal." They said his name with awe, and it made her smile as she hugged them close. Even Duncan, who generally tried to avoid the "babyness" of hugs and caresses, warmed to his vibrant aunt, and thrived with the feeling of being held close.

"We've got to keep them away from this jerk of a DJ at the local radio station," Frederick had admonished her, as if he had their best interests at heart. "You can help me with that. They are too vulnerable, after the loss they've had, and this guy seems to like to fill their heads with a lot of garbage, making them arrogant and disobedient. That's the last thing I need, some do-gooder interfering and having power over my kids. They think he's some kind of god or something."

"No one should have too much power over kids." Diana had said softly. Frederick took it as agreement. She let it stand.

"We'll keep an eye on it," she promised him, and meant it. She meant to monitor the station, especially Cal's show, because that was her only link to Cassandra now. Phone calls were out of the question. They had told her that incoming calls had been routed to Frederick's office, and she would not be surprised if he had outgoing calls monitored. There was too much at stake.

After their happy reunion, the boys had retired to their rooms and had full nights of sleep. For the boys, it was the first night of peace that they had. They felt safe. They felt protected. For Diana, however, sleep didn't come easy. Her mind was filled with thoughts and plans and ideas, and she carefully reviewed each step and its repercussions mentally.

She read a little, calming her mind and trying to reinforce herself, finally feeling hopeful and determined. She fell asleep at the very earliest hours of dawn, and was awakened by two emotionally starved boys who bounded into her room when the sun was high, carrying a full, if not professionally laid out tray of breakfast, prepared with love, if not with culinary skill.

"We made you breakfast, Aunt Diana," they said with enthusiastic voices. Her throat filled with emotion. These were good boys. These were her nephews.

"Thanks, guys!" she said with fervor. "This looks absolutely great." She ate every bite of it, exclaiming as she went, even about the banana pancakes. It was the least she could do, and she was rewarded by a look of pride and self esteem in two sets of eyes.

They would be OK. Between her and Cassandra, they would be fine. She'd see to it.

Chapter 35

The search of the river bank began early Sunday morning. The police team went over the rocks, dug into crevices, but could come up with nothing that indicated that Pamela Gravely had gone over the river bank at the secluded turnoff.

Marv stood on the highest rocky point above the river, looking fiercely in both directions. He must have been wrong. His gut must have been wrong. He was heavy hearted, and ready to call off the search.

"Over here!" came the voice of a rookie cop. He was off to the left, along the top of the river bank where the trees and heavy undergrowth began. "There's something over here."

There was the sound of trampling feet and excited searchers.

Marv followed the men, off to the left, up river, preoccupied.

"Look at this!" The man had lifted something, dangling it on the sharp end of his prodding tool. It was ripped and torn, had leaves and small twigs embedded, but it was obviously identifiable. It was a pair of women's pantyhose.

They excitedly placed the find in an evidence bag, not noticing the fact that Marvin Greenstein, the head of the investigation, was not rejoicing with them.

Two ideas were rattling around in his head. One was that the panty hose had not belonged to Pamela Gravely. Her corpse had still been pretty much dressed when she had been fished out of the river. They body had still worn panty hose.

The second idea in his head was a terrible one. The panty hose were evidence, that was for sure. He looked hard into the trees, trees still budding, and not yet covered with their full summer greenery. Cal's house was located on the far side of the trees, the edge of his deck visible to Marv, probably just because he knew it was there. The panty hose had probably belonged to Cassandra. She had been half delirious as she had crept through the darkness on the fateful night, finding sanctuary with his best friend.

The panty hose were evidence, all right. They were evidence that Cassandra Ellington had been on the top of the river bank. They were evidence that she was alive. His gut wrenched in fear. The timing was too bad. He still had too much to prove to be able to put the nails in Ellington's coffin, to make him unable to ever hurt Cassandra and the boys.

If anyone started sniffing around, started wondering about the panty hose, and put two and two together, it could be a disaster. The very suspicion that Cassandra Ellington was still alive could send Frederick into a tailspin. The fact that Calvin Johnson, who had been in contact with his boys, and who he had tried to blackmail, lived nearby, could be the straw that broke the camel's back. There was no telling what the man would be capable of doing. A cornered, injured animal was an dangerous thing.

Marv had ordered this search. He would be responsible for whatever happened to Cassandra, to Cal, to the boys, and to Diana, who he had helped place in the lion's den.

His gut was giving him a message again. He was nauseous.

"OK guys, let's call it a day. I don't really think that the pantyhose are a viable clue, but we'll check it out." He acted nonchalant, bringing the men together, and watching their excitement at their find die away. They believed him. He had never steered them wrong.

"Go get lunch, then back to the station. I have a couple of other spots to check out." He would get out the map, and find some other locations. Pamela had been dumped into that river, and if it wasn't from here, maybe it was from someplace else. That would be the logical next step, even if his heart wasn't involved.

He sat for a moment as the men drove away. The plastic bag with the panty hose sat on the seat of his car. He got out and put the bag in his trunk, hoping it would be forgotten about, but knowing that the likelihood of that was small.

Meanwhile, he'd organize another search, and make some plans for Diana to be able to keep in touch with them. He was worried about her, and doubted himself for allowing her to put herself in danger. It had seemed like a good idea at the time, but now, it just seemed like too many things could go wrong. But she was there, and there was no pulling back now. He had to find the answers soon, and bring this thing to a head.

****

Frederick felt like he was losing his cool. His nerves were shot. It was taking much more effort than usual to keep his calm, rational exterior for the world to see. He heard on the news that they had discovered and identified Pamela's body. Too quickly. Almost immediately. Bad luck, it had not disappeared as Cassandra's had. As he had hoped.

A contact at the police station had left Frederick a cryptic message on his office answering machine. The man was a simple minded patrolman, who lived in fear that Frederick would expose him for his philandering. He had used a local call girl who had, Frederick always thought, missed her calling as an accountant, kept the most excellent records on her customers that Frederick had ever seen. She had been a wealth of information about individuals in the community, complete with the little sordid details about personal preferences, exact times and meeting places. It was the kind of detail that made people easily believe in the existence of pictures and videotapes about their escapades..and made them especially willing to pay his price, whether it was financial or a "little favor" in regards to confidential information that they may have access to in their job.

To Frederick, the news he provided was not good.

It seemed that during a search for evidence in Pamela Gravely's death, the police had once again gone over the site where Cassandra's car had crashed. The police had found, but then had discounted as evidence in their current case, a tattered pair of women's panty hose, tangled in the undergrowth nearby. But Pamela's body had still been clothed in her panty hose, according to the police records, and so the tattered pair were not hers.

The man thought Frederick might like to know, however, since his wife had perished from that very same spot only a short time ago.

Frederick hung up the phone thoughtfully. The odds were, the panty hose had been lying hidden in the undergrowth for weeks, maybe for months. Synthetic in nature, they would not have disintegrated from the elements. The odds were, they had nothing to do with Cassandra Ellington and her accident. But then again...

What if, by some miraculous stretch of the imagination, they were Cassandra's panty hose? What possible scenario could be drawn, that would leave a pair of tattered panty hose at the top of the cliff? Cassandra's body had not been found. Had she been mysteriously rescued from the accident? Had she, perhaps, staged a fake death, and then disappeared? He had read of that kind of thing happening, seen it in a movie, actually. Cassandra?

He smiled to himself. It was out of the question. It was ludicrous. Cassandra Ellington did not have the gumption to plan or to carry out that kind of thing. He thought back to the last time he had seen her, sniveling about being told she couldn't cut her hair. No, that was not a woman with a plan.

And Cassandra loved her sons. He was sure of that. She would never be able to plan a future that would not include them. She cared nothing for herself, actually. Maybe that was why he had married her, he thought philosophically. She could spend all her energy caring for him, pleasing him. He liked it that way, and that was the way she was.

No, Cassandra had gone over the cliff, and the panty hose were coincidental, at best. Still, he'd keep his eyes and ears open...

Chapter 36

Cassandra spent the early morning hours alone. Cal had gotten a call at dawn from an AA friend who was in trouble, and he had taken off to help. Cal amazed her. With his job, his assistance to her, the stress of being threatened with a smear campaign that could once again destroy the career he had worked hard to build, he never seemed to lose his sense of calm, of rightness.

He had come to her door to whisper his intentions before leaving. He figured, and he was right, that the ringing phone had awakened her.

"It's a new guy who got out of detox last week. He was just dumped by his girlfriend, and he's desolate and sitting alone in his apartment, looking at an unopened bottle of Scotch. I've got to go to him. I should be back in a few hours."

"Why?" she had asked him once before, when he had spent hours on the phone with another member. "You can't make someone stop drinking."

"True. Very true. That's a personal decision," he had agreed. "But sometimes you can give a perspective to a problem, help a person think through consequences, let them know that they are not alone with their fears and pain. I know it worked with me, knowing someone cares."

"Bye," she said softly, as he turned to leave. "You're a special man, Calvin Johnson," she said to herself as he went down the steps. But he had, as he often prided himself, superb hearing, and her words registered with him. He went off to his labor of love with a smile on his lips.

Cassandra had made a quick breakfast, and had donned a sweat suit and sneakers. She had some cute clothes, courtesy of Janie, but sometimes, there was a kind of solace in wearing Cal's well worn sweats. The morning was a beautiful one, the spring air warm and moist, the sun clear and bright. She had a cup of coffee out on the deck, watching the river flow by.

The deck was built off the back of the house, extending out over the river cliff. There was a steep wooden flight of steps that led from the corner of the deck down to the rocks and undergrowth below. From the bottom of the rough stairway, she could see it was only a short, if rocky walk to the edge of the river. The water beckoned her, and she decided to explore.

She picked her way through the undergrowth, finding a pathway which was passable, if not well used. Coming out to the edge of the water, she found a small dock, hidden from view from the deck. A battered red canoe was tied tightly to it. She laughed out loud, liking the boat immediately. Like his car, this boat was "Cal", battle scarred, and all the better for it. She sat down on the edge of the dock, and watched a family of baby ducks make a valiant attempt to follow their efficient mother in a swimming lesson.

She sat down on the dock, with her feet over the edge, dangling down. The water rushed by about 3 feet below. It was peaceful, her ears filled with the sound of the river, and the occasional squawk of a frustrated duck. But other than that, she was in her own personal world, unaware of anything around her. She lost track of time as she sat and enjoyed the peace.

She had changed a lot in the past few days, taken a giant leap; changing the direction of her life since the fateful moment when she had summoned the courage to take a giant leap from the plummeting car. Her eyes were wide open now, able to face the reality of what her life with Frederick had been. At moments, she found her heart aching for the lost years, the hours of agony and fear and self doubt that had stolen so much of her adult life.

She felt sad for the anger and fear that her sons had grown up with, and vowed to herself to do whatever she had to do to be sure that the three of them could be safe and happy. She would wait anxiously for Marv Greenstein to tie up the facts that he needed to permanently remove the fear of Frederick from their lives, hopeful that her confidence in his abilities as a detective was not ill placed. She knew that Diana was with her boys, and that her strong willed sister would keep them safe.

So she turned her thoughts to herself, to the personal changes that were happening to her, as she dared to review her life, and had the courage to face the facts about herself.

She had stopped growing, really, when she had become involved with Frederick. She had been overwhelmed with both his attention, and with his overpowering confidence as he faced the world. She had simply done his bidding, first as a wife, and then as a mother, stifling her opinions, her needs and her judgment.

No more. She could see that now. The Cassandra who had been a loved starved and approval seeking young girl was finally growing up. She smiled as a brightly colored cardinal flew by the dock, perching in the branch of a budding tree that draped itself out over the river's edge. She had a lot of life ahead of her, a lot of decisions to make.

She had been interested in writing when she had begun college. She had been considering a career as a journalist, pleased when her attempts at writing had been met with positive comments from her teachers and fellow students. But then the pleasure and excitement she had once found in writing had dulled, replaced by the all encompassing drive to please Frederick, to win his precarious approval. Her goal then had been to merely graduate, and to move into the role of wife.

She sighed.

She would write again. She felt the feeling begin to flow in her again as she sat quietly, like a river that had been undammed, letting the pent up current flow. A warm feeling came over her as she realized that deep inside of her, she still had the confidence and belief in her innate talent to create. Instead of a flame being totally snuffed out, an ember had remained smoldering, and now it was being fanned to life. She would write.

She would take a class, maybe, to begin, to refresh and reawaken what she had learned in her earlier journalism classes. Maybe she'd be able to take a position with a weekly newspaper as she learned. She felt her heart beat increase with excitement.

It would take a long time, she knew, to overcome the years of repression and unhappiness. She would have to do a lot of work to overcome it. She didn't fool herself about that. But for the first time, life was beginning to makc sense. She felt connected to good friends, connected to her sons, and most importantly, connected to her own feelings and needs and talents. It was an amazing feeling, this feeling of hope.

A lot of time had gone by as she had sat on the dock, and when she realized it, she stood up, brushing off her sweat suit, and looked out over the river once more before beginning the arduous climb back up the pathway to the deck stairway.

Preoccupied with her thoughts, she didn't bother to look up or down the river from her dock, or she may have seen the glint of the sun on a pair of binoculars that were focused on her. The reflection came from up at the secluded turnoff at the curve downriver, at the top of the cliff, where her car had gone over the edge, only a few days before.

****

Cal had returned back to the house on the river, and had found Cassandra curled up in a chair in the living room, a tablet and pen in hand, in deep concentration as she wrote and wrote and wrote.

"You ought to keep this door locked, Cass," he said softly as he shut the front door behind him. His voice broke her concentration.

"Hi, stranger! How did it go? Sorry about the door lock, I guess I wasn't thinking. Actually, I WAS thinking, just not about the door. I've been writing. How'd it go?"

"My time with my new AA friend was a great success. He's really going to do OK, I think. What are you writing?"

He plopped down on the floor in front of her chair, and listened carefully as she described the thoughts and feeling she had been having about writing. She talked about beginning a career and starting a new life. He asked a question or made a comment here or there, but mostly he just listened. She glowed when she talked, and he felt very, very happy. Cassandra Ellington was beginning to heal.

He had to admit, though, that he was worried about her, worried about the next few days, and the things that were coming to the surface about Frederick Ellington. He had a feeling that the man was right on the edge, and under a lot of stress.

Marv had assured him that they were making progress in breaking down small links in the grid work of control and blackmail that Frederick Ellington had constructed, enough to topple his power.

But Marv had even bigger ideas, and they were waiting to hear from him, giving him the time he needed to collect solid information on the man. He was sure that he could come up with enough evidence to put Frederick Ellington away forever, and remove his ability to hurt Cassandra or the boys for good.

They both jumped when the phone rang. It was Marv, but he was not calling about the case. Instead, he was calling Cal with a plea for help.

"I'm sorry to bother you, man. I know you spent time helping someone already today, but we have another problem. It's about Mr. Gravely. He's the father of Pamela, the woman who drowned the other day in the river. He's drunk."

"Is he asking for help?"

"It's his wife. She's beside herself. She called me to tell me that she thinks he's going out of his mind. I know he was having a war with a bottle the other day when I was there. It looks like the bottle's winning. I'm too connected to their daughter's case. I thought maybe.."

"I understand, man. You keep your official capacity, and I'll go see what the horizon is with the guy. Address?" He wrote quickly. "I'll call you in a while when I see what's needed. Will you be home or in the office?"

"Office, Cal. I think I may as well move in here and work round the clock."

"You need a wife, Marvin."

"You need a psychiatrist, Calvin." Marv retorted.

"I AM a psychiatrist, Detective." Cal said without missing a beat.

"You're also a good friend. Thanks for trying to help this guy. He's been through a lot. He really needs someone."

"I'm on my way. That's how it works, man. I'll talk to you later." He broke the connection and turned to look at Cassandra.

"I've got to go.."

"I figured it out from this end of the conversation." She smiled softly at him, and his insides turned to mush. She didn't know many details about the AA program, but she seemed to understand how important it was to him..to them all. "Do what you have to do, Cal. I'll be right here when you get back."

He kissed the top of her head softly, and slipped back out the door without saying a word. He was choked up with feeling, looking at her there, perched in the chair with her tablet in her lap, and the soft glow of the afternoon sun reflecting on her hair. He couldn't trust his voice. He locked the door behind him. "Stay safe, Cassandra," he said as a silent prayer as he stepped to his car.

Chapter 37

Earlier in the day, Mrs. Hannah Mae March had been out on the back deck of her house, enjoying her morning cup of coffee, and fighting the agitated feeling that she always felt on the day each week she planned to clean the floors.

The wall to wall carpet had been Herbert's idea, and they had had it installed a few months before he died, covering the hard wood floors that used to peek out from around her ancient area rugs.

"They've got to go," he had exploded one day, watching her on her hands and knees as she cleaned the cracks in the random width floor, and hand buffed the wood until it glowed. "This is simply too much work for you. We'll have wall to wall installed. You'll love it, you'll see."

Well, they had gone ahead and done it, choosing a soft beige color and had had it professionally installed. And while she had to admit, taking care of it did cut down on the wear and tear on her knees, she had never really come to love it. She had gotten used to it, maybe. Perhaps she could even admit that the lighter color gave the room a cheery, airy look. But she couldn't say that she loved it...simply because of the vacuum cleaner.

She would pull out the long corded monstrosity that Herbert had purchased with the carpet, and begin the wrestling match of the century as she tried to maneuver the maniacal machine around the room. The noise it made was deafening, and right at the most inopportune moment, she would discover that it had thrown a belt, needed a new bag, or that the cord wouldn't quite reach into the corner of the room.

It had a self propelled feature that she had never quite master, she always felt like she was jogging around the room behind the errant machine, or trying to pull it in a direction that it simply didn't want to go.

No, despite the fact that the room was light and cheery, and she didn't have to wear out her knees, she would have given anything to go back to her old and faded area rugs. They could be beaten on the back line every so often, or kept in daily good condition with her little manual carpet sweeper.

But the carpet was installed, and the vacuum cleaner was of the quality that was supposed to "last a lifetime", and so she faced each cleaning day with determination, if with a little bit of agitation. It was time to begin.

With a last swig of her coffee, she looked out over the river, enjoying the view. A slight movement caught her eye and she looked to the right, slightly down river, to the dock that lay below Mr. Johnson's house, next door. The bank of the river was covered with light underbrush at this point, and the dock was slightly visible. In a few weeks, she knew, the dock would be totally out of sight, as the rest of the trees came into full bud. But today, she had a slight view of it.

There was someone sitting on the edge of the dock, feet swinging free. From the distance, and because of her not-so-young eyes, she couldn't identify the person, couldn't even see if it was a man or a woman or a child. The person was wearing grayish, shapeless sweat clothes, and had short brown hair.

That counted out that nice Mr. Johnson, who was a little short in the hair department, she knew. He joked about it on the rare occasions that they ran into each other. He was a nice, gentle man, with twinkling eyes and a helpful look about him. Solid. Understanding. She liked that about a man. Her husband had known him well, she knew, they had often met down on the river bank, discussing their canoes and their mutual love of the river.

She had sold the canoe after Herbert's death, and she hoped it had brought some degree of happiness to the cute young couple who had purchased it. That would have made Herbert happy, she knew, to know that his canoe was put to good use.

So it wasn't Mr. Johnson on the dock, but maybe it was a guest or a friend. She didn't think he had any particular women friends, which was a bit of a shame, because he was such a nice man. Young people sometimes didn't look for the right things in a man today.

But the visitor didn't look like anybody making any kind of trouble. Whoever it was, swinging their feet in such a spritely way on the dock, they looked confident and natural to her, so she decided she wouldn't worry about it. People who lived here on the river road were rather the private type, and kept to themselves.

And so she forced herself to turn around, walk back into the house that she loved, despite the beige carpet, and tackle the vacuuming for the week without any more distractions.

The vacuum cleaner leaped to life a few minutes later, pulling her around the room as usual, until it make a funny whirring sound and she could smell the unpleasant smell of burned rubber. She had broken the belt on the vacuum again. She turned it over, and retrieved the lodged penny that was the culprit. She needed a new belt.

It had happened before. She felt like it was a kind of ritual. She would go to the store, get the belt, and then go next door and ask kindly Mr. Johnson to put it on the blasted monster machine, which he always seemed happy to do. It was little things like that that could leave a widow in the lurch. But Mr. Johnson was a wonderful neighbor.

Almost thankful for an excuse to stop vacuuming, she donned her lightweight jacket and picked up her purse.

She started the car easily and pulled out the long, tree lined driveway, out onto the river road, heading toward town. She passed Mr. Johnson's driveway, and then the turnoff at the corner. That was where the pretty young woman had driven to her death the week before. She had seen her picture in the paper. The thought made her shudder. The river was, in general, such a quiet place. It made her sad to think of it as the setting for such a violent death.

Two deaths, actually, she remembered. A young student had been drowned too, in the spring currents. It was very sad. She noticed a car parked at the turnoff. She probably wouldn't have paid the least bit of attention to it under normal circumstances, but just having been wallowing in sadness about the two deaths (not to mention being agitated about the vacuum cleaner), she turned and looked when she saw the car. A man had gotten out of the car, and was standing on the very edge of the cliff. It was not the greatest place to stand, and she had to fight the urge to pull over and tell him to be careful. For some reason, she kept wanting to get into everyone else's business today.

He was holding up a long pair of binoculars, and from where she was, it looked like he had them trained up river, up toward her house, along the shore. Her house, she knew from years of walking the banks of the river, couldn't be seen from this point, even at this time of the year. But Mr. Johnson's house, that might possibly be visible And his dock most assuredly would be, sticking out a bit into the water like it did.

She thought suddenly, of the unknown person swinging their feet on the dock, and wondered if that was who the man was looking at.

He turned, suddenly, and started back toward the car, and she just glimpsed his face as her car drove past. It was a face filled with anger and frustration. Instantly, she didn't like the man.

She drove on to the hardware store in the shopping center in town, telling herself all the way there to mind her own business, get the vacuum cleaner belt, and finish the dreaded job of vacuuming.

By the time she travelled up the river road again, the car was gone, the man was gone, she had the new vacuum cleaner belt, and nothing but a memory of the angry looking man at the top of the cliff.

****

Being in Cassandra's house felt like stepping back into stopped time for Diana. The last time she had left here, her heart a jumble of outrage and painful emotion, she had reconciled herself to the fact that her sister's living situation was abhorrent and unacceptable to her. She had mentally accepted, or so she thought, the fact that she might not ever see her sister again. Watching what was to her a macabre scene of masochism as Cassandra served, pleased and groveled to please her handsome and demanding husband, her mind and being had rebelled, and she had run.

Maybe with the same response as she had had when her living situation in high school had been intolerable, she had picked up her things and had made herself scarce. She had run away. For her, it was a modus operandi that worked. Her MO, that wise guy cop Marv would say.

She had coped with the idea that she had given up going to college when she left home. She had coped with the string of interesting if illusive boyfriends who had crossed her path. She had simply always followed the same rule. Avoid it if it feels bad. Frederick had made her feel bad. And seeing Cassandra do cartwheels to please him had made her feel worse.

This time, running away could have been a real tragedy. Her sister, by her own admission, had almost willed herself over the damn cliff and into the river. Left alone, with that battering ram of a man she had been married to, Cassandra had almost ceased to exist physically. God knows, she had ceased to exist emotionally years before.

The thought felt like a hot knife in her stomach, and she had to keep reminding herself that Cassandra was truly alive, despite what Frederick thought. She could have been walking into the house when her sister was truly dead. It could have been too late.

It was early Sunday morning, but Frederick had already been out. He came in the front door, threw his keys on the kitchen counter, and methodically checked the telephone and answering machine. There was no evidence of calls. He tried to look casual and nonchalant, but Diana had heard about his actions already. He was controlling the calls to and from the house, monitoring the boys.

"I wish I had known about Cassandra earlier, Frederick. I'm sorry I missed the funeral and all. But I guess I'm not real big on that kind of ritual, anyhow." She tossed her blonde head, and stuffed her hands into the oversized pockets of the arty, shapeless hand printed dress she wore over her high leather boots. She gave an expressive shrug, lifting her shoulders to her ears like a spunky waif. Her smile sparked and she spoke with exuberance. Out of the corner of her eye, she saw Frederick sizing her up, a look of distaste and disapproval peeking out under his "charming" facade.

"Good," she thought viciously, proud of her dramatic ability. "I haven't lost my touch. He has written me off as an eccentric airhead. Point, to Diana." She dismissed the urge to smile.

The boys came into the kitchen, and sat down at the table, wanting to be close to Diana. They were filled with questions.

"Where do you live? Are you in plays?" The questions started to tumble and Frederick took control.

"No badgering, boys. The woman is just off an airplane for heaven's sake. How about some tea? I think there are some biscuits in the cupboard, Duncan."

He practically sprinted to the stove to put on the teapot.

"Whoa," she said automatically, her skin feeling familiarly prickly as she watched him jump into action. "Slow down, tall person," she admonished gently. "There's no tea olympics going on here. Take your time. No hurry."

Duncan's eyes flashed a look of thanks, but Frederick's voice practically shook the room.

"I SAID make the tea, son. Now."

Duncan's head lowered as he turned back to the stove.

Peter sat at the table, instantly subdued, quiet and watching.

"It's not a national emergency, Frederick," Diana said softly into the silence. "There's no hurry. It's not like I'm in a rush going anywhere."

His eyes flashed. "The boys will do as I say."

She raised her eyes to meet his. "Your sons are human beings, Frederick, and are entitled to be treated with respect."

"My sons will follow my directions, Diana. That will never change."

She kept her eyes defiantly meeting his, but she kept her mouth shut. She had a job to do, and she would rile him as little as she could. The words were spoken only in the confines of her mind. "That will change, Frederick. That will change."

His mind, too, held silent words. "And don't think you aren't going somewhere, doll, when all of this is over."

"The tea is just about ready," came Duncan's nervous voice. "Should I put it in the dining room?"

"Yes." "Very good son." They spoke at the same time, normalcy again in their voices. They'd have tea. But the battle lines were drawn.

Chapter 38

Cassandra felt restless on Monday morning. She rose early, feeling invigorated and energetic. Since Cal was still asleep, she put on the coffee. When it was done, she poured a big cup, wrapped herself in an oversized jacket that hung by the back door, and climbed down the deck stairs toward the dock.

The air was early morning sharp, but the sun was edging its way into sight to warm things. Even more buds had appeared on the scraggly bushes that lined the river bank, and the trees overhead were filled with an amazing chorus of birds. The river looked high, but calm. There hadn't been any rain to challenge it's capacity lately.

She sat on the deck, willing the warmth from the coffee mug to transfer to her body. It was chilly. She missed her boys. She had the growing feeling of hope these past few days. The boys were going to be with her soon, and the nightmare would be over. She had trust in Marvin Greenstein with his smart, dark eyes and strong looking hands. She had trust in Cal. It was the first time, maybe, in her life that she didn't feel like she was standing alone. And the funny thing was, that feeling like she wasn't alone made her able and willing to stand up and be stronger as an individual.

"You've had it, Frederick Ellington III. It's almost over."

But she had to wait. She would see Diana later in this day, and then just have to wait it out until the closing tomorrow. The waiting would be the hard part now.

But the boys would be safe in school all day, and Diana would be with them at night. And in the early hours of the morning, a few compelling lines for a short story had been echoing around in her brain. Characters were growing in her imagination. There was a dialog beginning here and there, then a plot beginning to hatch with a frenzy. It was hard to describe the excitement she felt with the ideas racing through her brain. She would spend the day putting words to paper. She would write. Like an affirmation that she had not become permanently brain dead in the depressing life she had led, she genuinely rejoiced as the flow of adrenaline shot through her limbs.

She found herself getting up off her now favorite sitting place on the dock, and stretching her arms toward the sky, as the early morning sun beat down caressingly on her face. Tears started flowing down her cheeks. But they weren't the tears that she had shed so many times before. Those had been tears of frustration, tears of self contempt, tears of sadness rooted deep inside. Today, they were tears of happiness, tears of thankfulness. She started laughing suddenly, and dancing around on the dock, engulfed in a large, clumsy coat, Cal's oversized sweats, and wearing her favorite bulky red socks that overflowed her shoes. She felt totally alive.

Two people watched this seemingly strange performance, both unknown to Cassandra. One was a thoughtful neighbor, Hannah Mae, who had come out on her deck in the quiet of the morning to refill the bird feeder and check on her river. She recognized the waif like figure from the day before, and watched the spontaneous dance. She found her throat closing with emotion at the simple beauty of the woman on the dock, leaping with unrestrained joy. To Hannah Mae, it was a beautiful sight, almost a spiritual celebration. It endeared the tiny stranger and touched her soul.

The second person to watch Cassandra's joyous greeting of a new life was Calvin Johnson, who had wandered in a sleepy daze from his bedroom, awakened gently by the enticing smell of coffee having been perked in his kitchen. He knew Cassandra was up and about. He had wandered in, looking more for Cassandra than for coffee, and had caught a glimpse of her from the kitchen window when he was pouring a cup.

Silently, he had stepped out on the deck, intending to join her for a few minutes of peace and happiness by the water. But she had stood up suddenly, as he had watched from the height of the deck. Stretching like a sun worshipper, and looking like a reject from a used clothing drive, she had begun to dance, feeling and movement flowing deep from within her. He saw her joy and her exuberance, and the sight filled him with the same.

He watched silently for a minute, like a voyeur, while he felt himself filled with the same joy and exuberance she demonstrated.

It was in that very moment that Dr. Calvin Johnson realized, finally and forever, that he had lost his heart to the woman on his dock, dancing around once more in those crazy red socks. His own spirits soared with love, and almost instantly, a wave of desire surged through him like an electric jolt, a tightening in his loins so dramatic that he was almost out of breath from the shock.

"Hurry up, Cassandra," he said in almost a whisper, witnessed only by the chirping birds in the trees overhead. "Grow and get strong in your new life, but make sure there's room for me there." He said it almost like a prayer, and then he slipped back into the kitchen without being noticed, leaving her in privacy to find her soul.

****

For Diana, Monday morning dawned bright and sunny, the radio weather news gleefully promising an almost summer like day, the first of the season when people wanted to pull the tee shirts and shorts out of storage, and have a picnic on a blanket in the park. Diana awakened early, as she had almost every day of her life. Her mind was clear, and her body was ready for whatever the day would bring. She landed on the floor next to her bed in a flash, and put herself through a rigorous routine of exercises.

Her friends in the city had often laughed at her frenetic routine first thing in the morning, but she had always been able to scoff at them. She had learned what worked well for her, and she had the discipline to do it. She knew she had to be on her toes to do the things that she had to do, first and foremost, to protect her nephews.

God, had they grown. Duncan was practically a young man, and a kind, sensitive one at that. Even through the tension that hovered over him like a cloud, she could sense the goodness in him. Cassandra could be very proud of such a fine son. And then there was Peter. Full of personality, and with a brain to brag about, that clever and brave young man with his freckles and easy laugh was a gift, too.

Only Peter didn't have much to laugh about at the moment, and Diana yearned to put the twinkle back into his eyes. They deserved better than this life they were living, and between Cassandra and herself, they'd see that they got it.

She got up on her feet now, and was jogging in place. She glanced at the clock, giving herself ten minutes to aerobically exercise her heart. A lot of people jogged, she knew, taking for the parks and neighborhoods where they lived. But in her neighborhood in New York City... a young woman running alone was not a great idea. But Diana liked to be alone in her morning routine, because it was some of her best "thinking time". So she had long ago decided to stick to jogging in place.

The boys would be going to school today. She had been adamant that they should follow as normal a routine as possible. They were obviously glad for the chance to get out of the house. She was glad to know that for several hours they would be undeniably safe.

There was a knock on the door, and she opened it to find the driver from the car rental company who was dropping off the car she had ordered. She signed the form with a tight smile, and tipped the man well.

Fixing a cheerful breakfast, and packing the boys hearty lunches, they left Frederick at the kitchen table finishing his coffee. He had looked sour when Diana announced that she would drive the boys to school, but hadn't been able to come up with a reason to veto the plan.

Frederick had an early faculty meeting at the college, and was scheduled to meet with the publisher later in the morning.

He was irritated as he watched the three of them go out the door. His sister in law irked him in a way that few people ever had..so confident, so full of life..He'd like to take her down a peg or two. He made a quick call to James Jenkins before he left, catching the lawyer in his office, but on his way out to court.

"I have a big trial today, Frederick. I have to be in court for most of the day." Jenkins sounded tired.

"You have to do what I say, Jenkins. My pain in the ass sister in law is taking the boys to school. She'll be coming back. I want someone to watch her, really watch her. Every move she makes."

Jenkins sighed. "I'll have her watched, Frederick. I promise. This will be over tomorrow, we're almost there. Don't get paranoid on me."

"Don't lecture me, James. Paranoid does not describe me. Paranoid describes how you are going to feel each day when you open the paper, sure that you may find your own name in the headlines. Don't push me James. Just do what I say. Have the broad tailed."

****

Jenkins made his next call with a dry mouth, arranging for a man to follow Diana. He gathered up his things in his office, and quickly shut the door behind him, determined to be on time for his trial. His head was beginning to pound, feeling like it was clamped in a vise. Lots of pressure. His face was ashen by the time he entered the courtroom, but he was on time. The trial began.

****

The operative that Jenkins had called was already parked in the street when Diana arrived back from delivering the boys to school, but she was ready for him. Boy, that Marvin Cop knew his stuff. His warning about this had been right on. She was instantly glad for the precautions he had insisted she make.

She smiled as she acted as if she didn't notice the watching man. He was parked about 3/4 block down the street, unobtrusively facing away from the house, seemingly asleep in the driver's seat, a cap pulled low over his face. She memorized the license plate quickly and without making a scene. The car was dark blue, nondescript, ordinary. She felt like she was in a TV cop show.

Diana used the key Frederick had presented her with and opened the front door.

She crossed to the telephone, again following Marvin's directions. She dialed a number. "Just for You Hair Salon", a feminine sounding male voice answered. "How can I help you?"

She smiled into the phone. "I'd like to make an appointment. I'm from out of town, and I got your number in the yellow pages."

"Delightful, delightful," the cheerful voice went on. "Certainly we can arrange an appointment time for you.

This morning? Janique can do you at 10:30 AM. Would that be convenient?"

"Great. Really great. I'll be there."

She hung up the phone gently, watching the answering machine hum. Frederick had it programmed to record any calls that were made. The message was on the tape, just as Marv had wanted. She smiled again. Smart cop. Very smart.

She cleaned up the kitchen and organized a few of the boys' things. At ten, she left the house, carefully locking the door behind her. She backed out the drive and headed into town, cheerfully watching the generic car as it pulled behind her, always keeping a distance, but always keeping her in sight.

She pulled up to the hair salon, which was located in a small strip mall on the south side of town. The operative pulled into a donut shop across the street, hunkering down for a wait, and obviously wanting convenient carbohydrates to pass the time.

She entered the glass door, where a freshly painted sign that hung in the window announced: "Now open Mondays."

A burly looking man, looking a bit incongruous in a long white smock rose to meet her.

"Good morning," the large man said in the cheerful affected tone she recognized from the telephone. "I'm Bernard. Janique is ready for you. Come this way."

She followed him through a flowered curtain, and into the back shampooing room, closing the door behind her.

Janique, better known as Janie, was sitting on the sink, with Cal and Marvin in chairs nearby. It was the person who rose to greet her, though, who captured her attention. Cassandra lept across the room and into the arms of her sister, Diana. There were tears all around.

****

"Just like a typical broad," the long faced man in the surveillance car mumbled to himself. "World's going to hell in a hand basket, and they got to get their hair done."

He shook his head in disgust, opened the car door, and fished in his jeans for some crumpled dollar bills. In the donut shop, he carefully selected an even dozen, and meticulously instructed the waitress as she filled the box. Chocolates stayed on one side, powdered sugar on the end. It was important to keep the flavors separate. He was serious about his donuts. He ordered two hot cups of coffee, to go, and had them fitted with plastic lids.

He balanced his purchases carefully, box in one hand, coffee cups stacked on top of each other. He opened the shop door with his foot. The donuts smelled good, mingling with the heady smell of fresh coffee.

Back in the car, he bit into a jelly donut. He always ate his donuts in a certain order, too. Jelly first, vanilla cream in between, finishing off with the chocolate, which was definitely the best. He felt prepared now, ready for anything. God knows, the stupid woman could be in their forever. With his luck, she'd be getting a one of those newfangled perms. Or a color job. That took forever. He sighed, and ate another donut.

****

In the little back room of the hair salon, with its walls painted soft pink, Cassandra and Diana laughed and cried together. The spectators kept as invisible as possible, not immune to the emotion of the minute.

"Janique", better known as Janie, was the first one to speak. "Bernie, you better get back out front to the desk, in case anybody else comes in. I hope nobody really thinks we're open. If there are calls for appointments, tell them we are booked for the day. If there's a walk in, call me and I may have to take the appointment. It'll look better if the shop is busy."

"Bernard", better known as Bernie, her loving plumber husband, gave her a good spirited grimace. "Sure, doll," he said in an affected tone, fluffing his smock. "I aim to please." He sashayed out the door to the front of the shop, ignoring the giggles behind him.

"He's a riot," Cal said. "I really appreciate you letting us use the shop, Janie, it makes a good cover. Bernard, however, makes a better plumber than a hairstylist, I have a feeling."

"My boss is out of town, because we are always closed Sunday and Monday. I put the sign in the window, in case anybody watching has figured that out. I'll tell Marie I was trying out a new market strategy for customer convenience, if she catches wind of it. I'll also tell her it failed," she giggled. "I don't want to work extra hours on Mondays. It's busy enough at the title office."

"You'd make a good detective, Janie, if you ever get tired of typing and snipping." Marv said with a chuckle.

"No thanks. I'm starting to appreciate my quiet boring life."

As Marvin and Cassandra filled in Diana on the details they had learned about the closing, the legalities involved, and the evidence that they were searching for to convict Frederick, Janie quickly and efficiently washed and blew dry her hair. The blonde, carefree hair took on a soft, gentle look. Marvin sat mesmerized.

The hair change was a must. Another detail, Janie insisted. Diana had to look different walking out of the salon than she did going in. Secretly, Janie was getting an even greater kick out of seeing Marv's mystified face as he watched the feminine ritual. Janie saw how he was looking at Diana, and it made her smile.

When the hair was done, Janie excused herself, she had already taken precious time off from her office job, and she had to get back. She slipped a funny looking plastic scarf over her own head, the kind that little old ladies wear when they take their new do's out into inclement weather.

"I'll look like another satisfied client," she said with a smile. "Details, details!" She left in a rush, leaving Bernard behind to close the shop when the meeting was done.

They sat around a small round table, and continued their conversation.

"We've broken down the doctor, the liquor store clerk, and have tapes of the blackmail threats that were made to Cal. We can get Frederick on several small blackmail and extortion charges, and we're working on the property owners who originally owned the land, who were evidently coerced to sell, " Marv explained, "But bringing Diana in with the power of attorney means she'll be signing the forms. He won't be guilty of serious fraud. He's registered a phony power of attorney, but he hasn't used it. We can get a few small contacts to crack, and admit what he has over them, but it's tough."

"People are protecting life secrets," Cal added. "If they admit succumbing to blackmail, they admit there is something in their life worth blackmailing them for."

"We can call for an investigation after the land deal, because the city is really paying more for that land than it should. The deal should never have been approved. But that responsibility lies with the city commission, and they'll be held responsible. Again, he has probably blackmailed them into voting as they did, but they're still accountable."

Cassandra's eyes began to shine with unshed tears. "What are you saying, Marv? Are you saying we can't get him convicted of anything that will be serious enough to keep him away from the boys?" She could hear the beat of her own heart as she waited for his answer, which was almost a full minute in forthcoming.

"I'm not saying that we can't get him, Cassandra. I'm saying that blackmail is going to be one of the charges. But he can post bail when you are charged with blackmail, and be back out on the streets within hours. But I'm not going to have Frederick Ellington back on the streets when I get through with him. There will be no bail for this one. The charge is going to be murder."

There was a deathly silence in the room. "Murder?" Even Diana, hearty, unflappable Diana, had turned pale.

"But Cassandra is alive," Diana said softly, her eyes staring at Marv's. "Very alive."

"Yes, Cassandra's is alive." His voice was low and slow.

"But there is one person who is not, a young student named Pamela Gravely. She drowned in the river last week, right after Cassandra's car went over the cliff. I'm sure that her death was not an accident and I'm sure that Frederick Ellington is tied to it."

There was not a sound in the room except for a yelp of surprise from Cal Johnson, who found he had very quick reflexes, as he caught Cassandra Ellington before she hit the floor. She had passed out cold.

Chapter 39

Cal sat on the floor and held Cassandra in his lap, gently stroking her hair. She began to gain consciousness almost immediately with a heart wrenching moan. It escaped from the back of her throat as she slipped back into reality and relived the words that had shocked her system.

Murder. Frederick. Her skin felt clammy and cold, and her stomach was not exactly stable. She could hear Cal murmuring to her, and feel his patient hands comforting her. Murder. Frederick.

Slowly, feeling like she was in slow motion, she sat up. If this was reality, she was going to deal with it. She willed her stomach to stop its threatened upheaval, and commanded her mind to focus. It worked. The shock had passed.

In that blinding instant, she realized two truths. The first: That as horrified as she was to hear Frederick was suspected of murder, she accepted it. There was nothing that she would believe was beyond him. The second thought followed: She was strong enough to deal with it. She was strong enough, and getting more confident every day. She would claim her sons, and remove them from the evil that had surrounded them all. No matter what it took.

Marvin Greenstein stared at Cassandra. He was a cop who had seen a lot, and he knew that people had different thresh holds for stress. Being through what she had been through already, Cassandra Ellington may well have been ready to crack. Many people would have reached their limits. He had watched her lose consciousness with a heavy heart. Marv needed to break this case, and he was going to need her help to do it.

"Detective," she said to his ever evaluating eyes. "I'm OK now. It was a shock, but I'm ok. Tell me what you can about this murder."

He looked at her for a minute, reading her eyes, and then he smiled. "I'm glad you're ok. You had me scared there for a minute. This is not going to be easy."

"I know. I'm ok."

He told them all the details of the Pamela Gravely case. He painted the picture of a quiet, lonely, dedicated student, with no boyfriends, no activities, and two doting parents, a young girl whose body had turned up in the river. He talked about the lack of obvious motive, the fact that she had been in Frederick's writing class, the fact that her book had disappeared.

"But I don't understand how you can tie those thing together," Cassandra said thoughtfully. "Frederick has had many students in his writing classes over the years. Several have been students just like this girl. Some he has worked with quite intensely. Some have eventually dropped out of school. But none, none, have ever turned up dead."

"He killed this one."

There was a thick silence in the air. After a moment, Diana's voice broke the tension.

"Maybe Marv is trying to say that this one wasn't like the others he had worked with," she said gently to Cassandra. "Marv, are you saying that he was involved with this girl? Romantically?"

"No, he wasn't involved. At least not romantically in the commonly held sense. The autopsy showed that the young woman was a virgin. She hadn't been involved with anybody. She just wrote."

Cassandra felt a moment of amazement at the detachment she felt. Discussing the fact that Frederick may or may not have been involved with somebody else brought absolutely no reaction from her. She had to wonder how long ago her feelings, except for the blanket of fear, had died. He wasn't her husband, in her heart, and hadn't been for a really long time.

"What did she write?" Cal interjected.

"Good question. Her parents swear she had completed a novel. Full length, and she was mighty excited about it. Wouldn't let them read it. She wrote on a simple little home computer, and stored the chapters on a floppy disk. The disk is gone. So is any backup or hard copy she may have made. DeNada. There's nothing there."

"Maybe she didn't really have a novel finished," said Cal gently. "Sometimes people exaggerate..."

"Spent hours and hours on it. Purchased reams and reams of paper. She wrote something, that's for sure. Her parents have seen the piles of paper, and have heard her working late into the night. It takes a lot of time and energy to write a book, and she had done it. No one would spend all that time pretending to write a book. There was a book, I'm sure. But it's all gone. All gone."

"Writing can be a messy business," Diana added, thoughtfully. I've written a few screenplays, and when I'm into it, there are notes and corrections and pages of rough draft all over the place. Full trashcans, organized chaos. You can't hide that."

"And that's the state of things her parents described. Paper stacks and full trash cans one day, totally gone the next. And Pamela was gone too."

There was something nagging in the back of Cassandra's mind. She was listening closely to Marv's words, and a strange thought was forming in her mind. She was trying to picture Frederick, hard at work on a book manuscript. What did she remember? She was trying to picture the piles of manuscript pages, notes, research, trash....and she was coming up blank.

"You say you can't hide writing a book," Cassandra said thoughtfully. "You also can't hide NOT writing one. Frederick has supposedly written a dozen books. I've never really thought about it before, but I can honestly say that I have never seen him spend that kind of time writing. I have never seen any of that messy chaos that should go along with it."

Her voice got stronger as she got more confident. "As amazing as it may seem, I honestly am coming to think that Frederick has never written a book. I'm sure of it. I don't know whose books he has published under his own name, or how he obtained them, but he didn't write them himself."

There was silence in the room, every face registering shock, except Marv's. "I kind of hoped you'd come to that conclusion, Cassandra. Because that's what I think, too. I think that Frederick is a master at blackmail, and has picked talented students over the years who had completed a promising manuscript. Getting to know them, he had found the skeletons in their closets, so to speak, and had taken their original works as payment for his silence. Pamela, perhaps, didn't want to go along, or perhaps had no skeletons to rattle. He was desperate for money, and he took that final, ugly step. He traded her life for her manuscript. And when I can prove that, I will have stopped the killer in his tracks forever."

"But how can you prove it? What can you do?" Diana's voice was raspy, and her face was flushed.

"Diana, you're the only one who can do it. You have to find the original computer disk, the one that would have Pamela's book on it. It has to be in the house. He'd never risk leaving it in his office. You have access to the house until the closing tomorrow."

Cassandra was worried. "This is too dangerous. Frederick is simply unpredictable. We can't put Diana in danger like that."

"No, Marv is right." Diana said quickly. "As long as he needs me to sign the papers, I'm safe. I don't know if I can find it, Marv, but I'll try.

She smiled brightly now, determination flashing from her eyes. Marv looked at her with a kind of wonder. "You're some kind of woman, Diana Clark."

She tossed her freshly fluffed blond hair. "Don't you forget it, copper!"

****

Diana stepped from the beauty parlor a short time later, new hair swinging gently in the breeze. She looked straight ahead, climbing into her rental car, pretending not to notice the dark colored sedan that started up across the street at the donut shop, following the cab through the bustling mid day streets. She smiled to herself. Marv had been right. She was being watched, and closely. But their ruse had worked, and the tail was following her, unaware of the meeting that had gone on behind the pink and white walls of the tiny beauty parlor. She hugged her purse closely, adrenalin flowing as she thought of the papers Marv had tucked inside. Tomorrow couldn't come soon enough. She couldn't wait to get this over with, to get the boys away from crazy Frederick, to have Cassandra begin a new life without the cloud of fear over her.

Frederick Ellington was a murderer. She believed it, evidence or not. Her throat got a little tight at the thought of being cooped up with him another night. He was close to the edge, his anger barely hidden, the unflappable smoothness almost gone from his eyes. He was flappable, that was for sure. Like a keg of nitroglycerin needing only a slight bump to explode, she and the boys would have to walk gently around the man tonight.

"Be calm, Diana, " she cautioned herself and her famous temper. "Don't be a catalyst. Your job is to keep the boys safe, to snoop around if it's safe, not to beard the lion in his den."

She went straight to the Ellington house. She pulled up in front of the majestic house, and parked. Out of the corner of her eye, she saw the dark sedan pass by after her. He slowed until she went into the front door, closing it behind her. She went into the kitchen to begin dinner for her nephews, hoping to give them a moment of normalcy at dinner, in this situation that was absolutely abnormal. She hated the feeling of helplessness and waiting she felt. But it would be over soon. One way or another, it would be over.

****

Marv had gathered all the manpower available in the police department. Time was short, and nothing was going to keep him from finding the evidence he needed to close in on Frederick Ellington. He had many pieces of the puzzle, but key facts were missing. He needed to link the professor to Pamela's death. He needed to prove without a doubt that the books the man had published had been written by others. He had to break the wall of silence that protected his maze of blackmail.

"Ask questions. Take the gloves off. I want the truth, no matter how many cages it ruffles." The men and woman sitting before him, crowded into an almost airless meeting room, watched the detective closely. They took their assignments and left with determination. He had given them the information they needed. He had given them all that he could, withholding only one attention getting fact. And that was a fact that he shared with no one..no one who didn't already know...the fact that Cassandra Ellington was alive. He trusted his staff with his life...but he was not willing to trust anyone with HER life. Frederick's cast of characters in his power wielding blackmail and extortions seemed to be an amazing one. He would take no chance with Cassandra's life.

They were all racing the clock. It was late afternoon on Monday, and the closing was set for 12 noon tomorrow. They had to break Frederick Ellington before he could do any more damage.

It was up to him..it was up to Diana. His nerves were as tight as he could remember. He wanted a drink. He made a phone call instead, thanking God for the calming, honest, anonymous AA voice that helped him to hang onto his sanity. "You've got a mission, Marv," the voice said, the truthfulness piercing through his tension. "Sober you can save lives..."

Marv felt his body relax, acknowledging the words. "Maybe you just saved MY life, buddy. I'm ok now, thanks."

"Any time, man. You'd do the same for me. That's how it works."

Marv hung up the phone, his energy restored, and reached for his notes, ready to tackle the questions on his list.

****

Diana greeted the boys with a smile when they got off their bus from school, talking to them softly and briefly on the short walk back to the house. She told them she had seen their mom, that she was fine, and that they had to hold on and act as normally as possible. They halted their conversation as they reached the house, Diana following Marv's directions. The chance that Frederick had bugged the house to keep track of them when he was gone was far from remote.

When they huddled around the kitchen table, the boys doing homework, and Diana starting dinner, they talked about normal daily things like school, teachers, friends. They snacked as they worked, and Diana felt her heart swell with pride watching the two boys, heads bent over their work. Cassandra may have made some errors in judgment in her life, marrying Frederick, and staying with him for so long, but she had done well by these boys. They were wonderful. They were going to go through a bit more trauma, when the walls came crashing down around their father, but they would be ok. The daily, debilitating fear and tension they had lived with dealing with their father's abuse would be over, and they would be able to begin again.

****

There was a constant feeling of tension in the Ellington house. Late Monday night, the phone rang. Frederick picked it up in his bedroom, where he had stayed most of the evening. Diana had scurried around when he was out of the room, checking drawers and closets for the book information, either in paper or computer disk form, but she had had no luck. She was sure, if the evidence was in the house, it was tucked away in Frederick's desk, in his room, and she had no opportunity to investigate. The boys sat with Diana at the kitchen table, doing a puzzle, and reassuring each other quietly.

As soon as he answered the phone, they could hear the explosion of Frederick's voice from down the hall. "WHAT? They said what?"

Diana felt her stomach contract in fear. Peter jumped to his feet, however, bolting to the answering machine near the kitchen phone. Diana rose to stop him, suddenly afraid. Duncan put his hand on her arm.

"Don't worry, the kid's a wizard. He knows what he's doing."

Without wasting a second, Peter had extracted a new tape from the drawer, deposited it into the machine, and started to record the conversation, without lifting the receiver. With the sound turned down, there was no evidence at all, except for the small blinking light that showed that the machine was doing its job.

They couldn't hear the words, but he knew the instant his father had hung up the phone. Like lightning, he flipped out the tape, stuck it into his pants, slipped in a new one and flew across the room to the kitchen table, landing without a sound, just as his father stomped into the room.

Frederick had rage written all over his face. Peter raised bored eyes to look at him. "Going out, Dad?"

Frederick's open raincoat hung loosely on his usually elegant frame. He opened his mouth to spew his anger, then checked his words. Calmness. He needed calmness. He was almost there.

"Yes, I'm going out for a little while. It's important business. Diana, make sure they get to bed very soon. They have school tomorrow. They're not to miss another day." The words came out like a bark.

Diana nodded, not trusting her voice to speak as she watched his barely controlled anger. This was a disturbed man. She couldn't wait until the whole thing was over.

The door slammed behind him, and she turned to Peter, who was already scrambling and fumbling in his clothes for the hidden tape. "And I thought I could act," she said with a slow smile, watching the freckled face with admiration.

"Peter thinks he's Columbo," Duncan said in a teasing voice, though his eyes belied his pride in his younger brother.

Once she was sure that Frederick was gone, she bolted to his room, determined to search for the evidence of Pamela Gravely's book. The door was soundly locked.

"I could pick it." Peter's voice said behind her.

"Too risky."

"Well," said Duncan, "Let's hear what's on the tape."

In the shelter of the bathroom, with the water running in the background to protect them in case the house was bugged, the tape was played quietly.

"You have bungled this whole thing. I had no idea they were so close." Frederick sounded furious.

"They got to Beckman, your editor." The speakers voice was almost a whisper. "They asked him if it was POSSIBLE that you hadn't written all of the books. It made him think, and he started babbling about "style"."

"The hell with style. What's going on now?"

"He said he'd review his notes, think over what they said. They're coming back first thing in the morning. He's definitely suspicious."

"Holy Shit. We've got to get to the closing, get the money into the bank. It'll be a cashier's check, and deposited as cash. As soon as it hits the account, I've got someone who's going to wire it to the Cayman account. Meet me at the airport with the tickets. I've got the passports. No screw ups this time, you hear me?"

"But what about the cops, Ellington, and their infernal questions?"

"Questions don't matter as long as nobody gives answers."

"But what about Beckman in the morning?"

"Don't worry about Beckman in the morning. Don't worry about Beckman at all."

He had hung up then, with a bang, and the tape had turned off. The three sat quietly and looked at each other.

"Should we call Marv? " Duncan asked thoughtfully. "Dad would know we'd called."

Diana was nervous, the boys her first priority. "Guys, she said quietly, "Later we'll give this tape to Marv, but to contact him would be too dangerous right now."

"What does it mean? What does the editor have to do with it?"

They deserved to know. They were in the middle of the whole thing, and they had proved without a shadow of doubt that they could handle the stress. Diana believed in truth, and she believed in her nephews. They had already developed a shadowy image of what he was up to, Diana gave them the facts and brought the picture into focus.

"Geez," breathed Duncan. "He probably killed that girl for her book."

"We don't have the proof of that, yet, Duncan. But we do know that your dad is a very sick man."

"Tell me about it." He put his hand up to his face, where the bruises were fading.

"He's got to be stopped. He can't get away with it. He's dangerous. Why, if he ever found mom...." His freckled face blanched and his lip started to quiver.

"He's not going to find your mom. The police are doing a good job on this. And your mom is stronger now, not afraid. She's only worried about you guys, so you have to sit tight, and let the cops do their thing."

They nodded and got ready for bed, but Duncan was worried. Peter had that "wizard" look in his eye, and that could mean trouble. He heard his little brother in the hall, and opened the door to see him sneaking toward the closed door of his father's room. "Where are you going, punk?" he whispered.

"I'm going to look around."

"No you're not. He'll be home any time. If he caught you, he'd..."

The key sounded in the living room door, and Peter dove at his brother, who pulled him into the room with a yank and shut the door gently, and flipped out the light. They hopped into the bed, pressing their faces into the pillow.

The bedroom door opened, and Frederick looked in quickly, shutting the door when he saw they were "asleep".

They lay perfectly still for a long minute, then Peter whispered.

"Thanks, Dunc."

"Be careful, wizard."

Neither of them commented on the fact that they were both shaking with fear as they pulled the covers up more tightly, huddling next to each other until sleep slowly calmed them.

Chapter 40

Tuesday morning dawned as a beautiful spring day, but no one in the Ellington house was aware of it. Frederick was in a bad mood, angry and critical at everyone.

"No wonder you look like a tub. Look at that breakfast," he sneered at Peter, who was pouring syrup over pancakes. "Duncan, sit up straight, you look like a scarecrow."

His comments made Diana's eyes flash, but she held her tongue, saddest most that the boys seemed used to his callous remarks.

The boys were ready for school, but seemed hesitant when leaving the door. Peter had dawdled in his room, listening to the radio, and seeming to take forever to dress. "I'll see you later," Diana told them kindly, coercing them to get on their way. Whatever happened, she wanted the boys safe and sound within the confines of school.

Frederick was dressed and ready to go shortly after breakfast, once more looking like a model from an expensive clothing store. His suit was superb, his cuff links solid gold, his Italian shoes gleamed, and his hair was perfectly in place. Even his eyes looked successful this morning, Diana thought with a pout. He looked happy, invigorated, like a man who was sure he would win....it made her stomach turn.

She had hoped that he might go out for a a little while in the early morning, as he had before, to give her some time to search his room, but Frederick lingered at the breakfast table, reading the paper. She was simply not going to get the chance to search.

She dressed quickly, wearing a full skirted dress with deep pockets, made of multicolored woven cotton.

Her newly styled hair was easy to care for, and her makeup was very light. It was time to go. She took her identification, her power of attorney, putting them into the pocket of her dress.

Then she panicked. Fumbling around in her things, she was alarmed to find that she couldn't find the tape from the night before. Worried about the things she had heard, and worried about Peter's reaction, she had stayed up half the night trying to decide what to do. She had finally come up with a plan. She had written a short message and had wrapped it around the tape, planning to hand it off to Janie at the closing office, to get it into Marv's hands as soon as possible.

But the tape was gone, and there was nothing she could do about it. Exasperated, but still determined to follow through with the rest of the plan she had developed, she picked up a folded piece of paper from the bank that she had kept tucked away in her wallet for years. She put it safely into the other pocket of her dress, took a deep breath, and walked out the door to meet Frederick Ellington.

                    ****

Cassandra was curled up in what had become her favorite chair in the corner of Cal's living room, writing furiously. Awake since barely daylight, she had stolen from her room, careful not to awake Cal down the hall. He had come in well past midnight, after his show, and they had spent the next hour talking about every subject under the sun. Except Frederick. Somehow sensing the preoccupation and worry she felt, and realizing how many hours she had been spending alone to dwell on her muddled past life, he had encouraged her to tackle other topics, to discuss other issues in her life.

It was a wonderful time, thought provoking, sometimes argumentative. Just fun. He made her forget the pain and worry in her heart, at least for a little while. She slept deeply when she had finally drifted to sleep, and when she opened her eyes just a few hours later, she felt invigorated, excited, and full of hope.

Marv said that things would be brought to a head on this day. Diana was safely entrenched with the boys until the closing, and Marv had reported that they were closing in on Frederick.

God, she wanted it over. She wanted to hold her boys, to talk to them, to build a new life that was based on truth and love and positive energy. She felt so useless, hidden away, while Marv and Diana played the active role. But she knew what Marv said was true. She couldn't be found alive until the police were ready.

So she used the time the best way she knew how. She had written reams and reams in the last few days, mostly writing about what she had been through, and how she felt about it. She had talked a few times to the psychologist that Cal had suggested, and was following her suggestions to try to put her feelings down on paper. She had plans and hopes for the future, but she needed to understand how she had lived so far. It was a pretty painful undertaking. But she had garnered an amazing kind of strength as the words had poured out onto the paper. She found her courage mounting, her self esteem blossoming. Cassandra Ellington would not be the shrinking, scared woman of her past. She was stronger now, and she was ready to live...if she was given the chance.

Cal found her like that a short time later, nestled in her chair, head bent in avid concentration over her notebook. Watching her made him feel warm inside. He didn't say a word, but poured himself a cup of coffee from the pot she had brewed in the kitchen, bringing her one too. He set it next to her.

"You're up uncharacteristically early, Dr. Johnson," she laughed lightly, sipping the hot coffee.

"Don't tell anyone. I don't want it expected of me."

"Your secret is safe."

"Today's the day, Cass. Are you ready?"

She nodded, not trusting her voice when her throat got suddenly tight.

"It's going to be OK, Cassandra. You're not alone in this thing, you know."

She nodded. "I know."

He was kneeling on the floor in front of her, his hands resting assuringly on her knees. She reached out and touched his cheek gently. She could feel the stubble of whiskers with her fingertips. She reached up and ran her fingers through his thinning hair. He was so good. He was so real. He made her smile.

"What do you want to do this morning?" Cal said brightly.

"Don't you have a meeting to go to? I remember you mentioning it the other day. Some media thing.."

"I'm supposed to go to the station to meet with a TV news crew this morning. We are doing a joint fund raiser for the new hospital wing and we're going to work out an advertising schedule. But I was thinking about rescheduling it.."

"No way, My Pal Cal. You don't have to babysit me. Go to the station and have the meeting, and I'll be here when you get back. It'll be hours before Marv calls to let me know how things went, and what we're doing next."

"I hate to leave you alone. Want to come? Incognito?"

"Thanks but no thanks. Facing a TV media crew is not exactly what Marv wants, wise guy. I'm just going to write this morning, and try to pass the time. I can't wait to see the boys..." Her voice broke.

"It'll be soon, Cassandra. I'll go and get dressed and get back as soon as I can."

He gave her a hug when he left, and planted a kiss so soft on the top of her head, that she almost thought she imagined it. Almost...

****

Mr. Sloboski was just about as close to a nervous wreck as Janie had ever seen him, on Tuesday morning at the real estate office, and no amount of donuts was doing the trick. She had given him chocolate, creme filled, glazed, and then jelly, but had been unable to bring a smile to his frantic face.

The closing was the biggest his office had ever handled, and he was fraught with dismay at every turn.

"My god, is the deed finished?"

"Yes, sir. It looks good." Janie kept her voice low and calm.

"Janie, I don't think the bank papers are all in order."

"Perfect sir. Checked and double checked."

"Oh God, where did I put the bank check?" He started slapping pockets, and Janie actually felt sorry for the man.

"It's right here, sir." She placed the check on the conference table. "Now sit down and calm yourself. You're a professional, and you want to appear in control." She patted his shoulder in a motherly way. "Cinnamon twist?" She was pulling out all the stops now, but he was really getting on her nerves.

She had accompanied him (more or less dragged him, to be more exact) to the bank when it had opened, to have the certified check drawn for the land purchase. She had never seen such a big check in her life.

They had gone over every detail with the bank officers, as well as the city council. Everything was in order, as far as the land deal was concerned. What was not in order, and what was driving her crazy, was the fact that she had not heard from Marv this morning, to hear that everything had been solidified, and that he had enough evidence to arrest Frederick Ellington. And time was getting short.

Promptly at noon, Frederick Ellington walked in the door, tall, attractive, smiling, and looking like a million bucks. Or maybe you could say three million bucks. Diana was at his side, looking a bit breathless and excited, but still playing the part of the scattered sister.

They turned down the coffee and donuts that she offered, which was just as well, as Mr. Sloboski had made quite a dent in the supply, and sat making small talk with her anxious boss, until the City Commissioners and their attorney came in the door.

They made the usual polite greetings as they settled around the conference table, with it's piles of papers stacked neatly, ready for the real estate closing.

"Jenkins won't be with you?" the city's lawyer asked.

"No, our attorney is.. indisposed this morning. He regrets to miss this event, but it couldn't be helped. My sister in law, Diana Clark represents my wife."

"Yes," the lawyer stammered, "SO sorry to hear about your wife. Dreadful. Simply dreadful. I hope they find the poor woman."

Frederick began to nod when the man went on.

"And the news about your editor from Aarkvaark. Such a shame. Really a tragedy."

Frederick cleared his voice. "Yes, thank you. It was quite a sad thing."

"Your editor?" piped in Mr. Sloboski. "I hadn't heard."

"He was discovered dead in his garage this morning. Horrible thing. Must have slipped and hit his head, with the car still running. The carbon monoxide got him. A maid found him this morning. I guess you'll miss his expertise a lot, Ellington."

"Certainly."

Diana felt like she was going to be sick. Bile was churning in her stomach, making her almost weak with the upheaval. Frederick's editor. The one who was going to look over his notes. The one Frederick wasn't worried about. No wonder. She raised her head and looked into his eyes, which was a tactical mistake.

His dark, angry eyes bore back into hers, almost hypnotizing her. She felt fear begin to well up in her, rising from the very tips of her toes, through her body, closing her voice, and showing in her eyes. He knew that she knew. Had he taken the tape? Or had he simply read her reaction?

When she lowered her eyes for a minute, she saw him relax. He's used to it, she thought to herself. Like a snake ready to strike, the fear in the victim was what gave him his power. She took a deep breath and cleared her head. Her stomach began to resettle. She wasn't going to let him scare her, or to intimidate her. She would follow her plan, but she wasn't going to dare to look him in the eyes again any time soon.

The paper signing began.

Chapter 41

Cal was having trouble finding his usual enthusiasm for life as he sat in the media meeting at the station. Three disc jockeys, the station manager, and three TV personalities were busy hashing out a detailed schedule of radio and tv ads, mall appearances, and school assemblies for an cancer research benefit. Usually a leader in a meeting such as this, Cal was having trouble even focusing on the subject at hand.

Halfway through the meeting, the station secretary poked her multi-colored head in the door. "Young man here to see you, Cal," she said between gum snaps. "Says it's urgent. Name's Duncan."

Cal slipped out the door. Duncan stood in the hallway, hands jammed into his jeans pockets. Cal ushered him into a small empty office.

"Duncan Ellington! I'm glad to see you, but I'm surprised. Did something happen? What happened to school?"

"It's Peter, Cal. He's disappeared. We started out to school today, but he was really nervous, not wanting to go. It has to do with the tape." He explained about the taped conversation, and the fact that Diana had planned to pass it along to Janie to give to Marv at the real estate closing.

"But when we got on the bus, Peter had the tape. He must have taken it from Diana's room. He was determined to get it into Marv's hands right away. He said waiting for the closing would take too much time. He might even be right, Cal, but he's still a kid. He got off the bus at school and took off for the police station. I was afraid somebody would try to follow him, so I took off in another direction, in case dad has somebody watching us. You know, make them follow me."

"That was pretty brave. Did you see anybody?"

"Nobody. So I just walked and walked, and then I ended up here. But nobody followed me, either. I'm sure of it."

. "That was good thinking. So Peter, odds are, went to the police station, if he wanted to turn over that tape. How about if we call there?"

He dialed the phone quickly, talking to the sergeant at the main desk. He hung the phone up with a long face.

" He WAS there, Duncan. But Marv wasn't. Peter said he didn't want to talk to anybody else. I think Marv probably headed out to the River house to check on your mom. Do you guys know where my house is? Could he had gone there?"

"He has no idea where it is, I'm sure."

"Where else would he go? Think hard, Duncan." Cal could feel a slight sheen of perspiration begin on his brow, on the back of his neck. Where was Peter?

"Maybe back to the house. Last night, I caught him trying to slip down the hall to dad's room to find some kind of evidence. I made him come back just in time because dad came home...."

Cal's heart started hammering. He was thinking hard.

Without a sound, the door behind them opened, and a low pitched voice sounded. "Can I help?"

It was Charlies Upworth, one of the TV news anchors. "UH, I don't think so, Charlie, this is a kinda personal matter. Can we talk another time?"

Charlie stood silent for a minute, watching Duncan, whose name he'd recognized from the receptionist. He was a newsman, with a newsman's instinct, and he could smell trouble here. "Remember me, Duncan?"

"You're the TV guy who got my dad mad, right?"

"I'm the guy who could see he had hit you guys, and who warned him not to. And I told you if you ever needed my help..I'd be there."

Cal stared at the man for a full minute. A ton of life experiences had made him a good judge of character.

"Maybe we do need your help. It's Peter, Duncan's brother. He's taken off from school, probably to go back to his house, but there are extenuating circumstances, and it's not safe for him to be there."

"Does this have to do with Frederick Ellington? The questions the police have been asking?" His reporter's mind was working quickly.

The land deal for the zoo was scheduled for today. The pieces began to click into place. He didn't have all the details, but he knew it was going down today. The authorities were cornering Ellington, and the boy had gotten in the way.

God knows Cal shouldn't have been surprised about the press. Whether it was newspaper, TV or radio, the grapevine was the tightest, most extensive, most connected.

"This is off the record, Upworth, understood? There are kids at stake here."

"No problem. That's why I'm standing here. The kids matter."

"If we can get the boy out of there, he won't have to be a part of things when they all come crashing down. I want him safe. We have to find him."

"I'll go get him. I've been to the house. If anyone else is there, I'll concoct a story about talking to Ellington about the zoo deal. That way nothing will get blown. OK?"

Cal nodded slowly, looking from Duncan to Charlie. "Duncan can stay here with me, in case Peter shows up here. We'll get in touch with Marv, and let him know what's happened, and let Janie know so that she can slow things down as much as possible at the closing to give us time to get him out of there before they get home."

He gave Charlie some more details of the case, so he wouldn't be operating in the dark. Charlie took in every word, and his eyes were honest and trustworthy. Cal shook his hand.

"You're helping a lot, Charlie. These are good boys, and they deserve a lot better than they've got. But be careful. He's a dangerous man."

"I can tell, Cal. But I've seen my share of dangerous men in my day, and with a past like mine, I just don't scare too easily. If the boy is there, I'll keep him safe, I promise."

He was gone in a flash.

****

Back at Cal's house, Cassandra heard the crunch of Marv's tires as he arrived in the driveway. She uncurled herself from the chair, stretching to remove the stiffness she felt from the intensity of her writing. She walked to the door to let him in.

"Everything OK?" he asked as he pulled off his coat and started for the coffee pot.

"Nice and quiet. Just waiting for you to give me good news."

Marv's face was serious. "There's all kinds of news, Cassandra, but not all of it good. Frederick's editor was found dead this morning."

"Was it Frederick...."

"I say he was involved. He was responsible. The current evidence says maybe accident. It has to be investigated."

"And Pamela's death?" A tenseness was building in her stomach. Panic. She wanted it over. She wanted her boys. She didn't want anyone else to die.

"He would have been a key in it. We thought we had it pretty sewn up. We need some kind of information, some lead that would give conclusive proof that he wasn't the true author of his books. It's all about motive at this point."

"How about the closing? How is Diana?"

"Going off as scheduled. Cassandra, I think we are going to have to get the boys out of there whether we can tie this thing up today or not. Diana is ok right now. But my gut tells me this man is right on the edge, and it's just too dangerous to leave them there."

The phone rang.

Marv picked it up and heard Cal's voice. He listened for a minute, then said. "Good move. Keep Duncan there, and call here when Peter has arrived. I'll let Janie know that she should stall things as much as possible. I'll call the station and then I'll head for the house."

Hanging up the phone, he turned to Cassandra. "Maybe the boys have good instinct, too, Cassandra. They ran away from school today. Duncan went to Cal at the radio station, Peter went to my office, left a package, and then disappeared."

Cassandra turned white.

"He'll be ok. Charles Upworth, a friend of Cal's, went to head him off if he was headed back home."

He dialed the real estate office and asked for Janie. "This is her hairdresser," he said in a soft voice.

"Yikes, Marv" Janie exclaimed when she picked up the phone. "You're a man of hidden talents. Though I'm not going to let you touch my hair, no matter what hobbies you've taken up."

"Shut up, wise-woman. Listen, kiddo, we need a delay. Peter took off from school, and may have gone to the Ellington house. We've got to get him out of there before his father gets home, in case the fireworks start."

Janie sighed. "Of course, this just happens to be the one closing in a million that is going smoothly and right on time. But I'll think of something. Something. Nothing like a challenge. Go find the kid, Marv, and leave this little problem to me." With an airy tone, she hung up the receiver.

"Janie is going to assure us some time, Cassandra."

"He has to be found, Marv. He's only a child...Peter." Her voice broke.

"I'm going to go pick up the package he dropped off at the police station, Cassandra, then I'll go to the house. I promise you, we'll have both of your sons back to you safe and sound."

He picked up the phone. "Here. Call Cal, and have him put Duncan on the line, for starters. You two have a lot of catching up to do."

She took the phone in a shaking hand.

He gave her a worried stare. "I hate to leave you here alone."

"I'm ok, Marv. Go find Peter." She dialed Cal's number, hearing the crunch of tires as Marv pulled from the drive.

****

Peter hadn't slept much the night before. His stomach had been churning, and nightmares had hovered in the back of his mind every time he began drifting to sleep. So he stoically kept himself awake, and used the time in the darkness of Duncan's bedroom to think. He was pretty good at thinking.

Duncan's steady breathing provided a comforting background as he lay in the dark. His father. His father was nuts. Sometimes it amazed him, when he really stopped to think of it, that the man was his father. But he was. And he hated him. Really hated him. He hated what he had done to his mom, not just recently, but over a lifetime, for as long as he could remember. Peter hated what he did to Duncan, making him cower, using threats of violence to get his way. He hated, of course, the bruises and ugliness he had lived with...not just the physical pain, but even worse, the threat of it. And he hated the feeling of being a coward, of not being able to stand up to him.

Peter had picked up bits and pieces of information since his mom's accident, and the conclusion his twelve year old mind had drawn was clear..his father was crazy and dangerous. He was also very smart, and the police were going to have to work pretty hard to outsmart him.

He thought of the tape that Diana had taken, intending to get it to the police by taking it to the real estate closing. Diana was taking a risk. If he knew his father, he would be watching her like a hawk. A crazy hawk.

But the police needed that tape, that was for sure. An idea had begun to sprout in his mind.

But then, listening to the early news on the radio while he was dressing for school, he had almost panicked. The newsman reported that a man had died of carbon monoxide poisoning. Accidental, the report stated. But Peter, even at twelve, knew better. Because the man who had died was none other than his father's editor, the man he had spoken about on the tape. "Don't worry about him, he had said." Now he was dead. No chance for a coincidence there.

The police had to have the tape, and the more he thought about it, the more his idea began to grow. The next morning, it had been an easy thing to locate the tape in his Aunt Diana's room, and to stuff it deep into his book bag. He had gone to school with Duncan on the bus, but had had no intention of staying at school. "I'm going to go find Marv," he had whispered to Duncan as they had climbed off the yellow bus.

"The best place you can be is where Marv expects you to be, and that's in school."

"I've got the tape. He's got to have it. You didn't hear the news. The editor, dad's editor, died last night. Maybe this is the proof he needs. Maybe later will be too late."

He had turned and run then, leaving Duncan behind.

****

Duncan had been in a panic. Chasing Peter wouldn't help anything. He knew better than anybody how stubborn his little brother could be. He also knew that it was entirely possible that his father had someone watching them. So he had taken off in the other direction, hoping to draw attention away from his brave little brother.

Duncan put one foot in front of the other, and had walked and walked. He walked through the center of town, paying no attention to the sights as he walked by. After a while, he was sure no one had followed him. He found himself suddenly on the outskirts of town, and within a half mile of the radio station. Like radar he made his way toward Cal, and he walked the final distance with determination. Cal would know what to do. Cal would help him protect his determined little brother.

****

The man who had watched the boys get on and off the school bus was puzzled. He was sure his morning assignment would be a quick one, simply watching the boys until they went into their school. But they didn't enter the building. Instead, they split up and went to two different directions.

"Shit!" he said to himself. Heads or tails? He couldn't follow both. He chose the older one, and kept far behind him as he meandered around town, seemingly with no destination. A waste of time, watching a teenage kid who was playing hookey from school on a spring day. After several blocks, he was cursing to himself. He probably should have followed the younger one. He doubled back, but couldn't find him. It was going to be a great day, he could just tell. He could feel a headache coming on.

****

Peter had walked quickly to the police station, which was in the center of town. Huffing and puffing from the pace he set, he asked for Marv, and had been horrified to find out that he wasn't in. He left the tape for Marv, and quickly left, determined to find answers to some of the questions in his mind. If Marv wasn't available, he was going to investigate by himself. Heading out of town and toward his house, he thumbed a ride with a kindly lady in a minivan who gave him a lecture about the hazards of hitchhiking. He thanked her profusely for both the ride and the advice, and waved goodbye to her a short time later when he was deposited just a short distance from his driveway.

It appeared that no one was home, which he was counting on. The police were centering their investigations on his father's books, and were trying to tie in the death of the student Pamela Gravely. Now, the death of the editor could be added. And Diana had told them that there was question that his father had not even written the books he supposedly published. It was all tied together.

His father's room, and the office alcove that held his computer had always been considered off limits to the boys. His large wooden desk and leather chair was used by him alone. Even his mother left the area alone. If there was anything significant to be found in the house, that would be the place to begin searching.

The police needed a search warrant to do it, but by the time they got one, even with the evidence on the tape that Peter had dropped off, Frederick could have plenty of time to destroy anything that might be incriminating. Peter wasn't going to let that happen.

If his father was innocent, there would be evidence that he had indeed written the books. There could be notes, rough drafts, outlines, all the stuff he accumulated when he wrote a paper for school. If he was guilty....who knows what he'd find. And in his heart, he knew that the man who was his father was guilty. Very guilty.

His hand was shaking, and his heart was hammering by the time he located the key his mother had always kept hidden for emergencies, and let himself in the large front door. He'd get right to work, not knowing how much time he had before his father returned. He knew that if he was caught at what he was doing, not even his clever Aunt Diana could save him from his father's rage.

Chapter 42

Janie bit on her thumb nail as she hung up the phone. Delay. She looked around the corner to the conference room, where the pile of papers still needing to be signed was definitely getting smaller and the pile that was finished was definitely larger. The people at the table were talking in hushed tones as each issue was reviewed. Tax excrows, deed registrations, title searches. She was just too damn efficient, that was all. The deal was almost done.

She looked across the desk at the copy machine, its green light glowing on the instrument panel. She could sabotage the copy machine so that they couldn't make copies of the documents. Everyone would believe that one....the copy machine was old, and it was out of order more than it was working.

She could see Frederick Ellington glancing occasionally at his watch. He was in a hurry. No, copies wouldn't hold the man back. He'd simply ask them to forward copies of the transactions at a later date. She sashayed over to the conference room, thinking hard.

"How about some coffee and donuts for everyone here?" she said in a chipper voice.

"Well, that sounds right nice, Janie," said Mr. Sloboski, predictably.

"If you don't mind, sir," Frederick injected in a professional, charming voice, but with a tone that didn't suggest openness to argument, "We're almost finished here, and my schedule is quite tight. Could we please complete the transfer, and then those who have the time can take their much needed break."

The man even smiled as he said it, Janie realized with a grimace. His words blew a hole in her plan without any effort at all. Everyone at the table complied and got back to work.

She glanced at the almost completed pile of papers. What on earth was she going to do? What could slow things down?

Then she saw it. Off to the right, almost in the center of the table, sat a small rectangle of paper. It was the check she had placed on the table. It was the certified bank check, drawn for the amount of $3,000,000, and made out to Cassandra Ellington. Amazing that that little scrap of paper was worth three million, but it was. It was also the one thing that Frederick Ellington would not be willing to leave behind when he left.

Could she grab it? Ask to copy it? Reshuffle papers and perhaps lose it? The ideas ticked by, and she discarded each one. They would all call attention to her, and would probably meet with another one of those controlling statements from Ellington. She had to figure out something else.

She closed her eyes and said a short prayer, tilting her head upward in thought. Her eyes opened, and a brilliant smile flashed across her face. She saw the answer to the problem on the ceiling.

The fire sprinkler system.

Janie slipped out of the conference room again, and tiptoed to the small kitchen in the back of the office. Fireworks, Marv had said. He had no idea how right he had been.

This was going to slow things down, she knew, and it was also going to change her life. She was going to lose her job. Mr. Sloboski might even have her tarred and feathered by the end of the day. But she would have given Marv the time he needed. She routed in the drawers by the sink, pulling out a little box. Birthday candles. Now she was more than glad that she had presented cranky Agnes with a birthday cake the month before.

Out of sight in the little office kitchen, she scrambled up onto the counter to get closer to the ceiling. God, she wished Bernie were here. He would shake his serious head, and inform Mr. Sloboski in his best business voice, "I told you so, Sir. This system is antiquated and inadequate. It just dumps water at will. There's no way to regulate it, and only a plumber can turn it off once it's activated."

Maybe he'd even get a sale out of the whole thing. Though she doubted it.

But she was trying to put a roadblock in the path of a homicidal maniac, and she'd be happy to come out of this thing with all of her body parts intact.

She willed her hands not to shake. This was for Cassandra. For the boys. For Cal and for Marv, and for Diana. Maybe even for every woman who had been forced to live in the degradation of abuse. The hell with Frederick Ellington.

She held the candle right under the fire sensor and lit the match.

The candle burned for about 30 seconds, but it felt like an hour had passed before the sickly whine of the fire alarm began to bleep. Almost immediately, the sprinkler system blasted to life, a fact that Janie was more than aware of as the water plummeted out of the ceiling over her head, drenching her, and putting out the candle.

"Jesus!" "Oh, My God!" "What the hell?"

A series of yells and comments emulated from the conference room. Agnes ran past from the front desk with her hands over her head, crying. Makeup streamed down her face. "My hair, my hair!"

Janie checked the smile that was beginning to creep onto her lips. This was too much. She took large strides to the conference, both to see what damage had been done, and to position herself with the crowd for an alibi.

One look at the table told it all. The entire pile of papers now looked like papier-mâché. Including the check.

"Oh my goodness, oh my goodness," prattled Mr. Sloboski. "It's the fire alarm system, it must be on the blink. I've been warned about replacing that system. What timing! Oh my goodness, oh my goodness." Her boss' face was red as a beet. He looked like he might have a stroke.

Janie swallowed at the thought of all of the hours of extra typing she'd have to put in to rectify the mess, if, of course, she were still alive.

"I'll run to the basement turn off the building's water supply, Mr. Sloboski. That will at least stop it until a plumber can be called to reset the system." Janie volunteered, scurrying for the basement door. Within seconds, the water stopped.

As she came back into the room, she looked at Frederick Ellington. Now he looked ready to have the stroke. His eyes had lighted on the soggy check.

"This is an outrage. This is horrible. I have plans. I have a timetable.....Sloboski, you're an incompetent idiot... you'll answer for this..."

"Please, Professor Ellington, we will make all the arrangements we possibly can. We have the documents. They can be retyped so they are more professional, but even crumpled, they are still legal as they dry. We can consider the transfer complete, and can redo the paperwork as a formality..."

"The check..."

"Oh, the check." Mr. Sloboski looked crestfallen and momentarily puzzled. Nervously he lifted the phone and called the bank manager, explaining the problem. He hung up the phone with a look of gratitude on his face. "The bank will replace the check. We simply must take these, uh, remains, to the manager, and she will cut a new check. So there, you see, we can settle it. It's fixable. A minor inconvenience, a little wasted time...."

"I hope you're going to feel the same about the lawsuit I'm going to be initiating, Sloboski. But more than a little inconvenience. More than a little time." Frederick's face was hard and mad.

"Please, Professor. You know I'll do anything in my power to make up for this. If you wait right here, I'll go over and pick up the replacement check."

"I'll get the check. Give me the ruined check. I've got to get to the bank quickly. I'm running late as it is. Come, Diana!"

He roughly took her arm, and at first Janie thought Diana was going to react to him and pull away, but she kept her calm and docile demeanor and followed Frederick out the door.

Mr. Sloboski looked beaten, shaking his head, as he waddled back to his damp office. Janie had a moment of remorse for the aggravation she had caused the man. She'd have to bring him coffee and donuts every day for the rest of his life to make up for it.

"Good luck", she thought to her friends. "I hope I gave you enough time."

Chapter 43

There was no gentleness in the way that Frederick gripped Diana's arm as they walked the two blocks down the street to the bank. He had put the water damaged check into an envelope and into his pocket. At the bank cashier's window, he abruptly requested the manager, and was quickly ushered to her desk.

"I'll be happy to draw up a new check Professor Ellington, Ms. . It'll just take a minute."

"I wish to deposit the check right away."

"The check is drawn to your wife's name, Professor...In the circumstances..."

"I am Mrs. Ellington's sister, and I hold her power of attorney." Diana withdrew the paper from the pocket of her dress. "I'm sure you will find this in order. I believe it enables me to endorse the check for deposit in her absence?"

The manager looked over the document, inspecting it carefully. "Yes, I see. I will be just a minute."

"Cool, Diana. You were very cool and collected." Frederick pulled back and looked at her with new eyes. "I like your new haircut, by the way."

He had a suggestive grin on her face. It made her feel ill.

Diana wanted to belt him. "Don't get any ideas, Frederick. I'm doing this for my sister. I don't want any part of you."

Frederick smiled an enigmatic smile, as the bank manager returned. Quickly, he handed Diana a deposit slip. "You can endorse it immediately, and then it can be deposited."

"Sure." She started to sneeze suddenly, a series of little bursting sneezes that made her eyes well up. She apologized, groping in her pockets for a tissue. "I don't seem to have a tissue." She sneezed again, and by that time, the manager had produced a tissue.

"Allergy, probably," she apologized, as she signed her name to the back of the check. The sneezing had stopped. With lightning speed, she transferred the figures onto the deposit slip and handed it to the manager.

"We'd like this deposited immediately."

The manager exited to carry out the deposit.

Frederick was smiling now. "It's done. The money's in the bank." The manager returned with the deposit receipt and he slipped it into his pocket, quickly ushering Diana out the door, and into his car which parked a short distance away.

"I didn't know that Cassandra had owned so much property. That was a lot of money," she said softly, watching him out of the corner of her eye as he started the car.

"Don't kid yourself," he said.

The car moved swiftly through the traffic, out of town and toward the Ellington neighborhood.

"Cassandra didn't know a thing about that property. It was just part of a deal I put together. So don't get any ideas. Your job here is done, and the money is where it belongs. Now that it's in a joint account, it's in my hands, and that's where it's going to stay. You're free to go back to New York."

They had pulled up to the curb, and were walking up to the house.

"Of course I'm free to go back to New York. I was always free to do that, Frederick. I'm here for the boys, not the money, and I'll stay as long as I think they need me."

They entered the living room, and he slammed the door hard. She turned and looked at him. His calm mask had been removed, and he stared at her with menacing, hate filled eyes.

"You'll do as I say, bitch, and nothing else. The boys don't need you. They don't need anybody but me. The boys and I are taking a little trip right now, and you're not invited."

Her heart hammered, but she kept her face calm. The airport. The message on the tape had mentioned the airport and passports.

"But school..the boys have to go to school." She was fighting off panic.

"There are schools all over the world. They'll go to school. Right now, I have to pack. You should do the same. Because you are going back to New York."

He glared at her as he left the room.

    ****

Peter heard his father come into the house, and heard his gruff tone with Diana. He felt sick to his stomach. He too, remembered the tape mentioning passports. His father's reference to a trip made him blanche. Taken away by his father? He'd rather chew glass. He redoubled his efforts.

He was sitting at the computer at Frederick's desk. In the drawer, he had found a stack of computer memory sticks, mostly unmarked, though a few were marked with student's names. Popping them into the computer, he had been calling up their directories. Clumsy at first, once he got started, he was thankful for his cranky computer teacher who had insisted on "computer literacy".

He went through disk after disk. For the most part, the disks contained student work. This wasn't unusual for a writing professor. Mostly it was poetry, and occasional short stories, but none of the names were familiar. He was looking especially for large files, that would indicate something big enough to be a book. He had made his way almost through the pile when he heard his father arrive.

Sweat appeared on his freckled brow, but he was determined to finish. Memory stick after memory stick went into the drive, was checked, and removed. Disappointment welled up in him as he reached the end of the pile. He put the last disk into the machine, and pulled up the directory onto the screen.

He gulped. "Gravely, P." the file clearly said. He opened the file on the screen. "A first novel by Pamela Gravely. This book is dedicated to my parents, who have supported me in every way, and to whom I owe my undying thanks."

The story began. And Pamela's story had the same title as his father's latest book.

Tears began to well up in Peter's eyes. For all his determination, for all his suspicions, a part of his mind had wanted it to be untrue. But it was true. His father had stolen this book. And his father was a killer.

He slipped the memory stick out of the computer, and put it into the large pocket of his flannel shirt. He turned off the computer.

Out in the hallway, he could hear his father and Diana as they argued. The voices got louder. The clarity of the words could only mean one thing. They were coming closer, heading toward him. Was his father coming toward the bedroom? His father was planning to pack a suitcase, and Diana was trying to talk him out of it. He could hear the desperation in her voice.

Frantic, he looked around the alcove, searching for a place to hide. There was none. He flipped the remaining memory sticks into the drawer, and shut it. He could see the shadow of his father looming large on the wall as he entered the room. Peter threw himself up against the wall of the alcove, as much out of sight from the doorway, making himself as small as possible. It would only be seconds before he was discovered.

His father took a step into the room, still arguing with Diana, then another. Peter held his breath. The phone rang.

The sudden noise made him jump. Frederick turned toward the phone, away from the alcove, but Diana caught the movement from the corner of her eye. She saw Peter. Her face paled, but she didn't move a muscle.

"Just transfer it, you idiot!" Frederick screamed into the phone. There was a silence as the other person spoke. Then he exploded again. "What do you mean, the money is not in the account? I was there myself. I saw the check endorsed. I saw the deposit made. What is the delay?"

Another silence, and Peter was sure the beating of his heart could be heard across the room.

"Oh my god!" yelled Frederick, slamming down the phone, and grabbing Diana by the arm, yanking her back down the hallway toward the living room.

"What did you do with the money, you bitch!" he screamed.

Peter slipped out of the alcove behind them and crept silently toward the atrium doors that opened out onto a deck outside of his parents' room. He was in a panic, and he had to get help. But the sound of his father's voice froze him to the spot. Diana was in trouble here, in a lot of trouble, and he was afraid to leave her alone.

In the living room, Frederick had picked up his suit jacket from the place he had dropped it on the couch, and was furiously searching the pockets. He pulled out the small folded deposit slip the bank manager had given him.

His brow was wrinkled in thought. "Deposit: $3,000,000, Cashier's check" was printed on it. His contact at the bank was stating that his account was empty and he was unable to wire the money out of the country. If the man was playing games, he was playing a deadly one. Frederick looked again at the preprinted deposit slip.

"Cassandra Ellington" it said on the first line. "Diana Clark? " he hollered as he read the second line that was printed on the check. His eyes got wide, and very dark.

When he turned and looked at Diana, she saw true evil in his face. He took a step toward her.

Peter stood at the doorway of the bedroom, staring down the hallway, not knowing what to do. If he left, he was leaving Diana alone. If he stayed...well, he was afraid to think of the consequences of that, too. He blinked back the tears that were building in his eyes.

He looked toward the atrium doors at the back of the bedroom, praying for a solution, and saw the most amazing thing. Peering in the corner of the door was a face..a face that was just the slightest bit familiar. He squinted, and a hand came up beside the face, and waved.

It was the guy from TV. He could remember the guy from his mom's funeral service, and from the book publishing news, as well as from the TV screen. It was Charles Upworth, the man who had treated him and Duncan so kindly when their mother had been reported dead. Now, like a miracle, he was staring in the window, a concerned look on his face.

Without further thought, Peter lunged to the door and soundlessly opened the lock. No matter what or who, Peter was glad to have an adult on the scene. Charles slipped in.

"Cal sent me. They're worried about you. They're worried about what your dad is up to..Cal told me some of the details... they want me to bring you to the station."

Peter eyes got bigger, and he whispered back. "My dad's here. I'm scared. I have the proof that he stole the book from Pamela Gravely, and that probably means he murdered her." He patted the memory stick in his pocket. Charles stared at him. He had fear on his face, too.

"I'm sorry kid. I know he's your dad," the news reporter said.

Peter sucked in his breath. "No matter. If he's a killer, he's got to be stopped," he whispered. "He's in the living room, but he's got my aunt there. I'm not leaving her alone with him. He's nuts and I think he's going to hurt her."

Charles looked at the sturdy young boy in front of him, and his mind filled with a million painful memories about his own father. Love mixed with hate, fear mixed with pity. But like he had been, this was a strong boy and he'd find his peace.

"I'm with you, Peter. You're not alone. We've got to call the cops." Charles whispered.

They crossed to the phone, still hearing the angry voices from the living room. They called for Marv, and were told that he was on his way.

But Frederick's voice had gotten even more intense.

"You stole my money." His voice was low pitched, gravelly, almost like a growl.

"I deposited it into the bank, just as you asked. I simply deposited it into a different account. I used a deposit slip from the account that Cassandra and I opened years ago, the account that you disapproved of so vehemently back then, the account she was always afraid to use." She stood up straight, and tossed her blond hair. "The account is still open. The money was in Cassandra's name, and I have her power of attorney. Legally, the money is in a perfectly acceptable place."

For a moment, Frederick looked stunned.

Charles and Peter moved to the corner of the room, where they could just see down the hall, and catch a glimpse of Frederick's back. Diana made little darting glances their way, concerned for Peter, and seeing that someone was with him. Her voice got braver.

Charles got a brainstorm, reaching into his pocket and pulling out his hand sized recorder, used for interviews. He flicked it on and it began to record.

"Listen, you greedy thing." Frederick growled. "There is no way that you are going to escape with both your life and that money. I have worked long and hard for every penny of it. You have no idea of what I've had to do for that money. And it's mine."

"Legally, it's Cassandra's. The land was in her name, " Diana goaded him, trying not to gasp as he took a handful of her hair and yanked it, bringing her closer.

"It was in her name just to keep the press off my tail, to keep people from getting suspicious. I bought every damn lot, acre by acre. It was all my master plan, and no one else is going to benefit from it."

"You don't have enough money to pull off something like that, you egotistical maniac."

"I get whatever money I need. People do what I say. I know their little "weaknesses", the things that they would rather not have released for public display. It works quite effectively. I'm a master at understanding what works with people."

"And if they don't go along with your plans?" she asked breathlessly.

"One way or another, they will get out of my way. Even you."

"You're a liar and a cheat. You pretend to be a respectable professor and writer..and you're neither."

He was pulling her hair as he spoke, and the pain made her eyes fill with tears, but she would not give him the satisfaction of letting him see her cry. She sucked in her breath.

"You don't need to do the writing when you know how people think," he said. "You don't need to do the grunt work when you know their little weaknesses. Exchanging an unpublished manuscript for peace of mind is a price guilty people are more than willing to pay."

"How about Pamela Gravely. How willing was she?"

"Pamela was a fool. An innocent, naive, principled fool. But she was also a terrific writer. Don't think I didn't try to find another way. She could have written several more books. She had that kind of talent. She just didn't have any common sense. No way to deal with her. There was no way out. I was short of time."

"You killed her."

"I had no choice. Not only was she not going to give me the book, the little fool was going to turn me in. Me. Dr. Frederick Ellington. What a joke. But I won. I always win. It was my best book, too, don't you think? The critics are raving already."

His eyes held a lunatic light, now, and Charles was more than sure that Peter had heard enough. He had certainly taped enough for the authorities. He pulled the boy away from the doorway, back into the bedroom, and called Cal at the station, filling him in quickly. But where was Marv? The minutes were ticking by, and they were far from safe.

"Play me the tape, Charles, " Cal commanded.

Charles held the player up against the phone, hitting the play button. He closed his eyes, hoping wildly that the noise wasn't heard in the living room down the hall, as Cal's equipment began to record it.

"Can you get Peter to run to the neighbor's house?" Cal asked. "To keep him out of the way until Marv arrives?"

Charlie looked at Peter's determined face, still staring at the open doorway. "I don't think there's a chance. He's mighty stubborn, but he's one hell of a kid."

"I know. Well, take care of him. Marv should be there any second."

"I'll guard him with my life, man," he said, leaving the phone, but leaving it off the hook, still connected to Cal.

They moved back to the doorway to listen. Where was Marv?

Frederick was still ranting. "So you've got to die, little lady. There's no other way. You've signed your own death warrant. With Cassandra gone, and you dead, the money belongs to me, anyway. It'll just take a little longer to collect, that's all."

Diana didn't say a word, but even from the distance down the hall, Charlie could see the terror in her eyes. Frederick was now holding a gun.

Behind him, Charlie could hear Peter gasp. He motioned toward the phone, wanting Peter to pick it up. Peter sped across the room to tell Cal what was happening.

But Frederick had heard the slight gasp. He turned toward the bedroom.

Charlie swallowed hard, as he found the barrel of the gun pointed directly at him. But the madman still held Diana tightly by the hair. She found her voice.

"Don't shoot, don't shoot," she wailed, trying to break his hold on her, and to dislodge the gun. Charles took a step toward him, his legs feeling numb but driven to protect the blonde woman in front of him and the brave little boy in the next room.

"Killing Diana won't solve anything, Ellington," he said quietly, amazed at how calm his voice sounded. Because his insides were like jello.

"Where the hell did you come from?" Frederick waved the gun, his face enraged. "Keep out of this. She's brought it on herself, trying to steal my hard earned money. People don't cross Frederick Ellington. I trusted her, and it was a mistake. I don't like to make mistakes. This one has to be rectified." His face was mottled, and it was clear that he was a man who had become dangerously unraveled.

In the back room, Peter stuttered at Cal on the phone, then frantically obeyed Cal's calm instructions. "Get your boom box, and push it out into the hallway. Make sure it's tuned to this station. When I count to three, turn it on as loud as it will go."

Peter obeyed instantly, ready for the count.

"Let her go, Ellington, don't make it worse," Charlie Upworth was pleading. "You have nothing to gain by having her die."

"Nothing but a little matter of $3,000,000 in a joint account with my dead wife. But when Diana dies, the money's mine again." He raised the gun again.

Peter heard Cal's count," One, two, three." The boy closed his eyes and flipped the switch.

"Take it easy Ellington." Cal's radio voice boomed through the air. Frederick looked around the room in surprise, trying to identify the source of the loud voice.

The voice from the radio continued. "The money isn't ever going to be yours. Killing Diana is not the answer. Cassandra is alive."

Silence filled the room. Frederick dropped Diana, and she collapsed on the carpet. He charged down the hallway, then stared at the place in the carpet where the radio was sitting.

"The radio?" he barked, confused, frantic. "It's that Cal guy on the radio? What the hell did he say about Cassandra?" He had turned white as a sheet.

"It's over, Frederick," Cal's voice said firmly but calmly." No more killing. You can't get away with it. There's no way out. You've convicted yourself."

Suddenly, from the radio, Frederick's own words could be heard, "Pamela Gravely was a fool......"

Diana's voice, "You killed her..."

Frederick's voice, "I had no choice..."

Like a cornered man, Frederick let out a tortured, primal scream, running pas the radio, heading for the back of the house, toward the bedroom where Charles knew Peter still hid. He spun and chased the crazed man down the hallway.

"Watch out, watch out," he screamed to warn the boy. Peter heard the warning, and reacted quickly. He dove into the alcove as Frederick came charging into the room, heading for the back atrium doors, still brandishing the gun.

At that very instant, Marv and his back up officers had arrived, and had surrounded the house. A uniformed officer stepped onto the deck, just as Frederick reached the back door.

Cornered, with flashing, insane eyes, Frederick spun on his heel, suddenly sensing movement in the alcove to his right, and fired a single shot, aiming toward Peter.

Sensing the danger to Peter, the frantic young newsman made an adrenalin driven leap to put himself between Ellington and his hiding son. Charles dropped on impact, the bullet tearing into his flesh.

Frederick Ellington turned like a wild animal, crashing through the glass paned doors. Seconds later, there was the sound of a second shot. Frederick fell to the ground. Seeing the police surrounding the house, he had turned the gun on himself.

Instantly there were police everywhere. And ambulance sirens. Voices shouting orders. Marv grabbed Diana and Peter, his usually steady hands shaking, seeing that they were all right, and then helped to load the barely conscious Charles Upworth into a waiting ambulance.

Charles forced his eyes open as he felt himself being moved. He found Peter staring down at him, his face white, his eyes wide open with fear and doubt.

"You did great, kid." Charles said with all the energy he could muster. Peter tried to smile but his quivering face couldn't make it happen.

"You're shot," cried the horrified twelve year old. "He shot you."

"It'll be OK, Peter," the injured newsman went on, forcing the words out. "I know you feel mixed up right now, but it'll get better. Sometime I'll tell you about my dad. You're going to get through this. I promise."

Peter nodded, feeling close and wanting Charles to be ok."

"Thanks," Peter said, his throat tight. "You saved my life."

Charles smiled. "Yeah, kid. Go see your mom. Some story, huh?"

"Take good care of him," Marv barked at the paramedics, his usually level voice choked with emotion. He's one hell of a guy."

The ambulance took him away.

****

Marv had picked up the phone to talk to Cal. "You're a nut. Playing that confession tape over the radio. That had to break about a zillion rules. The FCC will have your hide. "

"It won't be the first time...or probably the last," Cal sighed. "It just seemed like the thing to do at the moment."

"Go to Cassandra, Calvin," Marv said. " It's over. Take Duncan, and we'll meet you at the house."

The police were roping off the area, and more than a few nosey neighbors had gathered to watch the ambulance and the coroner pull away. Marvin sighed, a deep cleansing breath that reached to the tip of his toes. He turned to Diana, and pulled her into his arms, kissing her smack on the lips.

"A bossy, macho cop. Who said you could kiss me?" She whispered in a shaky voice.

"It just seemed like the thing to do at the moment," Marv said, and kissed her again.

Then they took Peter and climbed into the police car to head to the river house.

Chapter 44

Calvin hung up the phone, and took the first deep breath he had dared to chance since he had gotten the taped confession on the phone from Charlie. He felt like his heart had stopped. Frederick Ellington was dead. It was over, Marv had said. Duncan had sat by his side through the whole ordeal, and now the young man was openly crying. It was relief, it was anguish, it was a reaction to the fear and the worry. And even the loss.

No matter how sick Frederick Ellington had been, he had been the boys' father. And they were going to have to process the loss, even with the anger and hate they had for the man. It was a complicated thing, and it would take time. But together, they would all make it.

Cal held an arm around him, and let him cry it out. "It'll be ok, Dunc. It'll be ok. I know this has been a tough, tough time. But now, let's go see your mother."

He called Cassandra immediately. Gently, caring, he told her the details of what had happened. He knew she would hear the words with a mindboggling mixture of emotions, too. The hold that Frederick had had on her was over, but the reconciliation of feelings was not. No matter how cruel and insane the man had become, he knew Cassandra, and knew that she, too, would have to go through the memories and pain of the many years of her life she had spent with him. It was a path she would have to travel, no matter how much it hurt, and so he gave her the chance to begin.

Cal knew that when she held her hurting boys in her arms in a short time, her feelings and concerns would be for their loss and understanding, instead of her own. Healing would take time.

Their pain mattered to him, Cassandra's, Duncan's and Peter's. They were connected in an invisible way, as they had been from the beginning. Maybe it was love. Probably it was love. He couldn't wait to see her. He needed to see her. He was still worried, and he didn't even know why.

"It's over." Marv had said. But something didn't seem right.

He wished that he was already with Cassandra, that she was not alone. He tried to calm himself, tried to muster some patience. As Cal and Duncan got into the aged suburban and began the several mile trip to the river house, Cal's anxiety level increased. He couldn't wait to get home to Cassandra, to see that she was really ok, and to believe that, like Marv said, it was over.

****

Hannah Mae March sat in her little house by the river. She was in the bad mood of bad moods. All day, she had watched for Calvin, her kindly next door neighbor to come home so that she could get the belt repaired on her monstrous vacuum cleaner. Usually, he was home at least part of the day. Not today. There had been no sign of his cute little visitor, either. Not that she was so newsy that she was watching. It was just that in this quiet neck of the woods, a person could sometimes see what went on through the trees, even without making an attempt. And if you were an observant type of person, as she was…you couldn't help but notice.

So she was fairly certain the pretty visitor was still there, since she hadn't seen her leave, and that Calvin was not, since she hadn't seen him come. She'd make a pretty good detective, she laughed to herself.

Despite her many years, she had a good head on her shoulders. She remembered what that cute Jewish detective had said. Not that he was truly "cute" in the absolute definition of the word. But that he was cute in the kind sense. A nice man, a gentle person. She liked that. She still had his card attached by a magnet on the fridge, from when he had come around asking about the woman who had crashed into the river. Detective Marvin Greenstein. Of course, detectives probably don't think of themselves as cute. They'd rather be "tough", she thought. So she'd keep that "cute" opinion to herself if she ever saw him again.

Bored, and more than a little frustrated that she couldn't finish her vacuuming, she went out onto the back deck. Again, she wasn't snooping, but she couldn't help what was plain to see. Two things were observed.

The first was that the visitor, was, in fact, home. The telephone rang, and through the side window, she could see the young woman get up off the couch, leaving a notebook of some sort behind, and pick up the phone from the end table. With a hand to her throat, she evidently heard some startling news, because she sat down abruptly, suddenly out of sight from Hannah's curious eyes.

Not being able to see the young woman any more, she turned her vision toward the river, behind Cal's little house, where she saw the second thing, actually even more remarkable. There was a man, a full grown man, dressed in a business suit. And he was picking his way along rocks that lined the river bank toward the back steps that led to Calvin's house.

Despite the fact that it would be unusual for any unfamiliar person, especially one in a suit to be traveling in such an orthodox place, it was his manner of walking that puzzled her. He looked sneaky. He looked like a person who was up to no good at all, and when he took a final step along the rocks and reached the pathway that meandered up to the steps to Calvin's back porch, Hannah got more nervous than curious. Who was it? And what on earth could he be doing?

The most unnerving thing was the fact that, although Hannah wouldn't want to swear to it, the man looked vaguely familiar, very similar to the man she had seen eyeing the dock earlier with a pair of binoculars, with a very mean look on his face.

And detective or no, putting together all those things didn't present a very nice picture. She picked up the phone and dialed 911. An efficient female voice came on the line.

"This is a message, an important and urgent message that must be delivered to Detective Marvin Greenstein. This is Hannah Mae March, from up on River Road. He'll remember who I am. He said for me to call if there was anything to tell him, and today there most certainly is. Tell him there is a man sneaking right up to the back door of the house next door, and if what he said about my instincts is correct, this man is looking for trouble."

She left her name and number again, and the kindly voice took the information with the kind of inflection one uses when one deals with people who are a few cards short of a full deck.

So Hannah Mae hung up, not feeling good at all about the call, and feeling even more worried about the visitor next door. What should she do? She put her instincts to work.

She'd act neighborly. For all she knew, she could be simply imagining trouble, but she couldn't take the chance. Making a fool of oneself was sometimes called for in the greater scheme of things. Muttering under her breath, she grabbed the first thing that came to mind, which happened to be the vacuum cleaner. She took the new belt, a black rubber loop that was still not attached to the torturous cleaning device, and pulled the vacuum cleaner out the front door. She walked quickly through the trees along the little used path that connected the two houses, pulling the big vacuum cleaner behind her. Arriving at the front door she balked, feeling like a fool.

At first the house sounded quiet, then she peered in the little side window by the door, and saw the young woman curled up on the couch, sobbing her eyes out. It didn't seem to be the time to disturb her.

But looking through the window again, she could see clear back through to the kitchen, and she could see the back door slowly opening. The dark suited man, now looking a little disheveled from his climb up to the back deck, was tiptoeing in through the door, right into the kitchen.

Hannah Mae swallowed hard. Now, for sure, she knew it was the same man she had seen with the binoculars. He had that same cruel look on his face. What on earth was she going to do? She took a very deep breath.

    ****

The girl at the 911 emergency switchboard had taken Hannah Mae's message with a smile, putting it into the pile of messages on her desk. A patrol car would be sent to check it out. Not that it sounded like a major emergency. She wouldn't bother the detective. The old lady's neighbor had probably locked himself out of the house, and was likely just trying to get in through the back door. One of the biggest problems they were having since the county had installed the 911 emergency program was the fact that people called with all kinds of bizarre complaints and problems, many of which could take time and energy and man power away from a real crisis.

But then, she overheard the call coming in to her coworker on the next phone, where the shooting/suicide of Frederick Ellington had been reported and ambulances assigned. The reporting officer was Detective Marvin Greenstein. That was the name she had just written in the old woman's complaint. Quickly she reached back into the pile and pulled out the message, calling police headquarters. Coincidence? She wouldn't take the chance. Within seconds, she was connected with Detective Greenstein, who was in his police car. She relayed the information.

"Holy shit!" the detective exclaimed. She heard the siren start to blare on his police car. "Get me some backups. I'm on the way there. 9228 River Road, on the double."

He was gone.

Chapter 45

Cassandra heard a noise. She had been crying for several minutes, oblivious to the world around her. Frederick was dead. It was over. He couldn't hurt them anymore. The tears flowed like a river as emotions rolled over her, sitting alone in the stillness of Calvin's house. Memories came flooding back, the scared college student she had been, so very impressed with the popular young professor who had taken an interest in her.

She thought about the early days, when Frederick had tried to impress her, too, and she had believed in him at first, and had tried to fit the role he had so carefully planned for her. When had the desire to please him turned to fear? When had the stars in her eyes turned to tears? She thought of the birth of her sons, each one a miracle to her, but each one another person for Frederick to control, to mold.

When had he begun to lose his mind? Why had it taken her so long to realize it, to realize that the problems were his and not hers, and that there were answers and changes that could be made? Beat down by all the years of abuse and fear, the constantly reinforced feeling of inadequacy and inability, she had been trapped. Trapped by worry for the welfare for her sons, for herself, trapped by the overpowering and paralyzing fear that life would only get worse, not better, if she dared to put all her energies toward change and rebellion.

So many times, in the earlier days, she had imagined relief of cutting free, of beginning a new life. But then the guilt had come, guilt for her "disloyal" thoughts, and she had lost even more faith in herself. He became stronger in his sickness, and she had become weaker.

But a miracle had occurred, and she had begun to grow, nurtured by the friends she had made, people who believed in her. Motivated by the love she had for her sons, and knowing how much they needed her, strong and well, she had begun to change. She felt connected now, connected to the good things in life, trust, love and self-esteem.

It was too late for Frederick, and he had paid the greatest price for his cruelty and insanity. But it was not too late for her, and for the boys. The vision of Cal's face passed through her mind. Maybe, just maybe, she could be a strong enough individual now to be a full-fledged partner in a relationship; deserving, giving, receiving. The sobs subsided a little as hope crept into her heart.

And then the noise had come.

It was the sound of tiptoeing feet. Cassandra raised her head, hearing someone moving in the house. A draft of air came through the room, evidence that the back door had been opened.

"Cal?" she said quietly, hopefully.

But in truth, she did not think that is was Cal who approached her. She had not heard the sound of his car. The hairs on the back of her neck prickled, and she felt the first waves of fear. But Frederick was dead. Cal had told her so on the phone. Frederick was dead. So who was walking in the kitchen?

She stood quietly and moved across the room. She turned the corner toward the kitchen. She came face to face with the intruder...Frederick's attorney, James Jenkins. Large and threatening, he loomed over her. And in his hand, he held a small silver gun.

"Cassandra, it IS you. You're alive." His voice barked, more gravelly than she remembered. She looked at the usually debonair lawyer, the man who knew more about Frederick's activities than anyone alive. His face was contorted. His eyes didn't seem focused. He looked wild.

Cassandra's heart was beating fast, but she found the courage to meet his eyes, pulling her shoulders up tall. She would never back down in fear again.

"What are you doing here, James?" She looked at the dark circles under his eyes, feel the panic that reverberated in him. Even from the distance of several feet, she could smell the liquor on his breath.

He moved toward her in a jerky fashion, his face in a snarl. "You shouldn't be alive, Cassandra. You can't be alive. You'll ruin everything. Frederick will really have it in for me if he found out you're still alive. Frederick will kill me."

"Relax, James," she said, attempting to keep her voice calm, but very aware that he was out of control. "I need to tell you about Frederick..."

"There's nothing you can tell me about Frederick," he shouted. "Nothing at all. I've given the bastard everything I have...my time, my energy, my money, my loyalty, my pride. He's like a bloodsucking leech who gets a hold on you and never lets go. Never."

He took another step toward her, waving the gun. Instinctively, she pulled back. "Steady, James."

Up close, she could see the sweat on his brow, his bloodshot eyes. She could see that the hand that held the gun was shaking.

"It is never enough. You can't do enough when you are owned by the devil. After all I've done, after all I've sacrificed, he turns on me. Calls me incompetent. Me. It was your stupid bitch of a sister who put the money in the wrong account. SHE did it. Right under his nose. Tricked him. Outsmarted by a woman. She put it in a joint account in your name and hers. So he's going to kill her..and he thinks that's the end of it." He ran one hand through his unruly hair.

"But the money is in YOUR name too, and you're still alive. But no one, not even Frederick knows you're alive. No one but me. You're not going to get that money, Cassandra, and have that vengeful bastard bring me down for it. I'll get blamed. I always get blamed. Unless you're dead. You've got to be dead. You're going in the river, where you should have been a week ago, and everything will be all right." He moved toward her.

****

Hannah Mae stood on the front porch with her vacuum cleaner, horrified at the words she heard. Now she was eavesdropping, really eavesdropping, and there was no doubt about it. Hannah squinted her eyes and peeked through the small window beside the door. The kindly little woman in Cal's house was being brave, but that girl didn't have much of a chance against the brute standing in front of her, big and crazy to boot. And with a gun.

Hannah closed her eyes for a minute, panic spreading through her like an electric current. On TV, a bad guy like this was easily thwarted, but in real life…. This was different, and horribly scary. But she had to do something.

Hannah thought fast. She had to create a diversion, and give the girl a chance to get away. That was her only chance. Problem was, the girl was standing there in her stocking feet. She wore no shoes, just a big, bulky pair of red socks on her feet. She wasn't going to get far in the woods in those. So there was only one way to get away fast enough. The river.

Hannah came up with her plan in a flash. Taking the black rubber vacuum cleaner belt from her pocket, she slipped it around the front door handle, then looped it onto the iron bracket that held the window shutter next to the door. It wouldn't totally keep the door from being opened, but was certain to slow him down. Next, she bent over and plugged the vacuum cleaner into the outside electrical socket beneath the porch light.

There was nothing, she had learned,, that was a more grating sound than her monstrous vacuum cleaner trying to suck up small articles. In the past it had happened by accident, like when she mistakenly rolled it over some spilled buttons or an occasional safety pin on the floor. But this time, she was going to make a racket on purpose. Like for instance, letting it suck up rocks and twigs. She placed the vacuum cleaner on the dirt and small stones next to the walk way. She took a deep breath and flipped the switch. Instantly the machine roared to life, sucking in everything in sight, puffing up with air, and making a horrible roaring, grinding sound that echoed in the country air.

Hannah climbed off the front porch and hightailed it around the house, almost sliding down the hill toward the dock and the river. Her knee gave a twinge, and she almost lost her balance, but she kept moving. In fact, she was surprised at her own agility. "I may be old," she thought to herself, "But I'm not done yet!"

Just as she hoped, the man lunged at the front door, trying to see what that noise was. He pulled hard on the handle to open the door. It opened a few inches, as the vacuum belt stretched. Then it snapped back and closed, pulled by the vacuum belt. He tried again, furious. The delay gave the woman in the red socks the miraculous seconds she needed to escape.

As Cassandra ran out the back door and plummeted down the deck steps. She slowed only a minute in surprise when she saw the spry little grey haired woman climbing down the rocky bank behind the house running toward the dock.

"Quick," the woman screamed, pointing toward the canoe that was tied at the dock. Cassandra didn't need a second invitation. They both jumped into the boat, picking up paddles. Together, they pushed away from shore into the river current.

A stream of curse words filled the air as Jenkins flew down the deck steps and onto the dock after them. He had a gun in his hand. They hadn't gotten far enough. They were only feet away.

Cassandra put the paddle in the water ferociously, paddling with all her might. "Get down," she screamed to the little woman who was trying to valiantly help paddle the canoe. A shot rang out.

Hannah heard the shot. She was terrified, and obeyed instantly, ducking down into the bottom of the canoe. Cassandra paddled with all her might, heading the craft straight out from the shore, into deeper water. She dipped the paddle deep into the water, straining to get the most from each stroke. She tried to ignore the angry curses that echoed from the man on the dock.

Instinctively, she knew that she had to get the boat away from the shallow river's edge, away from the rocks, and out into the faster current. Suddenly, the craft picked up speed. The wild spring current of the river had taken charge of the canoe, and they began moving downriver at a frantic pace. Two more shots rang out around her, but they only hit the water, as the speed of the canoe increased. Now, Cassandra fought the current for control. She struggled to keep the craft from overturning, as the rough water tossed them back and forth, shouting commands to Hannah Mae, who once more had her paddle in the water. Neither of them was going to earn a medal for their canoeing skill. But they were out of range of the gun.

"We're far enough away now," she yelled, watching the scenery slip by dangerously fast. "Pull back toward shore. Paddle hard!" It was important, she knew, to slow the canoe before it went around the far turn in the river, where rocky rapids were a threat and would make it impossible to keep from capsizing. The thought of Pamela

Gravely's river battered body passed through her mind, and spurred her on. She was using muscles that she didn't even know she had. Her arms ached, her shoulders ached, but she didn't give up.

The sound of sirens filled the air as the police arrived at the dock now far behind her. She could barely hear people yelling over the sound of the roaring river, but she looked back long enough to see James quickly subdued by two officers. Up on the deck of Cal's house, she caught of glimpse of Diana and Peter, but instantly, her attention was back on the swirling water around her. The canoe hit a rock and began to spin.

It was out of control.

"Oh, God, I can't swim. I think we're going to drown," wailed the little woman behind her in the boat. She started crying.

"NO we're not. This river didn't get me last week, and it's not going to get us now." This was Cal's river, and she concentrated on the peace and beauty she had felt since she had come to Cal's river house. Hannah Mae heard her words and took them to heart. This was the river of sunrises and sunsets. She wasn't going to be afraid of it.

"Come on, now, paddle for shore. We've come this far. We can do it. We're going to make it."

Cassandra and Hannah pulled at the water with all their might, trying to bring the canoe back toward the shore, and into the slower, shallower water. Finally, the canoe began to obey. Cassandra's shoulders ached, her lungs felt like they would burst.

"Come on river, be our friend." she growled at the churning water, as they made slow progress toward the shore.

It seemed like hours, but in reality it was only minutes before they were out of true danger. Cassandra lifted her eyes as the canoe reached calmer water and began to slow, to see that they had traveled downriver and were almost directly under the spot where her car had gone over the cliff a week before.

She squinted at what seemed to be two figures who were scurrying down the cliff toward them from the turnoff above. She recognized Cal and Duncan.

Cassandra smiled, a burst of happiness filling her heart. "We're going to make it," she yelled over the water. We're going to make it."

Cal and Duncan had reached the water's edge, and began to take tenuous steps into the water toward them, shoes and all. Cassandra began to laugh exultantly as she climbed over the edge of the boat into the now thigh high water to leap into their open arms. Then Cal turned and looked at the boat.

"Hannah?" gasped Cal, recognizing his little neighbor. He and Duncan began pulling the canoe with its elderly passenger toward shore. "What..."

"Oh, Calvin, your girlfriend and I outran the big bad man. We made a great team, didn't we?" She giggled, and her gray curls bobbed.

"The best," Cassandra called back as they sloshed toward the bank.

They reached the edge and helped Hannah Mae out of the boat. Once the canoe was anchored, they fell into each other's arms, laughing and crying.

"Now it's really over. It's really over! Oh, Mom!" Duncan cried. Cassandra hugged her son.

"Peter's fine," Duncan volunteered. "He's up at the house with Marv and Diana. He told me what happened with dad."

Cassandra stopped and put her arm around her tall son's shoulders. "Duncan, I'm sorry. I know, despite everything, you feel really bad about your dad. You and Peter and I have a lot to work out about this. He had a lot of problems."

"Yeah. But he was my dad. It hurts a lot."

"As long as you can face it, you can handle it, Duncan," said Cal softly, putting an arm around Duncan. "You'll all be OK."

They continued slowly up the rocky path for a few minutes, when suddenly Cassandra turned around, and looked back, surveying the rocky cliff, and watching the river rushing by.

"I can't believe it. This is the place where my car went over the cliff. This is the place where my life almost ended," Cassandra gasped, shivering suddenly, her clothes drenched and clinging to her body.

Cal pulled her close and put his arms around her. "Maybe this is the place where a new phase of your life is really just beginning," he said into her soggy, short hair.

"It's a good place to begin a life," piped in Hannah Mae, "On this wonderful river."

"Thanks, Hannah Mae, for your help here. You're a woman of surprising talents!"

"It hasn't been a dull day, that's for sure, Cal. Johnson." Hannah said with a twinkle in her eye.

"I'll never forget this. There has to be something I can do to pay you back."

"There certainly is. You can come and rip out my wall to wall carpets, Calvin. I'm going back to hard wood floors, and we'll give that vacuum cleaner a decent burial. Though it saved the day."

Calvin laughed as they made their way back up the path to the top of the cliff, Duncan and Hannah Mae before them.

"Oh no", Cassandra exclaimed, looking down at her now bare feet. "I lost my lucky red socks in the river."

"I promise you," he exclaimed, "I'll get you another pair. But right now, do you want me to carry you the rest of the way up this cliff? Your feet must be freezing. And these rocks are tough."

She looked at him, rumpled, and kindly and loving, and knew that he'd do it in a minute if she asked.

"Nope", she said with a smile, starting to climb toward the top. "I'm going to get back up there on my own two feet, and then we can go from there...But I'm holding you to the socks."

"I'm sure you will," he said with a wide smile. He bent his head, and kissed her hard.

The river roared its approval in the background.

The End

About the Author

Christine Bush is the award winning, USA Today Bestselling author of romance, mystery and suspense. When she's not writing, she can be found teaching Psychology at a local college, working with clients in private practice as a Marriage and Family Therapist, or enjoying her twelve grandchildren! She lives in the country in northeastern Pennsylvania with two crazy cats.

Christine loves to hear from reader! Email her at ChristineABush@aol.com or see her on facebook at https://www.facebook.com/Christine-Bush-Author-213919128638762/

Other Books by Christine

Cindy's Prince
Noah's Bark
Sunny's Smile
Love, Julie
Courageous Heart
Patient Heart
Daring Heart
Promise Forever
Where Love Prevails

Novellas

Meddling Mona
Fear of Flowers
Christmas Daisy
Christmas Rose
Christmas Laurel
Christmas Holly
Cowboy Boots

Easy Amazon Ordering
Print and Ebook

https://www.amazon.com/Christine-Bush/e/B001KHSLRG/

www.ChristineBush.com